WARBOSS

WARBOSS

MIKE BROOKS

BLACK LIBRARY

A BLACK LIBRARY PUBLICATION

First published in 2022.
This edition published in Great Britain in 2023 by
Black Library, Games Workshop Ltd., Willow Road,
Nottingham, NG7 2WS, UK.

Represented by: Games Workshop Limited – Irish branch,
Unit 3, Lower Liffey Street, Dublin 1,
D01 K199, Ireland.

10 9 8 7 6 5 4 3 2 1

Produced by Games Workshop in Nottingham.
Cover illustration by Tazio Bettin.

See Black Library on the internet at

blacklibrary.com

Find out more about Games Workshop
and the worlds of Warhammer at

games-workshop.com

Printed and bound in the UK.

Thanks to Pidge for help with the tank stuff.

For more than a hundred centuries the Emperor has sat
immobile on the Golden Throne of Earth. He is the
Master of Mankind. By the might of His inexhaustible
armies a million worlds stand against the dark.

Yet, He is a rotting carcass, the Carrion Lord of the
Imperium held in life by marvels from the Dark Age of
Technology and the thousand souls sacrificed each day so
that His may continue to burn.

To be a man in such times is to be one amongst untold
billions. It is to live in the cruellest and most bloody
regime imaginable. It is to suffer an eternity of carnage
and slaughter. It is to have cries of anguish and sorrow
drowned by the thirsting laughter of dark gods.

This is a dark and terrible era where you will find little
comfort or hope. Forget the power of technology and
science. Forget the promise of progress and advancement.
Forget any notion of common humanity or compassion.

There is no peace amongst the stars, for in the grim
darkness of the far future,
there is only war.

DA KAST

ORKS

Waaagh! Gazrot

Gazrot Goresnappa, Da Snakebitten	Warboss, Snakebite
Old Morgrub	Warphead weirdboy, Snakebite
Genrul Uzbrag, 'Da Genrul'	Big boss, Blood Axe
Mag Dedfist	Big boss, Goff
Zagnob Thundaskuzz	Speedboss, Evil Sun
Skabrukk	Stormboy drill boss, Goff
Badzag	Skarboyz nob, Goff
Nuzzgrond	Trukkboyz nob, Goff
Skulsnik	Kommando kaptin, Blood Axe
Skrappit	Mekaniak, Evil Sun
Duffrak	Thundaskuzz's driver, Evil Sun
Rukknut	Shokkjump dragsta driver, Bad Moon
Uzgul	Beast snagga boy, Goff
Urlukk	Spanner, Deathskull
Gutzog	Spanner, Deathskull
Zukrod	Runtherd, Snakebite
Lootenant Kabrukk	Nob, Blood Axe
Lootenant Gubzag	Nob, Blood Axe
Skitta	Zagnob's fuel-mixer, grot
'Sarge'	Killa Kan, Da Genrul's attendant

Da GrotWaaagh!

Snaggi Littletoof	Da Grotboss, Chosen of Gork and Mork
Skrawk	Grot
Guffink	Grot
Kruffik	Grot
Snippa One-Ear	Grot
Lunk	Grot
Pukk	Grot
Wizza	Grot

Da TekWaaagh!

Ufthak Blackhawk	Big boss, Bad Moon
Nizkwik	Grot

HUMIES

Aranuan 25th Astra Militarum, 'Golden Lions'

Grozer Sudliff	Colonel
Armenius Varrow	Captain, Third Platoon
Deralee Bruja	Major
Sentra LaSteel	Tank commander, Seventh Company, *Golden Thunder*
Darrus Greel	Armour sergeant, Seventh Company, *Lion's Fury*
Kat Pallas	Driver, Seventh Company, *Golden Thunder*
Gravers	Gunner, Seventh Company, *Golden Thunder*

'Two Hands' Tayne	Loader, Seventh Company, *Golden Thunder*
Xanin	Sponson gunner, Seventh Company, *Golden Thunder*
Sanavar Deltis	Enginseer, Seventh Company
Elushka Bone, 'Old Bones'	Regimental commissar

Aranuan Citizens

Ama Junier	Planetary governor
Eza	Hunter
The Seer	Chief of Emperor's Gate

SKRAWNIEZ

| Ilaethen Arhien | Autarch of Lugganath craftworld |
| Yria Nightsong | Farseer of Lugganath craftworld |

The orkish mind is something that many of my esteemed colleagues will argue barely exists. They will maintain that the orks and their kin are little more than instinctive animals, carrying out the tasks and functions in which they have evolved to specialise without independent thought, somewhat in the manner of colonial insects. In this matter – as in so many others – it is in fact the magi biologis in question who are acting mindlessly.

Orkish society is considerably more dynamic than our own; my learned peers might deride it as chaotic, if they deigned to accept the truth of such a statement, but even that would indicate limited understanding on their parts.[1] The simple truth is that an ork is far more capable than an unaugmented human of recognising when a situation is not to their individual benefit and taking action to remedy that fact.

It might be argued that this cannot be true, since orks will readily throw themselves into perilous situations with little regard for their own safety, or indeed, in a combat situation, tactics. The key issue here is that this is a highly desirable state of affairs for an ork, for whom the outcome of a battle is of substantially less importance than experiencing said battle in the first place. However, should an ork 'boss', 'big boss' or 'warboss' (the closest translations of their very loose command structure) not provide their followers with an appropriate level of excitement, combat or plunder – in other words, the things their followers desire – they can expect an attempted coup from within

1 I have separately catalogued seven hundred and forty-three instances of current recognised members of the Biologis holding or stating incorrect assumptions or observations about the orks and their related subspecies, which I have placed into the appendices of this work.

the ranks of those followers. This is a universally observed truth, wherever it has been possible to study the behaviour of orks with any degree of accuracy over a period of time.

If one compares this with the behaviour of, for example, the massed ranks of the Astra Militarum, for whom combat or even the potential of combat will provoke extremely negative physiological reactions, the difference is startling. Notions such as 'duty' might hold them to an undesirable course of action with poor outcomes; so too might fear of lethal censure by an officer such as an Imperial commissar, despite the fact that, should they act as a unit – as they have been trained to – the troopers could easily overpower and kill any such officer. The unaugmented human, enslaved to the whirl of emotions in their brain, is far more likely to go against their own wishes and interests rather than disobey a figure of authority.

For orks, that position would be unthinkable. So far as this xenos species appears to be concerned, although senior orks are larger than their subordinates, no ork – no matter how large – could maintain authority over its fellows without providing them with what they want. Indeed, since orks gain in size the more they fight, being a large ork indicates that you fight regularly, and therefore following you is likely to bring any other ork into combat.

It would be an interesting state of affairs indeed if unaugmented humans were to show the clear, logical reasoning possessed by orks, and act on it accordingly...

– Extract from the works of Magos Kazadin Yallamagasa, later known as the Biologis Diabolicus, declared heretek in M38

DA BIT WOT
COMES BEFORE DA FING

It was dark.

This was mainly because something was tied over Snaggi Littletoof's eyes, and therefore he couldn't see, but that was not a great deal of comfort. *He* certainly hadn't tied it there. Nor had he shoved the gag into his mouth, which foiled the efforts of even his needle-pointed teeth to bite through it, and condemned him to drool ceaselessly. He had not been the one to tie his hands behind his back, either, or attach them to something firm. He couldn't move, and he certainly couldn't escape. Not for the first time, he wondered what in the names of Gork and Mork a simple grot like him had done to deserve this.

Actually, there was probably quite a long list, now he came to think about it.

His eyes might be covered, but his ears were unstopped, and he could tell from the acoustics that he was inside something: probably a hut, or maybe part of a wrecked vehicle. He was sitting on dirt, although that didn't mean that much in these circumstances. He could still hear noises from outside, but it sounded like the fight was over. He wondered who had won. He hoped that it was his side, assuming there was still a side to which he could claim he belonged.

Something *whoomped* softly, like a hanging swath of cloth being shoved aside, and Snaggi sat up a little straighter, trying not to tremble in fear. His experiences of such things were limited, but he was fairly certain that you didn't get bound, gagged and blindfolded just to then be offered a hot squig skewer and your pick of the battlefield loot.

His ears told him that someone had come to a halt in front of him, and his nostrils picked up the scents of bang-powder and smoke and shoota grease, but even had they been blocked too, some other sense still hinted at the *closeness* of another being. A moment later, hands were reaching around to loosen the gag, and it was pulled free.

Snaggi didn't say anything. If you'd been gagged, and the gag was then loosened, it probably did not mean that you were in a position where shouting for help was going to do you any good. Either help had already loosened the gag, or you were about to get asked some serious questions by those uninclined to help. Besides, who would help him?

Then the blindfold was pulled off, and he found himself staring at another grot.

Hope leaped in his fast-beating heart. They'd found him! One of his ladz had found him, and was about to get him away from all this...

His brain realised that he did not recognise this grot at about the same time that his eyes focused on the hulking shape that loomed further back, in the shadows of what was, he now saw, an ork hut. The hut was a crudely assembled but sturdy affair of looted scrap, fairly unremarkable as such things went, but the ork was something else. It was massive, one of the largest

Snaggi had ever seen, and although its armour was painted in the black and yellow of the Bad Moons clan, that armour looked to be primarily composed of beakie bits.

'Dat fing out dere,' the grot said, snapping Snaggi's attention back to him. 'How's it work? How'd ya get 'ere, an' where'd ya come from?'

Snaggi licked his teeth nervously. If he was being asked this, then that implied he had some value: value that might evaporate as soon as he coughed up what information he had. He grinned at his captors, readying his mind for the battle of wits that would ensue.

'Tell me now, or I crush yer skull,' the ork rumbled, taking a tectonic step forwards. 'Ya ain't da only captive we got, yoo're just da one I'm askin' first.'

Orks were not given to idle threats in general, and Snaggi could immediately tell that this one was deathly serious: Snaggi's death, to be precise. He hastily revised his strategy from 'bargain for your life' to 'tell the scary ork what it wants to know and hope it then forgets about you'.

'Well,' he began hastily, 'dat's a bit of a long story.'

'Shorten it,' the ork suggested, folding its fingers into a fist that was roughly the size of Snaggi's entire upper body. 'Or I shorten yoo. By a head.'

'Yes, boss!' Snaggi gabbled, the honorific cutting in by reflex, even though he hated himself for it. 'So, uh...'

ONE

Warboss Gazrot Goresnappa had descended on the Imperial world of Aranua with all his forces and had, in the words of Major Saras, proceeded to give it such a thorough kicking that most of it didn't know which way was up any more.[2] The northern seas were now in xenos hands, including their promethium-extraction rigs. The main southern continent had been overrun, with neither high mountains, baking deserts, nor humid swamps providing any manner of meaningful defence against the invaders. Hive city after hive city had been taken. The populace either died in the fighting, were killed during the looting, or were enslaved.

Only one sizeable stronghold now remained: Davidia Hive, rising eight miles into the sky out of the blasted grey of Aranua's industrial heartland. It was a towering edifice of human engineering, and had stood in defiance of everything the galaxy could throw at it for seven millennia. Governor Ama Junier

---

2 The major was executed immediately following this statement, but that did not make it any less accurate.

thought she should probably take some heart from that, but the simple fact of the matter was that up until now, the galaxy hadn't thrown orks.

And now here they were, virtually on her doorstep. She looked out of the window of her quarters. Above her, the sky darkened to a deep, deep blue. She could make out the curvature of the planet from up here. And yet despite the distance, despite the patchy cloud cover beneath her feet, if she looked down she could see the shifting mass of the orkish forces. There were so Throne-damned many of them!

'I take it there has been no word from the astropaths?' she asked carefully.

'No, ma'am,' Colonel Grozer Sudliff of the Aranuan 25th replied. His voice was level, but Ama could hear the tension within it. He was resentful of her question, because he would of course have informed her had there been any manner of communication to indicate that reinforcements were coming. However, unless she asked such questions, she risked looking like the clueless aristocrat she knew the general suspected her to be.

'And the tactical situation has not meaningfully altered?'

'No, ma'am.'

Ama sighed. An Imperial governor was supposed to lead and defend their world, but there was very little she could do in such circumstances. Colonel Sudliff had been in military command, and he had been pushed back and overwhelmed in short order. Not that Ama blamed the man for it: he would have needed to be the rebirth of Macharius himself to have succeeded against such odds, and Sudliff most certainly was not that. He was a solid and unremarkable man, born into an officer family. From there he had taken up a military position, which he held with no great problem until called upon in earnest, at which point he failed in a solid and unremarkable manner. Ama had needed to use every part of her wit and ingenuity to achieve the role of planetary governor when the previous incumbent had passed away, including the discreet assassination of three rivals. At least she'd had to do some thinking in her life.

Their options ranged from laughable to piteous. The might of the orks' ground forces dictated against any notion of a sortie or counter-attack, despite the fact that the remnants of Sudliff's troops were now holed up in the lower sections of Davidia, in cramped and unsuitable conditions. They had no Titans, no Knights, no super-heavy tanks: all the ordnance of that scale had either been destroyed or, to Ama's great displeasure, captured. Above Ama's head, the mobile, heavily weaponised agglomerations of scrap and junk that the orks used as warships, which had annihilated all merchant and military shipping that had stuck around to fight them, were patrolling, if 'patrolling' was the right term for 'moving unpredictably and haphazardly'. There were at least two warp-capable ships currently berthed in Davidia's space docks, but even the *Tennavar's Smile*, pleasure yacht of rogue trader Priam Huzinka, lacked the armour or weaponry to survive the orks' attention for long enough to get to the system's Mandeville point. There would be no escape off-world for Davidia's nobility, including Aranua's governor: at least, not unless an unheralded arm of the Indomitus Crusade arrived.

Ama tapped her fingers on the thick crystalflex in front of her. 'What do you suppose they're waiting for, colonel? They've barely hesitated before attacking a hive city up until now, by all accounts.'

'Can't say for sure, ma'am.'

Ama turned to him. Colonel Sudliff was the very image of the Imperial military: his hair was grey but still thick, and his mutton chop sideburns brushed the stiff, gold-embroidered collar of his dress jacket. His epaulettes sparkled, his creases were so sharp that he could have shaved with them, his boots were shined to a mirror finish, and his jacket's buttons were the maned heads of the animal that gave its name to his regiment, the Golden Lions. It was a shame his tactical wisdom was no match for his sartorial grandeur.

'Can you say at all?' she enquired. 'We await near-certain death at the hands of xenos invaders, colonel. I feel it is not unreasonable to hold some curiosity about what might be staying our execution, at least briefly.'

The colonel cleared his throat, and his usual direct – even impertinent – stare wandered from her face for the first time that she could remember.

'They seem to be building fires, ma'am. So far as we can understand these creatures, they... Well, if they were human, I'd say they were having a party.'

'A party.' Ama turned away from him to stare out of her window once more. Darkness was falling on the ground far below, and she could indeed see the tiny sparks of light that must have been, if one were standing next to them, huge conflagrations. 'These creatures fall upon my world, they kill my people, and now they mock me by having a *party*?'

'If it please you, ma'am,' Sudliff offered, 'I doubt they're mocking you. These orks – they're barely more than animals. Nothing that they do here will be considered with us in mind. They're simply doing it because they want to.'

'I know,' Ama murmured. She'd been underestimated, maligned, avoided, and outright threatened in her life, but never had she simply been *ignored*. 'If anything, that just makes it worse.'

TWO

'Get dose fires nice an' big! I want all dem humies to know we'z here, an' I want 'em shakin' in dere boots!'

Gazrot Goresnappa, also known as Gazrot Da Snakebitten, was without question one of the greatest orks to ever venture out into the galaxy and punch it in its face. A member of the Snakebite clan, he rose to violent prominence early in his life by regularly winning headbutting contests with smasha squigs. He had strangled the seven-headed serpent of Kryyk using one of its own necks, and had gone to the trouble of harvesting its venom glands, not to coat his blade or poison his enemies, but simply to add a bit of kick to his fungus beer. He quickly gained a strong following, based in part on his skill in combat, and in part on his propensity and ability to raise squiggoths of a size rarely seen. When he was slighted by Warboss Kurzan, Gazrot had ridden his herd right over the other ork's battlewagon, crushing it, and Kurzan inside it, in the process. After that, there had been little doubt in anyone's mind who should take the old warboss' place.

What this meant was that when Gazrot Goresnappa, close to

ten feet tall in his hulking, fur-draped, smoke-belching mega armour, yelled at you to make a fire nice and big, you zoggin' well made that fire nice and big.

All around him, orks scurried to do his bidding, and the sight brought a smile to Gazrot's face. This was what it meant to be an ork! It wasn't like he was one of those self-important types, like the freebooter kaptins, or the Blood Axes that enjoyed mimicking the humie way of doing things. Gazrot didn't give himself fancy hats, or medals, or any other frippery. Gazrot just enjoyed a good scrap, and the more orks that followed him and did what he said when he said it, the more scraps he could win.

He'd very nearly won this one, which was why he was taking a moment to enjoy himself. There was one big humie camp left on this entire planet, so far as he could tell, which was the one looming above them all at this very moment. Gazrot would say this for humies: they knew how to build big. The 'city', as the humies called it, must have been larger than any of the ships in his fleet, which was impressive in and of itself. It was taller than a mountain, with its summit lost in the clouds; it was practically a mountain in its own right, a gargantuan structure which wasn't just tall, but *wide*. Simply being near it would probably be enough to intimidate any normal creature.

Gazrot wasn't any normal creature. So far as he was concerned, the sheer size of this thing just made it more of an obvious and impressive target. He'd bring it down, just like his ladz had brought down all the others. Then the meks would strip out anything useful, and they'd get some of the fuel that Magzak's lot were pulling off the humie rigs in the big water to the north, and they'd build a whole bunch of new war engines, repair the ones that had been damaged, wait around a bit for a bunch of new boyz to show up – they always did, sooner or later – and then get back out into the stars in search of the next planet to conquer. That was life as it should be lived; that was the ork way.

In the meantime, though, he wanted to remind every ork exactly who it was that had led them here and crushed the humies. That wasn't him being self-important, that was just proper and sensible. It made it more likely that they'd do what he said, when he said it. Da Genrul had a humie word for that: 'dissipline'. Gazrot wasn't buying into any of that humie crap, though.

Da Genrul. Now, that was an ork who needed watching, Gazrot thought. Genrul Uzbrag was a typical Blood Axe, in that he liked the orks under his command to walk in straight lines and hit their heads with their hands when he told them to do something, and a whole load of other stuff he'd picked up from humies, and elsewhere for that matter. It didn't sit well with Gazrot, borrowing stuff from other species. What was wrong with being an ork, and doing things in the ork way, like Gork and Mork intended? Snakebites were traditionalists at heart, and Uzbrag's tendency towards innovation rubbed Gazrot up the wrong way. Still, there was no denying that the git was successful. He could clobber an enemy with the best of them, and sometimes his strange inventions and 'battle plans' actually worked surprisingly well. There was a reason he was one of Gazrot's favoured big bosses, but that didn't mean Gazrot trusted him. Although to be fair, he didn't trust anyone.

He certainly didn't trust Mag Dedfist. The massive Goff big boss was yelling at a bunch of his ladz to build the fires higher, which was all well and good, but Dedfist was a dour son of a squig who Gazrot reckoned wouldn't be content playing second shoota to him for much longer. One day soon, Dedfist would get it into his incredibly thick-skulled head to take a swing for his warboss, with the goal of taking his place. Gazrot had no intention of letting that happen, of course, but it wasn't like there were many options. He'd thrown Dedfist at the hardest knots of humie resistance, and the big Goff had gone through them without much pause, and certainly without taking any sort of noticeable harm. Dedfist had simply reinforced his own reputation with the boyz under his command, which wasn't going to do Gazrot any favours. No, when it came to it, he'd have to let Dedfist take his swing and then just stomp him flat into the ground, as tradition dictated.

He also didn't trust Zagnob Thundaskuzz, the Evil Sunz speed-boss, but that was less because Gazrot thought that Thundaskuzz was gunning for him, and more because simply getting any concept into the speedboss' head was virtually impossible. You couldn't trust him to do anything other than accelerate off into the distance and kill things while going at an incredibly high speed, which, granted, was sometimes a very useful trait. It wasn't much good when you were trying to make sure the right bits of a Waaagh! hit the enemy at the right time to cause maximum impact, though. Nonetheless, the Kult of Speed had a sizeable presence in Waaagh! Goresnappa, and Thundaskuzz had a correspondingly high amount of influence. He could neither be conveniently ignored nor disposed of, so Gazrot would just have to make use of him as best he could.

All of those were considerations for another time, though. Right now, the raging infernos that had been built had achieved the desired effect: namely, a whole load of orks were starting to congregate, wondering what was going on, and if there was going to be any food or, preferably, a fight.

Gazrot looked around, then tapped his shouty box to make sure it was working. It responded with a pleasing static squeal, which sounded almost exactly like a grot that had been stepped on. Dedfist had been watching him ever since he'd stopped yelling at his boyz to make the fires bigger, but now Gazrot could see the strange peaked hat of Da Genrul approaching in the midst of a big knot of Blood Axes, accompanied by the Killa Kan he called 'Sarge', which followed him around with that ridiculous captured humie in a cage on its back. A rumble of engines and the stink of badly refined fuel smoke announced the arrival of Zagnob Thundaskuzz, resplendent on the back of his Deffkilla wartrike, and at the head of a veritable host of bikers.

Good. Let them all come. Let them see the might of the Great Goresnappa, Da Snakebitten, the ork who led them here. Let them be reminded who was in charge, and whose boot would be kicking their arse if anyone thought they fancied being warboss.

His own Snakebites were flooding in now, too: they didn't outnumber the other clans in his Waaagh!, but they were certainly the most numerous of any one faction. And of course, a truly great warboss didn't just have one clan behind him, he had many. They were all here, Bad Moons, Deathskulls and all, even a few freebooters hanging around the edges, but this was the main core of his force. Goffs for the really close-in fighting, Evil Sunz for the quick stuff, Blood Axes when you needed a sneaky git, and Snakebites to hold it all together: proper orks; true orks; orks you could rely on not to forget about the old ways, and how Gork and Mork wanted things done.

Still, for all the fact that Snakebites were undoubtedly the best clan, and that the war beasts his particular part of it bred were the biggest and stompiest around, there was something to be said for a bit of teknology now and then. No one had ever before seen a squiggoth the size of Tankbreaka, Gazrot's personal mount, but even that massive creature was dwarfed by the Mega-Gargant in front of which Gazrot was currently standing – *Da Kroolfang*. It somehow seemed even bigger than the massive human city, because that was just a *thing*, and things could be as big as they were: a planet was a thing, and no one would blink at that. The Gargant, however, was a giant effigy of Gork (or possibly Mork), and was shaped accordingly, with huge eyes that could fire energy beams, a gigantic bitey jaw, arms of death-dealing weapons, and a massive body which housed not only the infamous belly gun, but could also transport a whole host of boyz right into the thick of the fight, assuming any enemies were foolish enough to get close to such a gigantic machine of destruction. It was utterly titanic.

Gazrot had no doubt that some orks wouldn't like to stand directly in front of such a monstrous war machine, in case it made them look small by comparison. Gazrot had no such compunctions. He told the zoggin' thing what to do, where to go, and what to stomp: that made him the most powerful ork around. So far as he was concerned, the sheer size of the Gargant made him look *bigger*.

He flicked his shouty box again, and the resulting squeal-edged *thud* drew everyone's attention to him.

'ALRIGHT, LISSEN UP!' he bellowed, and the shouty box amplified his voice so magnificently that it was as though he were shouting directly into the ear of every ork present: every warboss' heartfelt desire. *'Now, I told ya all wot was gonna happen 'ere, right? We was gonna come down, give all da humies a right good kickin', and take all dere stuff! An' we did it, didn't we?'*

His words drew a mighty roar of approval from the assembled orks. Out of the corner of his eye, Gazrot saw the crooked staff of Old Morgrub approaching, belting other orks on the head to get them out of his way. The weirdboy was the Waaagh!'s most senior warphead, at least so far as these things could be determined. He certainly seemed a little more grounded than a lot of the rest, although that was a bit like saying that one trampla squig smelled better than most of the others. Still, Morgrub had enough control over the power that built up within him to not explode too many heads by accident, and although sometimes he made less sense than a squig that had fallen in the fungus beer, he was capable of providing decent advice every now and then. Gazrot knew that his big bosses weren't fans of Morgrub's rantings, but that was just further evidence that, unlike Snakebites, they'd forgotten the ways of Gork and Mork.

'*So now we got just one more fing to do,*' Gazrot continued, as Morgrub finally clobbered his way to the front of the packed ranks of orkish faces, all lit up by the roaring flames. '*One more bunch of humies to stomp, and den all dis planet's ours!*'

That brought some cheers as well, but also some grumbling, because no more humies meant no more fighting. Well, actually it didn't mean that at all, because any ork could pick a fight with any other ork for just about any reason, including because both of them happened to want a fight, but that was just scrapping. That wasn't the full-throated bloodlust of the Waaagh!, where the orks all banded together and showed the other species in the galaxy exactly why they were the very best. A scrap was fun, without question, but it wasn't quite the same thing as charging into battle with the thunder of guns as your heartbeat, your mates beside you, and getting covered in someone else's blood, or ichor, or whatever turned out to be inside when you hit 'em.

'*Once we're done 'ere, we'll get ourselves sorted out an' back onto da ships, den go an' find some uvver place to conquer!*' Gazrot bellowed, to reassure his ladz. '*Dis ain't da end of the Waaagh!! Dis ain't even da beginnin' of da end! It might be da end of da…*'

He tailed off, because Old Morgrub was looking upwards with a strangely intent expression on his scarred, leathery face. Normally it took a lot to throw Gazrot off his stride, but there was something about the warphead's sheer focus that made him uneasy. Still not quite sure why he was doing it, and heedless of the impact such uncertainty would have on his standing amongst his boyz, he too turned and looked upwards to see what Morgrub was staring at.

THREE

Gork and Mork did not speak loudly to everyone. Many orks lived out their lives without ever really hearing the voices of their gods, save in the background roar of battle. For others – the weirdboyz whose heads exploded, for example – they spoke a bit *too* loudly. But for some rare orks, like Grand Warlord Ghazghkull Mag Uruk Thraka, the voices of the ork gods were their guidance, the fuel that powered the furnace of conquest and violence burning in their hearts, and which was crucial to their success at bringing others under their sway and dominating the galaxy.

Snaggi Littletoof knew in his heart that Gork and Mork were speaking to him, as well. The trouble was, he was a grot, and no one cared.

He'd tried to tell others about it, of course. The thing was, the volume of Gork and Mork speaking *to you* didn't seem to be anywhere near as important as how loudly you could talk about it to *other orks*. And when you weren't even an ork to begin with, that wasn't very loud at all. Snaggi was surrounded by hulking green giants, bellowing and roaring and kicking him without thinking – or sometimes thinking about it and then kicking him again, just to be sure – and not one of them was prepared to listen to the words of their own gods, just because they were coming out of the mouth of a grot. It was enough to make you sick. He'd had more than one hiding for 'bleedin' cheek' when he'd mentioned the gods, and he'd learned to keep his mouth shut now. More or less, anyway.

Still, he'd managed to get himself a fairly cushy little number, at least so far as things went for grots. No desperate clutching of an unreliable grot blasta and trying to get close enough to shoot some giant humie in a suit of armour, or a deadly-fast bugeye with four arms and knives for hands for Snaggi Littletoof, oh no. No, he'd managed to blag his way onto the Mega-Gargant known as *Da Kroolfang*, which was an awful lot of metal between him and anything that might want to kill him.

Of course, he wasn't a passenger. Snaggi and the rest of his little crew were under the theoretical oversight of Mek Zagblutz, a cantankerous old Deathskull with three eyes (two of them mechanical, but that was meks for you) and expectations of the level of work required from those under his command which were so high that Snaggi sometimes wondered if the old git had missed his proper calling as a stormboy drill boss. Right now they were greasing and polishing a collection of cogs and gears, the purpose of which Snaggi wasn't quite sure, but might have had something to do with turning the Gargant's head from side to side so its Gaze of Mork could incinerate whatever its kommander chose.

'Ow long d'ya fink it'll take to kill dat last humie city?' Guffink asked, scrubbing at a gear with his shiny-cloth. Guffink was hard-working and industrious, and generally made the rest of them look bad in comparison.

'Dunno,' Skrawk replied. The others waited for a moment to

see if he was going to qualify that with anything else, such as musings on exactly what might cause a variance in the time taken, but nothing else was forthcoming. Skrawk wasn't much of a conversationalist.

'I fink it's da biggest dere's been yet,' Snaggi offered. 'So it'll prob'ly take longer.' He looked around to make sure no one was watching, then took a swig from his oil can. He spat it out hurriedly a moment later, because it tasted foul. It had done every time so far, but he made a point of trying it once a day, just in case one of the others had come up with a cunning plan to sneak some booze under Zagblutz's nose by putting it in a can. Snaggi wasn't going to risk missing out on some good stuff just because he got a mouthful of oil if he was wrong: that would have been cowardly, and that was not the way of Gork and Mork.

'See, I was finkin' dat,' Guffink replied amiably, 'but den I fort, well, as it's da last one, none of da ladz are off doin' anyfing else, are dey? So dere's a lot more boyz to kill it, an' dat means it might even be quicker!'

'"Da ladz",' Kruffik chuckled mockingly. Kruffik was big, at least for a grot, and liked to throw what weight he had around. 'Stop talkin' like yoo're one of 'em, Guffink. Any of 'em hears ya talkin' like dat, dey'll twist yer head clean off yer neck.'

'An' wot's it to yoo if dey did?' Guffink demanded, ceasing his polishing and rounding on the bigger grot. 'Eh? Why're ya so worried about wot an ork's gonna fink if he hears me talkin', Kruffik? Yoo ain't worried about *me*, I know dat much!'

Snaggi exchanged glances with Skrawk. This little exchange held the promise of livening up their work a bit.

'I reckon ya fancy yerself as an ork's runt,' Guffink continued, warming to his subject. 'Does that sound good, eh, Kruffik? Ya wanna do wot a nob says? Ya wanna carry his ammo around? Wanna polish his shoota for 'im? Workin' on a Gargant's not good enuff, is it? Ya wanna go pick up after a boss nob, den come back an' lord it over da rest of us like dat makes you all *important*?'

Snaggi was expecting Kruffik to belt Guffink round the face, but to his surprise the bigger grot just folded his arms and glowered. 'Yoo'z a snivellin' little whiner, Guffink, an' ya always have been. Yoo'z da one wot finks he's important – yoo'z as bad as Snaggi dere.'

Snaggi felt his brows rise, as he was unexpectedly drawn into this conflict. 'Wait a second, Kruffik, wotcha mean by dat?'

'Wot I *mean*,' Kruffik said, squaring up to Snaggi, 'is dat we'z all heard ya talkin' about da gods, Snaggi. We'z all heard ya saying dat dere talkin' to ya, like yoo'z somefing speshul. But ya *ain't*.'

Snaggi grinned toothily at him. 'Dat's okay, Kruffik. Yoo're just jealous cos da gods ain't talkin' to ya.'

'Dey ain't talkin' to *yoo* either!' Kruffik barked, his temper fraying. He reached out with one sharp-nailed finger, and jabbed Snaggi in the chest with it. 'Yoo're makin' it up to try an' make yerself sound important, so cloth'eads like Guffink 'ere might lissen to ya, an' do yer work for ya!'

Now, that statement wasn't born of any concern for Guffink, Snaggi knew. So far as ork kultur went – and grot kultur along with it – if you couldn't stand up for yourself, you got walked on. That was the way of the galaxy, and no one with any sense had any problem with it. The only reason Kruffik would object would be because he was jealous he hadn't thought of it himself.

The thing was, cunning plan though it might have been, that wasn't what Snaggi was doing. He wouldn't dare invite the wrath of Gork or Mork by claiming to hear their voices when he didn't. He knew exactly what he'd heard.

'Dey're talkin' to me right now,' he told Kruffik. 'Dey're tellin' me just wot to do.'

'Oh?' Kruffik's snort of derision was so forceful that it splattered snot all over his front. 'An' wot's dat?'

'Dis.'

Snaggi kicked him in the shin as hard as he could, which given he was wearing metal-capped boots, and Kruffik's shins were completely unprotected was, when everything was taken into account, pretty zoggin' hard.

Kruffik howled and hopped backwards, clutching his shin in both hands. Snaggi laughed at him, enjoying the other grot's pain, but Kruffik's rage quickly overcame it. Kruffik grabbed a wrench, a piece of dirty metal nearly as long as he was tall, and swung it in both hands, screaming as he did so. Snaggi stumbled backwards, fear replacing his amusement just as quickly as Kruffik's pain had disappeared, and ducked a moment before the wrench could connect with his head. The *whoosh* of air displacement hinted at exactly how heavy the impact would have been had the blow landed, but the force of the missed swing carried Kruffik around, off balance. Snaggi had no intention of letting him have another go, so he charged and put his shoulder into the other grot's ribs as hard as he could.

Kruffik let out a great huff of air, and they both went down onto the greasy plates of metal that formed the floor in this part of the Gargant. Guffink and Skrawk were cheering, as was the way of any grot when encountering a fight in which they were not a participant, but they weren't on anyone's side: it was just good old-fashioned appreciation of a brawl. Snaggi couldn't count on any help, even though it had been Guffink squaring up to Kruffik a few moments before, so he grabbed one of Kruffik's wrists in both hands and bit it as hard as he could. Kruffik howled and relaxed his grip on the wrench, dropping it completely, but Snaggi quickly realised that this was possibly a bad development for him. The wrench was big and clumsy, and although Kruffik would have clung to the weapon instinctively, it wouldn't have served him well at such close quarters. Now, however, the larger grot had his hands free to claw and strangle, and that wasn't going to go so well for Snaggi.

Snaggi went for his eyes instead.

Kruffik howled in pain as Snaggi's nails gouged at his face, but he flailed and thrashed and kicked so vigorously that Snaggi was thrown clean off him and landed hard on the deck again. He staggered up, looking for some sort of weapon of his own, but to no avail: Kruffik was too quick, and was already coming for him with fists balled.

A grot's punch would barely register to an ork, and even a human would probably shrug it off and swing one back with considerably more force, but they were plenty hard enough to another grot. Snaggi ducked the first and landed a pointy elbow into Kruffik's ribs, but then the other grot managed to get hold of him by the back of the neck and pulled him up sufficiently to send his next blow, with his other hand, right into Snaggi's gob.

Pain flowered, and Snaggi staggered backwards as the entire Gargant swayed around him. He spat out a toof, stumbled sideways, and caught at a lever of uncertain provenance in order to hold himself up. The last place he wanted to be was on the floor when his head was swimming, and Kruffik was still coming at him. Then an idea struck him, and he wrenched on the lever, trying to break it loose. Zagblutz's engineering wasn't always the most secure, and it would make a handy bludgeon...

The lever *moved*.

Kruffik stopped as something overhead *creaked*. It was a deep noise, one that reverberated around the Gargant's frame like an episode of particularly explosive flatulence in a squiggoth stall. It spoke not of the slight settling of a sturdy metallic superstructure, but of the beginnings of something more, something greater, something decidedly more emphatic than just a *creak*.

Very, very slowly, the ceiling began to move.

It was almost infinitesimal at first, only the faintest of shifts in shadow and light to suggest that something was happening. Then, as the movement became more obvious, more sounds sprang up. Scraping sounds, groaning sounds, the sounds of bolts and rivets *pinging* off from their fixings, the sounds of metal flexing in ways it was not supposed to flex, and tearing in ways it most certainly was not supposed to tear.

Snaggi didn't move. He was frozen in place by the fear that most commonly consumed a grot, which could be divided into two parts: firstly, that he was going to be crushed by something much larger and heavier than him; and secondly, that even if he somehow survived the current peril, he was going to be blamed for it.

'Oh, zoggin' 'eck,' Snaggi muttered weakly, as a thin crack of darkness appeared above him, and rapidly widened. That was the night sky, and one thing Snaggi was pretty certain about was that you weren't supposed to see *outside* a Gargant when you were *inside* a Gargant, unless you were looking through a window that a mek had specifically put there.

'Da head's comin' off!' Skrawk wailed, showing uncharacteristic perceptiveness and communication. 'Da zoggin' head's comin' off, ladz! Wot're we gonna do?!'

There was nothing they *could* do, of course – at least not to stop the landslide of metal which was even now carrying an untold tonnage of prime scrap, at least two high-power energy weapons, probably several orks, and quite possibly one very angry mekboy, forwards and then suddenly and quite terminally downwards. Snaggi managed to force himself to move and, along with the rest of his krew – hostilities abruptly forgotten – ran forwards to the front edge of the Gargant as the gigantic construction above them scraped onwards.

Snaggi got to the rail of what had been a viewing deck just as the ceiling began to tilt, and the head began to plummet. He looked over the edge and at first, of course, saw nothing but the underside of the Gargant's head. Then, as it fell and got smaller, he saw the rest of the Waaagh! spread out below, thousands of orks all gathered around blazing fires. They all seemed to be organised – insofar as orks were ever organised – into a loose semicircle around the base of the Mega-Gargant, and they began scrambling backwards as the head fell towards them. None of them were under it, but they'd been looking at something which had been…

'Oh, Gork's Green Grin,' Snaggi breathed, clapping his hand over his mouth. 'Da zoggin' warboss is down dere!'

For just a moment, Genrul Uzbrag thought that the enormous visage of Gork (or possibly Mork) falling off the Mega-Gargant was something Gazrot Goresnappa had orchestrated. He was still waiting for a squiggoth head to appear in its place, and Da Snakebitten to announce he'd created the galaxy's first Squig-Dread, or something equally ridiculous, when he realised that Gazrot's expression as he looked upwards at the massive hunk of falling metal was not one of triumph or pride, but one of confusion, rapidly overtaken by pissed-off comprehension.

Da Genrul had done enough yellin' back and forth in loud warzones to have picked up an understanding of what shapes an ork's mouth made when forming certain words, and so he was quite certain that he did not imagine that Gazrot said 'Oh zog' just before the Gargant's head landed on top of him.

Fire blossomed upwards, accompanied by roiling clouds of

black smoke. Shards of metal were flung out, scything through the ranks and cutting down the ones at the front (mainly lower-ranking boyz, since any boss with half a brain kept a few footsloggers between him and Gazrot Goresnappa, just in case Da Snakebitten decided he needed to make an example of someone). A lot of orks cheered on general principle, since something loud and destructive had happened, and that was always worth cheering.[3]

Genrul Uzbrag's brows lowered, and not just because he was squinting against the cloud of dust and dirt blasted outwards by the impact. The presence of the warboss was the lodestone to which the rest of the Waaagh! was inexorably drawn: an invisible force, sort of like gravity, only not one the mekboyz could duplicate with a trukk full of spare parts, a free afternoon, and a plentiful supply of fungus beer. And now, in some way that Uzbrag could not quite verbalise even within his own head, that pull was gone.

Well, not gone, exactly. It was more…

…*inwards*.

'You killed 'im,' Kruffik said, his tone one of bleak and utter dread. 'You killed da warboss, Snaggi.'

Snaggi's first instinct was to deny it. That was what a grot did: if something happened then you denied it, unless you were absolutely sure that the biggest ork paying attention was happy with it, in which case you claimed credit for it. He should deny that the lever had moved, and if it had definitely moved then he should deny being the one to have pulled on it; and if it was impossible to argue that he hadn't been the one who'd pulled on it then he should *definitely* blame Kruffik for hitting

---

3 Exactly what had been destroyed was always an after-thought, since if you were still able to cheer, it wasn't *you*, and that was the main thing.

him so hard that he'd had no option other than to grab at the lever – no, better, that he hadn't even *realised* that he'd grabbed at the lever.

But he didn't feel like denying it. He could hear the great green voices of the gods, and the gods were telling him that he shouldn't be trying to hide this. Who could say they'd killed a warboss? Precious few! There were mighty beakies who'd never killed a warboss! There were flashy skrawniez who'd never killed a warboss! There were stompy metal gits with the glowy guns who'd never killed a warboss! So what if Snaggi couldn't actually *prove* that pulling on the lever was what had caused the Gargant's head to fall off? So what if it made no sense for Mek Zagblutz to have set up a lever that would make the head of his pride and joy fall off? Maybe the mek hadn't done it on purpose: maybe he'd made a mistake. Perhaps this was Snaggi's *destiny*.

He liked that.

'Yeah,' he said, tasting the word as it passed his needle teeth, relishing the thrill of danger as he admitted – no! Claimed credit for – killing Gazrot Goresnappa. 'Yeah, I did. I killed da warboss. An' ya know wot?' he continued, warming to the rebellious glow in his chest. 'Ya know zoggin' *wot*?'

He rounded on Kruffik and grabbed the horrified grot by the front of his rags.

'I ain't finished! I've had it wiv bein' kicked for fings I ain't done! Or even for fings I have! I've had it wiv bein' yelled at, and fightin' da squigs for me food! Dere's more of us dan dere are of dem! It's time for us grots to rise up, ya hear me? We're gonna show dese overgrown gits who da *real* bosses are round 'ere! An' if any of 'em don't like it...' He smacked the back of one hand into the palm of the other. '*Blam!* Dey're gonna get flattened, just like dat git down dere! Dis is just da beginnin'! Dis is da *Revolushun!*'

Far below, the orks of what had up until very recently been Waaagh! Gazrot weren't paying any attention to the tiny, animated figure screaming far above them.

They had suddenly acquired much more pressing concerns.

FOUR

Gazrot Goresnappa was given every opportunity to prove that he wasn't dead. Those orks who hadn't been crushed, incinerated by the explosion, or perforated by flying debris watched the fallen Gargant head expectantly, waiting for the warboss to angrily swat aside a piece of panelling or a broken strut and emerge from the wreckage, angry but largely unharmed, in an unquestionable sign of the favour of Gork and Mork.

As the smoke continued to billow out and the fires continued to burn, and there remained absolutely no sign that Gazrot was now anything other than an extremely flat green smear somewhere beneath the pile of metal, it began to dawn on the assembled mass that they were a Waaagh! which now lacked a warboss.

Some other clans might call the Blood Axes 'opportunistic'. They definitely called them 'sneaky'. So far as Genrul Uzbrag was concerned, those were just words used by orks angry that someone else had thought of something they hadn't.

'Dis is a sign!' he bellowed, striding forwards out of the

mass of boyz to stand in front of them. He knew he was an imposing sight: a big ork with an axe-bladed choppa as tall as he was, which he could energise with a flick of a switch to envelop it in a crackling power field that would allow it to slice through pretty much anything. In his other hand he had a humie double-shoota, the sort carried by the really tough beakies in immensely thick armour. More than one ork had scoffed at him carrying a humie gun, but they hadn't laughed after Da Genrul had demonstrated its effectiveness: indeed, they hadn't been in much of a condition to do anything. Beakies were much tougher and shootier than normal humies, and Uzbrag saw no harm in nicking their stuff after he'd killed them.

'Wot sorta sign?' someone shouted.

'A sign from Gork an' Mork to say dat Goresnappa weren't da one to be leading dis Waaagh!' Da Genrul replied loudly, smacking himself in the chest. 'It should be *me*, instead! Cos I ain't fick enough to stand under a Gargant when its head's gonna fall off!'

'*Oh yeah?*'

Another disturbance in the green sea led to the mass of ork bodies parting, and the intimidating shape of Boss Mag Dedfist strode through, his mega armour hissing vapour as he came. Uzbrag immediately sized up his potential opponent.[4] Dedfist was broader than him, and very likely heavier even without the weight of his mega armour, but he wasn't quite as tall, and probably not as quick. On the other hand, if the massive power klaw that made up the left arm of his armour[5] managed to land a blow, that would probably be the last blow of

4 Any ork in a disagreement with another ork is a potential opponent.
5 Also called the Dedfist, since Mag was of the opinion that if you'd found a good name you might as well get some use out of it.

the fight. The question would be whether he'd get the chance, or whether Uzbrag's choppa would strike home first. But then again, what about Dedfist's skorchas, the nozzles of which were mounted in the twin horns that jutted forth from the jaw of his armour? They could put even an ork as tough as Uzbrag right off his swing.

'Dunno what sorta fermented fungus beer ya been drinkin', but dere's no way dat *yoo* are da ork wot's gonna lead dis Waaagh!' Dedfist proclaimed, swaggering towards Uzbrag. 'Typical sneaky Blood Axe, wiv yer silly choppa, an' yer humie shoota, an' yer *hat*.' He sneered at Uzbrag's headgear, which lacked any of the horns, spikes, jawbones of large animals, or other accoutrements that would normally adorn such an item for a more traditionally minded ork. 'Ya ain't gonna be da one leadin' da charge, an' clobberin' da gits on da uvver end of it! Yer gonna be *hidin'* behind yer ladz!'

A collective ripple of anticipation and amusement rippled through the watching orks, because although fighting and talking were two very different things, that was very definitely fightin' talk, as in the thing you said in the full knowledge that the other ork was then going to try to punch you in the mouth.

Uzbrag's eyes narrowed, and his fingers tightened on the haft of his choppa. He could feel the anticipation of the orks around him: was he going to settle for clonking Dedfist around the head, a swift blow to establish his quickness and superiority of skill, or was he going to power up his weapon and go straight for a killing swing?

Neither, as it turned out, because someone else had something to say.

'*Both of yoo zoggin' grots should go an' herd squigs!*' a mighty voice bellowed at the top of its lungs. Both bosses turned, their violent intentions briefly postponed by the desire to see which other fool wanted his head kicked in, and were rewarded by the sight of Speedboss Zagnob Thundaskuzz standing upright on the back of his Deffkilla wartrike and staring balefully at them.

'Dat's strong words comin' from an ork standin' all da way over dere on his rokkit trolley!' Uzbrag retorted, to a general chorus of laughter. 'If ya got somefing to say, why dontcha come over here, an' say it to our faces?'

Shouts and hoots from the crowd accompanied that invitation, but they only rose in volume when Thundaskuzz actually *stepped off his wartrike* and began to shove his way through the assembled boyz. Speed freeks didn't get off or out of their vehicles without very good reason, and they generally weren't very impressed when they had to. The speedboss had his snagga klaw on one arm and a twin boomstikk in the other hand, with a second such weapon shoved in the back of his belt. New mutters began to fly backwards and forwards, and Uzbrag heard a few quick bets taking place as well. If it came to a three-way punch-up, the logic seemed to go that Thundaskuzz's snagga klaw could strike from distance and then pull his enemy in for a proper goin'-over. Plus, everyone knew that speed freeks put all manner of chemicals into their blood to make themselves faster, didn't they? It wouldn't be a surprise if Zagnob could leave even Da Genrul in the dust when it came to reflexes.

'Goffs don't see nuffin' wot ain't in front of dere faces, an' Blood Axes can't be trusted to fight wot's in front of dere faces!' Thundaskuzz declared. 'When ya want somefin' done quick an' proper, who d'ya want doin' it?'

'*SPEED FREEKS!*' his loyal retinue of bikers yelled, waving their weapons in the air. One or two of the more excitable ones triggered their bikes' dakkaguns as well, which mowed down several of the orks in front of them and sparked immediate and violent retribution from the survivors, who turned around and began hauling the warbikers off their vehicles to give them a thorough pasting.

Violence, never far from the surface in any orkish gathering, bubbled up instantly, and rapidly spread out. The warboss was dead and there was no immediately obvious replacement yet, which meant that any sort of mass Waaagh! attack on the humie city probably wasn't going to be happening in the next few minutes. Given that, no ork was going to pass up the chance of a fight with his neighbour, as much to while away the time as anything else. If a bigger fight started, the survivors could always leave off and join it.

As slugga shots flew, punches landed, and choppas rose and fell, the three big bosses of the collection of orks formerly known as Waaagh! Goresnappa triangled up to each other, each waiting for someone else to make the first move. It wasn't that they didn't want to fight – all orks wanted to fight, it was the simplest, most primal instinct they had – but you wanted to make yourself look your best when you were scrappin' over rank. It was fine and proper to charge into humies or beakies or skrawniez before they knew you were there – although good luck with that against skrawniez, those pointy-eared gits always seemed to know something – because if they weren't paying attention then they obviously didn't deserve to even have a chance to stay alive, but it was a bit different when it was one ork against another, like this.

Being warboss wasn't just about hitting hard, it was also about being *tough*. You didn't want to make the first move, in case it looked like you were scared of being hit. So each one of them eyed the other two, muttering insults, and waiting for someone else to finally lose their rag and swing first. When they did, it was going to get extremely violent very, very quickly.

Or at least, it would have done, had all three of them not

suddenly suffered a piercing headache and spontaneous nose-bleeds.

'Wot da zoggin'…?' Uzbrag spluttered, wiping at his nose with the sleeve of his coat.

'It's Morgrub!' Dedfist spat, pointing with one finger of his power klaw at the figure of the old weirdboy, who was glowing with green energy. 'Dat bloody warphead's gonna blow everyone's skulls!'

Everyone knew that weirdboyz got all charged up when the orks around them were agitated. That was what made them such good weapons, because you could haul 'em into the middle of a fight, point them at the enemy, and hope that they'd be able to aim the power building inside them at the other gits instead of your own ladz. Even the mightiest sorcerers of other races would be hard-pressed to stand up to a weirdboy when he was surrounded by fighting orks, as at least one pointy-eared git would have been able to attest to, had Old Morgrub not burst his head open with a surge of pure Waaagh! energy during a duel. All that was left of him now was a funny-looking stone, which Morgrub had hung off his staff and sometimes licked when he wanted inspiration, or was bored.

The thing about Old Morgrub, though, was that he wasn't just any weirdboy, he was a warphead. Weirdboyz had a fairly short life expectancy, since the overload of Waaagh! energy could easily explode their skulls, but warpheadz were those who had survived for long enough to properly master their abilities, and were even more dangerous as a result. Whereas most weirdboyz were a bit uncomfortable with the building sensation of Waaagh! energy within them, and tried to avoid it, warpheadz couldn't get enough of it. They actively sought out any sort of fight simply in order to get charged up and let off a few blasts, which looked to be exactly what Old Morgrub was doing here. The problem was, he might just take a few dozen ork heads with him.

'Get 'im outta here!' Dedfist barked.

'Who're ya givin' orders to, ya git?' Thundaskuzz demanded, working the action on his snagga klaw even as he winced from the increasing pain inside his skull.

'Oh for Mork's sake, I'll do it me zoggin' self!' Da Genrul yelled, advancing on Old Morgrub with the intention of grabbing the warphead and hauling him as far away as possible from the massive ruckus that had broken out. However, before he could reach him, Morgrub threw back his head, spread his arms, and opened his jaws wider than would seem anatomically possible.

'Oh, zoggin' 'eck!' Mag Dedfist was heard to complain, as a pillar of lightning wrapped green fire shot up into the air from Morgrub's gape, sizzling and spitting as it went. It rose straight and true, and as it did so it ignited the air around it, causing a titanic thunderclap that struck the assembled orks with a sound so loud it manifested as a physical force. The shockwave flattened boyz and rocked buggies on their suspensions; it kicked up dust and sent it spinning through the air in fractal spirals. It succeeded in stopping the fight in its tracks, which was a remarkable achievement in and of itself, and when everyone had turned around and picked themselves up off the ground, Old Morgrub was staring at them with eyes that were slightly too wide and a grin apparently directed somewhere slightly beyond every ork's left shoulder: or, indeed, the other way around.

No one moved, just in case it set Morgrub off and somehow singled them out for an exploding head. No ork minded the idea of dying, but there was such a thing as *style*. Dying with three different enemy weapons stuck in you and having left a trail of bodies in your wake was one thing; dying because a weirdboy hiccupped at the wrong moment would be just plain embarrassing.

'Da warboss is dead,' Old Morgrub said, in a sing-song voice like coiling serpents. His stare was discomfortingly unfocused, but carried the inherent threat that it might suddenly *become* focused, and on you, and that that would not be a good thing. 'Da warboss is dead. Long live da warboss.'

Dedfist, Uzbrag and Thundaskuzz exchanged glances. None of them had a great deal of time for Old Morgrub, but that was mainly because the old git had been Goresnappa's closest advisor, and the Snakebite had taken the warphead's deranged rantings as deep insights rather too often for their liking. On the other hand, Morgrub was a well-known figure within the Waaagh!, and even with Goresnappa gone his words would likely carry a great deal of weight.

Uzbrag decided to wait for a moment and see what Morgrub said. If the warphead spoke in favour of him, then clearly Gork and Mork wanted him to lead. If he didn't... Well, there was no point in heeding the ramblings of a demented old fool who couldn't tell a squig from a splatta kannon.

'I saw dis comin',' Morgrub declared. 'I saw a *lotta* fings.' He paused to lick the skrawnie stone on his staff, and giggled as a green spark earthed itself from the tip of his tongue. 'I didn't see who da next warboss would be...'

Da Genrul tensed, and felt the other two do the same. If Morgrub wasn't going to say their name, none of them had any current use for him.

'...but I did see how he will reveal himself,' Morgrub continued, still in that same sing-song voice. 'I seen it, right? A propha-see.'

It was difficult to hold the attention of a large group of orks, at least without that attention being focused on a fight. Morgrub was managing it, though.

'An' it's not gonna be by just duffin' up anuvver ork!' Morgrub said loudly, and although his gaze still didn't really light on anyone in particular, it definitely drifted towards the three bosses. 'Dat's not wot dis Waaagh! needs. We need an ork wiv *vision*.'

Everyone looked at each other, somewhat confused. Of the three obvious candidates who might step up to become warboss, none were missing even one eye, let alone both. Having vision didn't sound like a particularly specific requirement. What was the old weirdboy on about?

'A warboss ain't just da best fighter, he's gotta be da best *finker!*' Morgrub shouted. 'He's gotta lead da boyz to da best scraps, and da best loot! An' he's gotta do it quick, so we don't get bored!'

That was hard to argue with, at any rate, and there was a general nodding of heads and murmur of agreement. Few orks liked being cooped up on a ship. It was entertaining enough if there were any other ships to fight, because you could look out of a see-hole and see them get blown up, but it still wasn't really the same for the average boy with his slugga and his choppa. Unless some enterprising boss decided to go boarding, most of them just had to hang around and wait for the krews to do their thing.

'So da way we're gonna find out who da new warboss is gonna be, is like dis,' Morgrub said. He waved his staff imperiously, causing the various trinkets and gewgaws suspended from it on lengths of wire and leather to rattle together. 'Da Great Green spoke to me, an' it showed me somefing *speshul*.'

Now the old weirdboy's stare *did* focus, as ferocious and concentrated as the cutting-torch on a burna when the nozzles were closed down tight so it got all small and blue and mega-hot. He turned that stare on the three big bosses, so intense that Uzbrag could almost feel it pinning his thoughts to the back of his skull.

And then it wasn't just his own thoughts inside his skull any longer.

* * *

Everything went green. Not the green of an ork's skin, or a grot's skin; and not the green of leaves, or the green of mould. This was the proto-green, the greenest of greens. This was the green that came before, and the green that would still be hanging around after everything else had given up and gone. This was a green so rich, so vibrant and so powerful that nothing that actually *existed* could come close to it. It wasn't a colour that would submit itself to anything as mundane as simply being seen; it would mount an assault on optic nerves until it was the only thing left.

And out of that green emerged shapes.

Uzbrag was angry at them, at first – angry that they had ruined the green with their imperfection. Then he began to perceive what they were. Shootas and choppas, kannons and klaws, stikkbombs and just sticks with spikes through them, sleeted towards him faster than thought itself. With them came other shapes: the tiny forms of grots; hulking, angular Deff Dreads; massive, solid Stompas; enormous, towering Gargants; bulbous-headed squighogs; and most of all, the boyz. Ork after ork after ork whirled past, the vision giving Uzbrag enough clarity to realise that each and every one of them was slightly different, an individual. This was the Waaagh! itself, *his* Waaagh!, and every ork he saw here represented one of those around him. The Waaagh! knew its own, and it knew that it was strong.

Then the vision shifted. The centre of the strong green was overtaken by a weak, sickly grey, out of which emerged a towering shape. It was washy and indistinct, but Uzbrag recognised it after a moment: this was the one remaining humie city. The Great Green didn't know it so well as it knew the Waaagh!, but he could feel that it was showing him something important. The humies weren't a threat, they couldn't be a threat, but there was something he needed to do…

The vision lurched forwards, rushing towards the city, and then *through* it, *into* it, as though the walls themselves were inconsequential. Then it plunged downwards, not up to where the humie bosses would be, but into the city's half-abandoned guts. And there, buried so deep that it had been forgotten by any of the humies who came as close to mattering as a humie ever could, there was... something.

This was at the edge of what the Great Green could show him. It was something so different, so alien, that it was little more than abstract impressions in his mind. He got an image of glowy stones, like the one Morgrub had on his staff... of boots crossing a threshold... of stars... then, more certain again, of new planets, ones he had never seen before, with flames spreading across them and the vivid green following hard in the fire's wake... And behind it all was the laughter of Gork and Mork, laughter that filled the galaxy from edge to edge, laughter that charged him with fire, laughter that could kill whoever heard it. It was both the greatest thing Uzbrag had ever experienced in his life, and the most terrifying.

And then it was over.

Uzbrag shook his head, trying to get his bearings. Both Dedfist and Thundaskuzz were doing the same, like they'd just woken up from a bite from a dok's sleepy-squig. Had those gits seen the same things he had?

'Dere's a gate under dat city,' Morgrub said, his voice seeming to come from a long way away. 'Built by da pointy-eared skrawnie gits. If we find it, dat gate means we ain't gonna need to rely on da ships to move about! We can just go froo it, walk for a bit, an' den come out somewhere dere's a bunch more gits to stomp. An' after dat, we can do da same fing again, an' again, an' again!'

Da Genrul looked around. Most of the rest of the Waaagh!

were looking interested, but without any indication that they had any idea what Old Morgrub was actually talking about. There was certainly no sign that they had seen what Uzbrag had seen. Was it just him, Dedfist and Thundaskuzz who had been granted the vision?

'So da ork wot's gonna lead da Waaagh! is da boss wot gets to dat gate first!' Morgrub declared forcefully. 'He's da one wot's gonna take the Waaagh! to da stars! He's da one wot's gonna turn planets green, one after anuvver! He's da one wot's gonna burn da galaxy down!'

Whether it was the concept of a new way of war, the method of Morgrub's delivery, or some leftover surge of Waaagh! energy that was bleeding off the warphead without him even realising it, his words resonated strongly through the assembled orks. A mighty cheer greeted his last words, as the Waaagh! forgot about kicking each other's heads in for now, and began to concentrate once again on the idea of doing it to everyone else instead.

'So dis gate!' Mag Dedfist bellowed, loud enough for everyone to hear him over the noise. 'It's under da humie city? Where?'

'Dunno!' Morgrub shouted back gleefully. 'Yoo're gonna hafta go lookin'!' He spread his arms, encompassing Dedfist, Uzbrag and Thundaskuzz all together.

'May da best ork win!'

FIVE

The proclamation ran through the camp like buggy fuel through a sick squiggoth. Every ork and grot was talking about it: how Old Morgrub had called down the power of the ork gods and they'd spoken through him in voices like thunder, declaring that this Waaagh! was the mightiest the galaxy had ever seen, and how it was destined to crush everything in its path; how the orks would rise and, through the power of their combined might, would conquer all other living beings and embody the Many-Fist Destiny of their species. No one questioned the veracity of the stories, or the fact that two different orks might be telling three different versions. The main thrust of the narrative struck right at the heart of every ork's beliefs, so it *had* to be true, and if it was broadly true, who cared about the details?

The only question left was which one of the three big bosses was going to take up the mantle of warboss. None of them had tried yet, and for very good and kunnin' reasons.

When it came right down to it, each one of them was still playing the odds as best they knew how. If Morgrub was right, and there really was a gateway made by the skrawniez somewhere under the humie city that could lead them across the galaxy in no time, then finding it first – and staying alive long enough to make sure that every other git knew you'd found it first – was the best way of piggybacking off Morgrub's influence and ensuring a seamless transition of authority from Goresnappa. These were concepts that orks understood without even really thinking about them.

On the other hand, if one of the other two gits got there first, you could still throw down anyway. It might be a bit messier, and a fair few of the more traditional Snakebites might take issue with how the warphead's propha-see had been ignored, but so what? Knock enough heads together, and sooner or later everyone would fall in line, or would be lacking enough head to complain about it any longer.

One upshot of the excitement around this novel way of deciding a leadership contest, and the general frenzied preparations as each big boss began organising the orks under their command to pursue their favoured method of attack, was that no one had thought to investigate exactly what had happened to make the head of the Mega-Gargant fall off in the first place and instigate this entire state of affairs. And what *that* meant was that Snaggi Littletoof, Guffink, Skrawk and Kruffik had managed to get out of and away from it without being hung up by their toes and beaten, fed to the gnasher squigs, used as target practice, or any of the other painful and likely fatal punishments that would normally have been enacted upon them under such circumstances. It helped that Mek Zagblutz had almost certainly been in the Mega-Gargant's head when it had fallen to its fiery doom, and since no ork really paid much attention to which grot was which unless they were supposed to be doing something for him, that meant they were probably out of the drops on that one.

Not that Kruffik seemed particularly confident on that front.

'We're gonna die,' he moaned, as the four of them scurried through the camp, dodging the feet of orks as they rushed hither and thither. 'Dey're gonna kill us for dis! An' it's all yoor fault, Snaggi!'

'Who's gonna care?' Snaggi demanded. When Old Morgrub had been blathering about the Great Green, the gods had spoken to him again! It had only been faint, a brushing at the edges of his consciousness, but it had been there nonetheless: he had seen the gate that the weirdboy had been talking about, surely a sign that he was favoured! He felt amazing. He felt invincible. He felt five feet tall, and as though he were weightless, yet as strong as a meganob.

A thought flitted across his brain. Was this how orks felt *all the time?*

'Wotcha mean, who's gonna care?!' Kruffik squeaked. 'Everyone! Everyone's gonna care! Of course dey're gonna care!'

'Why?' Snaggi asked him, swiping a screwdriver that no one seemed to be needing right now. 'Dere's a bunch of big bosses wot all wanna be warboss – ya reckon dey're gonna be mad dat I killed Goresnappa? Dey weren't gonna get to be warboss uvverwise!'

'Keep yer voice down!' Guffink hissed at him, and even Skrawk looked a little uneasy. 'Yeah, alright, maybe no one's comin' after us, but dat don't mean ya can just go shoutin' about it!'

'Shoutin' about wot?'

All four of them whirled on the spot, because that voice didn't belong to a grot. It was deeper, and more resonant.

It was Zukrod, the runtherd.

Zukrod wasn't much more than a yoof, with the green of his skin still relatively unscarred, and his build more lanky than bulky, but he'd not gone the way of some young orks and joined the stormboyz. Zukrod was a Snakebite, and he'd found his calling in the traditional work of a Snakebite: squigs and grots, and successfully beating them until they did what they were supposed to. That clan produced the most runtherds, and was widely reckoned to also produce the best ones.

'Nuffin'!' Kruffik said immediately, and anxiously. 'We weren't shoutin' about nuffin'! Did ya hear us shoutin' about anyfing? I don't reckon so, cos we weren't!' He grinned widely.

'Sounded to me,' Zukrod said slowly, 'like ya was sayin' somefing about da warboss. Da old warboss.'

'Nah, definitely not,' Guffink said, shaking his head vigorously. 'Why would we be doin' dat? We ain't been anywhere near 'im, or nuffin' like dat.'

'Sounded to *me*,' Zukrod said, flicking a switch which sent lightning sparking across the metal-toothed jaws of the grabba stikk he carried as a mark of his trade, 'like ya was talkin' about how ya *killed* da old warboss.'

'Dat's ridicul-arrgh!' Kruffik hastily corrected himself as the grabba stikk jabbed out at him, because a grot did not call anything an ork said or did 'ridiculous' if he wanted to remain in possession of all his limbs. 'I mean, dat's not wot was goin' on! We wasn't sayin' dat! How would we do dat?'

'Dunno,' Zukrod said. 'Maybe you was up in da Mega-Gargant, an' made its head fall off onto 'im?'

He grinned the toothy grin of an ork whose job it was to hurt grots, who really loved his job anyway, and who now had an excellent reason to indulge himself.

'Oh crikey,' Guffink whimpered, as Zukrod took a step forwards. 'You've gone an' done it now, Snaggi.'

'Dere's no point in runnin',' Zukrod chuckled. 'I'll only catch ya.'

Something snapped inside Snaggi Littletoof. He hadn't killed Warboss Gazrot Goresnappa just to let some jumped-up runtherd who probably wasn't even as old as him get all zap-happy with his grabba stikk. Fire flared inside his chest, the sort of fire that, once ignited, wouldn't be doused until it had consumed everything in its path.

He pulled the stolen screwdriver from his belt, clutched it in both hands, and took a deep breath.

'Waagh,' he muttered, and charged.

Zukrod wasn't expecting it. No ork ever really expected to be charged by anything: mostly, other stuff tried to avoid being charged by orks. Other than bugeyes, of course, and some of the tougher beakies, and a few of the pointy-eared skrawniez that moved real quick – oh, and those weird Chaos fings that glowed and gibbered and just sort of disappeared when you scragged or dakka'd them, instead of leaving a body behind like anything decent would – but *mainly*, other stuff tried to avoid being charged by orks. And if there was anything in the galaxy that an ork truly didn't expect to get charged by, then it was a snotling; but if there was anything *else* that an ork didn't expect to get charged by, it was a grot. After all, they were half the height, a quarter the strength, and perhaps an eighth the weight of an ork. What was a grot going to do?

In this case, the grot ducked under the jab of the grabba stikk, which was more reflex than actual aggression, since Zukrod's brain was still trying to come to terms with what his eyes were telling it, and stabbed the screwdriver right into the runtherd's left knee.

'Gahhh!' Zukrod howled, but an ork's pain threshold was high, and they could shrug off wounds that would incapacitate a human. 'Ya bloody little git! I'm gonna–'

He swung his grabba stikk two-handed, and Snaggi ducked under it.

'–tear yer–'

Zukrod swatted at the grot with the butt end of the haft, but

Snaggi rolled to one side with an awareness and agility born of desperation.

'–zoggin' head off!'

Snaggi leaped athletically over a swing of the grabba stikk intended to take his legs out from under him, but Zukrod's body followed the momentum of the swing around. As the runtherd pivoted he lashed out with a kick, using the screwdriver-impaled leg, and it caught Snaggi square in the chest just as he landed. The grot flew backwards, landing in what might have been a pile of junk, or might have been some mekaniak's most prized possessions: it was often hard to tell.

'Right!' Zukrod bellowed, dropping his grabba stikk and limping towards Snaggi with his fingers outstretched. 'Try dodgin' me now!'

Snaggi was only too willing to try, but unfortunately his body had other ideas. It generally liked air if it was going to be doing anything athletic, and right now that was a substance in which it was distinctly lacking. He was unable to do anything much more than flail weakly as the runtherd closed in on him, with murder in his eyes.

Then, astonishingly, Zukrod staggered again as the electrified jaws of his own grabba stikk closed on his as-yet-uninjured knee. He collapsed sideways, convulsing, and the extra second or so's reprieve gave Snaggi the chance to haul himself back to his feet and lay eyes on his saviour.

'Long live da Revolushun,' Skrawk said quietly, releasing the grabba stikk's hold on Zukrod.

'No, no, don't do dat!' Snaggi wailed, but it was too late. Zukrod was already shaking his head and getting his wits back now he was no longer being electrocuted, and he was going to be up and dangerous again in a matter of moments. 'Gimme da stikk, gimme da stikk!'

Skrawk chucked it to him, and Snaggi caught it, fumbled it,

nearly hit himself in the eye, then managed to get a proper grip on it at the second attempt. Zukrod was pushing himself up, letting his arms do most of the work of getting him back upright since one knee still had a screwdriver stuck into it, and the other had jagged tears in the scorched flesh.

Snaggi aimed for the runtherd's neck, and pulled the grabby-lever back as far as it would go.

The jaws snapped shut just under Zukrod's jaw, and the full charge of the stick flowed out into the young ork's body. Snaggi held on desperately as Zukrod began spasming, every one of the ork's muscles straining against itself, and made sure he didn't accidentally flick the switch that would turn the current off.

Zukrod screamed as his flesh began to burn, and his eyes began to melt, but Snaggi held on. He held on until Zukrod stopped moving completely, and was prone on the ground with froth bubbling out of his mouth.

'Ya killed 'im,' Kruffik whispered in horror. 'Ya killed an ork! A *runtherd!*'

'I already killed a warboss today,' Snaggi told him belligerently, looking around in case the little altercation had been seen, but no one appeared to be paying any attention. It was dark, and although orks and grots could see better at night than humies could, it wasn't their best time. The camp was still in an uproar as well, and there were shouts, and roaring engines, and any number of incidental scraps going on as orks got in each other's way and 'accidentally' picked up the wrong shoota.

They'd got away with it. Again.

'Dis is wot I'm talkin' about!' Snaggi hissed victoriously at the others. 'I said dat Gork an' Mork talk to me, didn't I? I said I hear dere voices! Look at dis! We just killed a runtherd, and nuffin' bad's happenin'! I'm da Chosen Grot! I'm gonna lead us outta slavery and into...' He paused, because he wasn't quite sure about the rest of that sentence, but the other three were looking at him. 'Somefing better!' he finished, as confidently as he could.

'Lead who? Us?' Kruffik objected. 'Dere's only four of us!'

'Dere's a lot more dan four of us in dis camp,' Snaggi said gleefully. 'Wot was dat ya said just now, Skrawk?'

'Long live da Revolushun,' Skrawk repeated.

'Exactly,' Snaggi said, puffing up his chest. 'It's time to spread da word! And da word is "Revolushun"!'

Within seconds, there was nothing to be seen except for a badly burned dead ork, with a hole in one knee that, until recently, had had a screwdriver sticking out of it.

LOTZ

'Whose Gargant is dat?'

The mekboy so addressed turned around and stared up into the face of Mag Dedfist. It was a fearsome face, scarred and brutal, and underlit by the pilot lights of the twin skorchas built into the horns that jutted from beneath his jaw. There were a number of possible answers to the question, and the mekboy chose the wrong one.

'Mine–'

A power klaw ignited and lashed out, sending the mek's broken body a good thirty feet through the air, before it landed in a boneless heap not far from an unattended stew pot. The mek's two spanner boyz, who'd been getting some of the excess gunk off their tools, looked at each other uncomfortably.

'Gonna ask again,' Mag Dedfist rumbled. 'Whose Gargant is dat?'

'Yoors, boss!' the brighter of the two spanners piped up. They were both Deathskulls, with blue paint adorning their faces and bodies in the hope of attracting good luck. At the very least, they managed to avoid the same bad luck that had befallen their mek.

'Dat's right,' Dedfist affirmed. 'Clearly yoo boyz've got good futures ahead of ya. Now go an' get it ready to stomp stuff. An' make sure da head ain't gonna fall off!' he bawled as an afterthought, as the pair of them scrambled away towards the brooding metal monstrosity. It wasn't quite the size of the Mega-Gargant which had spelled doom for Gazrot Goresnappa, but it was the largest one left, and had an impressive-looking array of suitably killy weapons.

'Yoo're gonna try to get dat inside da humie city?' Badzag asked dubiously. He was one of Dedfist's boss nobs, and headed up a bunch of skarboyz known as Badzag's Krushas.

'Course not,' Skabrukk replied, before Dedfist could answer. Skabrukk was the drill boss of Da Skyklaw, the Waaagh!'s largest mob of stormboyz. 'It's too big, ya zoggin' idiot. But it's got dead big gunz, so da boss is gonna use it to break froo da walls. Right, boss?' he added.

Dedfist clouted him across the face with the hand that wasn't enveloped in a power klaw. 'Did anyone say ya could talk for me, maggot-brain?' he demanded.

'No, boss,' Skabrukk replied, spitting out a couple of teeth that had been prematurely loosened. The other boss nobs who answered to Dedfist snickered at his misfortune, although not quite loudly enough to get a clobbering in their own right.

'Now, Skabrukk's right,' Dedfist acknowledged, with a glower at the drill boss. 'But dat don't mean he can just open his gob when someone's talkin' to me. We needs to get inside, an' da Gargants are da best tool for da job. Once da wall's been knocked in, we'll get da ladz together an' go find dis gate fing wot Morgrub's been gabbin' about.'

The assembled nobs nodded and muttered in the manner

each thought was the most appropriate yet unremarkable way to signal their agreement. Boss Dedfist didn't like being contradicted, but he also had absolutely no time for sycophants. It was best to treat his pronouncements as common, orkish good sense, rather than some form of great insight.

'Dese humie cities've got fick walls,' Dedfist continued. 'It'll take da Gargants some time to get froo, so any uvver big gunz we can round up should give 'em a hand. Wot about da uvver two? Thundaskuzz an' Da Genrul? Dey tried to get dere hands on anyfing big or shooty, or bossed any of da ladz inta fightin' for 'em?'

'Don't fink so, boss,' Badzag replied. 'Thundaskuzz's gone off on 'is trike, and da Kult's gone wiv 'im. Dere's a bunch of trukkboyz who've followed 'im, but ya know what dose Evil Sunz is like – dey don't like big gunz, cos dey don't move quick enuff. It's mainly buggies an' some flyers an' dat. Nuffin' else could keep up!'

'Wot's 'e gonna do, drive round da city in circles 'till dey give up?' Nuzzgrond laughed, a little too loudly. He had a bunch of trukkboyz himself, and while hitching a ride to get into the middle of the fight faster was a perfectly acceptable thing for a Goff to do, he was probably a bit worried that Dedfist might think he was going to go off and follow Thundaskuzz on whatever form of high-velocity idiocy the speedboss was planning now.

'An' what about Da Genrul?' Dedfist demanded.

'Disapp… disappy… he's gone, boss,' Skabrukk managed. 'Some of the ladz were keepin' an eye on him, and said he went off south right after Morgrub said his bit. Most of da Blood Axes went wiv him, an' a whole loada grots, but nuffin' much dat was very stompy or shooty.'

Dedfist frowned, and scratched his chin. 'Wot's dat git up to?'

'Can't be much, can it, boss?' Nuzzgrond asked. 'He's not gonna get inside dat fing with a bunch of boyz an' grots. Or not quickly, anyway,' he added conscientiously, since it was a well-known fact that enough orks could do pretty much anything, given enough time and a suitable concentration span.

'Nah, I don't trust him,' Dedfist growled. 'He's a finker, dat one, and da only fing worse dan a finker is a finker wot's got a bunch of ladz followin' him. Da Genrul ain't gonna be leavin' da Dreads an' wotnot behind if he needed 'em to do wotever it is he's plannin' on doin'. So wotever it is, he's not tryin' to go straight froo da walls like a proper ork should.' He worked the action of his power klaw, the massive digits clanking against each other as his neurones fizzed and sparked. Finally, after several long seconds of deliberate cogitation, he raised the brutal weapon and pointed it. 'Skabrukk.'

'Me, boss?' Skabrukk asked uncertainly, wondering if he was about to get clobbered again for an as-yet-unrealised indiscretion.

'Ya see any uvver gits round 'ere called Skabrukk?'

'No, boss,' Skabrukk admitted, checking both ways just to be sure.

'Den I mean yoo. Yer stormies are a bit Blood Axe-y, ain't dey?'

Had it been any other ork saying that, Skabrukk might have taken issue with him. The members of Da Skyklaw were Goffs through and through, and liked nothing better than getting stuck into a fight as soon as possible. Indeed, much like Nuzzgrond's trukkboyz, they'd taken extra measures to ensure that they could achieve just that, although in the case of the stormboyz it took the form of high-powered individual rokkit packs rather than a large and somewhat ramshackle vehicle. However, it was Mag Dedfist saying it, and Skabrukk had already taken one clobbering from him since his last meal, so he wasn't looking for another.

'Maybe,' he muttered, as non-committally as he thought he could get away with.

'Dere's no "maybe" about it,' Dedfist growled. 'Ya all walk behind each uvver in lines, ya do dat salutin' fing, ya all wear da same clothes as da rest of ya mob, an' polish ya boots, an' are basically all sorts of odd. Don't tell me ya ain't,' he added menacingly, 'cos I was a stormboy once, 'til I grew out of it.'

'Well, if ya put it like dat den I guess yeah, maybe we'z kind of a bit like Blood Axes,' Skabrukk admitted, shifting uncomfortably. 'But dat don't mean we're gonna go off an' join Da Genrul! Yoo'z da best big boss, boss, an' dat's da honest troof!'

'I didn't fink ya would, not even a stormboy would be dat stupid,' Dedfist declared, to another round of general laughter from the rest of his boss nobs. 'But I want ya to *pretend* to do dat, right? Get yer boyz, an' go an' see wot dat git's up to.'

'Ya want us to go an' *spy* for ya?' Skabrukk asked, bewildered. 'Boss?' he added hurriedly, a moment later.

It was a loaded question. Spying was grot work, or more accurately what grots just did in general, in the hope of currying favour with someone somewhere. An ork might take a look at where the enemy was, simply to have some idea of which direction in which to charge or shoot, but he'd never dream of hiding his own presence in the process. Unless he was a Blood Axe, of course, in which case he might even be wearing clothes that looked a bit like whatever terrain he was in, and hang bits of bush off himself, and all sorts of other strange behaviour that only Blood Axes had any patience for.

Luckily for everyone concerned, Mag Dedfist was not simply an enormous ork with both a predilection and a talent for unbridled violence. He was also savvy enough to know how to get the orks under his command to do what he wanted without always having to beat it into them.

'Nah, it ain't spyin',' Dedfist said, laying a comradely power klaw on his subordinate's shoulder. 'Dis is *scoutin'*, an' dat's totally different. I want ya to go an' *scout* wot Da Genrul's doin', by lettin' 'im fink ya gonna join 'im. An' den I want ya to come back an' tell me wot he's up to, so we can scrag him if it looks like he's found a quicker way to get to da gate. Dat clear?'

Skabrukk, who was neither stubborn nor slow-witted enough to push his luck any further, nodded. 'Yes, boss. I'll get da ladz right on it.'

'Good,' Dedfist said, and turned away from him. 'Nuzzgrond!'

'Yes, boss?' Nuzzgrond replied promptly, having clearly learned from Skabrukk's hesitation on how not to respond to his big boss.

'Get yer ladz togevva an' do da same fing with Thundaskuzz. He might drink buggy fuel, but ya don't get to be speedboss wivout findin' da right sorta fights at da right sorta times,' Dedfist said. 'If it looks like he's got any clue how to get inside, ya come back and tell me, got it?'

'Yes, boss,' Nuzzgrond replied, doing his best to hide his disappointment. Nuzzgrond's mob would want to be right at the front line, watching the Gargants blow holes in the city walls and then piling into the breach, not driving around trying to find Zagnob Thundaskuzz and his convoy of speed freeks.

'We're gonna need to get da rest of da boyz up here, and have 'em hang around da Gargants,' Dedfist said, addressing his nobs as one. 'I dunno who da Snakebite bosses are, an' I don't much care neither. None of 'em is gonna be big enough to give me any lip, so unless dey've gone off wiv Thundaskuzz or Da Genrul for some reason, dey're mine now.' He turned and surveyed the humie city through the pair of dark-gogglez he'd had one of the meks build for him, his experienced eyes quickly and instinctively searching out the potential weak points in its massive form.

'Looks like dere's some sort of crack in it, over dere,' he said, pointing to where the hint of a darker fissure running more or less vertically down to ground level suggested some ancient structural damage from a hive quake. 'S'not anyfing da humies would've done on purpose, dey don't build like dat, not fings dis size. Dat's where we'll get da Gargants to shoot. Once dey've knocked a hole in da wall, I'll lead da Krushas in, wiv da rest of da ladz behind us.' His gaze tracked upwards, taking in the irregular sides of the hive, and the various outcrops that might be usable as gun platforms by defenders. 'I reckon da humies'll get some of dere gitz up dere to shoot down at us, so we'll need da stormboyz to go an' clobber 'em, maybe a coupla strafing runs from da fighta-bommas...'

'Boss?' Badzag piped up. The other boss nobs, recognising his tone of voice as one belonging to an ork who thought that what he was about to say could possibly be construed as being a bit foolish, but who was going to say it anyway, edged away from him.

'Wot is it, Badzag?' Mag Dedfist enquired, giving the boss of the Krushas his full attention.

'Boss, all dis...' Badzag began. 'I mean... Ain't dis a bit... Blood Axe-y?'

Everything went very quiet, or at least as quiet as it was reasonably possible for things to be in the middle of an ork camp preparing for battle.

'Wot did yoo say?' Mag Dedfist asked, very slowly.

'Ya know...' Badzag said, with a weak and ill-advised attempt at an ingratiating smile. 'All dese... taktiks, an' dat.'

'*Taktiks?*' Dedfist's bellow erupted forth like the wrath of a black-clad volcano. '*Taktiks?!* Who d'ya fink yer talkin' to, my lad?!' His power klaw shot out and grabbed Badzag by the throat, and only the fact that its power field was not currently activated prevented the boss nob's head from coming clean off.

'Just in case ya ain't clear, let me give ya a quick lesson! What I'm doin' right now ain't *taktiks*! Dat's somefing wot Blood Axes and humies do, an' I never wanna hear it outta yer mouf again, got it? Wot I'm doin' is called a *plan*! An' do ya know wot da difference is between a plan an' taktiks, boyz?'

No one said anything, because all of them – with the possible exception of Badzag, who was in no position to answer right now – were smart enough to realise when Mag Dedfist was being rhetorical.

'A *plan* is how we make sure we kill da uvver gits,' Dedfist snarled into the oxygen-deprived face of Badzag, who was struggling hopelessly against the big boss' grip. '*Taktiks* is tryin' to make sure da uvver gits don't kill *us*, an' dat sorta finkin' is for cowards, an' grots!'

He released his hold on Badzag, who collapsed into the dirt, then hurriedly picked himself up again. You didn't want to be scrabbling around in front of the ork who might well shortly be warboss, even if – especially if – he'd just squeezed your head half off.

'Ya got yer orders,' Mag Dedfist growled at his nobz. 'Go an' get 'em done. When da sun comes up, I want all da ladz ready to go, an' I want to know wot's goin' on wiv dose uvver two gits who've buggered off an' seem to fink dey've got some sort of clever ideas!'

His nobz turned and hurried off, each one making the internal transition from meek subordinate who knew better than to speak out, to a feared boss who'd clout a lesser ork around the head for looking at him the wrong way. Dedfist watched them go, to make sure none of them were slacking, then turned and made for the Gargant into which the two spanners had disappeared.

'Now den, let's see what sorta gunz dis fing has...'

LOTZ

'Alright, ladz, put yer backs into it! C'mon, get dose shovels movin'! I wanna see dat dirt flyin', an' if I don't den dere's gonna be heads rollin'! Ya hear me?'

Genrul Uzbrag leaned on the tall haft of his power choppa, and surveyed the excavations with satisfaction. For all the yelling and bawling he'd been doing to make the boyz think he was dissatisfied with their efforts, and that they'd better get a shift on, he was reasonably happy with the speed at which the trenches were being dug. It helped that most of the orks under his command were Blood Axes, and so were willing to put effort into things even if they couldn't see the immediate benefit to them, thanks to their respect for his authority. After all, Da Genrul was in charge, so it made sense that he knew best. Otherwise he wouldn't be in charge, would he?

Besides, it wasn't that orks didn't know how to dig, or weren't used to it. You had to dig the drops out somehow, wherever it was you'd set up camp; at least, unless you were near a handy natural cliff or ravine. Sometimes you had to find food underground, whether that was burrowing squigs or the more esoteric wildlife of whatever planet you happened to be on at the time. Blood Axes, in particular, were used to digging out trenches if there was any notion of protracted warfare that couldn't be won with a simple charge and stomping the gits on the receiving end of it. Any ork knew that the enemy would have a hard time shooting you if they couldn't see you, but only Blood Axes had really bought into the idea that you could make it harder for the enemy to shoot you *even if they knew where you were.*

So it was that to the eyes of most other orks, or humans, or indeed, many other species in the galaxy, what the boyz under Da Genrul's command were doing might seem a little unusual for orks, but nothing particularly ingenious. Digging in prior to a long siege of a city was hardly standard ork behaviour, but it made a certain amount of sense, given that they were in the wasteland where everything around the hive had long since been killed by industrial ash and toxic runoff. The nearest other humie buildings[6] were the best part of a day's march away, at the edge of this dead ground, so some other sort of shelter from speculative defensive shooting was probably a good plan.

However, that was not the point of the trenches: or at least, not the complete point of them. Da Genrul had different plans for them. Right now, however, he had yet another thing on his mind.

'Come on out, kaptin,' he said brusquely, pulling open the door of the cage strapped to the back of Sarge. Daggit, the gretchin pilot of Sarge, was one of the few grots who had managed to rein in his aggressive streak after being wired into the mini-Dreadnought: mainly because instead of getting his kicks through stomping on his former oppressors, the little runt got

---

6 Or the remains of them, at any rate.

to hang around behind Da Genrul, feel important, and make affirmative noises like 'Yeah!' and 'Dat's right!' when Uzbrag was giving his orders.

Da Genrul didn't have Sarge following him around simply for the dubious level of support, though. That honour was because of who he was carrying.

Captain Armenius Varrow, formerly of the Third Platoon of the Aranuan 25th Astra Militarum regiment, the 'Golden Lions', fell out of the cage and into the dirt, prompting general merriment in the orks around him. This wasn't anything new, since his sheer continued existence was the source of considerable amusement for the hulking warriors. They mocked his size, his lack of strength, the increasingly filthy uniform in which he was still dressed – basically everything about him.

Captain Varrow hadn't *intended* to be captured, of course. His regiment had been rotated to garrison his home world while it recruited to replace losses sustained against the forces of the Great Enemy near the Siren's Storm, and while the prospect of an ork invasion had obviously been a horrendous one, the 25th had nevertheless been eager not only to throw the xenos back, but also to prove themselves once more and blood the new recruits in the process. They had managed to stall the orkish advance at first, and there had been talk of it all being over by Sanguinala.

Then the problems started. Captain Varrow was leading the right flank of a pitched battle against the orkish aggressors on the Sacracian Heights, and everything seemed to be going well until it was very abruptly no longer going well at all. An advance by four platoons into what had appeared to be a mass ork retreat, caused by appalling casualties inflicted by sustained heavy weapons fire, was swamped when at least half of the apparent casualties got back up to attack Varrow's men as they advanced heedlessly into the trap. The heavy weapon teams were descended upon by orks borne aloft by crude, smoke-belching jump packs, the reinforcements ran into some sort of orkish flamethrower units, and his own command squad had been assaulted by orks wearing camouflage – camouflage! – who must have been waiting in place since before the battle had commenced. Varrow had killed two of those infiltrators, but when his power sword was knocked from his grasp he'd known the game was up. He had expected to die quickly and brutally, as had been the fate of his standard bearer and comms officer.

But that was not what happened. Either by luck or, he was increasingly being forced to accept, actual understanding and intelligence, the orks had neglected to kill him, the commanding officer. Instead, he had been subdued by frighteningly powerful hands, and bundled off to be presented, with considerable pride, to Genrul Uzbrag.

Now he was the Blood Axe boss' prize, halfway between pet and tactical advisor. Armenius Varrow knew, in his heart of hearts, that the Imperium would expect him to take his own life in order to deny any sort of satisfaction to the enemy. He countered those thoughts with the logic that, firstly, he had no easy manner in which to achieve this: the orks prevented him from coming into contact with any sort of weapon, and would in fact force-feed him if he attempted to refuse the food and drink they provided. Secondly, if he could escape, he could provide the Astra Militarum with unprecedented insights into the nature of orkish strategy and psychology, which could undoubtedly be used to fight them more effectively in the future. Thirdly, he could of course use his position to influence Uzbrag and suggest courses of action that would hinder rather than benefit him.

The only trouble was that Da Genrul was not, as a rule, easily taken in.

'Dis city,' Uzbrag said to him, managing to get the Low Gothic words out reasonably clearly, despite the presence of lips and tusks that were not designed for its syllables. 'You humies don't jus' build up, do ya? Ya build *down*, too. So dere's gonna be a lot of dis fing dat's below da ground, like one of dem...' He paused, and turned to look at the rest of the orks that made up what he referred to as his 'High Kommand'. 'Wot're dose fings where dere's only a bit of it above da surface, and ya can't see da rest of it?' Da Genrul asked irritably.

'Pot-squigs, sir?' suggested the ork known as Lootenant Kabrukk.

'...Not wot I was finking of, but it'll do,' Da Genrul conceded. He turned back to Varrow, who was trying to at least kneel upright on the ground, but struggling against the twin enemies of muscle wastage and malnutrition. 'One of dem. So, da uvver ladz are gonna try an' get in above ground, which don't seem like such a good plan to me, cos yer mates'll see 'em coming an' can shoot at 'em.'

The massive ork crouched down so that his head was roughly on a level with Varrow's, although his skull had to be about three times the size. Despite exhaustion, and the deadened emotional reactions brought on by being in the constant company of such horrors, Varrow could not suppress a shudder of fear. Orks had been bad enough when he had thought of them only as feral, albeit incredibly dangerous, green-skinned monsters. The fact that they could, at least in some cases, *think* and *plan* and even imitate Imperial mannerisms just made them all the more terrifying. Looking at Da Genrul and his High Kommand was like an obscura dream where Varrow's senior officers had morphed into crude, mocking monstrosities that sought to bring down everything he had ever loved and believed in.

'Dere's gonna be tunnels, right?' Da Genrul asked, his voice pitched low, and even, so far as it was possible for an ork, friendly. 'Tunnels goin' all froo da ground. Tunnels what'll get us *inside* da walls, if we find one an' follow it back. An' I reckon yer mates in dere will be so busy watchin' Dedfist's ladz, all bunched up an' obvious, and Thundaskuzz, who's gonna be drivin' round an' round lookin' for a way he can get all his buggies inside, dat dey won't be finkin' about what might be comin' from underneath 'em. Speshully when we're just sat 'ere goin' nowhere, from what dey can see.'

He leaned in a little bit closer.

'So, wotcha sayin', kaptin? Ya reckon dere's tunnels comin' out from dat city?'

Captain Armenius Varrow did his best to steel his nerve. He was an officer of the Astra Militarum, from an unbroken line that stretched back to his great-great-grandfather, with assorted aunts, uncles and cousins thrown into the mix as well. His family was *bred* for command, it was their natural purpose in life. He was guided by the Emperor, his training, his years of experience, and the uplifting words of the *Regimental Standard*. He was capable of outwitting this fiend, no matter what manner of low cunning it had proved to possess.

'Keep digging all you wish,' he sneered into Uzbrag's face. 'You'll reach the planet's core before you encounter a weakness in an Aranuan city. We are a military people, and we build for strength and durability. If you want this city to fall, you'll have to charge into the teeth of its guns, along with your deluded comrades!'

There was a brief silence.

'Was dat a "yes" or a "no", sir?' the ork called Lootenant Gubzag asked, studying Varrow with suspicious eyes.

'I swear t'Mork,' Kabrukk put in, 'dese humies don't even know how to make sense in dere own language.'

A wide grin spread across Genrul Uzbrag's face, displaying far more teeth than Captain Varrow was comfortable with, no matter what he told himself. Da Genrul rose back to his full height once more, and beamed down at Varrow.

'It's a "yes". Dere are tunnels down dere. Keep the boyz diggin', an' we'll find one before long.'

Varrow's heart sank. It was true enough that Aranuan hives were ancient structures, which had settled deeper over millennia, not to mention been gradually buried as the ground level rose around them. Old sewage channels, thermal exhaust ports, even former access points: all of these might lie somewhere beneath their feet.

'Yeah, but wot if da humie's lyin'?' Gubzag asked.

'He *was* lyin'!' Da Genrul replied, exasperated. 'Wot he said meant "no"!'

'So how d'ya know he meant "yes", sir?' Kabrukk queried.

'Easy,' Uzbrag replied, with a smug glance down at Varrow. 'Humies are really bad at lyin' to fings wot scare 'em, an' dis one's one of da worst at it. He gets all sweaty, ya see? An' he can't look straight at me.'

Had he been a true hero of the Imperium, a Castellan Creed or a Commissar Cain, Captain Varrow might have come up with some manner of searing rejoinder that would have communicated his contempt for the entire orkish species, whilst simultaneously undermining Genrul Uzbrag's standing in the eyes of his subordinates as they witnessed how ruthlessly he had been mocked by a human prisoner. However, Armenius Varrow was no such fine specimen of humanity, and he could do nothing more than lower his gaze to stare miserably at the mud between his knees. The ork was right: he couldn't look straight at Da Genrul, and not because of hatred. He was scared. He was scared, and he did not want to die, and those facts disgusted him.

'Time for yer exercise, kaptin!' Uzbrag declared, reaching down to clamp one massive hand around Varrow's shoulder and hauling him up to his feet, where he managed to just about maintain his balance despite his treacherous body and the uneven footing. 'Off ya go. 'Ave a walk around, stretch yer legs. Can't 'ave you gettin' too stiff in dat cage, or ya might not last to give me any more advice!'

The High Kommand chuckled dutifully. Captain Varrow stared at his feet, at the fine boots he wore that were now spattered with mud, and also, he grimly suspected, with the blood of some of his dead men. 'Exercise time' was the most soul-crushing thing of all. Every ork in Da Genrul's warband knew of Captain Varrow, and would not harm him. Varrow had attacked one, once, in a desperate and fleeting attempt to provoke a noble death for himself, but he had simply been overpowered and had his face rubbed repeatedly into the mud, then been pelted with some sort of dung.

If he tried to pick up a weapon, he was disarmed. If he tried to attack an ork, he was humiliated. If he tried to escape, he was quickly fetched back. He was so inconsequential, so utterly unthreatening, that the cage in which he spent most of his time was not actually necessary for his containment: it was simply a way of ensuring that he was available at Da Genrul's pleasure, without the big boss having to go to the trouble of shouting at another ork to go and find his pet. This pseudo-freedom was, perhaps, the worst form of torture the orks could have devised for him, and it was made all the worse by the fact that Varrow honestly doubted it was anything more than a practicality for them.

All the same, if he was going to cling to any notion of escape, no matter how unlikely and self-deluding it might be, he needed to remain in some sort of physical condition. So he began to walk as he had been instructed, trying to work the kinks and strains out of his joints and muscles, just in case the moment ever came when he could be something more than a bad joke.

LOTZ

'Here they come,' Commander Sentra LaSteel said, holding her macro-binocs to her eyes. 'Dirty xenos scum. They've just rounded the northern spur.'

'What are they hoping to achieve?' Armour Sergeant Darrus Greel asked, from beside her. They were crushed up together next to one of Davidia Hive's ancient windows, one of very few that had ever been present at this low level. It was nothing more than a small arch of inches-thick crystalflex, scratched so badly by millennia of windborne particulates it was barely possible to see through it. However, lacking any form of reliable auspex, Sentra had taken up station here when she heard that a mechanised portion of the ork force had abandoned the foul camp on the city's eastern side and was traversing it to the north.

'The Emperor only knows,' Sentra replied, 'and I certainly don't care. There's a large chunk of the enemy's most mobile units headed our way, with no air support, no footslogger backup, none of those Throne-cursed Gargants. It's the perfect opportunity.'

She passed Darrus the macro-binocs, and he took a look for himself. He had to kick the magnification up to full, and the scratched and stained window eliminated any hope of seeing detail, but with the aid of the night-vision setting there was no mistaking the cloud of dust kicked up by the orkish convoy. He could just make out the multiple dark shapes covering the ground at what had to be a tremendous speed, although given the distance involved they still appeared to barely be moving.

'What are you thinking, ma'am?' he asked. 'A sortie?'

'You're damned right I'm thinking about a sortie, sergeant,' Sentra said. 'The north-west road gate's sunken, thanks to this place settling on its foundations, so it's not even visible from a distance. If we time it right, we can be out and in their midst before they realise we're coming. Those pieces of ramshackle junk might be dangerous to the footers, but we'll see how well they stand up to a few battle cannons without anything with more punch to ward us off!'

Darrus nodded, and handed the macro-binocs back. 'As you say, ma'am.'

Sentra knew that tone of voice, and she looked at him sidelong. 'I'm sensing there's a "but" lurking behind your lips, sergeant. Out with it.'

'Is that an order, ma'am?' Darrus asked politely.

'It damned well is an order, sergeant. Say whatever it is you've got to say.'

'Well, ma'am,' Darrus said, 'the colonel was quite explicit about the regiment's orders to withdraw into the city. He said nothing about us leaving it again, even if the orks presented a tempting target.'

'The colonel,' Sentra said, checking over her shoulder to ensure she could not be overheard, 'is somewhere up in the spire right now, probably nibbling on Genuvian quail's eggs and sipping two-hundred-year-old amasec with the governor. He's given up, and you know it.'

'I'm not arguing with any of that, ma'am,' Darrus said levelly. 'I'm just concerned about what's going to happen when he finds out that you've disobeyed an order. Or for that matter, what will happen if the commissar finds out.'

Sentra snorted. 'I'm even less scared of Old Bones than I am of Sudliff. She didn't execute the colonel for ordering the retreat – what's she going to do, declare me a coward for going out and fighting? Old Bones outlived her old regiment, she knows how the galaxy works. And don't give me any talk about "insubordination",' she added warningly, as Darrus began to open his mouth again. 'You said yourself, the colonel said nothing about us leaving the city again, either to say that we should *or* that we shouldn't. As a tank commander, I'm entitled to use my own initiative in an attempt to better the situation for our regiment, and the Imperium.'

Darrus shook his head. 'I can't say I'm comfortable with it, ma'am, but it's your call, not mine.' He sighed. 'Besides, I can't argue that the troops would like another chance to take it to the enemy.'

'We need to be out there, sergeant,' Sentra said firmly. 'The footers are far more suited to repelling an actual incursion than we are – we're better off thinning out the numbers of any orks that might end up making it in.' She pulled back from the window and dusted down her fatigues from where the aeons of dirt layered onto the wall had darkened the crimson. 'Let's get down to the bay and get our ladies running again.'

'Nothing moves faster than a secret' was an old Astra Militarum adage, and it proved well founded as the Golden Lions' auxiliary armour began to hurriedly prepare. At first it was just the Leman

Russ battle tanks of Seventh Company – *Golden Thunder, Death Knell* and *Lion's Fury* – all of which came under the direct command of Sentra LaSteel. However, you couldn't start the engines of all three of your tanks without other crews becoming aware of what you were doing, especially when you were loading ammo hoppers as well. The bay, which during peacetime had been a holding area for land trains bringing supplies into Davidia and then exporting its industrial products to the Sacracia space port, had been half-full of silent combat vehicles and listless crews ever since the withdrawal had been completed. Not a one of them had trusted the locals not to interfere with their precious tanks, or even steal parts or ammunition for their own use, and so they had turned down the offer of billeting within the hive to instead make themselves as comfortable as they could on and around their mechanical charges. Anything that might break the tedium was seized upon, especially if it looked more interesting than the prospect of losing yet another game of snapper to 'Flash' Harvax of Second Company.

No one said the word 'sortie', of course. A couple of other commanders had shouted over to Sentra and asked her what she was doing, but she'd just given them a polite nod and continued her preparations without replying. She wasn't going to lie to them, because that wasn't the 25th's way. However, she certainly wasn't going to tell them outright what she was planning, because to give voice to a thing – at least to anyone beyond her own crews, whose opinions she might listen to, but whom ultimately were in no position to argue – was to give it a tangibility and form that could be challenged or countermanded.

Commander DeTay of Tenth Company was the first to join in. Only *Hammer of Aranua* was left of her command, but the battered old thing was possessed of the sort of indomitable machine-spirit that had seen it twice return to its own lines after it had been officially written off as a battlefield loss, and it coughed belligerently into life once more when appropriately coaxed. Not a word was exchanged between DeTay and Sentra, but there were faint smiles present on the faces of their crews as they worked to make their engines of war ready for another fight.

Flash Harvax was next, finally putting his deck of cards away and ordering his crews into action. Second Company's auxiliary armour unit was comprised of three Hellhounds – *Smoke Eater*, *Ash Kicker* and *Flame Rider* – and the stink of promethium in the air grew stronger as their inferno cannons were topped up. Then the two surviving Leman Russes of 16th had their netting pulled off, followed by the lone remaining Demolisher of First. All across the bay, tank crews that until a few minutes before had been the very picture of slovenly idleness were now once more moving briskly and with purpose.

Of course, no rousing of machine-spirits on that sort of scale was likely to happen without a member of the honoured Priesthood of Mars noticing. Sure enough, it wasn't long before Enginseer Sanavar Deltis was hurrying towards *Golden Thunder* with his hands tucked into his robe's voluminous sleeves.

'Cogboy's here,' Kat Pallas said in a low voice, without looking up from where she was attaching the newly refilled box magazine to Sentra's pintle-mounted storm bolter.

'Honoured adept,' Sentra greeted the enginseer, popping her head up from inside *Golden Thunder*, the Mars Alpha-pattern Leman Russ which was her command vehicle, where a moment before she had been swearing at the battle cannon's targeting auspex. 'What can we do for you?'

Deltis came to a halt and tilted his face – or what remained of it, given that it was now mostly cables, metal plating, and tiny lumens – up at her.

'There are an excessive number of possible answers to that question, Commander LaSteel, too many to be easily verbalised whilst making an efficient use of time, although the number of tasks that you could complete for me more efficiently than I could complete them myself is somewhat lower. However–'

'Forget it,' Sentra replied, then waved a hand before Deltis could inform her that the Mechanicus deleted nothing, certainly not data. 'I meant, why have you come here to speak to me?'

'Commander, the increase and manner of activity taking place suggests that you are preparing your vehicles for combat,' Deltis said briskly. 'I am here to enquire whether that is your intention.'

'Enginseer, are you aware of any orders being issued to the regiment's auxiliary armour units concerning preparations for combat?' Sentra asked, while Pallas tightened a bolt and tried her best to keep a straight face.

'I am not, commander.'

'And you are familiar with the command structure and protocols of the Aranuan Twenty-Fifth?'

'I am, commander.'

'Then it seems statistically unlikely, does it not, that we are preparing for combat?' Sentra asked. Beneath her, a sponson-mounted heavy bolter traversed a few degrees as someone checked its functions. Sentra deliberately avoided looking down at it, and stared at the enginseer instead, daring him to acknowledge that anything had happened.

'I see,' Deltis replied, nodding in as human a manner as he could still manage, since he had found that regular humans responded better to body language they could easily recognise. 'In that case, I will not offer to operate the road gate in order to assist the egress of any vehicles that might have been intending to leave the city to engage the hated xenos.'

Commander Sentra LaSteel had not got to her position in

the Golden Lions without possessing an impressive tarot face, and without one would certainly not have been the veteran of many long nights opposed to Flash Harvax whilst still retaining ownership of at least some of her personal possessions. As a result, she was able to maintain a calm and composed exterior, despite her brain stripping a gear as she struggled to realign her expectations with her perceived reality.

'I'm sorry, enginseer,' she said, surreptitiously nudging Pallas to get her to stop staring. 'Would you care to expand upon your previous statement?'

'The vehicles of the Twenty-Fifth's auxiliary armour units are blessed in the eyes of the Omnissiah,' Enginseer Deltis said calmly, although Sentra had never really experienced a cogboy who got what she might call *emotional* about anything. 'Their purpose is to defeat His enemies, which in this case, are most readily embodied by the column of xenos vehicles approaching our position. Had the vehicles of the Twenty-Fifth's auxiliary armour units been intending to engage these xenos in combat, it is likely that they would have encountered resistance from the civilian operators of the road-gate mechanism, who might lack the necessary understanding of the Omnissiah's glorious purpose with regard to war. I would have been ready to explain these theological details and, if necessary, assume direct command of the gate's operating mechanisms in order to facilitate matters with the utmost efficiency.'

Sentra chewed her lip for a moment. 'Enginseer, I'm about to ask you a question, and in order to properly understand it and respond, you will need to access your lexicon of Aranuan slang.'

'Understood, commander.'

Sentra folded her arms. 'Are you taking the piss?'

There was a momentary pause, in which Sentra could almost swear she heard clicking noises coming from Deltis' head.

However, after a moment the enginseer gave the binharic stutter that she had come to interpret, on the rare occasions it had occurred, as a chuckle.

'No, commander. Not unless you were attempting to deceive me with your responses to my original question.'

Sentra sighed. 'Fine, honoured adept, you win. I can't speak for anyone else here, no matter what they may or may not be doing, but I was certainly intending to give the xenos a taste of our cannons.' She laid a loving hand on *Golden Thunder*'s hull. 'It pains me to have these ladies cooped up in here when there's an enemy outside. We might not be able to engage them fully, but I'd rather be sent to a penal legion than let those scum ride around right under our noses without us bloodying theirs a bit.'

Enginseer Deltis nodded again. 'Then our intentions coincide, commander. I have been granted access to a part of the city's noosphere, and utilising this I believe I am able to monitor the xenos' progress with more accuracy than you. I shall ensure that the road gate is ready to operate at the correct moment, and I shall communicate this to you.'

Sentra smiled. 'That is much appreciated, enginseer. May the Machine-God bless you.'

'Thank you for your kind words, commander,' Deltis replied, with a slight quirk of his torso that could have been an attempt at a bow from a being whose spine no longer bent in the same manner as one composed of human vertebrae. 'I estimate that the most opportune moment for you to depart will be slightly in excess of seven minutes hence, although I shall update you with more detail as it becomes clear.' He turned and headed off towards the distant darkness of the road gate, a huge edifice of ancient metal at least three feet thick, and large enough that a medium-sized Battle Titan could have walked through it without having to duck its head.

'Right, the cogboy's onside, bless his circuits,' Sentra said in a low voice down into *Golden Thunder*'s crew compartment. 'That solves the problem of me having to pull rank on the door wardens. Pallas, is that ammo box secured?'

'Yes, ma'am,' Pallas replied, giving the bolt one last twist just to make sure.

'Good, I don't want it shearing off again. You go and tell Flash, get him to pass it on. Gravers!'

'Yes, ma'am?' the battle cannon's gunner replied.

'You go and give the good news to Commander DeTay,' Sentra said. 'I don't see the need to use a vox, even given how noisy it is in here. No point the brass getting wind of anything before they need to, right?'

'Yes, ma'am,' Gravers acknowledged, giving his weapon's targeting auspex one last ritual and rather hopeful thump.

Sentra caught the eye of Darrus Greel, currently checking the hull-mounted lascannon on *Lion's Fury*, and gave him a small smile. In just a few minutes, the 25th – or a part of it, at least – would have a chance to strike back at the foul enemy that had forced them to take refuge in this giant, stinking hive city.

And then, there would be a reckoning.

LOTZ

Zagnob Thundaskuzz had the wind in his hair squigs, a wrench between his teeth, and a song in his heart.

The song in question was the full-throated engine roar of his Deffkilla wartrike, the thrumming of its thick, nobbled tyres over the dirt and sand below him, and the howl of the jet engine powering everything along. His wartrike was the perfect blend of speed, power and killyness: it was tougher than a warbike, faster than a buggy, trakk or trukk, and while it might not have the sheer firepower of something like a boomdakka snazzwagon, it carried *him*, and that made up for it. The only thing better than driving really, really fast was driving really, really fast into a bunch of gits and charring them with the engine outputs, blowing holes in them with the boomstikks, or impaling one with his snagga klaw and dragging the unfortunate along behind him. So far as Zagnob was concerned, he was doing whoever-it-was a favour by helping them go faster than they probably ever had before; it wasn't his fault if they weren't up to it.

'See anyfing yet?' he bellowed at Skitta, his grot fuel-mixer, who was currently bracing a pair of make-bigger tubes against its eyes.

'Nuffin', boss!' Skitta squeaked. 'Dere's no doors!'

'How do dese gits get in an' out, den?' Zagnob muttered to himself, rubbing his chin. He glanced irritably upwards, to the blinking lights and faint reflections of whirling blades that signified where Da Red Barrun's flyboyz were keeping pace with his convoy in their deffkoptas. He was going to be incredibly displeased if this humie city could only be accessed by the air.

He forced himself to think, making his brain turn away momentarily from revelling in the speed and noise that surrounded him, and the never-ceasing black-hole draw of the horizon. Part of him wanted nothing more than to roar off into the distance, like all speed freeks, until he finally caught up with it and made the distance into his 'here'. However, the distance was a tricky quarry, and he hadn't caught it yet. On the other hand, it wasn't going away: it was always lurking there, within sight, but not as yet within reach. He had other ambitions he could fulfil in the meantime, if he could just concentrate on them.

Goresnappa had been alright as warbosses went: a bit of a traditionalist, like all Snakebites, but not to the point where he hadn't recognised the importance of having some fast-moving vehicles to surge around the enemy and clobber them from the side or rear. He'd led the Waaagh! to some good fights in his time, which was all most orks wanted from a warboss.

Zagnob was not most orks, though: he was a speedboss, the unquestioned leader of the speed freeks here, and held in high regard by any ork who had anything to do with driving a vehicle, or riding one into battle. Zooming into the middle of a scrap to show the rest of the boyz how it was done was all very well, but he chafed at how slowly everyone and everything else moved. It always took the Waaagh! too long to get to a fight, and then even when they found one, the speed freeks had to wait for the rest to get themselves sorted. It was an insult to him, to his machine, and to the Kult.

But what if Zagnob Thundaskuzz wasn't just speedboss, but the overall warboss? Well, that would be a different matter entirely. Then there would be a simple rule: any ork that fell behind, would get left behind. He would give the hordes of boyz the chance to build themselves a few trukks or wagons, of course, so they had a chance of keeping up, but the die-hard footsloggers could go their own way if they were going to deliberately persist in being so zoggin' slow. Then Zagnob could move at the speed that pleased him – really, really fast – and take on whatever enemy he found, as and when he found them.

In order to call the shots, he needed to become warboss. In order to become warboss, he needed to find this gateway that Old Morgrub had talked about, or at least be close enough to smack whoever did find it out of the way and claim it for himself. In order to find the gate, he needed to be able to get inside the humie city, and that was the thing that was currently stumping him.

There *had* to be a way in, though. The Waaagh! had kicked the humies' heads in and sent the survivors scurrying away to take shelter in this city: they certainly weren't anywhere else, so they had to be in there. Zagnob didn't reckon the humies could have airlifted everything back inside, not including all their big tanks and battlewagons, so there had to be a door that vehicles could use. He just couldn't *find* the zoggin' thing…

Something thundered, overhead. No, not quite overhead, Zagnob realised: it was coming from the upper reaches of the humie city, and it had the unmistakeable rolling quality of high-powered dakka. Humies had some appreciation for blowing stuff up with big guns, Zagnob would give them that. What was more, their guns usually made a satisfying booming sound, not like those fizzing energy wotsits the blue fishboyz used, or the nearly silent weapons of the skrawniez. You might as well not shoot at your enemy at all, if your gun wasn't going to make a good lot of noise while you did so...

'Dey're shootin' at us, boss!' Skitta wailed, as glowing projectiles began to arc down through the night towards them. Zagnob snatched the make-bigger tubes off the grot for safekeeping, then clipped it around the head so hard that said head cannoned backwards into the side of the trike.

'I know dat!' he bawled. 'Duffrak! Yoo seein' dis?'

'Yes, boss!' his driver said, over his shoulder.

'Gonna do anyfing about it?'

'Just wanna see where dey're gonna land, boss,' Duffrak replied, keeping his eyes on the sky. Zagnob grunted, but held his tongue. He'd given Duffrak the job of driving him around not only because he went very fast, but also because he generally managed to avoid driving into things by accident, and while Zagnob wasn't scared of a crash, crashing did mean that he had stopped going fast. He thought it was fairly likely that Duffrak would also be able to avoid getting hit by incoming ordnance. If not, then Zagnob would be giving a thorough kicking to anything of Duffrak that happened to be left afterwards.

He glanced over his shoulder at the loose wedge of vehicles following him: dozens and dozens of them, spread out in an attempt to avoid each other's dust clouds, because what was the point of going fast if you couldn't see how fast you were going? It might have been dark, but Zagnob's eyes were up to the task of picking out the different shapes and lines, and he could see the wide and varied scope of orkish vehicles that answered the call of his engine's roar.

There were sleek dragstas, low to the ground and aerodynamic, with the whirling gizmos of their shokkjump drives ready to be activated; the gun-heavy shapes of snazzwagons, their mek owners perched proudly behind their fearsome armaments and eagerly awaiting anything upon which they could unleash the full force of their deranged designs; megatrakk scrapjets, the now-wingless shells of aircraft whose fuselages had remained whole enough after a crash to be refitted for overland travel, armed with batteries of rokkits; the smoke-billowing kustom boosta-blastas, their oily fumes turning the night even darker; ramshackle squig-buggies, the grunts and squeals of their caged living ammunition loud enough to be heard even over the thunder of engines; and, of course, mob upon mob of warbikers, perhaps the most quintessential of ork speedsters. Zagnob had a certain amount of respect for any ork who threw in with the Kult of Speed, no matter how wild or outlandish their vehicle, but there was something simplistically appealing about a classic warbike's combination of high speed, ferocious firepower, and lack of obvious balance.

Even that wasn't the end of it. Da Red Barrun's deffkoptas were sort of like sky-buggies: they were not as fast or as heavily armed as the true flyers, the dakkajets and the burna-bommers and their ilk, but their pilots braved the air and its associated dangers such as flak, enemies, and unexpected avians without the protective surroundings of a cockpit, instead relying on their piloting skills and the favour of Gork and Mork to keep them from harm. And of course, back on the ground, there were the trukkboyz: Kult of Speed wannabes who lacked the know-wotz to build their own vehicle, or the teef to pay a mek to knock one together for them, but would cling onto the back of a transport simply to feel the wind in their faces and be able to jump out and clobber the enemy all the sooner.

Zagnob squinted. Trukks, like every other ork vehicle, were wildly varied in design, albeit broadly similar in terms of size and function,[7] and a good speedboss would know to whom every vehicle in a Waaagh! belonged, just in case he had to clobber the owner for beating him in a race. Zagnob had just seen one whose presence was unexpected, and it bothered him.

'Oi, Skitta,' he said, peering at a trukk that was powering up behind them. It looked like it was painted black, although it was hard to tell in the dark. 'Does dat look like Nuzzgrond's mob–'

The night erupted.

Flame and dirt kicked up, and one of the trukks following Zagnob's wartrike was abruptly and spectacularly rearranged into a blossoming flower of fire, shrapnel, and dismembered body parts. The humie artillery had finished its long arc down from the walls above, and was doing some proper krumping.

'Ya worked out where it's landin' yet?' Zagnob yelled at Duffrak, grabbing onto a handhold as the wartrike swerved to one side.

'Reckon so, boss!' Duffrak replied cheerily. 'But ya might wanna hold on for a minute!'

Hold on? Zagnob could have thumped his driver for such cheek. Oh, he certainly *was* holding on, but there was a difference between holding on because you, a speedboss, had decided to, and holding on because your driver had told you to. He had half a mind to–

Another explosion, and then another, and another. Night became day, briefly and repeatedly, and Zagnob caught momentary

---

7 Every ork knew at what point a trukk stopped being a trukk and started being a battlewagon, although verbalising it might be another matter.

glimpses of the blue checks of Deathskull vehicles, the leering yellow crescent of the Bad Moons, and the fiery reds of Evil Sunz like him, all lit up in flashes of destruction as their neighbours were blown apart by the fury of humie vengeance.

He raised his face to the sky and howled in delight. He had the thunder of guns and the roar of speed around him, and that was all a speed freek needed in order to be happy. He would have preferred the presence of an enemy he could clobber as well, of course, but given they were all hiding behind those ridiculously thick walls, he would take this as a stopgap. How could anyone know they were truly living, unless there was the imminent possibility of being dead?

The mighty guns far above spoke once more, and a new rain of ordnance began to arc down towards them. The humies had altered their aim to account for their targets' fast-moving nature, and these shells were coming down in a curtain directly ahead. The only sure-fire way of avoiding them would be to stop dead.

There was no way that Duffrak was going to do that, and no way that Zagnob Thundaskuzz was going to tell him to, either. Instead, the driver raised one hand, and yelled one word.

'Skitta!'

The grot was also howling, with terror rather than with excitement, but it had enough brain space left around the edges of its panic to slam both fists down on the big red button that was its primary responsibility. Valves opened, and supercharged fuel gushed into the wartrike's system. It was a special brew, refined by the most skilled mekboyz and only available, let alone affordable, to important orks like Zagnob: mainly because he'd promised to kick the teef down the throat of any ork who provided it to someone else. It would burn out an engine in short order if used to excess, but when administered correctly...

The wartrike jerked forwards like a scalded smasha squig,

flames as long as Zagnob was tall billowing from its jet outflow. They were almost flying now, getting huge amounts of air as they crested each ridge or bump in the ground; then the wheels would dig in again as soon as they touched down, and the acceleration would somehow increase. They were passing directly beneath the bombardment. Zagnob looked up and bellowed his defiance at it, at those rapidly growing miniature suns of blazing energy and high explosive that presumed to threaten him. Let the humies sling their dakka at him! If he had to die, then knowing the gits had needed to call upon their biggest guns in order to kill him was a decent enough trade-off. Zagnob wasn't sure what happened when you died, but if Gork and Mork were paying any sort of attention to him, he felt sure they'd think that being blown up while going really, really fast was a death you could have a laugh about.

The shells got lower and lower, causing the air to scream as it was torn asunder by their sheer speed and mass, and then–

–they were past.

The first shells ripped into the ground, inflicting yet more damage on it, but Zagnob Thundaskuzz's Deffkilla wartrike was out of blast range and gunning on into the night. Even Da Red Barrun's deffkoptas were taking evasive action in order to avoid being swatted from the sky as an afterthought; the rest of the ground convoy were either being blown to smithereens, had slewed to a shameful stop, or were engaging in a whooping diversion around the kill-zone.

'Waaagh!' Zagnob roared, a cry of simultaneous joy and challenge. The engine was cycling down again now, as the brief burst of acceleration granted by the speshul fuel began to wear off. Zagnob wanted to bring the sensation back, to feel his neck muscles once again at war with G-forces and air drag, but only a squigbrained fool pushed his machine harder than it could take.

Any grot could achieve a brief burst of glory and then burn an engine out: the mark of a true speed freek was knowing exactly what line you could walk to get the most performance from your vehicle without leaving yourself coasting to an embarrassed halt atop a coughing pile of metal. He was alone, supreme and unchallenged in his speed and skill and daring.

'Boss?' Duffrak said. 'We've got company!'

Zagnob lowered his gaze from the heavens and looked ahead. Beams of light were splitting the night, but these weren't static searchlights, peering down from on high in search of targets for the big guns to let fly at; these jerked and juddered and shifted sharply, as the vehicles on which they were mounted bucked and bumped and bounced over the uneven terrain.

A wide, toothy grin spread across Zagnob Thundaskuzz's face.

'Looks like da humies have decided to come out an' play after all!' he chortled happily. 'Let's go an' welcome 'em to da party!'

'We're all on our own, boss,' Duffrak pointed out. He wasn't contradicting Zagnob, merely reminding his boss of something which might have otherwise slipped his mind, but Zagnob was well aware of the situation.

'Da uvvers'll catch up,' he said, matter-of-factly. 'If we can't run rings around a bunch of zoggin' humies in da dark, den we don't deserve to be out 'ere at all.' He worked the action on his snagga klaw, hearing the satisfying *snik-snak* of its blades, and the hiss of gas as he twisted a valve to pressurise the harpoon attachment. Some of the humies liked to get a proper ork's-eye view of things by riding along with their heads and torsos sticking out of the top of their tanks, and while Zagnob could admire their enthusiasm for getting the wind in their faces like a proper speed freek, they made ever-so-tempting targets when they did so.

'Let's go an' have some fun,' he growled, and the wartrike leaped forwards once more.

LOTZ

'Ya can't rebel against da orks!' hissed the other grot. He was
called Snippa One-Ear, for reasons that even Kruffik had not
needed clarifying; he was very nominally in charge of the large
collection of grots that Zukrod would have been leading – or
prodding – into battle; and he was very obviously frightened.

'Why not?' Snaggi asked, trying to sound reasonable.

'Because dey'll kill us!' Snippa protested, tugging on his one
remaining ear in fear. He and his mob were cowering in the
shelter of a wrecked megatrakk, in the hope that everyone would
forget about them until the coming battle was over. 'Dey'll probably kill us all just for ya talkin' to us about it!'

'Den wot've you got to lose?' Snaggi asked. 'If dey're gonna
kill ya *anyway*, why not try an' get ya freedom?'

Several of the assembled grots looked at each other and
nodded, with the confidence of those for whom the consequences of such actions were as yet only theoretical, but Snippa
One-Ear was not so easily swayed.

'Dey *might* kill us for ya talkin' to us about it,' he argued, 'but dey'll *definitely* kill us if we try an' rebel! Dat's an important difference! It's like, numbaz an' dat.'

'Yoo're a coward,' Snaggi accused him.

'Yep!' Snippa replied, folding his arms and staring back challengingly. 'Of course I'm a coward! Grots are *s'posed* to be cowards! It's what keeps us alive! We don't get good guns, we don't get good armour–'

'We don't get *any* armour,' Kruffik put in.

'–right, dat,' Snippa agreed, without breaking his stride, 'an' da orks hide behind us an' let us get shot! Bein' a coward's da only way yoo're gonna get out alive!'

'So why do da orks hide behind us?' Snaggi asked, raising his voice so the entire mob could hear him. 'Dey're bigger dan us! *We* should be hidin' behind *dem*! Orks get armour! Dey get all da good weapons, so da enemies are scared of 'em! Dey get to ride around in trukks an' wagons, or on da back of squigs, so dey can get to da fight faster an' have less time gettin' shot at! Dey're da cowards, not us!'

'Wait,' Snippa said, frowning. 'Does dat mean dat you weren't tryin' to insult me when ya called me a coward, or–'

'Dat don't matter now!' Snaggi interrupted him, on the basis that momentum was more important that internal consistency. 'My point *is*, dat us grots get a bad deal! We get da *worst* deal in da history of deals wot've been done in da galaxy. We didn't even do da deal! Dere's not one grot here wot had an ork come up to him an say, "Hello little grot, would ya like ta get a gun wot a humie would larf at, an' a coupla bits of cloth to wear, and go an' stand in front of us when we try an' kill da rest of da galaxy?", is dere?'

'I wouldn't have said "yes" to dat,' Guffink said, shaking his head.

'Course ya wouldn't!' Snaggi agreed. 'Who would? Bein' a

coward ain't gonna help ya get out alive, cos da orks always make sure we get da dangerous jobs! We just get told wot to do cos da orks are bigger, an' dey fink dat means dey can do wot dey want!'

'Well, it sorta does,' Snippa pointed out. 'Dat's how it works.'

'But it don't have to!' Snaggi said, appealing to the mob in general. 'Da orks *need* us! Dey don't know how to do half da fings dey want done, or if dey do, dey ain't got da patience for it! Dey've only got da patience to kick a grot if da grot don't do it like dey want it done. Wot dis Waaagh! needs is a warboss wot's gonna take grots seriously!'

'Dere's no ork in da history of all orks wot's ever taken grots seriously,' Snippa One-Ear objected. 'Now, I'll admit dat I ain't met every ork wot's ever lived, but I'm still pretty sure I'm right about dat. Dere's no warboss dat's gonna make life any better for us, so yer Revolushun's pointless.'

Snaggi grinned triumphantly. He was still riding on the wave of adrenaline that had engulfed him in the aftermath of frying Zukrod. He felt like he could reach out and touch the spire of the humie hive city, and maybe pull it down with one good tug. Gork and Mork were muttering away in the back of his brain, giving him the strength and the determination he needed to see this through, to change the face of the galaxy.

'No *ork* warboss is gonna make life any better for us,' he corrected Snippa, sticking his chest out.

'Yeah, dat's wot I said,' Snippa said, nonplussed.

Snaggi felt his grin slip a bit. 'No, wait, I meant...' He sighed. 'Skrawk! Bring in da stikk!'

There was a moment's pause, and then Skrawk shuffled in from outside with Zukrod's grabba stikk clutched in both hands. Snippa and the rest of his mob shied back from it in sudden and deeply ingrained fear, and Snaggi took the opportunity to take the tool from Skrawk and plant its haft firmly in the ground. It was taller than he was by some way, but so far as he was concerned, that just made him look more heroic next to it.

'Where did ya get dat?' Snippa wailed, trying to look all ways at once, as though expecting the grabba stikk's previous owner to emerge from the shadows, bellowing in rage.

'Took it from Zukrod,' Snaggi announced proudly. 'After I *killed* him!'

The jaw of every single grot in Snippa's mob dropped open, and every eye bulged.

'He's dead,' Snaggi persisted, keen to press his advantage with an audience who were suddenly hanging on his every word. 'Ya can go an' find him if ya want, just make sure no ork sees ya near his body, cos dey might get funny ideas about wot happened to him. An' I don't want ya takin' credit for wot I did!'

'You... *killed* him?' Snippa repeated, incredulously.

'He didn't just give me his grabba stikk cos he was feelin' generous!' Snaggi said. 'But I didn't just kill him – I killed da warboss too!'

He was expecting even more shocked reactions, but instead the grots in front of him just looked puzzled. A grot killing a runtherd, Snaggi realised, was vaguely possible for them to conceptualise: it was something that most of them would likely have dreamed of doing at some point, but they had lacked the courage, ability, or opportunity to do so. A grot killing a warboss, though, was outside of what they considered possible. It was ridiculous, like saying he had just eaten a battlewagon, or knocked a moon unconscious.

'I pulled da lever wot dumped da head of da Mega-Gargant onto him,' Snaggi said, trying to reframe events into something his audience could understand, and was rewarded with a few horrified expressions. 'Orks ain't so tough as all dat, ya just need to know how to squish 'em, or cook 'em, or wotever. If we put our minds to it, dere's no reason why da Revolushun shouldn't succeed!'

'An' wot are you gonna count as succeedin'?' Snippa demanded. 'Cos all I can see dat's likely is da orks stompin' us all flat!'

Here it was. His chance to finally verbalise what Gork and Mork had been telling him. His previous attempt at setting up the line had been kiboshed a bit by Snippa's reaction, but now Snaggi had a clear run at it.

'Success is gonna be when I become warboss!'

Laughter. Not just laughter, hilarity. Grots bending double, hands on their knees. Grots holding themselves up weakly on their neighbours. Grots rolling on the floor wheezing, most of the air they needed in order to simply survive stolen by their bodies' reactions to the utterly ludicrous notion of a grot being– No, not of a grot *being* warboss, because that was a concept too far, but of a grot *thinking* he could be warboss.

'Snaggi, dis is da best day of my life!' Snippa gurgled, from somewhere around knee height. 'I ain't larfed dis hard, *ever!* When I can get up, I'm gonna shake yer hand!'

'I ain't jokin'!' Snaggi shouted desperately. 'I mean it! I'm gonna become warboss!'

'But *how?*' someone shouted back, through splutters. 'Ya fink ya can outfight Dedfist, or outrun Thundaskuzz, or outfink Da Genrul?'

'I don't need to do any of dose fings!' Snaggi screamed angrily, levelling the grabba stikk at them all. 'I just need to get to dat gate wot Old Morgrub talked about, an' I need to get dere *first!*'

Silence fell, like the abruptly loosened head of a Mega-Gargant.

'Dat's wot da old warphead said, weren't it?' Snaggi asked quietly. 'I've heard wot everyone's been sayin', an' more importantly, I *saw* it. Gork an' Mork showed me. Dere's a skrawniez gate of some sort under da humie city, and da big bosses are all runnin' around tryin' ta find it. Old Morgrub said da ork wot finds it first is gonna be warboss, an' Old Morgrub's got a lot of clout around here.'

'Yeah,' Snippa said a trifle hoarsely, pushing himself back to his feet. 'But he was talkin' about *orks*. An' you might've killed an ork, an' you might've dropped something really heavy on anuvver ork, but ya ain't an ork, Snaggi Littletoof.'

'Maybe not,' Snaggi admitted. 'But Old Morgrub's an odd sort. Are ya tellin' me dat if he finds a grot at da gate, dere's *no way* dat he's gonna say dat grot is da new warboss?'

A few mouths opened, and then closed again as their owners mulled this over. When push came to shove, there was no denying that Old Morgrub *was* an odd sort, even as warpheadz went. It was not, grot brains began to realise, completely outside of the realms of possibility. It wasn't *likely*, no one was claiming that it was *likely*, but it wasn't impossible.

For a group of beings for whom life consisted of a few painful certainties, mainly involving physical abuse and terrified death, 'not impossible' held a certain appeal that was hard to deny.

'Even if he does,' Snippa said slowly, 'dat doesn't mean da rest of da Waaagh!'s gonna accept it.'

'Course not,' Snaggi admitted, 'but dere's more Snakebites dan any uvver clan. Dere's no Snakebite big bosses, cos Goresnappa stomped any of his own clan wot got too big for dere boots, so da Snakebites'll probably back up wot Old Morgrub says, cos he's one of 'em. It's a long shot, but it might just work. Besides,' he added, 'I ain't just talkin' about gettin' to da gate. Dat's wot'll get dere attention, but we're gonna need to do uvver stuff to make 'em listen once we've done dat.'

'Wot sort of uvver stuff?' Snippa asked. He wasn't convinced yet, Snaggi could tell that much, but the very vague prospect of having someone in charge who might not send him to go and die somewhere on the simple basis of him being a grot was enough to pull him in for now.

'We're gonna need to be able to stop everyfing,' Snaggi said, lowering his voice to a more conspiratorial tone. Snippa's mob crowded in around him in order to hear, and he got a new flush of excitement and importance. 'We're da ones wot load da ammo, grease da gears, herd da squigs – all dat stuff. We need to talk to da riggers, da oilers, da orderlies, every other grot wot does somefing dat an ork can't do, or won't do. When da time comes, da orks are gonna have a choice to make.'

He took a deep breath.

'Dey can pay us grots some proppa respect… or dey can sit around with gunz an' vehicles wot don't work, while we head off on da first ever GrotWaaagh!'

LOTZ

Mag Dedfist was inspecting the weapons systems on *Gork's Hammer*, the Mega-Gargant he had commandeered as his own, when a flash of green light through the viewports arrested his attention. A couple of moments later, the metal of the hull above his head rang with multiple muffled impacts.

'Wot in da blazes?' the Goff muttered, then squinted in surprise as a howling shape plummeted past a viewport, clawing futilely at the air. 'Woz dat an ork?'

'Fink so, boss,' the spanner called Gutzog replied, pressing his face up against the viewport and trying to peer downwards. 'He can't fly, whoever he is.'

A few more thuds and scraping noises came from above them, and Dedfist growled in irritation. He pointed at a nervous, oil-spattered grot who was hanging around the command deck with the attitude of one who was unsure if it would get in more trouble for leaving or for staying, and who had been on the agonised knife-edge of indecision for several minutes now.

'Yoo. Get out dere and find out why dere's boyz landin' on dis fing.'

'Yes, boss!' the grot squawked, and sprinted for the access hatch in the side of the head with the *flap-flap-flap* of its large bare feet. It desperately spun the opening wheel, then threw all of its body weight – such as it was – against the door, which barely cracked open. It backed off, desperation to please the warboss-to-be writ large on its face, and took a proper run up.

The hatch was tugged open from the outside just before the grot made contact with it, and the luckless creature's momentum sent it stumbling across the narrow gantry, and then over the edge to sail down into oblivion with nothing but a wailing cry of terror and despair to mark its passing. The ork who had pulled the door edged around it from the other side, casting an incurious glance in the direction of the falling grot as he did so, then pulled up short with one foot inside the Gargant's head when he clapped eyes on Mag Dedfist's hulking frame.

'Er… Hi, boss.'

'Wot da zoggin' 'eck is goin' on?' Dedfist demanded. 'Wot's da big idea?'

The ork was a beast snagga boy by the look of his crude armour, heavy, hook-bladed choppa, and a left leg which was a prosthetic from the knee downwards where a large squig of some sort had taken a nibble at him. However, he was also a Goff, judging by the colour of his clothes, and in no way inclined to risk the displeasure of his big boss. He attempted an appeasing grin. 'Uh, not exactly sure meself, boss. Nob Badeye said he had a kunnin' plan, an' we all went to see Old Morgrub. Da boss – dat is, Nob Badeye, not you, boss – told Morgrub to jump us froo da humie walls so's we could get inside wivout waitin'. Morgrub called 'im a cheater, an' da next fing I know, we're all in da sky. Guess he must've jumped us up dere instead, to teach Badeye a lesson.'

Mag Dedfist's expression, which was never going to be accused of being naturally sunny, grew suddenly and unmistakably more thunderous.

'Not my idea...' the ork muttered hopefully, as Dedfist stamped towards him, even the sturdy plating of the deck beneath them flexing slightly under the weight of his massive armour and furious displeasure.

'An' where is Nob Badeye now?' Dedfist rumbled.

'Can't say for sure, boss,' the ork replied quickly, looking up at the big boss, who stood head and shoulders taller than him. 'Last time I saw 'im, he was headin' for da ground, proppa quick like. He missed da Gargant, ya see.'

Dedfist paused for a moment, the talons of his enormous power klaw flexing slightly as he considered this. Then he snorted dismissively, and prodded the other ork in the chest with his non-klawed hand.

'Get back out dere, and bring in any of da rest of yer mob wot landed on me Gargant. Den get down into da belly an' wait.'

'Wait for wot, boss?' the ork asked, then flinched backwards as Dedfist scowled at him. 'Just so's we know wot yoo're wantin'!'

'Wait until da doors open, cos dat's when yoo're gonna be chargin'!' Mag growled at him, and the ork beat a hasty retreat back outside to start hollering at any of his mates who had been saved from a fatal fall by the unexpected intervention of a giant ork-shaped metal head. Dedfist himself turned back to the spanners, who were watching him with a mixture of excited anticipation that they might be called upon to demonstrate the effectiveness of their creation, and fear that it was somehow going to be terminally disappointing, with emphasis on the 'terminally' part.

'Looks like some of me nobs have decided to play silly buggers,' Mag Dedfist declared, and the twin pilot lights of his jaw-mounted skorchas flared a little bit wilder, as if tuned to his mood. 'I ain't gonna hang around here an' wait for some jumped-up little zogger to sneak in like a bloody grot, finkin' dey can claim wot don't belong to dem! Sound da horns! We're gonna crack dat city open, an' I ain't waitin' for da sun before I get started!'

The spanner boyz grinned gleefully at each other, their excitement overriding their fear, and spun around in their seats. Each one reached up and grabbed a dangling loop of chain, then hauled on it with all their respective mights.

And the Gargant

ROARED.

It started as something felt rather than heard: a subsonic shake that began at the soles of the feet and rapidly climbed upwards, vibrating through limbs, shaking the spine, and dancing uncomfortably through and around internal organs. By the time it was resonating within the lungs, the ears had started to register its presence: first as a wave of pressure, and then as something that could more or less be described as sound, if sound was something that grabbed you by each side of your skull and headbutted you in the face. On and on it climbed, rising through the frequencies with the savage, uncaring grace of an apex ocean predator breaching the wave crests to snatch and crush a doomed warm, furry prey-thing between razored jaws, and then just when you thought it had reached its apex, it *kept going*. It was the throaty bellow of a volcanic eruption, it was the shuddering groan of a continent-sized sheet of metal being torn asunder, it was the tortured scream of a million overpowered steam whistles. It wasn't truly the voice of Gork, but it was, Mag Dedfist reflected, a zoggin' good imitation.

And it was not alone.

There were other Gargants in the Waaagh!, none quite so large as *Gork's Hammer*, but each one a malignant, brooding powerhouse of war in its own right. Beneath them were the Stompas: mini-Gargants that could scrag an Imperial Knight in a matter of seconds, and make a Warhound Titan think twice. Then there were the Morkanauts and Gorkanauts, the pride and joy of badmeks and outcast nobs, who preferred riding into battle within the thick metal hides of their own personal war machines rather than fixing up da boss' battlewagons, or leading a bunch of boyz. Their owners were still welcome, despite being somewhat antisocial even by ork standards, because anything big and shooty and stompy would have a place in an ork warband. There were dozens of Deff Dreads, fearsome hunks of scrap and weapons in their own right, each one equal to a whole mob of boyz in terms of durability and killing power. Even the Killa Kans, despite being smaller and lighter and undoubtedly more cowardly, were part of the Waaagh!'s mighty contingent of walkers. Every one, no matter the clan affiliation of the orks that built or crewed them, fitted in with Mag Dedfist's preferred approach to war: walk forwards, give 'em some dakka, then clobber 'em good an' proper.

They all raised their mechanical voices in answer to their over-lord's call, stentorian bellows mixing with static-laden roars and fuzzed-out screeches. As they did so, the main body of the Waaagh! – the orks themselves – took up the shout. Mag looked out of the viewport and saw a mass of bodies swarming around the distant feet of the mighty war effigy in which he rode. He didn't need to dispense any orders: the Gargant's horns were instruction enough for the thousands of boyz around him, who knew that the time had come to pile headlong into the fight. Dedfist might not be warboss yet by the reckoning of Old Morgrub, but what say did the warphead really have in the matter? Da Genrul had got his bunch of finkers and oddboyz, and Thundaskuzz had the Kult of Speed, but the majority of the Waaagh! were here, and all too happy to follow Mag Dedfist's lead.

Still, the gate that Old Morgrub had talked about was supposedly somewhere inside the humie city, and Dedfist was going to be breaking down the walls anyway, to give the gits hiding in there a good kicking. He might as well find the gate while he was doing so, just to make sure there was no doubt in anyone's mind. Beating down challengers was entertaining enough, but Mag Dedfist was of the firm belief that the most important thing an ork could do was stomp the various other species of the galaxy into oily puddles, and orkish infighting was a distraction for which he had only a limited amount of patience.

'Looks like we got everyone's attenshun,' he said as the Gargant's roar died away, now supplanted by the answering cries from the rest of the warband. He even allowed himself to sound vaguely pleased, which he tried not to do too often, in case it gave his underlings the wrong idea. 'Alright, ladz, dere's a big crack runnin' a long way up da walls, pretty much straight ahead of us. Hit it wiv everyfing we've got. Dat's gonna be da quickest way in, an' I'm in no mood for waitin'.'

The spanners hauled on levers and twisted dials with ferocious glee. Klaxons sounded, tinny and weak against the aftermath of *Gork's Hammer*'s true voice, but alerting the rest of the crew to what was about to occur. Behind them, the hatch creaked open again, and the first of what remained of Nob Badeye's mob began filing in. Mag Dedfist watched them hurry past out of the corner of his eye. The ork he'd spoken to was doing a good job of hurrying them along and bawling at them, a far cry from the meek and submissive display he'd put on when talking to Mag before. That was good: it was hard for a big boss to work out which of his underlings were decent commanders, since they all deferred to him (if they knew what was good for them). You couldn't get the measure of an ork until you saw how he was with his own mob, especially when their nob had just copped it. It looked like this one was the natural successor.

'Yoo!' Dedfist barked. 'Wot's yer name?'

'Uzgul, boss.'

'Yoo da nob now?'

Uzgul took a look at the others around him, then nodded. 'Yes, boss!'

Dedfist waited. He did not have to wait long.

'Yoo, nob? Dat's a zoggin' joke, Uzgul!' one of the others spat.

'Oh, an' ya reckon it should be *yoo*, Braggit?' Uzgul demanded, squaring up to him.

Mag sized them both up with an expert's eye. They were fairly evenly matched in terms of size and build, and there wasn't a great deal to choose between them on any other front either. Both had the traditional horned helmet of a Goff warrior, and both were thick with muscle. Uzgul had a simple choppa, a heavy hooked axe blade on the end of a thick metal pole, whereas his adversary had a more advanced sawtoothed chain-blade that rumbled into fume-belching life as he pressed the activation switch – but that meant little. One would cleave deeper more quickly, while the other would cause much more damage if plunged into an enemy's body. At the end of the day, the nature of a weapon like that was of lesser importance than the skill of the wielder.

Neither ork went for their slugga. They were Goffs, after all, and beast snaggas to boot, and much preferred to settle things up close and personal. Each one swung at the same moment, while the rest of their mob backed away hurriedly, chuckling and whooping.

The command deck of a Gargant was far from a spacious area in which to have a fight, but that was of little consequence to a pair of Goffs: the purpose of a scrap was to win, and you couldn't win if you were out of reach of your opponent. Uzgul caught Braggit's in-swinging chainblade on the haft of his choppa and turned it aside, then mashed the butt end of it into Braggit's face to make room for a killing blow. The other ork staggered backwards, ducked the swipe that would have taken his head clean off, and tore his weapon up and across Uzgul's ribs, shredding fabric and flesh with equal ease. Dark blood flew, spattering against bulkheads and being turned into a fine mist in the air by the whirling saw-teeth of Braggit's chainblade. It was Uzgul's turn to stagger now – he emitted a grunt of pain as his torso was sliced open to the bone, and Braggit seized his opportunity. He lunged, looking to bury his weapon in Uzgul's chest and have its whining teeth chew through his opponent's body in a decisive blow.

He was too slow. Uzgul twisted aside and brought his choppa down on Braggit's arm, with enough force that the sturdy metal blade sheared right through muscle and bone, and left Braggit stumbling forwards with one fewer limb than he'd had a moment before.

'Ow! Zoggin' hell!' Braggit bellowed, turning on the spot, then raised his remaining hand as Uzgul drew his choppa back for another blow. 'Yeah, alright, alright. Da best ork won. Yoo're da boss.'

'An' don't yoo forget it,' Uzgul said, in a tone of deep satisfaction. He turned to the rest of them. 'Get movin', we ain't got all day, an' ya don't want to be gettin' in Boss Dedfist's way! Down dose stairs, hup-hup-hup! Grubslakk, close dat hatch, dere's no one else out dere! Lugrukk, give Braggit his arm back. Yes, *an'* his choppa too! Braggit, see if ya can find a painboy to get da zoggin' fing stitched back on again, for Mork's sake. If it ain't ready by da time da boss gives us da signal, yer gonna be fightin' wiv one arm, so don't say I didn't warn ya!'

Uzgul's mob, as they now were, disappeared from the command deck with the efficiency common to any ork who knew that the quickest way to reach the next interesting fight was to get out of their boss' way as soon as possible. Dedfist could hear Uzgul harassing them all the way down the ladders that led into the Gargant's belly, but that wasn't uncommon: even having proven his worth through combat, Uzgul would still want to reinforce his new position in the minds of the others.

He turned back to the spanners, who had been watching the fight with the same eagerness as the mob whose leadership had been in question. 'Did I tell ya to stop doin' wot ya was doin'?' Dedfist demanded, scowling at them.

'No, boss,' Gutzog admitted, nudging his companion. The pair of them went back to work, doing all manner of teknikal things about which Mag Dedfist had no idea: but then, he didn't need to. A warboss didn't have to pay attention to mek stuff, any more than he needed to pay attention to painboy stuff, or runtherd stuff. Oddboyz weren't leaders – apart from the occasional exception like Mad Dok Grotsnik, or Da Meklord – they did what they were told, and the orks who were suited to end up as leaders – orks like Mag Dedfist – were the ones who did the telling. That was how ork society had worked for longer than anyone could remember, and Dedfist saw no reason for it to change now he was at the top.

Well. Nearly at the top. But that was just a matter of time.

Gork's Hammer shifted beneath him. The grumble of the mighty engines changed in pitch, the smokestacks thrummed as their output increased, and great cogs and wheels began to turn and grind together. Far below, even the least perceptive ladz were breaking into desperate sprints as they tried to clear a path in front of the titanic walker. Trakks and buggies coughed into life and pulled away.

The Gargant raised one enormous lumpy foot, thrust it forwards a couple of dozen yards, and thumped it back down again. The command deck rocked, but Mag Dedfist stood firm in his mega armour, and he grinned.

To either side, the rest of the Waaagh! was mobilising, following the lead of their new boss in his mighty transport. Engines roared, horns blared, and a few enthusiastic weapons barked into life despite the fact that they were not yet close enough to the humie city to achieve anything. More than that, Mag could feel power starting to surge up all around: power that was latent whenever orks were gathered together, and which only came to the surface when they were heading in a mass towards the enemy. This was the true energy of the Waaagh!, the connection that brought a warband together and transformed it from a rough collection of mobs and individual vehicles into a bellowing force capable of toppling entire worlds, even entire systems.

The attack was underway, and the power of the Waaagh! was his to command.

LOTZ

Captain Armenius Varrow had the beginnings, the very faintest beginnings, of a plan.

It was taking a lot of effort not to second-guess himself. This was hardly surprising, given the regular humiliation he had endured at the hands of his captors. He had lost a lot of his self-confidence, all of his swagger, and not a few teeth during his time in captivity with Da Genrul. All the same, he was from Aranuan officer stock, and while he might have shamed his family by being captured alive, Captain Armenius Varrow was not a man who would accept this fate. Men of lesser breeding might have capitulated mentally, but he had never given up.

Of course, there were those who might argue that by even answering Uzbrag's questions – especially since it had been established that Varrow was not good at deceiving the hulking xenos – he *had* given up. It was just Captain Varrow's good fortune that such naysayers were not present to further discourage him.

The orks under Da Genrul's command were certainly obeying

their boss' orders. Soil was being rapidly and methodically shifted, with the same sort of haphazard efficiency that Armenius had noticed characterised so many of their endeavours. The brutes were noisy, argumentative, utterly slapdash, appeared to have little concept of danger and even less of safety, and yet they were undeniably, even terrifyingly, effective. He was uncertain whether his regiment, armed with shovels and pre-existing plans, and under the intimidating gaze of the regimental commissar, could have moved as much earth in so short a time. The orks had no plans, and very little in the way of instruction from their superiors – not to mention the fact that they occasionally stopped for a rowdy punch-up because someone had shovelled dirt into someone else's face, or stolen someone else's food, or they were all a bit bored – but still, somehow, the work was getting done.

The trenches were, as Da Genrul had intimated, only the start of what the orks were doing. Armenius could see deeper shafts running into the ground of Aranua, braced to keep them open. Crudely welded ladders disappeared into the depths, from which came the dull, repetitive sounds of tools biting into soil, mixed with grunts of effort and even the occasional raucous burst of what Armenius had realised, with some horror, was supposed to be singing.

He was on 'exercise time' again, and the horizon was starting to lighten with the dubiously welcome promise of yet another day in the orks' clutches under the punishing sun of this latitude, when the air began to shake with distant noise. He looked to the north, but could see little other than the artificial mountain of the hive city's bulk. Still, were those lights, off to the east? A veritable horde of lights? That must be where most of the rest of the orks' forces were. And although it was hard to tell at this distance, it looked to him as though they might be moving...

Heads came up, all around him. Noise died down and squabbles ceased, as every ork turned to look in the same direction. Diggers emerged from the tunnels, shovels and other earth-moving implements still clutched in their massive hands, their subterranean work temporarily set aside. A tension seemed to flow through the encampment, something that caught every ork up in its grip and held them.

For a long few moments, Armenius Varrow had the sensation that he was not in the middle of a large group of individual xenos, brought together by an affinity for warfare and violence, but surrounded by some sort of colonial organism, or perhaps a super-predator with one malignant and terrifying purpose running through every cell of its body, and those cells were orks. He had a sudden vision of what that might look like on a larger scale, if all the ork warbands across the galaxy were to come together with the same unity of purpose that he could sense in the air around him now, and was filled with unexpected gratitude for their belligerent nature and constant infighting. Armenius was a devoted servant of the God-Emperor, and he firmly believed that His light kept the Imperium whole and was what would guarantee humanity's eventual triumph over the myriad foes they faced, but there was still something sobering about the focus of these orks.

Millions of worlds and trillions of people though the Imperium contained, shielded though it was by the might of the Adeptus Astartes, the Adepta Sororitas and the Astra Militarum, and guided by the wisdom of the Master of Mankind though it might be, it was hard to see how his species could triumph if every ork forgot about internecine disagreements and came for them.

Those thoughts passed through Armenius Varrow's mind in a matter of moments, while the orks around him were still paying attention to whatever their comrades – or rivals, or whatever the appropriate term was – were doing in the north-east. As the surge of fear and disgust began to fade, or at least subsided back down to what had become normal levels for him, he realised that he had the opportunity he had been waiting for. None of the orks were paying attention to him! They were hardly reliable watch-canids most of the time, but there were so Throne-damned many of them that it had previously been impossible to escape every red, beady eye, even for a moment. Now, however, the psychic pull towards the violence that their kin were about to unleash might serve him well, if he was smart and quick.

Being smart and quick was by no means as easy for him as it had once been, given the privation to which he had been subjected, but Armenius was still able to propel his tired limbs towards a trench entrance and stumble down rough-cut steps into the earthworks. The ground was hard-packed under his feet – the result of being repeatedly trodden down by orks twice his weight or more – and he was able to hurry along at a comparatively swift pace towards the next target for his impromptu plan.

A shaft entrance.

It was deep, and it was dark, and he had no means to light his way, but Armenius knew better than to look a gift grox in the mouth. He could already hear orkish voices starting to grunt and grumble again above him, as whatever partial trance they had been in began to release them again. He might not get an opportunity like this again, and he really would be failing in his duty as a Golden Lion if he let it slip through his fingers. With any luck, he could evade the orks as they came back down: even if he were caught, he told himself guiltily, there was no indication that the xenos would inflict any particularly damaging punishment on him. He would simply be hauled back to Genrul Uzbrag once more.

The thought of that humiliation spurred him on, and he half-climbed, half-slid down the ladder into the depths below. He had seen how fast the orks worked, and there was every possibility that they would have already unearthed one of the various outflows or service tunnels that would be snaking out from the city. He could not stop them from finding them, nor could he stop them from entering them, but perhaps he could carry a warning.

Armenius was not overly familiar with the layout or structure of the Davidian underhive – such a place had been far beneath him, both literally and figuratively, when he had lived in the lower spire as a child of an officer family, before his life in service began – but he would have a far better hope of understanding signs and markings than the orks would. While they blundered around the maze-like structures of old tunnels and abandoned, half-demolished hab-domes which formed the meandering, largely lawless, and very nearly stable foundations of Davidia Hive, Captain Armenius Varrow would be heading towards help, straight as a las-bolt. He would bring word of the vile xenos' intentions, contribute to saving the hive from their subterranean treachery, and regain his honour.

Of course, even if Da Genrul's plan was foiled, that did not mean that the enormous offensive rumbling into action in the north would not endanger the hive as well, but Armenius could do nothing about that. If he had to put money on which was more dangerous – Genrul Uzbrag leading an unseen invasion through the tunnels, or an unknown ork at the head of an extremely obvious charge straight at the hive's main walls – he would be backing Da Genrul every time. The beast was a foul piece of work, but he had, in an odd way, earned Armenius' respect. Not *actual* respect, he hastily added to himself, nothing that meant the ork deserved anything less than utter annihilation by any means necessary or available, but the respect you might show a mighty carnosaur which had been brought to bay on a grav-bike hunt. You did not have to like something, or view it as anything other than a monstrosity, to appreciate the danger it posed.

He reached the bottom of the ladder, and cursed for a moment that he had not remembered to get his bearings before entering this stygian darkness, but he was still fairly sure that the city lay more to his right than to his left, in relation to the line of the trench from which he had descended. He blundered forwards, one arm raised above and in front of his face to prevent himself from walking head first into a bracing strut or similar obstruction, although most orks were at least his height, if not larger. Any tunnel down which they could walk would almost certainly be suitable for him as well.

More likely to bring him to his knees, he thought with grim humour, was the thick stench of the brutes that filled the unmoving air: although it was not, he had to admit, as foul a smell as he would have thought before he had spent time in the company of orks. Their odour was bitter and earthy more than anything else, albeit often flavoured with the chemical tang of their ballistic propellants, or engine grease, or something else's blood. However, overtly unpleasant or not, it was still strange and alien, and powerful enough that it lodged in his throat and made him feel as though some amorphous, barely corporeal being was making a spirited, if unsuccessful, attempt to strangle him.

He swallowed, and pushed onwards. Onwards and downwards, that was the key. If only he had been able to bring a lumen with him! But he was lucky to still have both his boots, let alone a light. He would simply have to make do with what he had, and pray to the Emperor that he found any breakthrough the orks might have unwittingly made into the underhive – and hopefully not by simply stepping unsighted into a hole and plummeting to his death or serious injury – before any returning orks found him in turn.

His raised hand encountered earth. Particles of it came away at his touch and fell into his upturned sleeve. He grunted in irritation and shook them out again, then felt upwards and ahead more cautiously. The last thing he wanted to do was to accidentally cause a cave-in: the thought of suddenly being buried beneath tons and tons of soft earth, unable to move and choking to death on the soil of his home planet, was a viscerally unpleasant one.

There was no mistake, even under the questing fingers of a more careful investigation. The downward-sloping tunnel along which he was travelling was closing in above him and, he found as he stretched his arms out, on either side. He could still make progress, but his headroom had disappeared. Soon, he was having to stoop a little. What was this? An ork might be able to fit into this space, but it would be a struggle, and why would they not have dug this section out to the dimensions further back, and further up?

Then he caught sight of something ahead in the blackness; or more accurately, he caught sight of something which made the blackness less black. Catching sight of something at all was noteworthy in and of itself.

Light.

And not just light. As he crept forwards, his mouth abruptly dry with nerves at the thought of being discovered, Armenius heard something over the hiss of his own breath, the faint rasp of the remnants of his clothes rubbing together as he moved, and the thunder of his heart in his ears. There were voices down here, but these were no ork voices, deep and guttural. These were higher-pitched: harsh and choppy, yes, and certainly far from melodic or pleasing to the ear, but they lacked the depth or timbre of the warriors to whose presence he had become accustomed.

Gretchin. It had to be gretchin.

He had seen the little devils around, of course, but none of them – other than the thing inside the machine that carried his hated cage – dared approach too close to Da Genrul, and so Armenius had not had any real contact with them. They were sly-looking little beasts, with long and nimble fingers that seemed equally suited to theft or throttling. Every Militarum officer knew about gretchin, of course: they were poorly armed and had little in the way of armour, their marksmanship was only average and their general morale was considerably worse, but there were usually so Throne-damned *many* of the things that you could not simply ignore them. The orks would throw them ahead of the main advance to soak up gunfire and wear you down, before their more elite units[8] would steamroller right over their corpses to sweep away your half-exhausted troops who were now low on ammunition.

Armenius felt a momentary flash of pride as he remembered rank upon rank of the glorious Golden Lions, resplendent in their gold-trimmed crimson flak armour, each soldier bearing an M35 M-Galaxy Short-pattern lasgun, so very different from the ragged mobs of wretched gretchin he had seen driven into battle by whip-wielding overseers. Every one of Armenius' troops would give their life in service to the Golden Throne – officers like him, or the regimental commissar, would ensure that one

8 Anything that wasn't a gretchin.

way or the other. The Space Marines might be the las-scalpel with which the Imperium excised the canker of xenos or heretic incursions from the galaxy, but the Astra Militarum were the grist to the mill of conquest. It was through their glorious sacrifice that the Imperium's borders were protected, and its enemies worn down.

Now it seemed that there were a few more enemies in front of him, and Armenius had no intention of letting his life get ground between the millstones just yet.

The faint glimmer of stolen light from ahead of him illuminated a pickaxe that someone had carelessly left leaning against the tunnel wall. He picked it up, his fingers closing around the metal haft. It was heavy, but not unmanageable, even in his weakened state. It had to be a gretchin tool: an ork could probably shift more soil by just digging its fingers into the wall and making a fist. Presumably the smaller caste had been sent in to open up the first tunnels, and the orks followed along behind to widen them. That suited Armenius just fine. He stood little chance of troubling an ork with this tool – in his current condition, he would likely struggle even if he had his power sword in hand – but gretchin were small, and weaker than him, and easily spooked.

He crept towards the light and the sound of voices, both hands wrapped around the pick's comforting weight. He did not need to make an effort to move quietly, since the soil beneath his feet muffled any sound of movement, and his quarry was somewhat raucous.

He listened, concentrating. They were not far around the tunnel's next bend, so far as he could tell. All gretchin sounded alike to human ears, of course, but the time Armenius had spent around their masters had given him some unwanted insight into the ways in which the species' voices were subtly different. He was fairly sure he could pick out four different ones, layered over each other in the boisterous, squabbling manner that was the nature of orks and their kin. Four was a challenge, he thought, but as his grandfather used to say, *a Varrow never shirks a challenge.*

Armenius got as close to the tunnel bend as he could without giving himself away. There was a metallic clanging, as though tools had struck something made of a similar substance. He took a deep breath, and leaped into action for the first time in weeks.

To be entirely accurate, it was not a leap at all, since the headroom was not sufficient for anything like that. He realised even as he charged that the natural motion of a pickaxe, starting behind his own shoulder and brought forwards and down in an arc, was not going to work: he would hit the ceiling, and get his weapon stuck at best, and bring it down upon himself at worst. A Varrow always knew when to adapt, however, so he kept the pick down at his side, then brought it diagonally up and across his body.

The metal point embedded itself in the first head that turned towards him. The gretchin did not even have time to squeal in shock or terror as the tool punched up through its long jaw and drove through its skull into the brain, killing it instantly. It slumped, and its weight dragged the pick downwards. Struggling against it with muscles that had not been properly used in too long, Armenius found himself exposed and vulnerable, not to mention blinded as three more pairs of eyes with head torches blazing out above them turned towards him. He froze for a second, waiting for the sharp pain that would signify the end of his life as he was overwhelmed by the foul creatures, and his noble blood was spilled beneath Aranua's surface.

Instead, all three gretchin screamed in terror, and turned to run.

'Oh no you don't!' Armenius shouted gleefully, the sight of a fleeing foe catalysing his transformation from hopeless prisoner to avenging angel. He reached out and grabbed one by the ear, hurling it against the wall, then kicked the legs out from beneath a second. He managed to haul the pick free and dropped to one knee to hurl it two-handed at the last as it ran, and the agonised cry and suddenly falling light as it struck home indicated that he had found his mark.

That just left him with two of the little xenos to deal with, albeit now without the assistance of a weapon.

One jumped at him with a scream, its clawed fingers reaching for his eyes, and apparently now sunk so far into terror that it had come out the other side into the place where the drive to kill the thing that caused the fear outweighed the fear itself. Armenius swatted it aside into the tunnel wall, drove his knee into the jaw of the one that had been behind it – the things only came up to his breastbone, so it was not so great a feat of athleticism as it might have been – and felt something in his enemy's skull fracture, then grabbed the one he had just knocked aside and flung it again, this time bodily into its companion. They both went down in a hissing tangle of limbs, like an overlarge and intoxicated green spider, and Armenius seized a shovel that one of them had let drop.

'For Aranua!' he declared joyously, and began to batter them about their heads with it.

It felt so good to be able to once again vent the Emperor's wrath on xenos scum, after so long being forced to watch their kind walking shamelessly around as though they had a right to be on His planet! Each gretchin stopped moving after the first half a dozen or so blows, but he kept at it until he was panting and exhausted, which to be fair, was not that long after.

'Hah!' he shouted, and spat on the pair of bodies, then kicked

the one upon whom he had performed an impromptu lobo-
tomy, just for good measure. 'How do you like that?' However,
his victory celebrations would have to be cut short. He had
come here with a plan, and it would not do to jeopardise that
by being caught by an ork when he was on the verge of success.
He thought he had seen, in the swaying light of the struggle…

The head torches of the two last casualties had been crushed
beneath the onslaught of his righteous strikes, but the one he
had killed first still had a working lumen attached to the strap
that ran around its head. He pulled it off the corpse and directed
the beam to the opposite side of the tunnel, then suppressed a
quite un-captain-like squeal of glee.

The gretchin had found a large piece of metal, roughly on
the level of the floor of their tunnel. It was slightly curved, and
disappeared down into the ground and into the wall, but just
where the earth wall met the floor was a raised, round shape.

This was, unless Armenius Varrow was very much mistaken,
some form of outflow pipe. And that was an entry hatch.

He set to work with the shovel feverishly, hacking back the
wall and exposing the hatch. He had no qualms about what he
was doing: the gretchin had already found it, and their masters
would surely have the wit to work out what it was. There was
no stopping them from getting into the system, so he would
simply have to make sure that he got into Davidia ahead of
them, carrying warning of their coming.

He was panting and his hands were blistered by the time he
had uncovered the hatch and made enough space for it to be
swung open. When he laid his hands upon the wheel and tried
to turn it, and it did not move, his heart sank. The pipe had
probably been buried for centuries at least, subsumed beneath
the gradually accumulating soil; there was every chance that
it would have rusted solid. This was little comfort, though,

since the orks would undoubtedly find a way to get in, using high-powered weapons and explosives to which Armenius did not have access. Even if they brought the tunnel down in the process, Uzbrag would know it was here, and he would command it dug out again and opened. The beast had the capacity to be relentless, and was clearly invested in his plan. No, the wheel not moving for Armenius Varrow was no guarantee of safety for the people of Davidia.

He sat back on his haunches and prayed to the Emperor. It was a simple prayer, and while it might have technically contained more than *please, Lord of Terra, let me escape here alive*, that was certainly the dominant ingredient. He had no time for anything more involved, and the glow of triumph was being clawed back down by the fear of discovery and recapture. Da Genrul would notice that he was missing soon, surely, and then those laughing, hooting beasts would come for him once more...

He leaned forwards and tried again, gritting his teeth and putting everything his body had left into the effort.

The wheel moved.

It scraped and it groaned, but Emperor be praised, it moved! Armenius cackled with glee as he spun it, until finally something *clicked* and he was able to lift it up, pressing it back and away from him on protesting hinges to reveal an even deeper darkness beneath. It smelled awful – some form of effluent runoff, he presumed – but it was sweet, sweet freedom compared to the confines of his cage, bumping around on the back of that fiendish machine.

Armenius tied the headtorch around his skull and quickly scanned the dead gretchin bodies. The first one he had killed proved to have a simple firearm tucked into its belt, which it had never had time to even think about drawing thanks to the noble swiftness of his attack. It looked even cruder than a stub

gun such as might be used by a downhive scummer, but Armenius was – with any luck – about to head into realms where
such insalubrious specimens of humanity might lurk. Doing
so without a firearm of any sort would be unwise; this piece
of xenos hardware would serve for now, until he could get his
hands on something more reliable. He knew that the Emperor
would understand.

He took the shovel as well, since it would serve equally well
as a bludgeon and a tool if he ran across any obstructions.
Then, as well prepared as he could hope to be, Captain Armenius Varrow climbed into the pipe and closed the hatch again
over his head.

It was down to him to save Davidia.

Da Genrul sighed. 'Nah, look, ya can't all be lootenants. How
many lootenants do ya fink we zoggin' need? A major's more
important. None of ya wanna be a major?'

The assembled orks shook their heads. Uzbrag narrowed his
eyes.

'Is dis because "lootenants" has got da word "loot" in it?'

It was not often that burly ork nobs looked embarrassed, but
this was one of those occasions.

'Mork's teef, da state of ya,' Da Genrul groaned. 'Dis is war,
ladz, an' war is a serious bizness!' He hesitated. 'Well, it's
zoggin' good fun most of da time, but dat's only because we
do it proppa, unlike da rest of da boyz, who–'

He whirled around, his greatcoat flaring, and raised his double
shoota, finger tightening on the trigger and ready to unleash
high-explosive death at whichever fool was creeping up behind
him. Then he grunted in recognition, and lowered his weapon
again as a shadowy shape detached itself from the wall of his
kommand bunker.

'Kaptin,' Uzbrag said, his tone just short of a remonstration, because while being cunning and sneaky was a good thing for a Blood Axe kommando, there was such a thing as trying to be *too* cunning and sneaky. 'Any news?'

'Da humie's gone,' Kaptin Skulsnik reported, saluting. His voice was low and unobtrusive, very different to most orks.

'About time,' Uzbrag said. 'I was beginnin' to fink we'd have to point it out to him. Did he kill anyone on da way?'

Skulsnik shook his head. 'Only some grots.'

'Bet he finks he's da big nob right now, don't he?' Da Genrul chuckled. 'Yer ladz tailin' him?'

'Yes, genrul. Waited until he was froo da hole, den went after him. He never even knew dey were followin'. I'm gonna go catch 'em up, an' we'll mark da way into da city for ya.'

'Good,' Uzbrag said, grinning. Let Mag Dedfist batter his head against the walls! Da Genrul had his own way of breaching the defences, unwittingly guided by one of the city's own.

He turned to his excessive number of lootenants, and spread his arms wide. 'Get da ladz togevva. We're goin' in.'

LOTZ

Sentra LaSteel had no idea what communication, if any, had passed between Sanavar Deltis and the civilian crew of the road gate. All she knew was that when *Golden Thunder* turned the corner to approach it with the remaining mechanised might of the Aranuan 25th behind her, the massive metal plates were grinding apart to allow them egress. One way or the other, Deltis had been as good as his word.

'Reckon we should get the cogboy a can of oil to say thanks?' Kat Pallas asked over the tank's internal vox, which was the only way Sentra, from her position in the turret cupola, was going to hear her. Pallas was the driver, and under her expert guidance *Golden Thunder* was practically as nimble and responsive as any Scout Salamander.

'Let's see if we make it through this alive, first,' Gravers replied, traversing the battle cannon a few degrees. He had checked its functionality before they had set off, but he always made another quick check once they were in motion. It was a personal superstition to which Sentra did not object, since it was better to find a fault before an engagement with the enemy than during.

'Positive as always, eh, Gravers?' said Two Hands, who was jointly responsible for both loading the battle cannon and operating the forward-facing, hull-mounted lascannon. Sentra had no idea why Loader Tayne was called 'Two Hands' – he indeed had two hands, both flesh and blood rather than bionic, and both apparently his from birth, so there seemed nothing remarkable there – and he'd already been in possession of the nickname when he had joined her crew. No one on her crew had ever asked, he had never explained, and so he was simply Two Hands to everyone. If someone from another crew expressed curiosity, Sentra tried to change the subject to avoid revealing that she had no idea why one of the people in whose charge she regularly placed her well-being had a nickname she could not explain.

'Are you expecting to live through this, then?' Xanin asked. He was one of the two sponson gunners, the most junior role on the tank.

'As the Emperor wills,' Two Hands said calmly. 'I'd like to blow holes in a couple of these xenos bastards before I'm done, but only He knows whether I'll get my wish.'

'*Commander,*' Greel's voice said into Sentra's ear over the vox. '*You're aware that we're going to be running out into fire from our own side? Some of the city's guns are shelling the ork column.*'

'I know,' Sentra replied. 'For all the good it will do them. The orks are too mobile for the big guns to do much, curse their eyes. If we're out there as well, though, not only can we take them down one on one, but we might also be able to bunch them up or limit their manoeuvrability so the artillery can land more hits.'

'*We know the orks aren't fools, commander, and nor will they hang back and engage us at range. They'll head straight for us.*'

'Which is why we're bringing Flash,' Sentra said with a smile, looking over her shoulder at where Flash Harvax's three Hell-hounds were rumbling along in a line. Flash himself was not visible: crewing a Hellhound was dangerous enough as it was, given the truly terrifying amount of highly volatile promethium present in the vehicle to power its turret-mounted inferno cannon. Poking one's head out of the turret while jets of burning liquid were gouting around changed the designation from 'dangerous' to 'suicidal', and while Harvax was a man who seemed to have been behind the door when fear was handed out, he was a little too fond of his own face to have any desire for it to be burned off by a malfunction, misfire, or particularly strong gust of wind.

'I wasn't aware that we were capable of stopping him from coming.'

'We weren't, but you know what I mean,' Sentra admitted. She cast a knowing glance over at *Lion's Fury*, the turret of which was also firmly locked down. Darrus Greel was a cautious man, and preferred being surrounded by armour plating. For her part, Sentra would duck inside if the going got too hot and the air too full of shots, but she preferred to rely on the evidence of her own eyes as well as her auspexes when determining the next course of action for her engine of war, and those that followed it.

The road gate was coming up. Sentra took a deep breath through her respirator, tasting the rubber and cloth and plas-tek, and held it as they crossed the threshold. She had worn the respirator out of habit ever since the action against the so-called Plague Children on Hammus XIII, a heretic uprising that had been unquestionably foul, but thankfully brought to battle and eradicated before it had got too large or powerful. Her previous loader, Amman Duznik, had died choking on his own blood after failing to fasten his breathing equipment properly when the hull had been pierced. Sentra's first demand of Two Hands had been that he demonstrate to her that he could fasten a res-pirator securely with his eyes shut.

Orks had no known history of using biological weapons – hateful brutes although they were, there was at least a certain honesty about the way in which they made war – but in some strange way, Sentra would have felt more naked going into battle without her respirator than if she had lacked her uniform. Gravers was not the only one who had a personal superstition, rooted in practicality though they both might have been.

'Lights,' she commanded, and the tank's powerful lumens snapped to life, spearing out through the blackness to illuminate the gritty earth and occasional tenacious shrub that constituted the landscape for miles around Davidia Hive. Sentra could *feel* the hulking presence of the hive directly behind her, a gigantic shadow looming into the sky that was simply too large to think about directly. She had seen bigger mountains in her travels across the galaxy, but none that stood so alone, rising up sheer from the ground without slope or foothills. And Davidia Hive was just one of innumerable hive cities across innumerable worlds in the Imperium: masterworks of engineering, and constructed not for some galaxy-spanning great purpose, but simply to accommodate the people that inhabited the God-Emperor's domain.

Sentra realised, once again, how humanity was destined to rule the galaxy. What other species could match their industry, their creativity, the sheer size and scope of their achievements? No matter the outcome of this battle, whether or not she and her crew survived, she could take comfort from the knowledge that the xenos aggressors would never truly triumph.

She keyed her headset to broadcast to all the vehicles with her. The time for any sort of vox silence was past: the brass would learn of their sortie soon anyway, and communication was more important than secrecy now they were outside the walls.

'Heads up and look alive, everyone, they'll be on us within

moments,' she declared. The night erupted into light and noise not far to the north, as shells fired from above began to detonate, hopefully taking some of the orks with them. 'There's no space or time for fancy tactics, and you all know how to do what you do best. Keep them at distance if you can, keep out of Flash's way if you can't, and give 'em hell!'

A chorus of cheers answered her, as the various tank commanders and their crews responded to her with vigour. Sentra raised the macro-binocs to her eyes and peered through the darkness, trying to make out signs of the enemy – the lights were more so that Pallas had some idea of what terrain she was driving through. Robust and powerful though a Leman Russ might be, it would still be little use against the Imperium's foes if it ended up on its side because the driver had steered it into an unseen ravine.

It was hard to make anything out, what with the brilliant flashes of ordnance that were even fiercer through her night-vision scope, but in the gaps between detonations Sentra thought she could just make out a single vehicle, jinking and swerving through the low dunes. She frowned in concentration, and... yes! That was no after-image of her own side's weaponry she could see, but the distinct glow of a crude-but-powerful ork propulsion system. It looked to be a trike of some sort, as ramshackle as anything she had seen in the orks' forces.

'Gunner, target, forty degrees,' she said. The turret began to traverse beneath her, as Gravers set his auspex to the hunt.

'Throne, it's moving,' her gunner muttered a moment later. 'Target acquired, gun laid. Loader, high-ex.'

There was a *thunk* as Two Hands cycled the correct autoloader. 'High-ex up!'

'Firing.'

Sentra closed her eyes as the battle cannon spoke, to prevent herself being blinded by the flare in her macro-binocs. The noise of the discharge was muffled by her responsive headset, which was all that stood between her and permanent, profound deafness, but it was still loud, not to mention the shudder of it reverberating through her bones.

'Round out,' Gravers intoned.

'Miss,' Sentra reported. Her macro-binocs had picked the ork vehicle up again, some way past where dirt was still pattering back down in the aftermath of Gravers' shot. 'Fire again.'

'Target acquired,' Gravers replied. 'Probably. Gun laid. Loader, high-ex.'

'High-ex up!'

'Firing.'

Golden Thunder lived up to her name again, and once more spat devastation out into the night. And once again missed, Sentra noted with rising anger, as another explosion failed to even clip the elusive, fast-approaching ork vehicle.

'Round out. Sorry, commander,' Gravers said. 'Whatever's steering that thing is either a genius, or suffering some sort of seizure.'

'Well, we are about to be in a target-rich environment,' Sentra declared, as more and more blurs of movement appeared in her sights. The rest of the ork convoy had been lagging behind this front runner, but they were visible now, and by the Emperor and all the primarchs, there were a lot of them. Few, if any, would be a match for a single vehicle in her thrown-together squadron one on one, but orks never came one on one. They came in a mass, combining reckless speed with disproportionate firepower. You might total one with a single shot, but there would be two more behind it, and three more behind those. Before you had managed to take them all out, their guns would have wrecked something important with either some sort of physics-defying blast, or a simple hail of high-calibre bullets too ferocious for even cast plasteel to resist.

The rest of her vehicles opened up. For a moment, Sentra thought they had now all realised what Gravers had been firing at, but the shots were looping far longer: they were targeting the main group of xenos vehicles, leaving the trike unmolested. She wasted a second considering whether she should order it destroyed as some sort of object lesson, but decided against it. This was not an official operation, after all, and her authority over these dregs and remnants came more from seniority and respect than any true command structure. If the trike continued to evade Gravers and got close enough to be a menace, Flash's Hellhounds would incinerate it.

Her vox crackled, followed by the warning chime of a direct command override. This was not a call that she could choose to ignore.

'LaSteel, what in the name of Terra are you doing?!'

It was Colonel Sudliff himself. Sentra was almost impressed. She had not expected him to be paying such close attention to ongoing developments on the ground, let alone know her name.

'Engaging the enemy, sir!' she called. And then, because there was a principle at stake, 'Gunner, target thirty degrees.' The trike was still zigzagging, but it appeared to have changed overall course to head towards *Golden Thunder*. That suited Sentra just fine. The turret ground back a little, still doing its best to track the trike, but Colonel Sudliff was not satisfied with her reply.

'You had no such orders! Withdraw to the city at once!'

'With respect, sir,' Sentra said, as Gravers informed Two Hands that nothing in the horde they were facing would require armour penetration, and so he should continue to load high-explosive unless specifically informed otherwise, 'you can court-martial me if I make it back alive.'

'For the Emperor's sake, LaSteel! I have no interest in court-martialling anyone, I just want my tank crews alive for when we need you!'

'You need us now, sir!' Sentra insisted doggedly. 'We can do more good here and now than we can cooped up behind the walls!' The battle cannon roared, but it only took a glance to confirm that it had missed once again. Not that she could truly fault Gravers for it: the trike was hard enough to keep in her sights from second to second with her macro-binocs, let alone trying to draw an accurate bead on it with a weapon. The orks were firing back now, their mismatched and somewhat haphazard weaponry roaring gleefully away, almost loud enough to drown out the whoops and cheers of the drivers, gunners, and passengers.

'LaSteel, since you have clearly abandoned all respect for authority, it appears I must appeal to your glory-hunting nature,' the colonel's voice said in her ear, acid dripping from his tone. *'The main orkish rabble is currently launching an offensive against the hive's eastern boundaries. I had intended to order the armour out to take them in the flank and give them something to think about, rather than let them bring their full force against the walls. However, since you have chosen to engage in this* skirmish *instead of waiting for deployment orders, I can do no such thing. If you would* care *to disengage and actually contribute to the defence of the hive, rather than attempting to drown your own feelings of inadequacy in cordite and promethium fumes where you are, I do not believe you will have trouble in locating the conflict.'*

The connection went dead as *Golden Thunder*'s battle cannon thumped once more, and the lascannon stabbed a lance of light out with a similar lack of effect. Colonel Sudliff had said his piece, and he had no interest in further communication. Sentra's gut roiled with fury and fear. Fury, because how dare he accuse her of hunting glory when she was only trying to fight the Imperium's enemies, exactly as she was supposed to? Fear, because she had thought that she was discharging her duty in an honourable manner – far more so than she could have expected when stuck inside Davidia – but now she had learned that a major battle was about to commence, and she was not able to be present. What if the lack of the 25th's armoured units was the telling factor that allowed the orks to break the hive's walls? She knew the likelihood of that was low, given the sheer amount of the xenos present compared to the low number of tanks, but nonetheless–

'Incoming!' Greel yelled over the vox, and Sentra jerked in shock as something swooped down out of the blackness above her with a whirr of rotor blades, then blasted off a bunch of explosive rockets that screamed through the air and detonated somewhere behind her. She had not realised that the orks had flyers with them!

'Bring the bastards down!' she screamed over the vox, slapping off the safety of her storm bolter and elevating the twin barrels. The orks were flying without lights – of course – but now she was looking for them instead of concentrating on the ground force, they were easy enough to make out. She opened fire, sending a double line of bolt-shells roaring upwards even as *Golden Thunder's* battle cannon boomed out again. The heavy bolters in the sponsons were opening fire as well, now the orkish vehicles were coming closer, but her pintle-mounted weapon was the only thing they had with any real degree of fire upwards. What she would give for a Hydra or two! But their anti-aircraft capability was gone, lost in the battle of the Sacracian Heights, and so it was only weapons like hers that stood a chance of bringing their flying enemies down.

No air support, no footslogger backup, none of those Throne-cursed Gargants. It's the perfect opportunity. Those had been her words to Greel, but they had not been accurate. The orks might not have their over-boosted aircraft overhead, but they had air support of a sort. Sentra scored a hit, the mass-reactive round detonating on impact and tearing the flimsy ork vehicle nearly in half, and she let out a cry of savage triumph as it fell in flames, but her storm bolter alone was not going to be enough.

The chatter of other pintle weapons joined hers, as some of her fellow officers risked venturing beyond the armoured shells of their vehicles to help her swat the xenos from the skies. These rotor-bladed flyers lacked anything much in the way of armour, but in the manner typical of orks they punched far above their weight: one unleashed a volley of its rockets, which struck home almost certainly more by luck than judgement, and the Demolisher *Glorious Storm* detonated with concussive force. Sentra counter-rotated the cupola, leaving Gravers to find his own targets, and fired at the veteran tank's killer. It dodged her shots, but Darrus Greel was luckier: her second-in-command stitched fire down the flying machine's flank, and it too began to fall from the sky.

Sentra instinctively tracked its descent to see where it was going to land, and a shock of horror ran through her like a physical force.

'Oh no...' she whispered.

The wrecked ork flyer crashed down onto *Ash Kicker*, the second of Flash Harvax's Hellhounds, and its remaining rockets went up. A moment later, the Hellhound did too.

It was like an early sunrise, if the sun were close enough to scorch your eyebrows off. Sentra jerked backwards instinctively, jarring her spine against the far side of the turret, as furious heat washed over her, flash-drying the sweat on her skin and burning the air out of her mouth. *Smoke Eater* was gunning along in front and escaped the blast, but *Flame Rider*, following along in its comrades' wake, was inside the radius before it could take evasive action. For a moment Sentra clung to the hope that it might be sturdy enough to weather the hit and keep going, but it was not to be: before the first spasm of *Ash Kicker*'s death throes had even finished, *Flame Rider* went up as well, in another titanic explosion that engulfed a Scylla light tank and took that with it.

Sentra looked over at Greel. Her sergeant was open-mouthed with horror at the unintended consequences of his actions, and frozen in place with his hands still locked on his pintle-mounted storm bolter, the weapon idle in his grasp.

'*Commander!*'

That was Xanin, yelling over the vox-net. Sentra turned away from the blazing wreckage and her stunned subordinate, just in time to duck as *Golden Thunder*'s hull rang with the impact of heavy ballistics.

It was that Throne-damned trike! She got a brief glimpse of it roaring past, still unscratched by gunfire, and now it was between her and her colleagues the sponson weapon couldn't target it for fear of hitting their own. The massive ork perched on the back of it seemed to be laughing at her.

Then it gestured with one arm, and *something* flew out to impale Sergeant Darrus Greel, commander of *Lion's Fury*.

'*No!*' Sentra screamed, in terror and fury. Greel's eyes went wide, wide enough for her to see the whites, even through the darkness and across the distance between the two of them, and then a cable snapped taut and he was plucked from his turret. His body skidded across the ground, ricocheting off *Death Knell*'s tracks with bone-snapping force, and then he was gone.

And then the rest of the orks were on them.

At point-blank range, even the orks' erratic driving styles could not save them all: battle cannons might not be able to traverse low enough to hit a target directly in front of the vehicle on which they were mounted, but hull and sponson weapons had far easier kills to make. The night was lit up again as ork vehicles blew apart or went up in flames, but there were so many of them, *so* many of them, and only *Smoke Eater* remained to bathe them in burning promethium.

The left-side sponson heavy bolter exploded as something potent landed a hit, and *Golden Thunder* rocked on its tracks, coughing to a halt. Sentra spun the cupola around, hoping to at least partially cover them from that side, closing her ears to screams below that might have been panic or might have been pain, and were probably both. A larger vehicle roared up, a wheeled troop transport. *No footslogger backup*, Sentra thought desperately, firing the storm bolter, but although she cut down two of the hulking orks crammed into the machine, her firepower was not enough. The rest leaped across the gap, or tried to: three fell short, clawing vainly at the air and the Leman Russ' side, and at least one went under the wheels of its own machine. Those remaining, perhaps half a dozen of them, made the jump, and their boots thudded down onto her tank.

The closest one raised a massive two-handed cleaver above its head, and swung it down at her with a roar of rage.

Sentra had already drawn her sword. It was an antique power weapon, presented to her by Major Saras in honour of her actions in an engagement against the aeldari two decades ago, when *Golden Thunder* had loosed the shot that brought down a Wraithknight. She activated the power field with a flick of her thumb, and raised it to block the blow.

In terms of sheer strength, she was utterly outmatched. The ork was taller than any unenhanced human she had ever seen, and far broader. However, not even brute strength could always be a match for technology.

The crackling edge of her blade sheared straight through the heavy metal head of the cleaver, sending half of it clattering away over the tank's hull behind her, and the rest swiping harmlessly down past her nose as the ork's swing did not encounter the resistance it was expecting. The ork itself made a noise that was hard to interpret as anything other than dull-witted surprise, right before Sentra cut it off at the knees.

Muscle, sinew, and bone – even as sturdy as that which belonged to an ork – provided no more resistance to her sword's disruptor field than metal had, and her vicious swipe ended with dark blood spattering across *Golden Thunder*'s armour plates, and the ork toppling sideways with its lower limbs abruptly truncated.

Sentra did not see the next blow until it was too late. It was a blunt impact that caught her under her upraised arm and lifted her bodily out of the cupola, and the sharp pain that accompanied it suggested that it had cracked a rib or two in the process. She slid across *Golden Thunder*'s hull, her own desperate grabs no more effective than the orks' had been, and fell.

She managed to avoid spitting herself on her sword, but the impact jarred every bone in her body. She was on the opposite side of the tank to where the failed boarders had landed, but that was of little comfort to her. She scrambled to her feet, wincing and cursing, and looked up.

Guffawing orks primed their club-like grenades, and dropped them into the hatch out of which she had just been forcibly removed before she could unholster her bolt pistol and even make an attempt at shooting them down. The detonations within were near instantaneous. There was no chance that any of her crew would have survived if even one of the grenades had gone off, let alone three or four.

Sentra LaSteel gritted her teeth, fumbled for her sidearm, and prepared to sell her life as dearly as possible.

The rapidly approaching roar of an untuned engine grabbed her attention. She turned to her right just in time to see a red-painted bumper, across which was stretched a gibbering gretchin lashed in place with chains, and then the world was dark and spiky, and went away completely.

LOTZ

Zagnob Thundaskuzz bellowed with laughter, and reeled his snagga klaw back in. The humie that had been on the other end of the line was long gone, jarred free by one too many impacts, although it had been looking far from healthy even before that. Humies were so frail! One good hit would usually do for them, and if you chopped anything sizeable off them then they just keeled over and bled to death, instead of looking around for a spare like an ork would.

He fired his boomstikk at the nearest humie vehicle, but its armour was up to the job. Zagnob supposed it made sense that humies would surround themselves with armour given they were so breakable themselves, but it still wasn't much fun. He clapped Duffrak on the shoulder, leaned forwards, and pointed at his intended target. 'Burn 'em out!'

'Yoo got it, boss!' Duffrak replied cheerfully, opening the throttle. The wartrike jumped with a sudden burst of speed, then the battle skewed around them as Duffrak threw the vehicle into a skid and rammed the throttle half-closed again. The jet engines, burning hot and fierce, were concentrated down into potent spear of heat that ripped along the humie tank's flank. Paint blistered, metal softened and sagged, and–

BOOM!

–ammo cooked off, yielding yet another explosion to add to the many that had already lit up the night. A few stray bits of metal from it *spanged* off the rear of the wartrike, and one or two dug into Zagnob's arm, but he had more important things to do than pay attention to minor scratches. The stricken tank was already behind him, as Duffrak expertly wrangled the controls to bring them around and get them moving again, and Zagnob took a moment to take stock.

The humies were being overwhelmed and outmanoeuvred, as was usually the case when they went up against the Kult of Speed. Oh, tanks hit hard when they hit, but the ladz knew a thing or two about steering in a way that made the enemy miss most of their shots, which was a totally different thing to dodging, because dodging implied you were scared of getting hurt. Making the other gits look silly by missing, though, that was perfectly fine orkish behaviour.

One of the trukks was obliterated by a point-blank hit from one of the big turret guns, and pieces of boy flew everywhere, but Rukknut's dragsta fired its shokk rifle as it went past, and the weapon's weird warp tek simply ripped a piece of armour the size of three orks off the tank's flank. Then Skrappit's snazz-wagon skidded up, and Skrappit himself emptied the magazine of his mek speshul into the tank's exposed interior, and his grot hanger-on chucked in a flaming bottle of Mork-knew-what, and that was the end of that. The ladz hadn't even planned it, because planning was for gits and Blood Axes. This was just orks acting in perfect synchronicity, effortlessly complementing each other while also really sticking it to the humies.

Zagnob sighed as a buggy and a trakk collided head-on, and the drivers scrambled over their own machines in their eagerness to come to blows over whose fault it was that they had both stopped moving. Well, it wouldn't be a proper scrap if some orks didn't end up fighting with each other as well. If orks stopped doing that then they'd be like those blue fishboyz that made really shooty stuff for orks to steal – at least, Zagnob assumed that was the reasoning, as they certainly didn't try very hard to hold onto it when you got up close to them – and who thought everyone might want to be on their side. Apparently, you could trick them by saying you wouldn't fight them, and then they'd actually be really surprised when you *did* fight them. Zagnob had no qualms about that sort of low cunning. Anyone who believed that an ork wasn't going to fight them deserved everything they got, and while anything other than heading for the enemy straight-on might technically be cowardice – or Blood Axe thinking[9] – sometimes it was so funny that it didn't count.

'Wanna go back round for anuvver pass, boss?' Duffrak called.

Zagnob surveyed the scene, his expert speedboss eye understanding the swirling, explosion-ridden mess of mass vehicular combat with the same ease as a painboy understood what bone went where. 'Nah. Reckon these gits are pretty much done. I'm more interested in where dey came from, cos dat's wot's gonna get us inside.'

'Dere tracks ain't gonna be hard to follow!' Duffrak said eagerly, gunning the engine again, and sure enough the dirt ahead was all torn up by the myriad of humie tanks which had recently passed over it. The rest of the Kult of Speed fell in behind Zagnob's wartrike once more, leaving the pitiful and largely flaming remnants of the humie convoy in their dust.

---

9 Essentially the same thing.

There were fewer orks than there had been, of course, but that was the way of war. The best went on to the next fight, and the ones that didn't, didn't: at least, unless the rumours were true, and when you died Gork and Mork gave you a new body and sent you back to fight again. Zagnob wasn't sure about that, because he certainly couldn't remember being anyone other than Zagnob, but that in itself was comforting, in a way. If he hadn't been anything before Zagnob, then he was unlikely to be anything after Zagnob. Being dead and stuck in your own body unable to move at all, let alone go fast, was the worst thing he could think of, so with any luck he just wouldn't even know he was dead. And if you weren't going to know you were dead, why was being dead anything to be afraid of?

All the same, he wasn't in any hurry to stop being Zagnob, because being Zagnob was a lot of fun, so he was glad to see Da Red Barrun's remaining deffkoptas roaring away upwards to go and have a highly explosive conversation with the big guns that had been shelling them all. The tracks Duffrak was following were heading in more or less a straight line for the massive bulk of the humies' city wall, so the guns probably wouldn't be able to shoot at the Kult soon in any case, but a little bit of extra help never hurt.

They crested a rise and hit a firmer, more defined surface: one of the humie roads, which snaked away through the dust and bushes to… somewhere else, Zagnob had no idea where, but presumably there had been another lot of humies at the far end of it, before Waaagh! Goresnappa had come here. More importantly, however, it was a big road, which probably meant that the end of it which terminated at the humie city had room for a lot of vehicles to get in and out at once, and *that* was excellent news for the Kult of Speed.

Of course, he realised as they chicaned through a couple of

bends and the base of the wall in question came into view, it would be just like the humies to have shut the gate behind themselves after they'd left.

It was a massive thing, certainly tall and broad enough to walk a couple of Stompas through side by side when fully open, if he was any judge. But it wasn't open, and Zagnob needed it to be open if he was going to get inside and find Old Morgrub's special gate, and that was a problem which was going to take more than a bit of acceleration to solve.

Zagnob *hated* problems like that.

'Wot's da plan, boss?' Duffrak called.

Zagnob grunted. It galled him, but he was going to have to do the thing he liked least.

'Slow down a bit. Let's let da uvvers catch up.'

Duffrak obediently throttled back, without making any sort of comment. As a speed freek himself, he was going against his instincts too, but he knew better than to provoke Zagnob by saying anything. A speed freek who had to slow down would be edgy and prone to lashing out, and Zagnob's snagga klaw was too sharp to trifle with.

The rest of the Kult did not take long to join them, and near the front was the exact vehicle Zagnob had hoped to see: Rukknut's shokkjump dragsta, a low-slung machine that ran half on high-grade fuel and half, from what Zagnob could work out, on a simple and stubborn refusal to accept the limitations imposed by standard physics.

'Don't fink da humies are gonna open dat for us!' he yelled across at Rukknut, who stared back at him with the impassive, blacked-out gaze of his road gogglez, which he wore to protect his eyes from hazards like flying grit and bits of dead humie. 'Need ya to shokk froo it, den open it from da uvver side! Reckon ya can do dat?'

'Sure fing, boss!' Rukknut said, grinning so widely that it looked like his head might fall off. Any dragsta driver would jump – quite literally – at the chance to show off what his machine could do, and Rukknut was no exception. Zagnob had no idea what Rukknut and his grot gunner would find on the other side of the gate, but this was his first plan for getting the zoggin' thing open. If it didn't work, he hadn't lost much: only Rukknut.

The dragsta's engine screamed as Rukknut floored the pedal, since the shokkjump only ever worked if the machine was going pretty much flat out. Zagnob watched as it pulled away, saw the spinny wotsits on the back begin to rotate faster and faster, saw the blue lightning begin to crackle and sizzle around the rotating orbs, saw the guns on either side of the gate open up in a fruitless attempt to score a hit on the vehicle racing towards them, saw Rukknut raise his hand and then slam it down on his dashboard just before the dragsta reached the gate–

KRUMP!

'It weren't meant to do dat, was it?' Duffrak asked dubiously, as the dragsta abruptly became both the widest and the shortest vehicle outside the walls, and the rest of the Kult of Speed cheered lustily in the manner of orks who had just seen a spectacular death inflicted on someone who wasn't them.

'Nah,' Zagnob grunted. That was the problem with fancy mekboy stuff. If it worked, it worked really well, but if it didn't work when you needed it to, you were rarely in a position to be able to go back to the mek in question afterwards and have words with him about how many teef you'd paid him for the work, and whether he'd like to keep any of the ones currently gracing his own gob.

'We gonna shoot our way froo, den?'

'Nah,' Zagnob repeated, with a sigh. Much as he would have

loved to bear down on the massive edifice in a cloud of dust and engine fumes and blow it to smithereens with the enthusiastic application of some dakka, he doubted that approach would work any better. The entrance had the look of something that was considerably thicker than your standard humie vehicle armour. If he'd had a couple of Stompas on hand to pound it with deffkannons and supa-gatlers, that might have been a different matter, but all the walkers were on the other side of the city. It was going to take more than a few rokkits to get through this, Zagnob knew in his bones.

'Skrappit!' he bawled over the din of engines, twisting around until he laid eyes on the mek. 'Get yer wheels over here!'

Skrappit's boomdakka snazzwagon heeled over, bringing Skrappit himself alongside Zagnob. The mek grinned, and patted the multiple barrels of his mek speshul lovingly, and probably absent-mindedly. Zagnob resisted the urge to trigger his snagga klaw and knock the smug git from his gunner's perch. So what if his buggy was shootier than Zagnob's wartrike? It wasn't as fast, *and* he didn't have something capable of dragging an enemy along behind him.

'What's up, boss?'

'Need to get dat fing open,' Zagnob said, indicating the gate. 'Dere's gotta be some sorta controls on dis side, and since yoo're one of da best meks around–'

'Hang on, hang on. *One of* da best?' Skrappit repeated incredulously.

'Well, yeah,' Zagnob said, his voice as innocent as a snotling skipping through a mushroom field. 'I mean, dere's Skarbag–'

'Dat zoggin' Snakebite? He won't touch nuffin' what ain't been built by orks! He ain't gonna get ya froo humie tek!'

'Or dere's Wurznik–'

'Wurznik?!' Skrappit's eyes actually bulged with indignation.

'He ain't just unreliable, he's *shoddy!* He built da dragsta dat just wrecked itself!'

'Well, dat could've just been driver error,' Zagnob said reasonably.

'Driver error, my arse!' Skrappit barked. 'If ya told Wurznik ta get ya froo dat gate, he'd probably only make anuvver, ficker gate come across on top of da one what's already dere!'

'Sounds like a tricky job, dunnit,' Zagnob tutted. 'Ya sure yoo're up to it?'

'Humies don't know nuffink about elektrik an' dat,' Skrappit said loftily. 'Dey do all dere wirin' da same way! No imaginashun.' He slapped himself on the chest, twice. 'You get rid of da guns so I don't gotta worry about da gitz shootin' at me while I'm workin', an' I'll have dat gate open before ya can say...' he pulled a complex-looking tool out from his belt, '...eudatri-kamital polaroconverter.'

Zagnob mentally attempted the first couple of syllables a few times, and fell flat on his metaphorical face. 'Yeah, alright, square deal.' He racked the action on a boomstikk, raised his snagga klaw, and gestured for the advance.

More detailed instructions were not necessary. The Kult of Speed would drive up to the gate and would immediately and automatically shoot back at anything which dared to shoot at them. The sheer volume of firepower at Zagnob's command might not have stood a chance of punching its way through the obstacle in their path, but it would be more than sufficient to take out the fixed weapon emplacements, even with an approach to aiming that went something along the lines of pointing the gun vaguely in the right direction, pulling the trigger, and letting Gork and Mork take care of the rest. Now suitably motivated, Skrappit should have no problem in 'convincing' the gate's controls to do what he wanted, and then the way would be open for Zagnob Thundaskuzz and his convoy to race onwards, in search of the path to the stars.

'But, boss,' Skitta piped up, as the roar of engines rose up around them again, 'can you even *say* "eudatrikam–"'

Zagnob casually kicked out backwards and sent the grot head first into the fuel tank's cover. There was an audible *clang*, and Skitta slumped bonelessly to the deck.

'Shut up, Skitta.'

LOTZ

It was time for the Waaagh! to show what it could do, and it turned out that what it could do was level a truly stupendous amount of dakka at the walls of the humie city.

Mag Dedfist grinned with glee as the Mega-Gargant's gut buster belly gun boomed out yet again. The kickback from the massive weapon rocked even the mighty war machine on which it was mounted, but Gargants were built to withstand such forces. A moment later, the resulting explosion blew a chunk of wall the size of a Stompa into smithereens, and the skullkrusha mega-kannon mounted on *Gork's Hammer*'s right arm spoke in turn, further damaging the humies' rapidly weakening defences. They were right up close, pretty much point-blank range for a war machine this size, and not even recoil was going to ruin the aim by enough to count.

The city was an 'ard case, there was no doubt about it, but Mag knew that it was weakening. It didn't matter how thick your wall was: give a few Gargants a go at it, and it would fall before long. The sun was only just coming up, and Mag was already fairly sure

they could be inside before the middle of the day. The humies'
only chance would have been if they had enough dakka of their
own to keep the Waaagh! away from their walls, but that did not
appear to be the case. Oh, some of the ladz at the front had run
into and over those buried explosives the humies liked to put
down, and everyone behind had had a good laugh as they got
blown into the air, but once one lot of boyz had gone over them,
it was safe for everyone else: and besides, that was why they'd
started sending grots forwards first, instead. When it came to
actual kannons and the like, the city didn't have anywhere near
enough for the job. They'd krumped a couple of Stompas, and
a gunwagon or five, but the Gargants were protected by kustom
force fields, and simply shrugged the impacts off.

Not that Mag was willing to chance it. He'd ordered the flyers
in, and fighta-bommas and dakkajets had taken out most of the
humies' gun emplacements in short order. The stormboyz had
taken care of the rest, bounding upwards on their rokkit packs
and either killing whatever humies were crewing the guns, or
simply whacking a bunch of stikkbombs down the huge barrels
and letting everything sort itself out. Now the humies had no
way of fighting back, at least until the wall was well and properly broken down and ork and humie could come face to face.

That was what Mag was waiting for. As soon as the way was
open to the interior, he would leave the Gargant's command
deck and lead the charge in. In the meantime, there was no
point being down on the ground and hanging around directly
in front of the point being targeted by the biggest guns in the
entire Waaagh!, especially given how inaccurate a lot of them
were. Besides, Mag had not reached his lofty position of command without a certain amount of low cunning, despite his
no-nonsense Goff approach to things, and he was well aware
that any ork looking to put himself forward as another candidate

for warboss might arrange for some sort of 'accident' involving heavy artillery if Mag was standing too near the breach. Mag certainly couldn't envisage any ork having the guts to challenge him directly: Thundaskuzz and Da Genrul were definitely about to back down right before Morgrub had said his piece, no question about it, or if the fight *had* gone ahead then the gits would have undoubtedly ganged up on him – so some sort of duplicitous treachery followed by, 'Oh no, Mag's dead, wot a shame, guess I'll 'ave to be da leader now,' was the only way he could see it playing out.

'Hit it again,' he growled, his eyes fixed on the widening breach in the humie walls.

'Da gut buster don't reload dat quickly, boss,' said Urlukk, the spanner that wasn't Gutzog. He flinched sideways as Mag rested the Dedfist on his shoulder.

'Den make it happen *quicker*,' he said, in a tone that brooked no argument. Urlukk nodded hurriedly, then picked up one of the speaker tubes and began bawling instructions and invectives down it in roughly equal measure.

'Nuffin' else coming at us from da humies?' Mag asked Gutzog. 'Nuffin' on da scopes?'

'Not a fing, boss,' Gutzog replied, slapping his instruments in case that made them reveal a secret which they had until that moment been keeping to themselves. 'Dey ain't comin' out from behind dere walls.'

Mag grunted thoughtfully. 'Humies are tricky gits, an' dey know better dan to just sit dere and wait for us to get at 'em. Where's dere tanks and trakks? We didn't stomp 'em all before dey ran away da last time. Surprised dey ain't done a Thundaskuzz an' come out to hit us in da flank.' He frowned. The only thing worse than an enemy doing something you didn't expect, in Mag Dedfist's mind, was an enemy *not* doing something you *did* expect. Granted, that was generally because it meant they were then going to be a sneaky git and do something you *really* didn't expect at some later point, but–

Something dark flashed past the Gargant's viewing window, and he looked up sharply. 'Wot was dat?'

'Someone fallin' off da top again?' Gutzog asked, following his gaze.

'Nah, dis was movin' upwards,' Mag growled, flexing the talons of the Dedfist (having remembered to move it off Urlukk's shoulder first). 'Besides, dere's no one out dere now.'

Clank.

'Ya sure about dat, boss?' Gutzog enquired, looking up towards the noise. 'Cos dat sounded like–'

'I know wot it sounded like!' Mag barked, striding towards the access hatch. Was this the humies' cunning ploy? Had they sent one of their own bosses, or some sort of kommando-equivalent, to try to take him out? Well, he'd like to see them try! In fact, he absolutely would: he didn't imagine the fight would last that long, but it might amuse him for a few moments. Watching a Gargant under his command utterly pulverise something the humies had built was quite gratifying, but it felt like something a Bad Moon would do. Mag Dedfist didn't take the same sort of delight in outsized guns and the destruction they wrought, no matter how impressive. This was only a stopgap until he could get up close an' personal with the enemy, so if the enemy had been obliging enough to come to *him*...

He pulled open the access hatch and found himself looking at Skabrukk, the stormboy drill boss.

'Wot da zoggin' hell are *yoo* doin' here?' Mag demanded, although at least Skabrukk's still-fuming rokkit pack explained the fast-moving shape that had gone past the viewing port. 'I told ya to go an' see wot Da Genrul's up to!'

'We did, boss!' Skabrukk said quickly, with the harried grin of an ork who could see a power klaw attached to a bad-tempered big boss in front of him and a long fall behind him, and who had no intention of finding out if his rokkit pack would save him from a combination of both. 'We went an' checked on him, just like ya said! But da git's gone!'

'Gone?' Mag repeated. 'Just him, or all his boyz as well?'

'All of 'em, boss! Dey'd dug a bunch of holes in da ground, but dere didn't seem to be anyone in 'em. Or if dere was, dey'd gone down deep. We didn't follow down far,' he admitted, sheepishly jerking a thumb towards the rokkit on his back, 'cos, well, ya know how dese fings get caught on stuff if ya ain't in da air...'

'Down deep...' Mag Dedfist muttered to himself. What was Uzbrag up to? It would be just like Da Genrul to hide from humie guns, but the vast majority of the humie attention was going to be on Mag himself, and the massive wave of orks under his command. How was hiding underground going to benefit the Blood Axe and his crafty underlings?

Unless...

'Gork's teef!' Mag bellowed in fury, as realisation dawned. 'Dat sneakin' git! He's *cheatin'*! He ain't goin' froo da walls, he's goin' *under* dem!'

'Is dat cheatin'?' Skabrukk asked, perplexed.

'Of course it's zoggin' cheatin'!' Mag roared. 'Dat's no way for an ork to behave! We go froo walls! Or over 'em, over 'em is fine if necessary. I'd even accept goin' *around* one, dependin' on how long it takes, but *under*? Dat's outrageous.'

Skabrukk wisely kept his mouth shut.

'How long has he been gone?' Mag demanded.

'Dunno exactly, boss, but it took us a bit longer dan usual to get back cos Grukk Gitstoppa's rokkit was on da blink, an' yoo was a stormboy once, ya know how important it is to maintain unit co-hee-shun…' Skabrukk tailed off in the face of Mag's glare, which imparted in a wordless yet utterly expressive manner how very much he did *not* understand the importance of that. 'Well, anyway, den it took me a bit to find out which Gargant ya was in, cos it's kinda loud down dere an' no one could hear wot I was askin' 'em–'

'Never mind, I get da picture,' Mag said in disgust. 'Zoggin' good scout *yoo* are. Never send an ork to do a grot's job, I guess. Get back out dere an' get Da Skyklaw togevva,' he continued, ignoring the look of chagrin that crossed the drill boss' face, 'and be ready to move when I give da word. I was gonna try an' make dat hole bigger, maybe get a few of da wagons in wiv us, but if Da Genrul's long gone den dere's no time to waste. He ain't gettin' to dat gate before me, ya hear?'

'I hear ya, boss!' Skabrukk replied loyally. He saluted, which garnered a dirty look from Mag, but drew attention away from how he had very nearly objected to the insinuation that he was worse than a grot. 'I'll get goin', den, an' see ya on da ground!' He backed off, jumped into the air and fired up his rokkit pack, and corkscrewed off in a plume of choking black smoke before he could be blamed for anything.

Gork's Hammer shook again as the gut buster fired once more. Mag Dedfist barely glanced in the direction of the humie city, but slammed the hatch shut and turned to the two spanners.

'I'm goin' down dere an' I'm goin' inside. Yoo gitz coming?'

Gutzog and Urlukk looked at each other. Stomping humies sounded fun and all, but different things appealed to different orks, and what two orks who had helped build a Mega-Gargant wanted more than anything was to sit inside it and laugh their heads off while killing anything that came within a five-mile radius. What was more, each one was realising that with their former big mek gone courtesy of the Dedfist, and Mag himself about to depart, *Gork's Hammer* was going to be in need of a kommander – you know, to look after it until Mag came back – and that was not a position that could be shared.

Mag watched them for a second as their stares became glares, then growled in irritation. 'Fine. Stay up here like da zoggin' grots ya are. But if dis fing lands a shell on me while I'm down dere, an' it don't kill me, I'm comin' back ta knock both yer heads off yer necks!'

He left without waiting for a reply, clumping down the ladder that descended from the head. He passed teams of sweating boyz hauling on levers and pumping on pistons to move the massive arms and keep coolant flowing; he passed loaders ramming new shells into breeches as fast as they were kicked out, or feeding gigantic belts of oversized rounds into enormous hoppers as tall as they were; he passed grots clambering everywhere, oiling joints and adjusting bolts, greasing cogwheels and furiously shouting readings from gauges to junior spanner boyz. Then he was in the proper guts of the machine, climbing down past the closed-off section that housed the rear end of the gut buster, where shells the size of warbikes were loaded into the mighty kannon. Beneath that was the belly, where the boyz who had blagged a lift inside the enormous walker would mill about until it was time for them to pour out and overwhelm whatever had been beneath the Gargant's notice, or as a counter-offensive if enemy troops tried to force their way inside to bring it down from within.

The boyz in question in the belly of *Gork's Hammer* were Uzgul's mob and Badzag's skarboyz. Uzgul's orks were swaggering and posturing, and definitely trying to give the impression that they were not at all intimidated by the hulking, scarred warriors with whom they were sharing the space, with their extra-large helmet horns and black-painted choppas. The skarboyz, in contrast, were pretending to ignore the new arrivals, and treating them as beneath their notice. No ork was going to stand for that for very long, no matter the situation, and Mag was certain that if he had not arrived, violence would have broken out inside the Gargant before long.

However, he had plans for violence to break out *outside* the Gargant, and he swatted one of Uzgul's lot out of his way just to get everyone's attention. It might mean risking getting a shell dropped on his head by some nob looking for quick advancement, but better that than letting a Blood Axe get to the goal first.

'All dese uvver gits are in a zoggin' rush, an' doin' all sorts of cheap stuff tryin' to get inside dat city first, when everyone knows it should be me wot gets to dis gate da skrawniez built and becomes warboss!' he announced loudly. 'So here's da plan. We open dese doors, we charge froo da hole da Gargants have just made in da wall, we kill any humie who gets in da way, an' we find dat gate before anyone else does. Got it?'

A selection of nodding horned helmets indicated that the boyz had indeed got it. That was the sort of plan that Goffs could easily understand: charge at the enemy and do them over, and sort the less important stuff out afterwards.

'Good,' Mag said. 'If any of ya sees da gate before me an' points me at it, ya can be big boss when I'm in charge. If ya get some idea about havin' Morgrub say dat *yoo're* warboss instead, I'll rip ya in half. Sound fair?'

Heads nodded again. None of them had any intention of challenging Mag Dedfist for anything right now. Getting a bit of reflected glory by making themselves useful to him, on the other hand, sounded like a good idea. And if things went well, then who knew? At some point down the line, maybe one of them might find himself in front of Mag and telling him to go for his klaw, or similar. They knew this, and Mag knew this, but Mag couldn't kill all of his potential future competitors, because that would mean killing most of the Waaagh! And besides, any warboss who didn't want a couple of big bosses around him to keep him on his toes and in top fighting condition was an insecure warboss, and probably not worth following.

'Get dose doors open, den!' Mag instructed. 'We've got humies to scrag.'

Someone – either one of Badzag's boyz or an obedient grot who had heard the order – pulled the correct lever, and the doors began to grind open. The Gargant's interior was immediately filled with dust as the choking air outside flowed in. Mag inhaled, and smelled gun smoke and rokkit propellant, the ozone afterstink of kustom mega-blastas and their ilk, and an awful lot of powdered humie building material. He lumbered into the closest he could come to a run in his mega armour, and the rest of the boyz formed up around him, their previous rivalry forgotten. All that would matter now would be who could kill more of the enemy.

They ran over broken ground: first the chewed-up dirt of the planet's surface, pocked with craters where mines had exploded or ordnance shot at the walls had fallen short, and then the rubble of the walls themselves. What had once been a thick dark crack in the city's wall was now a gaping crevasse, and the sheer amount of destruction unleashed by the Waaagh! had left a carpet of debris that extended out from the target area for a hundred yards or more. It got thicker and higher the closer to the wall Mag got, and with a lot more hanging around as particulates in the air, it was like running through gritty mist.

Other orks fell in with him: ones he recognised, such as Da Skyklaw, and ones he didn't, like a bunch of Deathskull lootas, and a big mob of boyz in Snakebite colours, all furs and squig hides. A veritable tide of grots came scuttling along in their wake as well, presumably survivors from the mine-clearing mobs.

It might seem suicidal to run headlong into the breach of a defended city, but Mag knew the business of close combat like few others. Any humies on the other side of the wall would not be pressed up against it in a position to make it a choke point: they would be further back, fearful of the bombardment that had caused this damage, and wary of the wall collapsing on them. Once there were orks inside the walls the gap would be held, and more and more would flood in like a tide. The key was to make sure that the first orks through were the toughest and roughest of the bunch, to take whatever the humies could throw at them and still stand their ground.

That was why Mag was at the front. There was no ork, either on this world or aboard any of the kroozers orbiting it, who could stand up to him. He would be first through the walls, and the entire Waaagh! would know that it was him who drove the humies back.

The gap was directly in front of him now, a black chasm of uncertainty. The weak grey half-light of the pre-dawn was being filtered out by the smoke and dust from the bombardment, so the only illumination as Mag plunged in was from the pilot lights of his skorchas. It lit up the dull grey expanse of rubble that shifted beneath his feet, and reflected back off the angular, broken surfaces on either side of him. There was no resistance here, of course. If he'd been facing orks, they would have swarmed out as soon as the walls had been breached, but that was not the humie way. Although of course, if it had been orks inside this city, they wouldn't have been cowering behind the walls in the first place...

Something blocked his path: a length of metal the width of a grot's body, perhaps a piece of rebar that had either somehow survived the onslaught of the wall around it being blown away, or that had fallen here. Mag didn't know, and didn't care. He activated the Dedfist and punched through it. It sheared and shattered under the impact, and he tramped onwards. It couldn't be much further now. Even cowardly humies could only make their walls *so* thick.

There. He sniffed, and over the dusty scent of pulverised rock-crete and the permanent chemical tang of his skorcha flames, he could just make out a new smell. Stuffy air, air which had not been moved by a natural wind for centuries, if not millennia; the scent of humie gunmetal, which was a sharper, thinner smell than the good strong stink of an ork shoota; and most promi-nent, humie sweat.

Humie sweat, and humie fear.

Mag grinned. The enemy knew what was coming, and they were scared. Well, he would show them why, on this occasion, they had got things exactly right.

The breach had narrowed now, even the mighty weapons of the Waaagh! having had less effect the further into the wall they had got, and it was not more than a couple of orks wide. Or, as it turned out, approximately one Mag Dedfist. He saw the glimmer of light ahead of him, and accelerated as much as he was able to.

A flash of ruby red from ahead, and then another: thin lines that burned tiny blooms of heat damage onto surfaces never intended to be exposed to the air as they struck the sides of the breach. The humies couldn't see him quite yet, but they could hear him coming.

'Hold!' a humie voice bellowed in response to the stray shots.

'WAAAAAGH!' Mag replied, and burst through the final gap into the humie city beyond.

A blizzard of las-bolts came at him as soon as he emerged,

but they splashed harmlessly off his thick armour plate. Mag retaliated by triggering his skorchas and his kustom shoota at the same time, letting rip with all the firepower at his command.

The humies had set up a few defensive emplacements of sandbags, crates, and what looked like a couple of buggies without any guns – what was the point of a buggy without any guns? – in this space, which seemed to be a wide, tall roadway that followed the line of the exterior wall, with another branch running off into the city's interior a little further along. The closest barricade disintegrated under Mag's opening volley, such makeshift protection proving no match for the shells of his kustom shoota, and those defenders who escaped that fate were roasted by the flames that washed over them. Humies scattered, some burning and some simply terrified. It made no difference to Mag: he plunged into them, the Dedfist swinging and crackling with power, and cut them down.

Then the boyz behind him arrived.

Badzag's skarboyz were next, thundering through with their own raucous war cries, and heading left where Mag had gone right. None of them were a match for him in terms of size, toughness, or equipment, but there were many more of them, and the defenders they charged only managed to bring down a couple before they were overrun by the massive orks. Uzgul's mob didn't want to be outdone, and went straight ahead, into the teeth of increasingly desperate las-fire.

Mag heard the deeper coughs of heavier guns opening up, and looked across to see a bunch of humies manning larger versions of the guns that beakies carried. That was the sort of thing that might actually trouble him, so he waved his power klaw in that direction.

'Skabrukk!'

Da Skyklaw soared out of the breach and into view, skimming

along the ceiling and, in at least one case, misjudging it slightly
and bouncing off in a shower of sparks. However, their angle
of attack was successful: the humies didn't manage to get their
guns elevated in time, and the stormboyz descended on them
in a hail of flame, sharp edges, and well-polished boots.

A humie ran at Mag, yelling in anger. It looked like one of
their bosses, to judge by its fancy clothes – lots of gold bits,
and a rack of medals like Da Genrul had made for himself –
although it was not noticeably bigger than any of the others, and
so still only about half his size. Its weapon was a fancy-looking
long, thin-bladed choppa, which it wielded in a two-handed grip
that made it at least look like it might know what to do with it.
Mag found the notion of a humie trying to scrag him so entertaining that he decided not to roast this enemy as it closed with
him: after all, humies who actually *wanted* to fight were a rare
bunch, and the tendency should probably be encouraged. He
set his shoulders, flexed the talons of the Dedfist, and waited.

The power field on the humie's choppa activated just as it
made its first swing, either because it had been trying to take
him by surprise, or because it had only just remembered to
turn it on. It made no difference, since Mag easily knocked
the blow aside with his power klaw, nearly tearing the weapon
from the humie's grasp. Many of its kind would have backed
away at that point, overawed by his sheer strength, but this one
recovered itself and came at him once more, its face screwed
up with concentration.

'Good on ya,' Mag told it conversationally, parrying its attacks
again. 'But I got somewhere to be.'

He thrust the Dedfist forwards. The point of one talon
punched through the humie's carapace breastplate with a noise
like a boot breaking the ice on a puddle, and the humie sagged
around it, the weapon falling from its hands with a clatter. Mag

hurled it off to one side, sending a spray of blood along with it, and turned to see who was next.

As it turned out, who was next was a tank.

It wasn't a proper tank, not the sort that the humies normally brought to a fight, but it was a vehicle on tracks with a gun on the top, so by Mag's understanding, that made it a tank in humie terms. It was rumbling up from further along, perhaps only just getting here. Maybe the humies hadn't been able to get all their remaining forces organised in time, and so they were still arriving in dribs and drabs. You wouldn't get that with orks: they would all have already been as close to the enemy as possible, just waiting for a chance to have a go at them.

Mag charged.

The tank saw him coming, and its weapons opened up, but it didn't seem to have quite got itself ready. One of the las-blasts spat out by the turret gun clipped Mag on the shoulder and actually burned through his armour, but by the time it had got to his flesh, it did little more than sting. Then he was on it.

He reached out with the Dedfist and tore through the metal, grabbing the hull gun and wrenching it out in a shower of sparks. He shoved his kustom shoota into the gap he'd just created and pulled the trigger, pouring rounds into the interior, while reaching up with his other arm to shear the multi-barrelled turret gun off halfway along its length. It tried to fire again a moment later, over his head since it couldn't lower enough to reach him, but the lack of a full barrel must have caused some sort of catastrophic error. The base of the gun exploded, taking half the turret with it.

Mag laughed. More and more orks were pouring through – the lootas were in now, and chewing up any remaining cover with hails of fire from their deffguns, which more than made up for in quantity what they lacked in accuracy – and whatever hopes the humies might have had of stopping the incursion had been smashed almost before they'd begun. Now all Mag needed to do was press on into the depths, and find–

The crowd of grots had followed in hard on the orks' heels, which was odd in itself, given that Mag hadn't seen any runt-herds prodding them along. They were running through the remnants of the fighting, paying as little attention to it as they could, and heading for the passage that led away from the walls and towards the centre of the city. And... was one of them holding a grabba stikk?

Mag absent-mindedly uppercut the tank with his power klaw, flipping it over onto its side with a tremendous crash, and glow-ered as the last grot disappeared from his view, surging ahead with very un-grotlike eagerness. Something strange was going on here, and Mag Dedfist was a Goff, which meant he had a profound and innate distrust of the strange.

'Oi!' he bellowed, his roar of command cutting through the gunfire, explosions and screams. Any ork not actively involved in scragging a humie looked around to see what had provoked their big boss' anger, and Mag raised the Dedfist to point with one of its talons.

'Follow dose grots!'

LOTZ

'Zoggin' 'eck, zoggin' 'eck, zoggin' *'eck!'*

Snaggi's plan had been simple. For him and his ladz to get in he needed the orks to blow a hole in the humie city's wall, and thankfully that was exactly what that squigbrained lump Mag Dedfist had intended anyway. Once that was done, the brave grots under Snaggi's command would race ahead – and crucially, downwards – while the orks got stuck into the humie defenders. Snaggi had never seen an ork who was willing to pass up a fight for any other goal, and he hadn't imagined that would change here. Dedfist would get to scraggin', and would either lose interest in Old Morgrub's gate, or would forget about it until he had run out of enemies, which, given the size of this place, should hopefully take some time even for him.

Unfortunately, Snaggi had forgotten to take a few things into account.

The first was that although Mag Dedfist was not what you might call a *finker*, he was possessed of a certain stubbornness that ran right through his train of thought. He was not easily dissuaded or distracted from something on which he had set his sights, and the problem with this enormous humie city was that the gits were literally everywhere. Mag could walk in any direction and find enemies, so he could head for wherever he thought this gate might be and still get a fight of some sort.

The second was that grots running ahead without a runtherd actively driving them onwards was an odd enough occurrence that even orks would notice it. Now Snaggi and his ladz had a suspicious Mag Dedfist somewhere behind them, doing his best to hunt them down to find out what in Gork's name was going on, and that was not where you wanted Mag Dedfist to be.

The third, and most immediately pressing thing, was that running ahead of the orkish advance meant encountering humies *whom the orks had not yet scragged.*

'Didn't ya fink of dis?' Kruffik wailed, desperately pulling the trigger on his blasta. By chance – or perhaps due to Snaggi's inspirational presence, which Snaggi decided was an explanation he liked far better – the shot hit its intended target, and one of the humies that had been firing at them staggered and dropped with a hole in its chest.

'Waaagh!' Snaggi yelled, firing his own blasta one-handed, while the other hand firmly clutched the grabba stikk he had taken from Zukrod, and which had rapidly become his symbol of office as the leader of da Revolushun. Another humie dropped, and although it was arguable that Snippa One-Ear had fired in the same general direction at roughly the same time, Snaggi had no problem with claiming the kill as his own. 'Take dat, ya gitz!'

The humies, who were a somewhat more ragtag bunch than usual, had first retreated from the onrushing grots, then had apparently realised what they were facing and started fighting back. Now, however, the massed fire of grot blastas seemed to have dissuaded some of them once more. Half kept advancing, roaring in anger and firing, but the rest were backing off again and looking for cover. Their surroundings were not what Snaggi would have usually thought of as a 'humie place': less shiny metal and straight lines, more ruined and grubby, with dripping pipes, faltering lights, and patches of stuff that might have been slime and might have been some sort of organic growth. Maybe that was why the humies were less neat and tidy, too.

'C'mon, boyz, we've got 'em on da run!' he yelled, hoping that it would become a self-fulfilling prophecy. He thew the zap-lever on the grabba stikk, activating the charge around its metal-toothed jaws, and charged forwards. Gork and Mork had spoken to him: they had singled him out as the grot who was going to lead his kind to freedom, who was going to rise above the orks and become the first-ever grotboss. What did he have to fear?

Well, none of his ladz following him and thereby leaving him an isolated and obvious target, for one thing, but happily it seemed that was not going to be the case. A high-pitched cry of 'Waaagh!' went up from several dozen grot throats, and his own personal green tide surged after him, screaming and yelling and firing their blastas.

Had all of the humies either come to meet them, or backed off, taken cover and started firing, things might have gone badly. As it was, the humies' lack of discipline was fatal. The ones behind couldn't get clear shots, thanks to their more aggressive mates who were in the way, and a couple of the ones who drew their own weapons and ran to meet the charge of Snaggi's Grot Brigade actually went down from accidental shots in the back: at least, Snaggi assumed they were accidental, since humies did not tend to take the ork approach to marksmanship of 'if you get in the way of my gun then it's your own stupid fault'. The aggressive ones managed to cut down one or two of Snaggi's brave ladz each, but they lacked the numbers to really make an impact, and point-blank blasta shots combined with stabbas in the ribs ended the fight within a matter of seconds.

Snaggi himself caught a humie by the neck with the grabba stikk and chuckled with glee as its hair stood on end and the flesh melted off its face. He opened the jaws again and it dropped, stinking of burned hair and charred meat.

The rest of the humies wanted no part of it. They turned and ran, firing wildly back over their shoulders as they did so. The Grot Brigade hunkered down on the other side of the cover that the humies had just abandoned, braced their blastas, aimed, and fired. Grots might not have good guns, Snaggi reflected as humie after humie toppled head over heels, but they knew how to send a slug in the right direction, unlike orks. That just made it all the more outrageous that orks kept all the best guns for themselves, and this was a strong candidate for the first thing that was going to change when he became grotboss.

'See?' he told Kruffik confidently, puffing out his chest. 'Nuffin' to worry about. Da gods are wiv us!'

Kruffik looked at him dubiously for a moment, but apparently concluded that there was no obvious evidence to the contrary. 'Alright. So which way now?'

Snaggi paused, while his loyal followers looted the dead humies for whatever weapons they had been carrying. These ones had not generally been armed with the zappy light guns most humies had, although there were still one or two of them. In fact, they had weapons much more like ork ones, albeit on a smaller scale. The human he'd fried with the grabba stikk had one slung over its back on a length of chain, and Snaggi reached down to disentangle it, then inspected it. It looked like a twin boomstikk, but on a scale far more manageable for a

grot than the massive, hulking things orks like Zagnob Thundaskuzz carried around.

'Ya know, dis ain't half bad for humie work,' he mused,
cracking it open and peering at the shiny shells within. A further quick rummage revealed a pouch of spare shells on the
humie's belt, which he appropriated with glee. 'When I become
grotboss, I reckon we should take a buncha humies as slaves
an' get 'em to make guns for us! Dey've got da sizin' down
right, look–'

'Snaggi!' Kruffik hissed at him, breaking his reverie. 'Which
way?' The other grot pointed a taloned finger back in the direction from whence they had come, and Snaggi was about to
tell him that no, of course they weren't going back *that* way,
when he heard the distant bellow of ork war cries, and the guttural cough of shootas. Mag Dedfist, or some of his boyz, were
catching up to them.

'Yeah, yeah, alright,' Snaggi muttered, closing his eyes – mostly,
anyway, since no grot trusted other grots enough to properly
close his eyes around them, lest he be hastily relieved of anything he once thought he owned. 'Just need to talk to da gods.'

The trouble was that regardless of talking to them, listening to
them, attempting to interpret his surroundings as signs of their
intentions, or any other method that Snaggi could think of, the
gods were being remarkably close-mouthed about exactly where
he could find this gateway. They had been clear about his destiny as grotboss, there was no doubt about *that*, but it seemed
that Gork and Mork were not giving out any easy answers with
regards to Old Morgrub's little puzzle.

There were two possible explanations for that, Snaggi thought
to himself as he wondered how long he could wait for guidance
until it was definitely time to run in any direction that presented
itself. The first was that the gods knew he could do this, and

didn't need any help: in effect, any choice he made would be the right choice, because this was his destiny. The second was that Old Morgrub was nothing more than a squigbrained madboy who had made this whole charade up, and Snaggi's destiny was entirely separate from finding this gate thing the skrawniez might or might not have left here.

The more he thought about it, the likelier the second explanation seemed. Snaggi had killed Gazrot Goresnappa before Morgrub had said anything about this gate: in fact, the old warphead had probably come up with the idea as a desperate attempt to keep some form of control over the Waaagh!, since his pet warboss was no more. Yes, that was it: Morgrub knew who was responsible for Goresnappa's death and was therefore the obvious candidate to take over, and he knew Snaggi talked to the gods, and he knew that therefore Snaggi would have no need of his advice. This was all just a ruse! No wonder Snaggi didn't know which way the gate was: there was no such thing! He must have imagined that part of the vision, led astray by Morgrub's words in the aftermath of it. Morgrub was just a fraud, trying to buy time until he could come up with–

'Snaggi!'

'I'm workin' on it!'

'No, Snaggi, *look!*'

Snaggi properly opened one eye, then gasped in amazement. A green glow was building in the air in front of the Grot Brigade, crackling with power that earthed itself in the ground beneath their feet and caused little clumps of pale fungus to spring up wherever it touched. The surge of Waaagh! energy coming off it was invigorating, and Snaggi abruptly felt as though he could lift a humie with one hand.

'It's da gods!' he breathed in delight. 'Dey've come to show me da way!'

The curtain of power divided and parted, and Old Morgrub stepped through.

'Yoo boyz lost?' the warphead asked conversationally, leaning on his trinket-bedecked staff and showing a lot of teef in a wide grin.

The assembled grots glanced at each other nervously. Being addressed by an ork in a manner that was not preceded by some sort of kick and an expletive was an unknown experience for most of them. Being spoken to in a tone of voice that bordered on friendly, or at least as friendly as an ork could ever get, was utterly alien. And this was not just any ork: this was Old Morgrub, Gazrot Goresnappa's advisor and the closest thing to a senior weirdboy you got in that strange, non-hierarchical and often head-exploding bunch of oddboyz.

'Snaggi's lookin' for da skrawniez' gate!' Guffink piped up from somewhere to Snaggi's right. Snaggi immediately wanted to clock the other grot around the head with the grabba stikk, but he didn't feel that using the tool of their oppressor for its original purpose rather than turning it on orks or humies would go down that well with the ladz, so he nobly resisted the temptation in the interests of grot solidarity.

'Is dat so?' Morgrub asked, raising his eyebrows. He sniffed the air, then licked that shiny stone he'd taken from a skrawnie weirdboy. A fat spark jumped from it to his tongue, and he grinned even more widely. When combined with his stare, which permanently seemed slightly vacant, even Snaggi had to admit to himself that the warphead was rather unnerving, and that was without including the possibility that he might explode however many heads were in the vicinity if he got overexcited.

'I reckon ya might wanna try goin' dat way, and downwards,' Morgrub said, pointing ahead and to the left as Snaggi looked at it. Snaggi nodded – that was also the direction he had just decided was obviously the best way, but it was good to have his instincts backed up.

He raised the grabba stikk. 'Grots! Onwards!'

The Grot Brigade surged forwards once more, slightly fewer in number than they had been, but now battle-hardened and newly equipped with weapons taken from vanquished foes. Most importantly, Snaggi now knew that he had the favour not only of the gods, but also of Old Morgrub. The warp-head knew of Snaggi's plan and approved of it – as of course he would have to, seeing as how Gork and Mork had granted Snaggi their favour – and so Snaggi could rely on Morgrub's influential backing when the time came to declare himself as grotboss. None of the orks would dare to oppose him then! It was exactly as he'd always said: his destiny was calling, and it was calling him ahead, and to the left, and downwards.

Old Morgrub backed into some shadows and watched the grots go, then looked around. The first of Mag Dedfist's lot were already piling into this chamber, and the one at the front – Skab-rukk, a part of Morgrub's Waaagh!-energy-addled brain threw at him – was roaring along on his rokkit pack and seemed to have caught sight of the stragglers.

'Over dere!' the stormboy drill boss roared, pointing. 'Dat way, dat way!'

A mighty bellow announced the arrival of Mag Dedfist him-self, mega armour spewing fumes as he thundered along. Well, Morgrub thought, the grots knew which way to go, and that meant that Dedfist did as well, since he hadn't got bored of fol-lowing them yet. It was probably better this way: Dedfist, with typical Goff stubbornness, wouldn't appreciate the thought of being led by the nose.

Morgrub concentrated, doing his best to ignore the splinter

in his brain where the presence of the skrawniez' gate nagged at him, and the background roar of the Realm of the Gods. He could feel where the different parts of the Waaagh! were, thanks to the concentrations of energy that ebbed and flowed around the masses of orks, and after all this time his mind was so finely attuned that the different forces stood out to him like beacons.

Sadly, not all of them were where they should be.

'Gotta do everyfing myself,' he muttered, wrapping himself in power and disappearing again.

LOTZ

Captain Armenius Varrow was cursing everything.

He cursed his own body, which was weak and trembling after exertion that, although rigorous and extended, would never have troubled him before his incarceration. He cursed his lungs, which appeared to have more holes than a Masali cheese, judging by the way they seemed to let oxygen slip through their metaphorical fingers instead of forcing it into his bloodstream. He cursed the designers and builders of the Davidian undercity, who had created such a warren of tunnels and service vents, and he cursed the governor and every single official beneath her who had abandoned this part of the city and let it degrade into dirty, poorly lit squalor with thoroughly inadequate signage. Most of all, he cursed the orks that had driven him to such desperate measures, and since he was a soldier, he had quite an extensive lexicon of profanity on which to draw.

However, despite all the challenges that faced him, despite the towering odds against him, he was triumphing. His progress had not been particularly fast, and nor had it been without mistakes or backtracking, but he was getting there. He had managed to interpret the peeling, damaged, acid-scarred or lichen-obscured paint marks and metal plaques intended to give an indication of where in the system a person was, and rather than getting lost in that system, or even wandering the wrong way further out into where the tunnels and sewers terminated, he was getting closer to civilisation.

Or what passed for civilisation at this depth, anyway.

Armenius wiped a sweaty hand on his damp and stinking trousers, and took a new hold of the firearm he had procured from the gretchin. It barely even qualified for the word 'gun' in his mind, but 'firearm' probably worked: it was a word that he felt could more reasonably apply to such a primitive creation. He had no idea if the weapon would shoot, even less – if it was possible – if he could aim it with any accuracy, and none at all whether it would blow up in his hand, but it was all he had. At the very least, the thing *looked* imposing. It was nothing in terms of size when set against an ork gun – and Armenius had seen more of them, and at far closer range, than any human should have to, so he knew what he was talking about – but it still had a ludicrously large bore by the standards of the Imperium, and was basically a roughly made hand cannon.

He might need all the intimidation he could muster, for the inhabitants at this depth were unlikely to be welcoming to outsiders, or, for that matter, even to each other. Armenius had heard tales of the underhive, and knew it as a place of lawlessness, and likely of heresy, where mutation and deviancy ran rife. Contaminants and pollutants twisted human biology into mockeries of its true form, which was no more than those who chose to live down here deserved. Even worse were the ones who tried to leave and move upwards into the hive, as though they could be tolerated in any form of decent society. A nobleman

like Armenius knew that the menial labourers of the main hive –
Plasteel City, as it was nicknamed – were the sort of talentless
dullards who were only good for working in the forges and on
processing-plant lines, collecting refuse, and picking up a lasgun
and obeying the orders of their betters in the planetary defence
force or Astra Militarum. However, they were still human: they
had the appropriate number of correctly shaped limbs, eyes,
and other appendages,[10] they lacked mutations and the curse
of witchery, and they worshipped the Emperor. None of those
things were certain down here.

He trudged forwards, his nose by now almost inured to the
fresh scents of putrescence and effluent that were stirred up with
each step. It was astonishing what a man could get used to after
even a relatively small amount of time exposed to something.
After all, had he not got used to being surrounded by monstrous, murderous xenos? Although perhaps that was a greater
indication of his own steely nerves rather than the hardiness of
his species as a whole. How many of his fellow officers would
have managed to remain unbroken in the face of such horror?
Precious few, he thought fiercely.

It took someone not only of the correct breeding, but also
of resolute moral fibre, to maintain their composure when
under such pressure. Not only had Armenius continued to
deceive and lie to his captors when interrogated, but his spirit
had sufficient fire left to attempt this bold escape plan. Even
more than that, he had overcome the limits of his own body,
inflicted by the orks' mistreatment of him, *and* also multiple
dangerous xenos foes in order to get this far. And he was doing
it not just in the interests of his own freedom – no, he could
have sought that at any time – but to save the last bastion of

10 Barring industrial or battlefield accidents.

human civilisation on Aranua from its doom. He had picked his moment to strike, waited until his actions would have the maximum effect. This was worthy of a medal, an honour, perhaps a promotion! Although of course, Colonel Sudliff would have to actually defeat the orks and rebuild the Golden Lions before there was much that would be worthy of having Major Varrow command them.

There was light up ahead, reflecting off the walls of what looked like a junction, and it was not just the soulless, intermittent light of the few surviving lumens in this tunnel system. It was flickering, that much was true, but not in the haphazard, binary on, off, on again of a faulty fitting. This was a flowing flicker, the natural shifting and ebbing that came with flames.

Fire. A small fire, such as one might build for cooking or warmth. Where there was fire in the depths, there would be people. Or at least, things that looked like people, Armenius reminded himself. He was not out of the minefields yet, not by a long shot.

He debated how to approach. Should he sneak closer until he had some idea of who – or indeed, what – might be lurking around these flames, and whether he wanted to attract their attention at all? Or should he openly announce his presence, so they did not mistake him for some stalking predator come to snatch them away into the darkness? He was under no illusions that he had any great capacity for stealth left in him, for his legs were weary and he was unused to this manner of terrain. He would be unsurprised if locals knew how to pick out echoes and the faint slosh of water and sludge underfoot in this environment of strange acoustics, and would know he was coming well before he had any notion of who they were.

Openness it was. He was a captain of the Golden Lions, damn it, and although his uniform was torn and soiled it was still distinguishable to anyone who had any idea what an Astra Militarum officer looked like. He was not trying to rob these people, he was trying to help them: no one else was going to be bringing news of Da Genrul's intention to infiltrate Davidia Hive by this route!

'Ahoy, the fire!' he called, then cursed his voice as it cracked and broke. He tried again. 'Ahoy!'

The words echoed and tumbled away along the large pipe through which he was walking, towards the light ahead of him. Nothing happened for a few moments, other than his next few trudging steps forwards, lit mainly by the head torch he had appropriated from the dead gretchin. Then a harsh ratcheting sound met his ears: the noise of a shotgun being racked.

'Oozat?'

For a single heart-stopping second, Armenius thought he was back in the orks' camp. Then reality asserted itself once more, as his ears reminded his brain what they had actually heard, rather than what it feared they had: this voice did not belong to an orkoid, no matter how slurred its Gothic was. It might have roughly the pitch of a gretchin, but it was definitely human. The surge of relief he felt at hearing another human voice for the first time in... he truly had no idea how long... was enough to make him stumble forwards at a greater pace. He might even welcome being threatened at gunpoint, if it were only one of his own kind who was doing it.

'A friend!' he called hopefully, although he did not put his gun away. That would be foolish.

'Ain't got no friends down here,' the voice replied. 'Specially not one who don't know to keep his voice down!'

'Fine,' Armenius said, somewhat more quietly. 'But friend or not, I have no intention of harming you, if you can say the same.'

'Well come on slow then, Fancy Talk, an' keep yer hands where

I can see 'em when ya get 'ere. Assumin' you've got hands,' the voice added, suddenly suspicious.

'Yes, two of them,' Armenius said, almost giddy with delight at exchanging words with another human. He was coming up on the junction now, close enough for the slight curve of the pipe to no longer hide it from him. It was a confluence of four pipes, with a small fire burning off to one side that was contained within a metal bin, to keep it out of the layer of sludge on the floor. On the other side of the fire, backed into a corner where nothing could come at them from behind, was–

A monster.

Armenius' reflexes began to twitch his arm up, ready to risk the wrath of the double-barrelled shotgun his soldier's instincts had already identified without even thinking about it, until his brain managed to once more decipher the unclear signals from his senses. That was not a hideously deformed or mutated skull; rather, it was the chitinous head of a giant arachnid, hollowed out to form a crude hat or helmet, with the huge mandibles protruding forwards like the galaxy's most threatening pair of eyebrows. What Armenius had taken for a misshapen body in fact looked relatively normal at second glance, and was instead wrapped in some form of hairy pelt that had thrown off his original perception. The two hands that held the shotgun certainly seemed human enough, as did the wizened face that peered out from beneath the spider-helm.

'Oo'z you, then?' the underhiver demanded. 'No more steps, not just yet – not 'til I've had a look at ya.'

'I am Captain Armenius Varrow, of the Aranuan Twenty-Fifth,' Armenius said. 'The Golden Lions?' he added hopefully, when the expression scrutinising him offered no glimmer of recognition.

'Oo're they?' the other person said, looking him up and down.

'You've not heard of the Aranuan Twenty-Fifth?' Armenius asked, appalled.

'Dunno. What's an Aranuan?'

'I– What– *You* are an Aranuan!' Armenius spluttered. 'As am I, as is everyone in this hive!'

The underhiver cocked their head. 'That a fancy word for "person", then?'

Armenius did his best not to scream in frustration. Of all his luck, which had been tremendously foul despite his dogged determination to make the best of it, the first person he encountered had to be this simpleton! He should have expected nothing better from an underhiver.

'Do you know what this planet is called?' he tried.

Eyes that glittered with reflected firelight narrowed suspiciously. 'What's one o' them?'

Armenius gritted his teeth, and tried to recalibrate his brain to something better suited to his current situation.

'Do you know what an ork is?'

'Never heard of him. An' if I ain't heard of him, then I ain't hunted him, an' if I ain't hunted him, he don't exist.' The underhiver cackled, a curiously lilting and high-pitched sound which was nevertheless soft, and did not carry far. Armenius wondered, for a moment, what kind of life a person had to lead in order for even their laugh to be modulated so as not to draw attention from beasts that lived in the shadows, whether those beasts wore human shape or otherwise. Not a life he would care for, he felt sure, despite the fact that his own had hardly been short of misery in the recent weeks and months.

'Orks exist,' Armenius said. He intended his voice to sound firm and authoritative, striking a tone that would make even the most sceptical, backward downhiver reconsider their position on something. Instead, the words came out weary and haunted.

The underhiver's head tilted back the other way. 'Seen that look before. That's the look of someone who's gone through hell. Or might still be there. Fine then, Fancy Talk, orks exist. What are they, an' why should I care?'

'They're… monsters?' Armenius ventured uncertainly, suddenly unsure how to describe the xenos threat to someone who lacked the comprehension of what a planet was, let alone which one they were on. 'Big. Green skin, tusks. Fierce, tough.'

'Ow many legs?'

'…Er, two?'

'Two?' The underhiver frowned, insofar as their expression could be made out under their spider-helm. 'Two arms, as well?'

'Yes.'

'You sure you've not just seen some people what looked a bit green? There's a family down by the Great Send what's got a bit of a green cast to 'em, on account of–'

'No!' Armenius shouted, his frustration boiling over. 'No, they are not *people!* They're aliens! Xenos! They are a blight on the cosmos, and I was captured and I have escaped, and they are coming, do you understand me? *They are coming!* I have to warn everyone!' He raised the firearm, not to threaten the underhiver with it – for their shotgun's barrel had not moved away from him, and Armenius had no intention of risking it – but to display it, crudely hewn barrel pointing at the ceiling. 'You see this? I took this from one of them!'

'Lemme see that,' the underhiver said immediately, their eyes flashing to it. They held out one hand, although the other kept hold of their shotgun.

'I'm not giving you my gun,' Armenius scoffed. 'You can see it well enough from there!'

'No, I can't,' the underhiver said calmly. They crouched down slowly, and set the shotgun down, then held out their hand again. 'There ya go, Fancy Talk. I've put me own gun down. Gimme yours. Lemme see it.'

There was a curious intensity to them, and the way their eyes had not moved from the gun in Armenius' hand. He walked closer, growing in confidence as he did so. He was larger than this person, and considerably younger. Weathered and toughened by their life they might be, but if it came to a quick and desperate grapple over a weapon, he might actually have a better chance than trying to win a shootout with a gun of such uncertain provenance. Once he was close enough to feel the warmth of the flames from the fire, he allowed the firearm to be taken from him.

'Hmm,' the underhiver grunted, weighing the gun in their hand. They turned it over, back and forth, then ran a finger down the barrel. They sniffed it, screwed up their face at whatever they smelled, then stuck their tongue out.

'Oh, I really wouldn't–'

They licked the back of the chamber in which the rounds were stored, but instead of recoiling in horror as any sensible person surely would, merely pursed their lips as though in thought.

'This is new,' they said.

'Well, I don't know about that–'

'Not in age,' the underhiver snapped, looking up at him. 'This is *new*. Not seen one like this before. Not this size, not this weight, not this build, not this taste. That's not cordite being used as propellant, neither. No, I ain't never seen a gun like this, an' I've seen a lot of guns in my time.' They chuckled again, high and soft as before, but their eyes were cold and hard. 'Something strange about you, something strange about this. Ya don't last long here if ya don't respect the strange.'

Armenius felt like he was being weighed and judged by this odd person in their spider-helm and rat-cloak, and he found himself straightening his shoulders. It was preposterous: what right did this underhiver have to judge *him*, a captain of the Golden Lions, and from a noble family to boot?

Circumstance, that was what.

'Alright, Fancy Talk,' the underhiver said after a few moments more, and handed the gun back to him. Armenius took it with relief, which was an odd sensation to experience when receiving a piece of xenos technology – in the loosest sense of the word – but his world was now very small, and very dark, and somewhat tunnel-shaped. He knew what this gun was, and where it came from, and what it meant, and that was something he had to hold on to.

'Alright?' he repeated, hopefully.

'Maybe there's somethin' down here I don't know about,' the underhiver said, picking their shotgun back up. 'So what're you tryin' to do about these monsters, these orks o' yours?'

Armenius' knees almost gave out, and not just from fatigue. He had found another human, and although that human had no real idea what was going on, or what the danger was that threatened them all, they seemed willing to help!

'I need to get uphive,' he said immediately. 'I need to get in touch with the people in charge, and tell them that the orks are trying to invade from down here. They're digging in from outside. I got away and I got ahead of them, but they'll find their way in sooner or later.'

'The people in charge, eh?' the underhiver said. They licked their lips, and squinted. 'Alright. I know the way. You seem kinda in a rush, Fancy Talk. Wanna get goin' right off?'

'Yes,' Armenius breathed. 'Oh Emperor, yes!'

'None o' that!' the underhiver snapped. 'You don't take His name in vain!'

Armenius opened his mouth to protest, stopped, opened it

again to ask how this person even *knew* about the Emperor when they didn't know what a planet was, and in the end thought better of that as well. He probably could find his way uphive on his own, eventually, but his new companion's accoutrements were testament to just a couple of the potential perils that lurked down here, so alienating someone who had just agreed to guide him seemed foolish.

'Of course,' he said, politely. 'My apologies. It won't happen again.'

The underhiver grunted, and began belting things onto themself: packs, tools, and all manner of other paraphernalia.

'What do I call you?' Armenius asked. *What name do I shout if a spider bigger than I am is about to pounce on us?*

'Eza.'

'Eza.' Armenius nodded. 'And, uh, I don't mean to be rude, Eza, but just so I know, you understand… are you a man or a woman?'

'Hah!' Eza chuckled once more. 'Don't matter. There's only two things what matter here, Fancy Talk – are you alive, or are you dead? If you're the first, and you're not careful, you'll end up the second before long.' They paused for a moment, then spat. 'For that matter, if you're the second, and you're not careful, you can end up the first. Or somethin' that looks a bit like it, and walks a bit like it, but don't sound or smell right.'

Armenius wasn't sure how to respond to that, so he said nothing. Tales of underhive revenants had made for enjoyably spooky ghost stories when he was a child, but now he was down here with nothing for protection but a firearm for which the term 'dubious provenance' was probably being charitable, and an ancient hunter wearing a spider's head over their own, such things no longer seemed so harmless.

Eza finished their preparations and straightened up, took their shotgun in both hands, nodded at Armenius, and took the tunnel leading off to the left of the one from which he had emerged. Armenius followed gratefully. He was a man used to a command structure, and although as captain he had made his own decisions, that had still been within the framework of orders coming from above. Being on his own for so long had worn him down, and so having someone else make the decisions for a while – even decisions so simple as which way he was supposed to walk – was almost blissful.

He did not let down his guard completely, of course. It was possible that Eza was leading him into some sort of cannibal ambush. However, his options were few. The one thing Eza could not do was lead Armenius to somewhere *more* isolated. Armenius might never make it to the main hive, get a chance to vox the colonel or the governor, make his report, or receive his due reward. However, the more people he met and told about the subterranean ork threat, the greater the likelihood that someone somewhere who actually knew what was going on would hear the news, and take action.

For now, that would have to do.

Kaptin Skulsnik and his Guttas came from the shadows, from the same tunnel out of which Armenius Varrow had emerged, but they moved far more quietly, and they did not announce themselves by shouting ahead. There were ten of them, their green skin smeared haphazardly with mud to mimic the play of shadows in a dark, poorly lit environment, and the blades of their weapons dulled to minimise reflection. They spread out near-silently, sniffing the air, examining the ground for tracks or other telltale marks in and around the semi-liquid sludge. Skulsnik drew his knife down across the wall twice with a faint scraping noise, scoring through the centuries-old patina of dirt and into the surface beneath to leave a large 'X'. Further back the

way they had come, his sensitive ears could just make out the
faint susurration that spoke of a loud noise at distance. Other
orks, even other Blood Axes, were not as subtle or stealthy as
kommandos, but they didn't need to be. They were well on the
path now, and it would not be long before they could abandon
trailing the humie, and start to choose their own route.

In the meantime, however, the Guttas still had a job to do.

'Dat way,' Skulsnik said softly, and the kommandos pressed
onwards, tracking the humies deeper into the hive.

LOTZ

'I fink I got it!' Skrappit shouted. The humies had inconsiderately not left a control panel on the outside, so the mek had battered and burned his way into the wall in an effort to find the wiring that operated the road gate. Now, head and shoulders into a ragged hole excavated with a tightly focused burna flame and a sturdy choppa blade, he finally sounded hopeful.

'About zoggin' time,' Zagnob Thundaskuzz muttered. The Kult was getting restless, and it was all he could manage to keep some of them from tearing off into the dawn. They'd swiftly taken out all of the humie guns, and now there was nothing to do except that mortal enemy of the speed freek: waiting. So far, Zagnob's authority and the promise of an imminent scrap with whatever humies were inside was winning out over the lure of the distant horizon, wind in their faces, and dust in their teef, but he could feel the mood changing. Speed freeks lived for the rush of acceleration, and orks – speed freeks in particular – rarely had much notion of delayed gratification.

He looked around and his eyes lighted on the black-painted,

spiky shape of a Goff trukk he had seen earlier. 'Oi, Nuzzgrond! Dat you?'

'Yeah.' The nob's horned helmet poked out around the slabs of metal welded onto the side of the vehicle in an attempt to give the occupants some sort of shelter from gunfire until they could get into a position to jump out and apply their choppas to the enemy. 'Wot's da hold-up?'

'Skrappit's doin' somefing mekish,' Zagnob said dismissively. 'He'll be done any minute. Wot're yoo boyz doin' here wiv us, den? I fort yoo'd be hangin' around wiv Dedfist, seein' as how yoo're his pets an' all.' He laughed nastily, just to put a point on it, and several of the other speed freeks within earshot chuckled merrily as well, enjoying a bit of trash talking when they heard it.

'We ain't no ork's pets!' Nuzzgrond barked, glowering back at Zagnob from beneath his helmet's rim. 'Followed ya cos we fort dat maybe yoo'd know a quicker way into da city, since ya like speed an' dat, but I'm startin' to fink we should've stuck with Mag!'

'Hmph.' Zagnob simply sneered at the nob, mainly because he didn't have that good of a comeback. Mag Dedfist was a plodder, but he was a plodder who'd been left with access to an awful lot of dakka, and heavy-hitting war machines. It wasn't unfeasible that he might have managed to batter his way inside by now, through sheer brute force and ignorance. Not that Zagnob wanted to let on to that, just in case the ladz with him decided that Nuzzgrond had a point. Besides which, even if Dedfist had managed to get in somehow, he wasn't going to have found an entry like this, through which the Kult of Speed could easily get all of their vehicles. All Zagnob needed was for that zoggin' mek to hurry up and do what he'd been so confident he could do...

'No, I def'nitely got it!' Skrappit called happily. There was a flash of light and a sizzle of electricity which coincided with a yelp of pain from the mek, and nothing else happened.

For a few seconds.

Then, the massive doors began to shudder and shake, and a deep metallic groan rang out. It was sufficiently loud to cut through even the low thunder of idling engines, and every driver, gunner and passenger looked up eagerly, their various squabbles and arguments forgotten. Orks could easily get distracted, it was true, but it might only take one thing to refocus them. For speed freeks, the prospect of being able to drive really fast at an enemy and fill them with dakka would do it every time.

Zagnob had ordered the wrecked shokkjump dragsta to be dragged and shunted out of the way well before now, because he was a canny speedboss with the kind of vision and preparedness that marked him out from his underlings. As a result the route in was clear, and as soon as the doors were wide enough apart, warbikes began to zip through with their dakkaguns already blazing.

'Right!' Zagnob shouted at Duffrak. 'Let's get–'

He didn't have to finish the sentence, because Duffrak had already opened the throttle. The Deffkilla wartrike lurched forwards with a howl of engines, and immediately collided with a megatrakk scrapjet which had clearly had the same idea. The impact jolted Zagnob loose, and he fell over the side of his kommand platform, landing on the scrapjet with a thud. The fuselage was roasting under his hands, the cool of the Aranuan night having done little to leech away the excess heat from the trakk's abused engines.

'Fink yer some sort o' brain boy, do ya?' Zagnob bawled at the scrapjet's driver, raising his snagga klaw. 'Get dis fing–'

'*Boss!*'

The high-pitched squeal came from Skitta, and Zagnob looked around just in time to see the grot waving helplessly as Duffrak, oblivious to his speedboss' predicament and eager to make up for lost time, accelerated away towards the widening gap in the doors. The wartrike jinked around a buggy, squeezed through a space it had no right to get through, and was lost from view. A moment later there was an almighty rending noise as other ork vehicles smashed into each other, each one trying to be the next through into the interior.

'Zoggin' idiots!' Zagnob snarled. He rounded on the scrap-jet driver, who largely consisted of a manic grin and a pair of goggles. 'Wotcha waitin' for? Get us inside!'

The driver howled with glee and fed power to his engine with a howl of turbines. The immediate way in front of them was blocked by a pair of buggies that had come together and were now interlocked by their twisted chassis, but it seemed the scrap-jet pilot had a solution for that.

Granted, the solution involved firing his rokkit kannon at point-blank range.

Zagnob yelled in alarm, and ducked instinctively as pieces of machine flew everywhere. Then the scrapjet's nose-cone drill hit what was left in their way, and the vehicle chewed through the wreckage without slowing. The huge, widening gap of the gate loomed up, through which was coming intermittent bursts of gunfire, but nothing in any sort of volume that would trouble the assembled speed freaks. Whatever resistance the humies had mustered within had either been blown apart by the opening volleys of the first few warbikes inside, or had never amounted to much in any case.

They screamed through the gates, flanked on one side by a trakk mounting nothing more than a giant skorcha as a weapon, and on the other by the trukk containing Nuzzgrond's mob.

Zagnob caught a glance of the chaos that had ensued within, and grinned with glee.

It was a giant road tunnel, as wide and as tall as the gates themselves, and the sort of place that could have been held quite effectively if enough firepower had been concentrated here. Unfortunately for the humies, that had not happened. A few crushed corpses bore silent witness to the doomed attempts to defend the tunnel, with only one smoking warbike wreck beside them in exchange for their sacrifice. The fight here was not completely over yet, though: a searing flash of light grabbed Zagnob's attention, and he saw three of the spindly walkers the humies used advancing out of a side passage. Their concentrated firepower took out another bike as it roared past them, the rider going too fast to adjust his trajectory in time to get any shots off before he died.

The skorcha trakk accelerated ahead and strafed the walkers with flame, but to no apparent effect. Nuzzgrond's trukk, on the other hand, slewed to a halt and disgorged its black-clad contents. The Goffs piled in, swarming the larger constructs and hacking at fuel lines and hydraulic cables with their choppas, firing their sluggas into any available opening, and clamping tankbusta bombs wherever they could. One was crushed beneath a giant metal foot, and another had his skull split by a feverishly waving kannon as one of the machines thrashed about trying to defend itself, but it was over in a matter of seconds. Nuzzgrond might not be a true speed freek, but he and his boyz knew choppa work well enough.

They were past the fight in a moment, barrelling on into the tunnel so fast that the regularly spaced lights the humies had placed overhead blurred into one flickering line of illumination. Zagnob looked up and caught sight of his wartrike ahead of them, where Duffrak was clearly going full throttle unless and until he received an order to the contrary from behind him: an order which would never come, given Zagnob was all the way back here. He half-turned to look at the scrapjet driver, and pointed with the hand with which he was not clinging on to the fuselage.

'Get after dat trike! I want–'

He never got a chance to finish the sentence, because something leaped at him.

It came from the side in a blur of red, the motion expertly judged to intersect with the scrapjet's progress despite the speed at which the vehicle was travelling, and with the sort of bound that could not have been powered by any form of natural limbs; at least, not unless it was one of the bugeye monsters, and Zagnob was fairly sure he would have noticed if any of *those* had been kicking around. It landed on the scrapjet directly in front of him with a clank of metal-on-metal as its feet magnetically locked to the hull, and Zagnob met the gaze of several metallic eyes within the depths of its hood.

Cogboy, his mind informed him within a split second: one of the humie mekboyz, who seemed just as prone to altering and upgrading their bodies as their ork counterparts. They exhibited rather un-humie individualism in that respect, despite their tendency to act as mindlessly and predictably as buzzer squigs about other things. Zagnob had already seen how enhanced its physical capabilities were in comparison to its weaker, squishier kin, and it was safest to assume that any part of it might be a weapon, so he was already ducking out of the way when it raised one arm to point at him.

Ruby red light beamed out, narrowly missing Zagnob's left shoulder. He heard a bellow of pain from behind him as it struck the scrapjet driver, which was abruptly truncated. That was probably a bad sign, at least for the driver: the only reason that any ork hurt badly enough to yell out in pain was not just going to switch to yelling in anger once the pain had stopped was because they were dead.

Zagnob swung his snagga klaw at the cogboy's legs, but the humie pistoned its left leg up and down within a moment, trapping his klaw underneath it with another metallic clang. Zagnob gave it a heave, but the cogboy had him trapped fast, and his attention was rapidly attracted to the arm weapon redirecting to point at his face. He grabbed where a wrist would have been on a normal humie and twisted, and the cogboy's next shot sizzled wide of him again.

Two metallic tendrils whipped out from the cogboy's back. One snaked down Zagnob's free arm, trying to anchor it in place for the humie to tug its weapon arm out of his grip, while the other wrapped around his neck like a constricting serpent. Zagnob tensed his neck muscles against it, daring it to try to suffocate him, but he was at a severe limb disadvantage: the humie's arm that he did not have hold of flashed out, slamming a metal fist repeatedly into his face.

It was painful, yes, but it was also infuriating. This humie cogboy had the zoggin' cheek to gobsmack him? Zagnob tightened his grip on the wrist of which he had hold, and felt metal begin to crack and bend beneath his fingers. There was a gun in there somewhere, and guns could do annoying things like explode if you squeezed them too hard, but he wasn't going to tolerate this any longer. He wasn't exactly getting much use out of his hand at the moment anyway...

Something *crunched* in a way that apparently went beyond an ability to easily repair, because the cogboy bleated mechanically and yanked its arm back, but left the hand – and the gun built into it – behind in Zagnob's grip. He dropped the scrap and tried to hoist his other hand free, but the humie's magnetic clamp of a foot had him pinned.

There was a jolt accompanied by a tremendous juddering shriek, and a spray of sparks from his left. The scrapjet was still powering along, but it had veered into the tunnel wall, and was now scraping along against it. The friction and heat could easily cook off any remaining wing missiles on that side, which would cause an explosion that... Well, it would be hilarious, but also probably lethal. Dying in a big bang was far from the worst way to go, but Zagnob Thundaskuzz hadn't got this close to Old Morgrub's mysterious gate to be blown into squigfood by accident, so he needed to get himself free.

The cogboy's head snapped around, and it clearly saw an opportunity. Its body twisted strangely, joints moving in ways that no bipedal vertebrate should have been able to manage, and Zagnob found his snagga-klaw arm wrenched up off the scrapjet's fuselage, only for his entire body to be pivoted around and his face rammed against the wall by the cogboy's remaining hand.

'Gaaaah!' he bellowed, as the side of his face began to be abraded away by the metal panelling. He kicked out, and scored a hit against whichever leg it was that was still supporting the cogboy, but it wasn't enough to snap the limb. His face was agony, and he didn't have time to muck about. The skin on that side was gone and the muscle tissue was being worn away fast; it would be down to the bone of his skull within seconds.

However, the snagga klaw on his right hand was free again now, albeit being held harmlessly away from the cogboy by the humie's unnaturally angled other leg. But it didn't necessarily need to be pointing at the git for it to be useful.

Zagnob triggered the firing mechanism in his klaw and felt the slight kick of it run down his arm as the grapnel shot up and away. It caught on something a moment later, and the sudden, extreme force exerted on his shoulder, as his momentum courtesy of the scrapjet was brutally arrested, might have dismembered a being from a less hardy species. However, orks were as tough as they came, and Zagnob Thundaskuzz was one of the toughest orks going.

In this case, he was going upwards.

He was plucked skywards, or at least ceilingwards, and the cogboy came with him, its magnetic clamp foot having been insufficient to keep them both rooted to the scrapjet. That saved its life, at least for the moment, because they were only just clear when the scrapjet's remaining munitions detonated and turned it into a high-speed fireball.

Not that the cogboy appeared at all grateful for Zagnob's timely intervention, since it still seemed intent on trying to kill him, but it was finding that more difficult now. The humie still had more limbs than Zagnob did, but it had lost its leverage. Zagnob wrapped his legs around its waist and yanked backwards with his left arm, ripping the mechanical tendril gripping it out from the socket where it attached to the humie's back, then grabbed hold of the one still around his neck. The cogboy squealed mechanically and clawed at his face with its hand, but it wasn't enough to prevent Zagnob from tearing that tentacle loose as well.

The humie wasn't done. Its feet came up behind Zagnob, knees and ankles twisted and bending unnaturally, in order to sink metal claws into the flesh of his back. He bellowed in pain and headbutted it. The impact was a single extra spark in the pre-existing agony that was his head, and barely worthy of notice to him, but something within the cogboy's hood cracked as his forehead connected with it. It burbled again, even its cry of distress sounding less precisely formed than before, and some sort of fluid squirted out over him. Suddenly it was not clinging to him any longer, but trying to get away. Zagnob aimed a punch at it, but it somehow slithered out of his grip and dropped, wailing.

It landed on the floor beneath just in time to be hit by the spiked ram of a boosta-blasta, and disintegrated into an assortment of limbs, various mechanical fluids, and surprisingly little blood.

Zagnob sighed and lowered himself down again with the snagga klaw, making sure all the gits coming his way saw him and knew to steer to one side, then went in search of one particular part. He found it just as a boomdakka snazzwagon pulled up alongside him.

'Alright, boss?' Skrappit the mek shouted gleefully. 'Told ya I'd get us inside, didn't I?'

'Dat ya did,' Zagnob admitted, wincing. Speaking was wreaking merry hell with the ruined left side of his face. 'Now give us a lift, me trike's gone an' zogged off cos I got busy killin' dis git.' He held up the cogboy's head. The statement was not technically true, of course, but Zagnob would salute a grot and call it warboss before he admitted that he had *fallen off his own vehicle*. That way lay mockery and humiliation.

He tossed the cogboy's head underarm to Skrappit, who caught it. 'Can ya do anyfing useful wiv dat?'

'Reckon so,' Skrappit said, prising one of the cranial plates off and peering inside. 'Should be able to get us froo any more doors, for one fing.' He produced a bunch of wires from his belt, and began plugging them in with the happy air of one for whom true joy could only ever be found alongside the risk of electrocution.

'Good, now move over.' Zagnob hauled himself up alongside the mek, and Skrappit's driver took this as his cue to floor the accelerator once more. The snazzwagon leaped forwards with a squeal of tyres, and Zagnob made sure he remained upright, because Gork take him if he fell off this zoggin' thing as well.

'Da tunnel's forkin'!' the driver bellowed, after they'd been going for a few seconds. 'Which way, boss?'

Zagnob peered ahead of them. Both possible routes had the humies' lights running along the ceiling, like the one through which they were currently travelling, but the fork to the right appeared to have a greenish glow to it as well.

'Go right!' he yelled, and the driver hauled on the wheel to obey. It seemed that the rest of the Kult had already made the same decision, judging by the black tread marks and haze of fumes down that tunnel, so if nothing else, Zagnob reckoned he had a good chance of catching up with that wretched Duffrak if they went this way. It looked like he wasn't the only one who had naturally gravitated to green, which only made sense, because what ork wouldn't?

As they whipped past the other entrance, Zagnob narrowed his eyes. 'Hang on, wot's dat?'

'Wot's wot?' Skrappit asked, looking up from his work.

Zagnob peered backwards. The other tunnel mouth was already behind them and out of sight, and even his finely honed ability to see things and interpret them in a split second had not been fully up to the task, but he could have sworn something had been lurking in the shadows back there. Something that might have looked a bit like an ork, trying not to be seen, and holding a staff from which dangled various oddments and trinkets.

That made no sense. There were no orks on foot on this side of the humie city, and no ork would stand by quietly and let a cavalcade of vehicles go past without trying to blag a lift, or at least cheering and firing whatever weapon it had to hand.

'Wot's wot?' Skrappit repeated.

'Never mind,' Zagnob said, turning back to face the way they were going, like a proper speed freek should. 'Prob'ly nuffin'.'

But that did not prevent the uncomfortable and decidedly un-orky feeling of unease in his gut that something was going on which he did not fully comprehend.

LOTZ

Governor Ama Junier was tired. Throne, but she was tired. Sleep was both a distant lure, taunting her with its unavailability, and an enemy to be shunned. How could she sleep when Davidia Hive, the seat of her authority and the last known redoubt of humanity on this planet, was under attack by orkish invaders? To sleep now would be to give in – to acknowledge that there was nothing she could do, to admit her uselessness, because who could sleep if they had any hope of influencing the outcome? And simultaneously, she could *not* sleep, even had she tried, because her brain whirled around and around over the same simple but insurmountable problems.

Too many orks. Too few defenders. Too little time.

'What is the situation?' she asked, approaching the main tactical hololith with a slow pace that she hoped indicated deliberation and calm, rather than an effort to not fall over her own feet out of weariness. 'Have the orks breached the main city?'

Colonel Sudliff turned towards her. Even through the haze of utter tiredness, Ama could tell that the man was puzzled.

Puzzled might actually be a good thing, she decided, with the strangely floaty thoughts of one in the grip of overwhelming fatigue. Puzzlement indicated something other than abject acceptance of their doom.

'No, governor,' Sudliff replied, his tone of voice mirroring his expression.

She frowned, and surreptitiously put out one hand to steady herself on the edge of the hololith table. She ignored the binharic cluck of disapproval from the Mechanicus adept lurking on the fringes of the room to make sure everything ran smoothly, and that none of the Golden Lions' high command damaged anything too valuable to the Omnissiah with their uncomprehending prodding.

'Please explain,' Ama said, hoping for once that he would take it as snootiness, since the alternative was admitting that she had absolutely no brainpower left to work anything out for herself.

'I'm not sure I can, governor,' Colonel Sudliff admitted, turning back to the hololith. He tapped something, and the overview of the hive, with its many turrets and spires, expanded to focus solely on the lower regions. 'The orks came in at ground level on opposite sides of the hive. A main force incursion here' – he gestured, and a section of the eastern wall turned red – 'where they exploited an existing weakness in the hive structure, and overwhelmed the defenders we were able to station there.'

'Why were we not defending this weakness in greater force?' Ama demanded.

'A matter of logistics,' Sudliff said. Ama glowered in a way that she hoped expressed her refusal to be fobbed off by such dissembling, and the colonel coughed uncomfortably. 'We simply had too few defenders, spread out to cover too many areas. The orks could have hit us anywhere along the eastern flank, and they will pass up an obvious weak point as often as not, so we had no way of knowing they would attack there. We tried to reposition other units to bolster defences once they had committed to the attack, but at that level of the hive, the infrastructure of roadways and the like is... somewhat lacking. By the time reinforcements arrived, the xenos had already established a beachhead.'

Ama sighed. 'And the other side?'

'A breach through the north-western road gate by a high-speed mechanised force.' Sudliff tapped something else, and a smaller red icon flashed up. 'They somehow managed to override the gate controls after Commander LaSteel disobeyed direct orders, left the hive to engage them on their approach, and got our armoured reserve annihilated.'

'How long has it been now?' Ama asked.

'Twelve hours, give or take,' Major Deralee Bruja replied, from the other side of the hololith table. She was a tall woman with rich umber skin, and cheekbones that looked sharp enough to cut anyone who got too close to her. Ama had no idea if the Lions' second-in-command was more tactically astute than Sudliff, but she certainly did a better job of looking like a leader. Sudliff resembled any number of the stuffy, aristocratic officers Ama had dealt with as she fought and clawed her way into power – the sort who relied on nothing more than his rank and his bloodline to get things done. Major Bruja looked like she could land in the underhive in rags, snap a bunch of orders at the first group of gangers she saw, and have a reasonable chance of being obeyed.

'I'm confused,' Ama admitted. 'Have the city's defences held better than expected?' Sudliff was right about one thing, at least: the lower parts of Plasteel City, at ground level and below, had been abandoned to dereliction, and only the routes up from the road gates were maintained with any care. With such a warren of pre-existing shafts, vents and full-blown transit routes to follow up from their breach points, the orks should have had their pick of options to rise through the hive and slaughter everyone in their way. The defenders did not even have enough bodies to place one solitary soldier at every potential entry point, let alone resist with any sort of strength.

'Plasteel City's defences have not been tested,' Colonel Sudliff informed her, which at least explained his look of puzzlement. Ama couldn't wrap her own head around it, either.

'They have not?'

'No, ma'am,' Sudliff confirmed. 'Our intelligence is limited, of course...'

Ama did not think she imagined the grimly amused glance Major Bruja shot her.

'...but all the reports we have been able to gather are suggesting that instead of ascending, the orks are going *downwards*,' the colonel concluded, apparently unaware of his subordinate's wordless humour.

Ama swallowed, barely able to believe what she had just heard. 'They are... not coming for us?'

'So it would seem,' Sudliff said, spreading his hands with the air of a man who had no answers, and was not inclined to question the mercy of the Emperor too closely.

Ama was not of a similar mindset. If there was one thing she had learned on her long path to planetary governor, it was that something which looked too good to be true usually was.

'Why?' she demanded. 'They have always previously targeted the highest population densities, the greatest concentrations of our troops. These monsters live for fighting and slaughter. What is in the depths of this hive that can attract them away from us?'

'We don't know, ma'am,' Major Bruja said simply, although her tone indicated that she did not share her commanding officer's relief at this state of affairs. Ama met her eyes, and suppressed a smile. Yes, Deralee Bruja was a very different breed of officer to Colonel Sudliff. Ama would have enjoyed the chance to match wits with her over a regicide board and a few glasses of amasec, under different circumstances.

'I want to find out,' she heard herself saying.

'Ma'am?' Sudliff asked, in the special tone of voice that the military reserved for when they had just heard a high-ranking civilian say something that sounded incredibly foolish, and were waiting for confirmation of exactly how foolish it was before committing to any definite response.

'Colonel, I am aware that I can make no strategic or tactical demands of the troops under your command,' Ama said primly. 'However, I feel most strongly that tempting although it is to hide up here and hope that the xenos have somehow forgotten about us, it is not the behaviour of loyal citizens of the Imperium. If the orks are not killing us then it is because they have found something better to do, and that notion is more terrifying to me than the thought of them breaking in here right now and slaughtering us all.'

Colonel Sudliff harrumphed and grimaced, and studied the hololith as though he could pull an answer for her out of its delicate web of light. However, it seemed that he could not, any more than he could totally dismiss her words. He looked at Bruja.

'Major, your thoughts?'

'The governor has a point, sir,' Bruja replied, straightening her spine and shoulders with the automatic reflexes of someone who would probably have a reasonable chance of coming to attention even while asleep, should a superior officer walk into the room. 'Even if we should die, the Imperium may be able to retake the planet, but only so long as the orks leave us a planet to retake. Who can say what manner of devilry they might be up to in the depths? There are thermal shafts that sink deep into the planet, and these beasts revel in destruction, after all.'

'They're barely more than animals,' Sudliff muttered.

'Are you telling me that the Golden Lions have been mauled and beaten back by *animals*, colonel?' Ama asked sharply. 'That is hardly a glowing reflection of your command!'

It was a strong statement, and not one that she would have ordinarily made. But Ama was tired, and it was hard to corral her thoughts before they slipped through her lips, and she very definitely had a bad feeling about the notion of orks choosing not to kill her people. The galaxy did not just… *let you off*.

The flash of Sudliff's eyes suggested to Ama that had she been one of his officers, or even a colonel from another regiment, he might have responded violently to such words. However, even an Astra Militarum colonel would think twice about taking any sort of action against a planetary governor, so long as the governor was not actively interfering in military matters, which Ama was not doing. She was simply trying to prod him in the direction she wanted, and her weariness had robbed her of any subtlety.

'Very well,' Sudliff said, through gritted teeth. 'It may be a fool's errand, but Emperor knows that the loss of a few bodies won't have any impact on our ability to withstand an assault if it should come. My main concern is that sending anyone down to reconnoitre might simply attract the bastards' attention, and draw an attack onto us which might not otherwise have occurred.' He looked at Bruja. 'Major, put the word out. I want volunteers only. Standard suicide mission detail – anyone earmarked for the penal legions gets their record scrubbed if they come back with useful intel, anyone without a mark against them gets promoted if they live, full honours and hero's bonus to surviving family if they die.' He flapped his hand. 'Make it happen.'

'Sir.' Major Bruja saluted, turned sharply, and left.

'I acknowledge the logic of your thought process, ma'am,' Sudliff said stiffly into the resulting silence, 'but I hope you're prepared for what this might bring down on us.'

'I am planetary governor, colonel,' Ama replied, trying to focus on the hololith. It was so damned complicated! So many domes, chambers, and tunnels... but the red icons indicating hostile activity definitely seemed to be converging inwards and downwards, so far as they could tell. 'I cannot govern a planet which no longer exists, and I have no illusions that the orks will not blow it up if they can find a way to do it. Nor do I have any trust that their infernal ingenuity will not be up to that task. Do you?'

Colonel Sudliff sighed, and closed his eyes.

'No.'

LOTZ

Eza led Armenius steadily through the darkness for hours, not always upwards, but never downwards. As time wore on, their surroundings grew gradually less wretched, although still hardly anything that Armenius would not have classed as 'wasteland'. Still, he began to appreciate the subtle differences in the under-hive environments. A thermal shaft bringing up heat from far below not only raised the ambient temperature enough to bring him out into a sweat, but also attracted swarms of flying insects which then got tangled in the webs of orb spiders as big as his hand. However, the dry heat led to less fungus growth: it clustered around the dank corners instead, and where moisture in the air condensed onto cooler metal surfaces, and was fed on by molluscs with jagged shells that looked oddly rusty. Armenius tapped one with his finger, and found to his shock that it felt like metal.

'Iron snails,' Eza remarked, watching him. 'Absorb the metal they crawl over, then strengthen their shells with it.'

'Fascinating,' Armenius murmured. He pointed at another

group of slimy creatures further up the wall, which were as long as his forearm, and strobed gently through greens and yellows. 'And them?'

'Glowslugs,' Eza said with a shrug. 'Harsh poisonous, so don't go eatin' one, Fancy Talk.'

'Hadn't intended to,' Armenius replied weakly, eyeing the creatures, and trying not to imagine what depths of starvation he would have to sink to in order to view one as an appetising meal, or indeed, as a meal of any sort.

'Good,' Eza said, their voice conveying enough surprise at Armenius' apparently good sense that Armenius felt he should probably take offence at it. What was he going to do, though? He was still reliant on the hunter's guidance to get him to where he wanted to go, so there hardly seemed any point in sticking his nose in the air and wandering off in a huff. He fell in behind Eza again, and took some comfort in the fact that his instincts not to trust anything organic which glowed appeared to be correct.

It was not long after the iron snails and glowslugs that they found the first signs of human habitation: or at least, the first signs that Armenius recognised, since Eza had already been muttering to themself about more tracks than usual, or how no one had harvested that growth of fungus lately. To begin with, there was a light far up and to the left when they emerged into an old hab-dome. It was the steady pale burn of a lumen, not the strobing pulse of a glowslug, and Armenius expected Eza to head straight for it. When the old hunter kept picking their way forwards, however, Armenius cleared his throat quietly.

'Should we not be talking to whoever lives up there?' he asked.

'No one lives up there,' Eza answered, without even turning around to see what he was referring to. Armenius looked back, and the lumen light was gone.

'Then what was–'

'Nothin' we want to concern ourselves with,' Eza said shortly, and Armenius decided to hold his tongue. The underhive was a strange place, and he did not need to poke into every corner and secret it held. Many of its residents would not be as accommodating as Eza, whose assistance had in any case only been procured by the sight (and smell, and apparently taste) of a gun they did not know, and what that might mean in terms of an unknown threat. Armenius just needed to get a message uphive, and leave the underhive to its ways.

They had to climb out of that dome, up what had once been a wide and undoubtedly grand staircase, but which was now simply a collection of trip hazards lined up one after another, a seemingly endless array of crumbling rockcrete, loose slabs and missing sections. Eza navigated their way up with the casual ease of one who had gone that way many times before, and Armenius swiftly realised that following in their footsteps was the fastest and safest way to travel. Once at the top, however, he found that the tunnel by which they passed through the wall between this dome and the next was well traversed, even to his eyes.

'Oh yes, we're gettin' close now,' Eza said, when he remarked on the footprints in the dust. 'Not far to go.'

That was music to Armenius' weary ears, and especially to his even wearier feet, but confusing as well. They had not yet reached the kind of population density he would have expected close to the wall – actually innumerable walls, barriers and blockades – that prevented the lawless folk below from passing up into Plasteel City without the permission of the hive's security forces. Everything he had learned of the depths suggested that the upper levels of the area designated as 'underhive' were not that dissimilar to the lower areas of Plasteel City itself in terms of quality of life, the main difference being that while both theoretically came under the purview of the governor, only in the latter was there much chance of laws actually being enforced.

When they came out into the next dome, Armenius was not prepared for what he saw.

This was undoubtedly a populated area. The hab-blocks and old factorum buildings which had been nothing but abandoned ruins in areas lower down were occupied, with lengths of cloth, pieces of scrap metal, or boards of freeze-dried fungus starch covering up holes in the architecture to give those who lived within some semblance of privacy. Lights split the darkness here and there: not just the ancient lumens in the ceiling up above, coaxed into life with prayer and semi-understood mechanical knowledge, but handheld devices, or those worn on the head like his own pilfered xenos tech, and cookfires, flickering warmly beneath pots or the skinned carcasses of some downhive creature judged fit for consumption.

Under normal circumstances, Armenius Varrow might have regarded such a place as a nest of scum and vermin, undoubtedly fallen far from the light of the Emperor and in all likelihood crawling with heretics and mutants. After so long with nothing but orks for company, however, the sight of a settlement populated by his own kind was enough to bring tears to his eyes. Humanity! Glorious, smelly, flawed, beautiful humanity! This was what he had been fighting to defend; this was what he was still defending now, through his quest to alert his superiors to the danger posed by the Blood Axe force.

'Checkpoint,' Eza said quietly, as they approached the first building. 'Try not to look dangerous, an' let me do the talkin', lest the guardians take a dislike to ya.'

'Guardians?' Armenius blinked, his eyes still not yet having readjusted to the level of light they were approaching, dim though it was by the standards of the surface. He made out a crude barrier drawn across the road, and two figures standing by it. Their helmets were little more than beaten metal, coming together into a point above their heads, but the weapons they held were long-barrelled lasguns which looked deadly enough. The settlement's security then – either some form of community force, or muscle for whichever gang leader had taken this place as their own. He swallowed, and prepared himself for a potential shakedown, not that he had anything of value they could take.

'That you, Eza?' one of them shouted, half-raising his weapon.

'Shangai,' Eza called back, and the two guardians relaxed again. 'Got someone with me, but don't alarm yourselves about it – he's harmless.'

Armenius bristled at that, but refrained from disputing it. He was supposed to be trying not to look dangerous, after all. Granted, he was carrying a massive handgun, but someone walking the Davidian underhive *without* a gun was probably much more worthy of fear.

'Outsider, eh?' one of the guardians said with a contemptuous sniff as Armenius drew closer. He was a wiry man, his skin dark as shadow, with a tuft of beard on the end of his chin. 'Where're you from, stranger?'

'Found 'im down in the tunnels, when I were huntin' spider-spawn,' Eza replied, without letting Armenius speak. 'Got tales of monsters, he has, an' says he needs to speak to the people in charge.'

'Monsters?' the other guardian said dubiously. She was far paler than her companion, and only had one eye, which was a brilliant green and was studying Armenius intently. 'What manner of monsters?'

'Eh, no one knows monsters like Eza,' the first guardian said, waving them through. 'If you think he needs to be heard, he needs to be heard. Get in with you, then.'

'C'mon, Fancy Talk,' Eza said, beckoning, and Armenius

hurried after them, with a quick nod to the guardians which he hoped conveyed professional respect.

Armenius had no idea what manner of reaction he would have garnered within the settlement had he entered it on his own, but his companion seemed to be attracting most of the attention as they walked through. People hailed Eza, often with the same 'shangai!' greeting they had used with the guardians, called out to enquire about their health, or whether they had slain anything impressive lately. The spider-helmed hunter replied to all such greetings with a dusty chuckle or a few quick words, but did not slow their pace.

'What is this place called?' Armenius asked in a low voice, as he hurried after Eza.

'Emperor's Gate,' Eza replied, mere moments before waving and replying to a young woman leaning out of a window above them.

'Why is it called that?'

'Oh, you'll see,' Eza replied, looking back at him and flashing a grin. 'At least, assuming the direguards let us in.'

'Direguards?' Armenius frowned. 'More guardians?'

'Dontcha know nothin', Fancy Talk?' Eza demanded. 'The guardians keep us all safe, the direguards keep the seer safe.'

'The seer?' Armenius' stomach clenched. Should he have paid attention to his instincts about mutation and heresy? Was this a stronghold of witchery?

'Aye, the seer,' Eza said, as though it were unremarkable. 'She and her council are the people in charge, an' that's who you said you wanted to talk to. Dontcha have seers where you're from?'

'I think we maybe call them something different,' Armenius said cautiously. It did not necessarily mean anything: everyone knew that underhivers were a suspicious bunch, and would be just as likely to swarm and mob a sanctioned psyker to burn them as a witch as they would be to follow a witch and proclaim them as a prophet of the Emperor. It could be that 'seer' was simply a title used for a leader with great vision in a more metaphorical sense.

And if not? If the leader of Emperor's Gate was actually a witch? Well, Armenius still had his duty to perform. If dealing with a witch was the only way to get a message uphive, then so be it: he would just have to direct the Emperor's cleansing fury here afterwards, in the form of a few flamer teams.

'Here we are,' Eza said quietly, as they turned a corner on what appeared to be the settlement's main street. 'Now, you remember what I said about not lookin' dangerous?'

'Yes.'

'That goes double for now.'

They rounded the corner, and Armenius came to halt in utter shock.

He had expected a large, impressive building: perhaps a former office of the Administratum, from the time when this level of Davidia had been in use by such officials. He had certainly *not* expected the sight that met his eyes.

It was a huge arch, which Armenius had only not seen previously due to the cluttered nature of other buildings getting in the way and his low angle of vision. The structure must have towered over a hundred feet high in total, right up towards the roof of the hab-dome, but it was not its scale that so shocked Armenius, for he had seen the Spatian Gate on Thracian Primaris.

'What... is that?' he managed.

'*That* is the Emperor's gate,' Eza said, with a hint of smugness. Then they hastily raised their hands. 'Shangai!'

Their voice was a little more hesitant this time, and Armenius understood why when the shadows cast by the portico and columns of a nearby building disgorged two warriors.

Armenius disliked them immediately. Each carried a heavy

autorifle with a bayonet slung under it which was so long as to practically be a sword, but it was not their armament which set his teeth on edge. Their helms were of a similar conical shape to the guardians at the barricade, but these fully enclosed the wearer's head behind an impassive mask broken only by eye slits. From the crest of the helm fell a long tail of what looked like hair, although presumably not attached to the scalp of the wearer. Their flak vests and the ballistic plates added over the chest were orange, but the helms were painted black, and the design made them look positively inhuman.

And combined with that damned gate…

'What is it made of?' he asked. When Eza did not answer him immediately, he repeated himself more urgently. 'The gate! What is it made of?'

'*Not now,*' Eza muttered. They moved forwards and engaged the two warriors – direguards? – in hasty conversation, with the occasional jerk of the head back at him. Armenius paid no attention, and gave no mind to not looking dangerous. His eyes tracked back and forth along the gate's length, taking in the seamless construction, the pale surface on which no dirt or dust seemed to have collected, and… were those markings on it, set into the substance itself? Armenius was too far away, and the available light too dim, for him to make it out for sure.

'Right, what were you gabberin' on about?' Eza demanded, turning back to him as the direguards disappeared into the building from which they had emerged. 'That's the Emperor's gate, like I said.'

'What's it made of?' Armenius repeated, not looking away from it.

'Damned if I know,' Eza said, with a shrug. 'Legend says it can't be marked or harmed, though all of us know better than to try. I mean, why would you want to mark it?'

'No human made that,' Armenius said, feeling the certainty inside him crystallise as he verbalised it.

'Well of course we didn't!' Eza laughed. 'The Emperor made it! It was His gift to us.'

'His gift?' Armenius was trying hard not to sound too sceptical, since he knew better than to openly scoff at underhivers' beliefs when he was in the middle of their town with an important message to deliver and only a questionable xenos firearm for protection, but his credulity was being stretched. The damned thing was making him uncomfortable just by its proximity. 'How do you know it's from Him?'

'Because long ago, He would send His great warriors through it.'

That voice did not belong to Eza: it was softer, and feminine. Armenius turned, and nearly recoiled at what he saw.

This black helm was more ostentatious than those belonging to the direguards, with a forward-curling ridge at the top, and large eye-lenses that were opaque, at least from the outside. Shiny chunks of metal ore had been affixed to it in an arrangement which was either haphazard, or deliberately – and, Armenius felt, aggravatingly – asymmetric. The newcomer wore robes of the same shade of orange as her guards, and a polished, oval stone sat over her breastbone.

'Shangai, seer,' Eza said, bowing.

'Shangai, Eza,' the seer replied, the sightless eyes of her helm turning towards them for a moment.

'What do you mean, the Emperor sent His warriors through this gate?' Armenius demanded. 'And what's this "shangai" thing you keep saying?' He knew that he should not ask such questions, he knew that he should just get on with his mission and have done, but even his great weariness was not enough to fully blunt the anger edging its way up to muster between his teeth. And to think Eza had told him not to take the Emperor's name in vain!

'It is the greeting of the Emperor's warriors, passed down to us through the generations from those who witnessed their last arrival here,' the seer said calmly. 'The Emperor sent His warriors to scourge the world of the unworthy. Our ancestors escaped His wrath, and we have lived in accordance with His values ever since.'

Armenius looked around, and properly took in what he saw for the first time. There were people here, for sure, but where were the signs of faith and devotion? Where were the aquilas? Where was the stake at which heretics would be burned? Why was everyone wearing a polished stone of some size or colour, somewhere on their person? The Imperial creed varied from planet to planet, he knew this: you could not expect the inhabitants of a feral world who interpreted the Emperor as the sun in the sky, or those of a mighty munitions factory in which they churned out shells through processes of which they had no true comprehension, to worship in the same manner as a cardinal world where the Ecclesiarchy ruled all. Even so, this was a perversion of faith worse than he had ever seen. Did these people still count as faithful? Was it enough to hold the name of the Emperor in reverence, if nothing that you did held any relevance to how He was to be worshiped?

Focus, Armenius. Nothing has changed. This is no worse than when you were given latrine supervision detail when the colonel caught you at his amasec. Just hold your nose, do what needs to be done, and get out the other side.

He opened his mouth to speak, but a flicker of movement caught his eye, away beyond the so-called Emperor's gate.

Green movement.

It was instinct, at this point. Armenius whirled, raising the weapon he had carried for so long in his right hand, and fired.

The concussive noise was tremendous, and the recoil brutal for someone used to the smooth whisper of a laspistol. It felt like the bones of his wrist had been pulverised, but it was not that which knocked him off his feet. That was Eza, tackling him down to the ground, as the seer screamed and stumbled away from him, and her direguards ran forwards with the barrels of their autorifles coming up to target him.

'You stupid *mon-keigh*!' Eza shouted into Armenius' face, their own face screwed up in rage and fear and sorrow. 'You've killed us both!'

Armenius ignored them, so much as it was possible to ignore someone on top of you. He did not even pay attention to the direguards as they placed themselves between him and their charge, and took aim at him. He shoved Eza out of the way enough to look in the direction he had fired, desperate to at least see whether he had been correct before he was killed by these damned heretics.

A cluster of green bodies was gathered around one of their own number on the ground, looking down at it. One of those still upright was holding a twin-jawed pole considerably taller than it was.

'Orks!' Armenius howled, pointing desperately. 'Look, Emperor damn you! *Orks!*'

The xenos looked back up and at him, and Armenius saw once again the red eyes and pointed green ears that had haunted so many of his dreams of late. Grots rather than orks, it was true, but where grots went, the orks followed. How had they got here so fast?

That was not important right now. Grots had little stomach for a fight. If Armenius could only direct the fighters of Emperor's Gate towards them, the little bastards might be scared off or killed, and he could get away before their larger cousins arrived.

The grot with the pole raised it into the air and howled something. Its companions – and there were a lot of them, Armenius realised with a sinking feeling, and the guns they held looked less like the rough firearm in his own hand, and rather more like Imperial hardware – echoed its cry.

Then the entire mass of them, in contravention of every piece of information or experience Armenius possessed about their mentality, charged.

LOTZ

Ilaethen Arhien waited, and the host of Craftworld Lugganath waited with him.

The webway was neither warm, nor cool. It was not a natural place, did not *feel* like a natural place, no matter how many millennia had passed since it first laced its way through and between and under the galaxy, halfway between the material universe and the realm of the immaterium. It was a lesson that something did not become natural merely because it had existed for a very long time, even by the standards of the children of Asuryan. Ilaethen had trodden the surface of countless worlds in his life: beautiful maiden worlds, still unspoiled; the far-flung Exodite worlds, simple and severe; and, far too many times, the lost worlds that had been invaded and devastated by the warlike lesser species. Even those last, though they might be wrapped in the fumes of war, though the air might taste of smoke and death, though the very ground might shake from the thunderous tread of monstrous war machines and the impact of colossal munitions, still felt more natural than the webway.

The fact that the webway had become a second home for his kin despite this was not a reflection on their affinity for this place. It was instead a testament to what had been inflicted upon them by usurpers, raiders and predators. The galaxy had been in flames since the Fall, and the younger, hungry species wished for nothing else. Other craftworlds still had some hope for the future, still entertained notions that even if they could no longer rule the stars, they might at least be able to set their own boundaries and live within them, safe from fear or threat.

Lugganath's people knew this to be folly. There was little for the aeldari out there save for bloodshed, sorrow, and a reminder of how they were fading from power. However, that did not mean that the material universe could be ignored completely. After all, damaged and lost though much of it now was, the webway still spanned the galaxy, and was accessible from innumerable points. If Ilaethen's people were to be kept safe, then they had to ensure that no one accessed the webway other than aeldari. Theoretically, that should be impossible in any case, but Ilaethen had learned long ago that comfortable theories rarely stood up well to the indifference of an uncaring galaxy.

He shifted his gaze to Yria Nightsong. The farseer stood tall and sombre, her shaved head revealing the smooth planes of her skull and orbited by wraithbone runes. They meant little to Ilaethen, who had never progressed far along the Path of the Seer. The Path of the Warrior had always called to him, but his self-control had sufficed to see him turn away from each aspect after he had studied it. Now he walked the Path of Command as an autarch, one of the hands that guided the blade of Lugganath's forces. However, he did not dictate where the blade should be deployed.

He raised an eyebrow slightly, the miniscule movement as

clear as words to someone such as Yria, whom he had known for centuries. *The runes remain unchanged?*

Her lips pursed. *They do.* He could read the regret in her face, though it would have been an impassive mask even to some of his own kin, let alone an alien. Her expression cleared, and she looked directly at him. *This course is necessary, although it saddens me.*

He inclined his head a fraction, once. *As it does me.* Ilaethen had no regrets about killing those who threatened what remained of his people's way of life, but it was a rare occurrence indeed when such an action cost no lives of Lugganath in return – and Lugganath had no lives to spare. Every engagement that could be foreseen was weighed to a nicety by their seers to determine the benefits, and the price. Which were the threads of fate that could most efficiently be severed to bring about the desired result, or stave off the greatest disaster? How likely was it that the act of engaging would itself spark disaster?

Some foes were largely predictable, albeit implacable: the brutal Imperium ploughed forwards and drowned the galaxy in its own blood, throwing their brief lives away to achieve short-sighted dominance. Common ground might be found with them in the most desperate of situations, against foes the mon-keigh perceived more horrific than the aeldari, but in the end their shallow, bitter hatred of anything even remotely different from themselves would lead them back to violence and treachery. The reawakened ancient enemy of the Great Dynasties were even worse: near-mindless machine bodies, led by those few who retained some semblance of wider comprehension. Ilaethen was not certain which was worse: the tragedy of so many lives being lost to a species that did not realise its time was past, or the possibility that they might yet truly rise again. The swarms of the Great Devourer were predictable, certainly, but that did not mean that they could be easily stopped. Against such hunger, foresight was of little use other than guiding the children of Asuryan out of its reach.

Then there was the foe against whom the forces of Lugganath had mustered; a foe whom the foolish underestimated, and of whom the wise were wary. Predictable in their lust for violence and conquest they most certainly were, but even the arts of the most skilled seers sometimes availed aeldari warriors little in terms of how that violence was going to play out, moment to moment. How such beasts might gain access to the webway was unclear, but the runes seemed certain that they had the capacity to do so, and that could not be tolerated.

Ilaethen sighed. He had learned, in years past, that the mon-keigh had a saying: 'no battle plan survives contact with the enemy'. It was emblematic of their species, in that it made excuses for failure before such an event had even occurred. Ilaethen himself had planned, overseen, and executed whole wars that had fallen within acceptable and predictable parameters, from the timing of the first raid to the climactic and crucial slaying of the enemy general.

But when it came to the orks, he conceded that the mon-keigh might have a point.

There was nothing for it now, however. In a way, he was glad that Yria's runes had not changed, despite the losses which were sure to follow. He could feel the hot, heavy beating of his blood in his chest, rising up to ensnare his mind. Lugganath had roused for war, and once so roused, war could not easily be set aside.

Ilaethen's people might be as at home in the webway as they were in their craftworld, but the craftworld still bound them with some ties that could not be broken.

LOTZ

'For da GrotWaaagh!'

Snaggi Littletoof screamed his war cry, and it was taken up by the loyal ladz all around him. He had been guided here, right to the gateway, by the knowledge of Gork and Mork – and, alright, a bit of a hint from Old Morgrub, but he was a warphead so that was practically the same thing – and he wasn't going to let a bunch of humies get in his way now, especially since one of them had shot Kruffik. Snaggi wasn't going to miss Kruffik at all, but it was the principle of the thing. Besides, always good to let the underlings think you might care if they died.

'Get 'em!' he bawled, and his mob, the first members of what would surely come to be one of the most feared warbands in the entire galaxy, surged forwards with screams, and yells, and the crack of gunfire. They had crept past the humie guards to get into this settlement, and slit a couple of throats when needed in order to remain unseen, but the time for subterfuge and conceal-ment was over. Snaggi aimed the humie boomstikk one-handed and pulled the trigger with a joyous grin: the recoil nearly jarred his shoulder out of its socket, but by the gods, what a *noise* it made! Not as much kick as an ork shoota, but at least that meant he had some hope of shooting straight with it.

Most of the humies panicked and ran, fleeing from the righteous wrath of Gork and Mork's chosen like the cowardly gits their species were when they didn't have superior numbers, or some of those well 'ard beakies in their supa-armour. A few chose to stand and fight, which was zoggin' foolish of them, because they weren't enough to have a hope of standing up to the GrotWaaagh!. One of Snippa One-Ear's mob bought it, courtesy of a rattle of small shells from a humie wearing an orange vest and a weird helmet that looked a bit like those the skrawniez wore, if it had been built in the dark by a grot who had only heard a rough description of one. That was not enough to turn back the green tide, however, and the humie and its mate both fell as grot gunfire tore into their bodies. The second one was still moving when Snaggi reached it, and he gave it a good old zap with the grabba stikk until its flesh was smoking and it had stopped spasming, to make sure it was properly dead.

'Secure da perimeter!' he yelled at his troops.

'Uh, wot?' Skrawk asked, scratching his head. Snaggi sighed, and bopped him on the skull – but gently, because Snaggi decided that a future grotboss would favour correction, not punishment.

'Spread out, an' make sure da humies don't get near da gate,' he clarified, pointing at the enormous arch of that weird bone-stuff the skrawniez made things out of. It wasn't actually bone – at least, he had never found a bit of it which had been any good to eat, and Mork knew he had tried – and it wasn't metal, and you couldn't do a zoggin' thing with it that was any use, but it was hard-wearing, he'd give it that. Bloody skrawniez, they had to be all special and have their own thing that no one else could have, didn't they?

'But dey ran away!' Snippa pointed out.

'Dey're easily scared, but dey'll be back soon, an' wiv a bunch of dere mates,' Snaggi said grimly. 'Dey built dere town around dis fing, dey've gotta fink it's important. I ain't havin' any humies around to get in da way when da rest of da Waaagh! turns up an' we show Old Morgrub dat it's da grots wot got it done, am I right?'

The ragged cheer which went up suggested that he was indeed right, and his mob spread out with their weapons aimed at the surrounding buildings and streets.

'Snaggi?' Guffink said quietly, after a few seconds of fierce concentration had passed.

'Wot?'

'So we keep da humies from gettin' dere gate back, I unnerstand dat...'

'Yeah?'

'How're we gonna keep Mag Dedfist from takin' it off us? Only he's a lot bigger dan da humies, an' he's basically got all da boyz from da Waaagh! wiv him wot weren't in Stompas an' dat, an' he weren't dat far behind us last time we checked...'

Snaggi sighed. 'Ya just gotta put yer trust in Gork an' Mork, Guffink. Dey know dat I'm dere chosen one, an' Old Morgrub knows I'm dere chosen one, so when Morgrub sees us wiv da gate, dat's gonna be an end to it.'

'But I'm just sayin', wot if Mag gets here first? Like, before Old Morgrub? Or wot if he don't listen to Morgrub? I'm just tryin' to fink dis froo, an' dere's a lotta very-ubbles.'

Snaggi frowned at him uncomprehendingly. 'Very-ubbles?'

'Yeah, it's somefing Zagblutz used to say. Fink it means "stuff wot changes a lot".'

Snaggi opened his mouth to deliver a stinging retort,

something that would leave Guffink shamefaced for questioning the will of the gods. The problem was that the will of the gods, which Snaggi knew to be true, was nevertheless struggling to hold up in his mind against Guffink's ragged logic, despite the fact that the deliverer of said logic was currently investigating the contents of one nostril with his finger.

Intellectually, yes, *intellectually* Snaggi knew that he was the chosen one of Gork and Mork, because, well, he had to be, didn't he? He had dropped the Gargant's head on Gazrot Goresnappa, and grots didn't get to do something as momentous as that without the favour of the gods. It was logical, it was sensible, it was bleeding obvious.

However, Snaggi's brain also possessed the intellectual knowledge that Mag Dedfist was perfectly capable of arguing against the logical, the sensible, and indeed the bleeding obvious; and what was more, that Mag Dedfist was big enough and mean enough that he just might *win*.

'S'gonna be fine,' he said. 'Cos...'

He paused, searching for inspiration. What he found instead was dakka. And while dakka might serve in the stead of inspiration for a lot of orks in a lot of situations, it was not what Snaggi was hoping for right now given that it was not any of his ladz who were the cause of it.

'Yoo hear dat?' Snippa One-Ear asked, perking his remaining ear up as the sound of shots began to ring out. It was joined a moment later by the roar of a mass of orkish voices, coming from the same direction from which they had entered the town, which meant it was highly likely that Mag Dedfist and his boyz had managed to follow Snaggi and his mob here after all, despite the distance they had tried to put between them.

'Nuffin' to worry about!' Snaggi said, as confidently as he could manage. 'Dey're just gonna take care of da humies for us!'

His head jerked around as a new noise reached his ears. This also contained elements of dakka, but the hearing of a grot was sensitive to more than just gunfire, and Snaggi could make out the throaty roars of many, many engines.

'Speed freeks,' Guffink whispered. 'But Mag didn't have any buggies an' dat wiv him, did he? Dey all zogged off with Speedboss Thundaskuzz.'

'Dat's comin' from a different direcshun!' Snippa wailed. 'Dat *is* Thundaskuzz! Da git must've found a way to get da buggies inside!'

'Well, den da two of 'em can scrag each uvver for all I care!' Snaggi spat, hastily reloading his boomstikk. It was just his luck that that oil-drinking gearhead had managed to make it here as well! Honestly, you would have thought that Gork and Mork might see their way to giving their chosen one a slightly easier time of it, but perhaps that was the way of things. Greatness was forged through challenges, and Snaggi Littletoof was about to experience the greatest challenge of his existence to date.

Still, at least Da Genrul hadn't made it this far. Snaggi had heard that the Blood Axes had been digging holes around the south end of the humie city, for whatever reason Blood Axes had for doing anything, so it wasn't like they were going to be showing up anytime soon–

A building exploded, directly in front of him.

The harsh bark of shootas rang out, and humie voices could be heard screaming and shouting. It wasn't Mag's lot responsible for this – not unless some of them had circumnavigated the town to attack it from two sides at once, which was hardly a Goff strategy, given that Goff strategy usually extended to 'hit 'em really hard, an' if dey ain't dead, hit 'em again'.

It seemed that Da Genrul had arrived with a typical lack of fanfare, and an equally typical application of violence.

'Snaggi?' someone whispered.

'Look, we're no worse off dan we was,' Snaggi managed.

'Yes we are!' Snippa hissed. 'Last time dese gitz were at each uvver's froats, we weren't standin' between dem an' wot dey wanted to get to!'

A humie appeared, running full pelt away from the Blood Axe onslaught, with three orks in pursuit: it was, Snaggi realised with a start, the one who had shot Kruffik. One of the orks threw something blunt, perhaps a small chunk of what had recently been building, which clocked the humie on the back of the head. It fell headlong, clearly dazed, and something spilled from its grasp which looked very much like a grot blasta, but it still flailed weakly to try to get up and keep moving. Snaggi levelled his boomstikk to shoot it, but the purposeful look of the Blood Axes moving up behind their quarry made him reconsider. It seemed like these orks wanted that humie alive for something, and it was a foolish grot who killed something on the rare occasion an ork wanted it alive. Even if Snaggi was going to become grotboss and lead the entire Waaagh!, it didn't make sense to push his luck before that had been confirmed, did it?

Then Da Genrul hove into view, one hand on the haft of the power choppa balanced casually on one shoulder, the other clutching his beakie-made twin shoota, and with Sarge the Killa Kan clumping along behind him on its piston-driven legs. One of the other orks hauled the dazed humie upright and turned it to face Genrul Uzbrag, whereupon it promptly began to wail.

'Ah, kaptin,' Da Genrul said genially. 'Good to see ya again. I fink exercise time is over, don't yoo?' He knocked on Sarge's hull, and the Killa Kan obediently turned around to present an empty cage.

The humie howled and thrashed and wept, but nothing it did could prevent it from being stuffed into the cage, and the door closed and locked. With that done to his satisfaction, Uzbrag at last deigned to notice Snaggi and his ladz.

'Who left dis buncha grots here?' Da Genrul asked, non-plussed. Another building collapsed some way behind him, and a handful of fleeing humies found that the shadows into which they were desperately running contained kommandos with sharp knives and sharper grins.

'Uzbrag!'

Snaggi was not certain if he was relieved or alarmed by the bellow that rang out and dragged Da Genrul's attention away from him. On the one hand, it meant he did not have to face down the Blood Axe big boss there and then. On the other hand, it meant that Mag Dedfist had not fallen down a hole, or been blown up by his skor-chas malfunctioning, or even, outside possibility though it might have been, been killed by a humie, and *that* meant that the Goff was going to be trying to lay his own claim to the gateway.

'Dedfist!' Da Genrul retorted with a grin. 'It's kinda impres-sive how ya can be so fick dat a wall can't stop ya!'

'We'll see who's larfin' when I take ya head off!' Mag Dedfist bellowed, advancing from the far side of the gate with the thunderous tread of a mega-armoured ork in a great hurry. He pointed at the nearest of Snaggi's ladz as he passed them, causing them to shrink back from him in fear. 'Dese your grots den, muckin' about an' messin' fings up?'

Uzbrag cast a puzzled glance at Snaggi. 'Nuffin' to do wiv me.' He shrugged the power choppa off his shoulder. 'Now, we can all see dat I got 'ere first, but since I can already tell dat ya ain't interested in fings like dat, d'ya wanna get down to it now, or wait for Thundaskuzz to show up?'

'Thundaskuzz?!' Dedfist guffawed. 'Wot makes ya fink dat git's comin'? He's still drivin' around in circles lookin' for a door, cos he don't have da brains to make one of his own!'

'He might not have brains, but all dat time clankin' around in yer armour means *yoo* don't got any ears,' Da Genrul said smugly, and looked meaningfully to his left.

The howl of engines had already been growing louder, but it rose to a crescendo as a Deffkilla wartrike screamed between two buildings and screeched to a halt in an extended skid that crushed one of Snaggi's ladz who didn't manage to get out of the way in time. Zagnob Thundaskuzz, who now had rather less face than the last time Snaggi had seen him, glared down at the other two big bosses from his platform and worked the action of his snagga klaw with an audible *klik-klak*. He was not alone, either: his convoy of heavily armed and lightly armoured vehicles pulled up behind him, with the bad nature of speed freeks compelled to stop.

'Who let da runts in?' were Zagnob's first words, his surprise at seeing Snaggi and his mob standing around the skrawniez' gate apparently greater than his desire to exchange unpleasantries with his rivals.

'I figured dey were his,' Mag Dedfist rumbled, pointing at Da Genrul.

'Ya need to stop tryin' to fink, cos ya clearly ain't any good at it,' Uzbrag scoffed. 'Alright den, boyz, we're all here again, an' nuffink's been settled, so where's da warphead? Or am I gonna have to do dis da old-fashioned way, like Gazrot would've wanted, an' beat some sense into da pair of ya?'

He flicked the switch on his power choppa to activate the crackling energy field around its blade, an action that was reciprocated by Mag Dedfist and his power klaw. Zagnob Thundaskuzz racked the action on his double boomstikk, and eyed the pair of them, waiting to see who he should plug first.

'Alright, alright, stand back dere! Let me froo!'

Some of the orks who had gathered around to see the three

big bosses go at it began to shift out of the way, which was not a particularly orky thing to do, unless the ork demanding that you do so might just make your head explode if you didn't. The shape of Old Morgrub emerged, his staff still rattling with trinkets and his eyes slightly too wide and slightly too vacant as ever.

'Well done!' he cackled, shaking his staff until it rattled. 'Yoo all got here! So, who got here first?'

'I did!' Snaggi shouted, leaping into the gap while Da Genrul was still taking a breath.

Every single ork head turned to look at him. For the first time in Snaggi Littletoof's life – quite probably for the first time in history – a grot found himself the centre of orkish attention.

It was... not entirely pleasant.

Options capered through his brain like a snotling after too much fungus beer. He could run. Just turn and run. None of them would pay any attention to him: they would all go back to their quarrel, because grots simply weren't worth paying attention to. If any of the three big bosses saw him tomorrow, they wouldn't even remember him.

Or, another possibility, he could quickly size up which of the three he thought was most likely to win, then declare that he'd claimed the gate for him. If his chosen fighter lost then he could still disappear with the same chance of anonymity, and if he turned out to have backed a winner then there might be something in it for him.

Something... Like a half-chewed humie leg. Or a shiny rock that the ork didn't want.

Neither of those options were acceptable. Not because he had an outsized and unrealistic appetite for glory and recognition, no: it was because Gork and Mork had spoken to him, damn it all, and they had made it very clear that he was their chosen one. *He* was supposed to lead the Waaagh! *He* was supposed to turn things around and bring grots to their rightful place on top! This was bigger than his own individual thoughts and fears: this was about *destiny*!

'I am Snaggi Littletoof!' he shouted into the silence. 'I killed Gazrot Goresnappa when I dropped da Gargant head on him! I killed Zukrod da runtherd wiv his own grabba stikk! Gork an' Mork have spoken to me, an' told me dat I'm gonna be Da Grotboss!' He pointed behind him at the huge arc of the skrawniez' gate. 'An' I found da gateway first! Dat *proves* it!'

There was a further silence, as the assembled orks considered what they had just heard. Then Da Genrul looked at Old Morgrub.

'Yoo're a Snakebite, Morgrub, ya know about runts an' stuff. Ya know dis little git?'

Morgrub's eyes swivelled towards Snaggi, without the rest of his head moving. They roved over him for a few moments, and then the warphead opened his mouth to deliver his judgement. Snaggi squeezed the grabba stikk tighter, waiting for the vindication and acclamation which would surely emerge.

'Never seen 'im before. Kill 'im if ya want, he's in da way.'

Snaggi's mouth dropped open. How could– But he– This wasn't *fair*!

'Enuff said,' Da Genrul grunted, raising his twin shoota. 'Zog off, runt.'

Light flickered. Not the lights far above in the dome's ceiling, dirty and yellow and very, very humie in their tone. This was cold and clean, and seemed to banish shadow, leaving anything it touched illuminated with a clarity that was not exactly bright, but which hurt the eyes nonetheless. It cast stark, unpleasant shadows on the ground.

And it was coming from directly behind Snaggi.

He turned away from the confused expression washing over

Da Genrul's face, something pulling at him hard enough to look away even from his own impending death. The arch, which until now had been nothing more than hollow, if still imposing, was now filled from edge to edge with a shimmering veil of light. It was not bright, but nor was it hazy, or lazy, or faint, or gentle. It shifted from steel-grey to ice-white, and from chilly blues to a cold green that was no kin to any shade of orkish skin.

'I knew it'd work!' Snaggi heard Old Morgrub cackle behind him. 'Get enough of us here, an' I knew dey'd come to protect da doorway! Dey can't let us get in, ya see? Dey're too scared, cos dey know I've got me stone, an' if we *do* get in, dere's nowhere we can't go!'

Snaggi frowned. There seemed to be… shadows behind the light? How did that work? Snaggi was not the most well versed in exactly what light did to make things look the way they looked, but he was pretty sure that you only got shadows if things were standing *in front* of the light.

'Oh,' he heard Old Morgrub add, 'ya might wanna take a step back for dis next part.'

The light parted, and death flowed out.

LOTZ

Everything had gone according to plan, even if Genrul Uzbrag said so himself.

Kaptin Varrow had played his part perfectly, almost as if he were one of Uzbrag's own, rather than a captive. The key thing to outwitting humies, Da Genrul had come to realise, was that they were always incredibly eager to assume that they were more intelligent than you were. They would often fall into even reasonably obvious traps, simply because they could not wrap their heads around the idea that an ork was capable of laying one.

For that, Uzbrag supposed the Blood Axes should be thankful to the other clans. There were certainly some warlords here and there who had a grasp of grand strategy – Ghazghkull Thraka was as cunning as any Blood Axe, despite being a Goff, but then Ghazghkull was the Prophet of Gork and Mork – but in general, most orks, even warbosses, just reacted to what was in front of them. That was often still enough to scrag humies, since they seemed to expect orks to be slow and lumbering, but it wasn't what you might call 'taktiks'. No, for forward planning and sideways thinking you usually needed a Blood Axe, and the fact that the rest of the clans didn't bother with such niceties just made it all the easier to hoodwink a humie.

It had taken a bit of effort to get everyone into the tunnels – Sarge the Killa Kan had been especially tricky – but it was worth it. Uzbrag's ladz had followed the trail laid down by Skulsnik's Guttas, and didn't even get too distracted on the way. They didn't have any vehicles with them, no buggies or trakks or flyers or Deff Dreads, and nor did they have any mek gunz or other fancy bits of big dakka, but Da Genrul knew that those things were not essential, when it came down to it. He had mob after mob of ladz, ranging from the masses of regular boyz who wanted nothing more than to empty their sluggas and shootas into an enemy, and then maybe get a bit of choppa work in too, to the more specialist mobs like the tankbustas with their rokkit launchas and high explosives, and the burna boyz who could and would immolate anything that moved. He had meks, and painboyz, and runtherds, and every one of them had the sort of orkish ingenuity that would one day bring the galaxy to its knees. The gubbinz he had left behind could be replaced, given a bit of time and a few resources.

All he needed was orks. Everything else would take care of itself, sooner or later.

The humies down here barely counted as opposition. Uzbrag's military mind almost despaired of how pitiful this town's defences had been. Had the humies not known he was coming? Well, of course they didn't know specifically, that was sort of the point of sneaking in via the tunnels rather than battering his way in through the walls, but did they not even know that there were orks outside, who might theoretically get inside at some point? Honestly, Da Genrul had expected better than this of humies. They might be a bit naff in a fight most of the time, but normally they at least knew that there *was* a fight. Skulsnik's ladz had slit the sentries' throats, and no one else noticed the Blood Axes until they were blowing up buildings and letting rip with dakka.

It was convenient in a way, though. He hadn't even had to go searching for the skrawniez' gate, since Varrow had led him directly to that as well, and the lack of resistance from the humies meant there was no argument that he had got here first. Not that it seemed to make any difference, since Mag Dedfist was utterly incapable of accepting that Uzbrag was the better ork. As for Zagnob Thundaskuzz, Uzbrag was surprised he had even managed to remember the gate for long enough to get inside and try to find it, let alone actually succeed.

As it turned out, however, the gate might not have been what the three big bosses had been led to believe. Which just showed what you got if you were foolish enough to trust a weirdboy.

'I knew it'd work!' Old Morgrub cackled as the gate lit up with strange lights. 'Get enough of us here, an' I knew dey'd come to protect da doorway! Dey can't let us get in, ya see? Dey're too scared, cos dey know I've got me stone, an' if we *do* get in, dere's nowhere we can't go!'

Uzbrag glowered at him, hoping for some sort of additional explanation that actually made, y'know, *sense*, but it seemed that was too much to hope for. Morgrub just licked the stone he had taken from that skrawnie weirdboy, and giggled as it sparked on his tongue. Uzbrag considered shooting the grot at which he was still aiming his beakie shoota, but the runt wasn't even looking at him any longer, and shooting a grot in the back was so pathetic that it wasn't even funny. Besides, Uzbrag had more pressing concerns than disciplining one runt with ideas above its station, so he rapped on Sarge's hull to get the Killa Kan to pivot around on the spot.

'Look at dat!' Da Genrul ordered the cowering Kaptin Varrow in humie-speak, pointing at the shifting lights in the gateway. 'Wot's goin' on?'

Varrow's eyes went wide as he beheld what was going on, but he appeared to be either unable or unwilling to communicate exactly what 'that' was. Uzbrag growled in frustration, and spun his power choppa to loosen his wrist up for whatever was about to go down. In the process of doing so he accidentally split the skull of one of the grots which had been surrounding the gate (for reasons he still had not quite puzzled out) and was now fleeing away from it (for reasons which were at least a little more understandable, at least bearing in mind the general mentality of grots).

'Oh,' Old Morgrub said conversationally, to the assembled orks in general, 'ya might wanna take a step back for dis next part.'

Uzbrag opened his mouth to ask the old git what he meant by that, but was brought up short when it became obvious. The shimmering curtain of light filling the giant archway began to boil – Uzbrag had not seen light boil before, but he couldn't think of a better term to describe it – and figures stepped out of it.

They were tall and slim, lithe and athletic, clad in figure-hugging armour of dark shiny cloth and hard orange protective plates. Their weapons were long and slender, all organic curves and smooth edges, not like the blocky, angular equipment of the boyz. They were possessed of the sort of fluid grace that reminded Uzbrag of a buzzer squig swarm: no movements were sharp or jerky, everything was smooth from one moment to the next, almost as though a small body of liquid had taken flight with a callous disregard for concepts like gravity. However, whereas buzzer squigs lacked intelligence, and their apparent unity simply came from a shared instinct to head for the nearest food source and avoid threats, each of these beings was obviously under the control of a conscious mind.

Well, and they were solid, rather than being made up of thousands of tiny bodies, but Uzbrag thought that distinction was fairly self-evident.

He knew what they were, of course. He had fought and killed them before, or at least things that looked and moved a lot like them, although he remembered those ones being a bit spikier. Given the context of where they were, and what they were emerging from, it was a fairly easy conclusion to draw.

'*Skrawniez!*' he bellowed, for the benefit of any of his mobs who were a little slower on the uptake, or did not have a sufficiently good view. He raised his beakie-shoota to open fire.

The skrawniez beat him to it.

The first ones out let rip with a hail of their slicy-disc things, the sort of ammunition that could take your hand off if you weren't careful. Uzbrag felt a *thump* from his chest and looked down to see three of them sticking out, all in a neat little row, where they had cut through the fabric of his greatcoat and embedded in the breastplate of the armour he wore beneath it.

'*Oi!*' he bellowed, outraged. 'Dat nearly got me!'

He opened fire, and he was not the only one. The skrawniez had been their usual annoyingly speedy selves and got their shots in before the ladz could react, and orks were already fumbling their shootas as arms fell away, or falling over as a leg got sliced off, or even just toppling backwards because a few internal organs had taken the brunt of the volley. However, there were still a lot of orks on their feet, or who were more angered than incapacitated by whatever had hit them, and they all had guns. The whisper-sounds of the skrawniez' slicy-discs slipping through the air like a rippy-fish through water were drowned out by the cough and roar of sluggas, shootas and big shootas getting their own back. Agile and elusive though the skrawniez were, and surprisingly tough though their flimsy-looking armour might be, there was only going to be one outcome. Slim bodies fell, ripped apart by munitions that prized efficacy (and a great deal of noise) over elegance. Trying to get into a dakka contest with a Waaagh! at close range was never a good idea.

Unless, of course, you brought tanks to a gunfight.

Uzbrag obliterated the closest skrawnie with a volley from his beakie-shoota, then blinked in surprise as the gate lights darkened once more. However, this did not resolve into another wave of skrawnie infantry: instead, the light slid apart and flowed around the twin-scythe prow of a floating vessel, its heavy guns already spitting death as it *thrummed* over the heads of the skrawnie troops who were still standing.[11] Uzbrag fired upwards into its hull as it passed over him, but his shots simply glanced off in showers of sparks without even leaving a scratch. A door at the rear hissed open as though in response to his attack, but his attempts to shoot through it were foiled by some sort of force field.

However, at least it seemed that the skrawniez inside were not content to let the tank's gunners have all the fun. A whole bunch of them jumped out clutching pistols and chain-choppas, and they were even wearing a shade of dark green, unlike the orange vehicle in which they had been riding. Uzbrag nodded in approval: it stood to reason that even skrawniez might behave in an appropriately orky manner if they wore green.

They landed like a thunderbolt in the midst of Da Genrul's ladz, their helmets spitting flashes of light even before they hit the ground. Boyz fell howling, clutching their eyes or their

11 And also over the troops who were no longer standing, but not all of those had heads left.

necks, and the skrawniez gave no time for the rest to sort themselves out. They plunged in with blade and pistol, decapitating and eviscerating. Slicer ammo punched through ork torsos in a fine spray of blood and went on to strike other victims; spindly chain-choppas met the trunklike limbs of boyz and prevailed in a shower of gore, leaving the bewildered amputees toppling sideways, or lacking a weapon with which to parry the next blow that was aimed for their necks.

'Now *dat's* more like it!' Uzbrag exclaimed with feeling. Blood Axes might think tactically, but he enjoyed a good scrap up close as much as the next ork: in fact, probably more than the next ork, since he was more likely to win. He raised his power choppa and pointed at the skrawnie mob.

'*Officerz! Get 'em!*'

The skrawniez had done a lot of damage to the boyz, striking hard and fast before their victims could react, and pressing the attack to prevent their victims from getting themselves organised and applying boot leather to the problem. What this situation needed was a bit of leadership by example, which was exactly what was about to arrive in a flurry of shiny medals and grimy choppas.

Da High Kommand was five of Genrul Uzbrag's most hard-bitten nobs: four lootenants led by Zorlag, who had finally accepted the rank of major, wielding choppas that probably weighed as much as a skrawnie, and clad in the best 'eavy armour that teef could buy. They were outnumbered two to one by the pointy-eared gits, but chain-choppas that had ripped apart lesser orks glanced off them with skittering noises, and it was skrawnie blood that flowed when they struck back. Uzbrag would be the first to admit that orks didn't move as smoothly as some of the things they clobbered across the galaxy, but that didn't mean that they were slow. They were certainly fast enough to chop a skrawnie in half if they let their guard down for half a second, and that was what the major's power klaw had just done.

Still, one of the skrawniez was on a different level to the rest. It flowed aside from strikes and ducked under point-blank shots, always avoiding harm by the narrowest of margins, then lashing out and leaving death in its wake. One of the lootenants took a swing at it, a diagonal downward blow which should have been unavoidable, should have left the skrawnie as nothing but two asymmetric pieces in a pool of its own blood. The lootenant in question was Kabrukk, one of the biggest and strongest under Da Genrul's command, and a towering piece of ork-flesh. The green-armoured skrawnie almost looked like a grot when set against him, so different were they in size and bulk, and it didn't dodge the blow.

It caught it.

Kabrukk had the briefest of moments to register what had happened, and for shock to spread over his face as he realised that the haft of his weapon was held fast in the clutches of the skrawnie's own power klaw. The skrawnie held him there for a moment, making a point of demonstrating its strength in a manner that Uzbrag found almost admirable. Then it flowed into motion again, using Kabrukk's choppa to hoist itself off the ground and deliver a back-flipping kick into his jaw. Kabrukk staggered backwards, teef flying, and the skrawnie fired a volley of slicers into his neck before its feet even touched down again. Kabrukk's head began to slide off his shoulders, and Uzbrag had seen enough.

'Dat one's mine!' he bellowed, holstering his beakie-shoota, and spinning his power choppa to make the point and attract its attention. The tank the green skrawniez had arrived in was still dakka-ing its way through his ladz, but a series of concussive explosions sent it rocking and announced that the tankbustas had found their range. Then dark shapes soared through the air in long rokkit-propelled arcs, and the ladz of Mag Dedfist's stormboyz known as Da Skyklaw landed on it. Uzbrag thought he could probably leave that to others to handle: this git looked like a challenge, and it had been too long since he'd had a proper fight.

The skrawnie nob heard his yell, and its strange crested helm whipped around to focus on him with insectoid lenses. It decapitated another boy with an almost casual backswing of its chain-choppa, and sprang towards him.

Uzbrag stepped to meet it, bringing his power choppa around in a two-handed swing at chest height. The skrawnie's helmet guns, which had flared as though about to fire, disappeared from view as it threw itself into a graceful roll and evaded his blow by the width of a grot's promise. Uzbrag let his momentum carry him around, and he aimed the point of his weapon at the skrawnie's chest as it came back up to its feet. His enemy nodded once, as though in recognition of a worthy adversary, then attacked again.

Gork's teeth, but it was fast! It had two obvious weapons, the chain-choppa and the power klaw, but the klaw also had that slicer-thrower built in, with which the skrawnie let rip at the slightest opportunity. Then there were its helmet guns, which were not going to have enough punch to seriously trouble an ork as big and tough as Uzbrag, but certainly had the potential to throw him off his swing at a critical moment.

Finally, there was the skrawnie itself.

It had already demonstrated the surprising amount of sheer strength contained in its skinny body, and it was not above throwing elbows, kicks or knees at an opportune moment. None of those blows in and of itself would put Uzbrag down, but the skrawnie was not going for one big hit to take him out. It was trying to wear him down, to bleed him from several cuts, debilitate and disorientate him before moving in for the kill. It was a good strategy, like Uzbrag had seen beast snaggas utilise when faced with massive prey animals, enemy war beasts, or even vehicles.

However, he was none of those things. He was Da Genrul, and he was *always* one step ahead.

He ducked his head, and the needle-thin slivers fired by the skrawnie's helmet guns glanced harmlessly off his reinforced hat rather than embedding in his flesh to provide the conduit for the laser sting intended to follow. He whirled his axe-headed power choppa two-handed, an almost casual move that parried and blocked strike after strike from his enemy's klaw and chainblade with the head or the haft, then struck back with a blow that left a long, deep gouge across the skrawnie's breastplate. The skrawnie leaped into the air to deliver a spinning kick to Uzbrag's head; he caught the git's shin a hand's breadth from his ear, then wrenched it around to slam his enemy bodily into the ground by its leg.

He lashed out with his power choppa again as the skrawnie raised itself back to one knee, and the force of his blow ripped its parrying chainblade from its grasp. He turned the motion of that strike into a second one, bringing his weapon around to raise it overhead in both hands, then slashing downwards.

The skrawnie's power klaw flashed up and caught the haft before the axe head landed, just like it had done with Kabrukk.

Uzbrag wrenched backwards to pull the skrawnie towards him, and lashed out with a knee at what was now its head height.

The skrawnie's helmet guns discharged into his thigh at the exact same time that he connected with the snout of its helm.

Something cracked, and it wasn't his knee. Uzbrag bellowed in pain as the sting flashed up his leg like fire, but the skrawnie had caught the worst of the exchange. It was flung backwards, and it flailed ungracefully for the first time as it tried to get its legs back under it. Its ruined helmet fell away from its head to reveal sharp cheekbones and the ubiquitous pointy ears of its kind, as well as slightly glazed eyes and a nose from which a trickle of blood was running.

'Come on!' Uzbrag roared, stomping unsteadily towards it. 'I don't need two workin' legs to scrag ya, ya little git!'

To its credit, the skrawnie nob didn't do what a lot of enemies would have done in this situation, in that it didn't turn tail and leg it. It probably could have outpaced him, unsteady on its feet or not, given he was limping now, and there were few things in the galaxy as fast as a skrawnie which had decided that it did not want to be caught. Instead it came to meet him one more time, power klaw extended and spitting slicy-discs, a snarl of rage twisting its lips.

Some of the slicers lodged in Uzbrag's armour again, but none of them found a weak point, and he ducked away from the rest. The blow he'd delivered to the skrawnie's head had clearly scrambled its perceptions: he was on top of it before it realised, and his choppa swept around and up to take its power klaw off at the elbow.

Even then, with one limb missing and blood gouting, the skrawnie did not cry out. It simply hissed with rage and malice, and reached for his eyes with hooked fingers.

Uzbrag's arm was longer. He grabbed it by the throat with his free hand, and tightened his grip. The skrawnie's eyes bulged for a second. Then its vertebrae snapped, and it went limp. Uzbrag nodded in satisfaction, turned around, and hurled its corpse back towards the gateway. He was hoping to send it right back through, which he thought would be quite funny, or if not, maybe take out one of its mates on this side. Instead, it bounced off the prow of another one of those floating tanks.

There were now several of them, Uzbrag noticed with the closest he ever really came to concern. There were also a lot more skrawniez than the last time he had looked. In fact, the pointy-eared gits were everywhere, pushing the boyz back as they came. The ground was awash with orkish blood, and the skrawniez were fighting with grim determination, paying little attention to their own losses.

'Dey really want dis, don't dey?' Skulsnik observed, arriving at Uzbrag's elbow. His knives were wet with skrawnie blood, and he'd lost an eye to someone else's blade since Da Genrul had last seen him.

Uzbrag cast a glance in the direction of Old Morgrub. The warphead was not hard to find: his chilling cackle rang out as his mouth opened wider than should be possible, and then he vomited a tide of green fire which washed over the nearest mob of skrawniez and melted them where they stood.

'Dat git knew dat somefing like dis was gonna happen when we got 'ere, an' he said nuffink,' Uzbrag observed angrily. 'I ain't got no problem wiv a scrap, dat's all good, but I ain't havin' a zoggin' weirdboy finking he can lead me around like a squig-goth! We're gonna have words wiv him once we're done 'ere.'

'Sounds good to me, genrul,' Skulsnik agreed.

'In da meantime, we'd best take care of dis lot,' Uzbrag said, shaking his head. 'Dey're all the same zoggin' size! How're ya s'posed to know which one is da boss?'

A new sound rolled out across the battlefield. It was a war cry, but it was not the voice of a mortal creature: no lungs of flesh and blood had produced that bellow of pure rage, hatred and bloodlust. It was like a furnace with a thirst for vengeance, or a volcano out for blood. It was fire and destruction given form and thought.

The light in the gateway parted once more, and *something* strode out.

It was titanic, a bipedal monster taller than any ork. High, jagged crests rose on either side of its head, and its body was molten red, glowing with heat and hate. It bore a gigantic rune-encrusted sword in its right hand, its left hand dripped with blood, and when it opened its mouth to roar again the very air trembled as the white-hot heat of its innards gusted forth.

'Never mind,' Uzbrag said. 'Found 'im.'

LOTZ

Ilaethen Arhien felt the war song rise in his blood as the Avatar of Khaine strode out of the webway portal and into the midst of their foes.

The decision to rouse the craftworld's shard of the Bloody-Handed God was never taken lightly. The presence of the avatar, and the psychic echoes it carried of Kaela Mensha Khaine's rage, inspired their warriors to greater deeds and ever more tenacious ferocity when they faced their foes. However, there was always a cost to such an impact: great deeds were not heroic if they led to portions of Lugganath's forces being overextended or exposed, and ferocity was a poor substitute for strategy. As was always the case for the asuryani, strict mental discipline was essential if they were not to be swept up and carried away by the sheer intensity of the experience.

Ilaethen felt it now, as he soared above the battle on the wings he had been gifted by the Temple of the Nine Winds, banking close against the ceiling of the dome and effortlessly evading the wild and sporadic attempts of the orks to shoot him down. His blood raged with the desire to crash down and wreak havoc on the filth that heaved beneath him, to slaughter them and drive them back, and save his people from their belligerent menace. However, his focus was laser-sharp, and as unyielding as chains of adamant. This was a desperate fight with no scope for error, and little room for manoeuvre. His tactical insight was needed from this vantage point, and when he did commit to the battle himself, it had to be in a surgical strike of great value.

The avatar ploughed forwards, the Wailing Doom in its hand sweeping back and forth, seeming to torment the very air through which it cut. Orkish lives were reaped as though they were wheat to a harvestman's blade, and the asuryani formed up behind the avatar in a wedge that drove into the thickest concentration of the foe. Ilaethen's lips twitched into a grim smile behind his war mask, but he was not unaware of the dangers posed by such an offensive. They had to hold the webway gate, they *had* to. If they could break the enemy and drive them away, then this aggression would serve their purpose. If not then it might simply weaken their defence, should the orks show the tactical wherewithal to circumnavigate the fiercest fighting and strike for their target. Assuming the gate *was* their target, that was.

He focused his thoughts, reaching out for the mind of Yria Nightsong. He lacked any great psychic gifts, but she was powerful and skilled enough to hear him if he called for her.

+Have you determined the crucial thread?+

There was a momentary pause, and then he heard her voice in his head. It was as though she were standing next to him, but this psychic communication also allowed him to feel the frustration in her soul.

+No. These beasts are a tangle of potential futures, and many could rise to ruin now the gateway has been opened.+

Ilaethen frowned.

+Now the gateway has been opened? We have widened the scope for disaster through our actions?+

+Widened the scope, but lessened the severity. You know that all our actions can change the weave of fate. Not acting unless the orks breached the webway was too great a risk, for there was one who held the power and the desire to do so, and it could have brought disaster. Now more of them have the potential to affect our future, but many would do less damage, and the creature who previously posed the greatest danger is now a lesser threat. If the orks do not believe it to have a unique power, they are less likely to follow it.+

+But we should still prevent them from gaining access to the webway.+

+Of course. Some things are immutable.+

The orks had, of course, noticed the arrival of the avatar, and most were surging towards it. Their species was drawn to conflict as though each and every one of them followed the Path of the Warrior, and Ilaethen momentarily considered what that might be like. How would it feel to know that this Path was all that you would ever need, and that to tread it could bring no disaster beyond your own death? If the aeldari abandoned their rigid discipline and all followed the Warrior Path then they would be extinct within a century or two, for they could not replace their populations at a rate that would permit that scale of warfare. There were always more orks, however, and Ilaethen had never seen a sign that any of them cared anything for the survival of their species. They did not care, and did not have to. Whatever nature or altered biology had given rise to them had ensured that they remained untroubled by the wider concerns of the universe.

Ilaethen Arhien, who agonised over minute details of defence and war, who keenly felt the loss of every spirit that fell in battle and was laid to rest in Lugganath's infinity circuit, felt the twin blades of envy and hatred pierce his heart. Envy, for a life so uncomplicated; and hatred, for the destruction they wrought with it. And hatred too, for himself, for envying these beasts.

+Ilaethen! Beware!+

Yria's warning to him came a moment before even his comparatively dull psychic abilities felt a swelling of raw, brutal power directly beneath him. He banked to one side, seeking to evade whatever crude sorcery an ork psyker was directing at him, but no bolt of power came lashing upwards. Instead, his head was enveloped by agonising pain, and his vision faded into the glowing darkness of a stygian blue.

His mastery of the wings of a Swooping Hawk was such that he could fly while blinded, of course, but to fly blinded whilst also in great pain, and above an enemy intent on shooting him down, was another matter entirely. He cut into a tight circle, hoping to avoid collision with any tall objects. His path through the air was predictable, it was true, but how much difference did that make when his foes' shooting was so erratic in any case?

'Yria!' he whispered, resorting to messenger waves rather than attempting to focus his thoughts. Not only would it be more difficult to do so while in such pain, but the psychic resonance of it might bleed across to her.

He felt the surge of her will, and then he was blinking rapidly clearing eyes as the alien malignancy was blown away like foul air banished by a fresh breeze. His keen vision, now returned to its full power, swiftly picked out the ork responsible for his brief incapacitation, since it was staggering to one side and slapping itself in the head as it dealt with the psychic backwash of having its conjuring severed. One of the beasts' psykers had been the strand of fate which sent the craftworld down this path, and although Ilaethen could not be certain that it was this one, it was clearly a dangerous foe.

He tucked his wings, and descended like the wrath of Asuryan himself.

None of the orks saw him coming. He threw himself into a forward somersault at the last moment before he touched down, to give his star glaive extra momentum, and the keen-edged weapon bisected the ork psyker down the middle. The two halves of its body dropped away from the path of his blade, the damage too severe for even its unnaturally rugged constitution to have a hope of surviving. The orks around it gaped in shock for the moment it took them to register the arrival of the winged warrior in their midst, and Ilaethen punished them for it.

They wore black, and although no ork shunned melee combat, it was the black-clad ones who seemed the most brutally and enthusiastically skilled at it. Ilaethen's long-handled blade swept out and took the heads from three of them before they could react. Then they piled into him, crude blades raised high and simple firearms blasting.

He could not dodge all their attacks, and nor could he block them all, but he could block some and dodge others. One ork might find their weapon's swing touched aside by the gentlest of nudges from the haft of his star glaive, and then that its blade had buried itself in the torso of one of its fellows. Another might fire two shots at his body only for Ilaethen to have jinked from side to side in the time between it pulling the trigger for the first and second time, and two other orks on the far side of him now had new holes in them, while Ilaethen had thrust the tip of his glaive through the shooter's throat. He danced among them with the same grace and skill as one of the children of Cegorach, and left a trail of destruction as he went. He broke bones with kicks, he swept out legs and bowled his enemies over with calculated blows from his wings, and always his glaive was flashing, like the light of ancient stars.

There were some twenty orks around him when he began. When he stopped moving, less than ten seconds later, none had more than a few breaths of life left, and for some it had already departed. For his part, Ilaethen had one wound on his left arm, where he'd had no option but to take a glancing blow from his last enemy a moment before he killed it.

A trio of wind riders screamed by overhead, their jetbikes' weapons discharging razor-edged shuriken into another mass of orks, scything down nearly half with one run. Ilaethen dipped the tip of his glaive in a salute to them and leaped skywards once more, fighting down the urge to give himself over to the lure of the avatar's aura and launch himself headlong into the nearest foes. He could ill afford to get bogged down fighting the rank and file of the orks' troops, despite the damage he could do to them. He was not invulnerable, and to be an autarch was to know your own worth without arrogance or undue humility. Few indeed were those individuals who could master the Aspect Paths without being subsumed by one, and their value to a craftworld was nearly incalculable. Only the certain elimination of a grave threat to his home would justify the loss of Ilaethen's life: any lesser prize would be a folly.

Once aloft, he took in the shape of the battle once more, and saw that it was far closer than he would have wished. This once-abandoned gate was buried deep beneath a mon-keigh city, and the orks had not cracked the structure open to a sufficient extent to bring their great machines of war within; but although not the smallest, the gate was far from the largest, and its dimensions meant that the host of Lugganath had not been able to deploy their mightiest weapons either. The presence of a

Wraithknight would have surely secured the outcome, but it had not been possible to bring any of the craftworld's few remaining specimens through. This battle would be carried by troops and vehicles, and while the aeldari had far superior quality and finesse, the orks had greater numbers and sheer brute force on their side.

Ilaethen saw one of their filthy four-limbed war walkers, belching noxious black fumes and painted in ugly splashes of brown, clanking towards the main concentration of asuryani. Its bulky weapons thundered, but lacked the accuracy to trouble its targets. A support platform's D-cannon shot wide, missing the Dreadnought but ripping a momentary hole into the warp through which a group of luckless orks were sucked; a hail of shuriken from the Guardian teams was more accurate, but their shots failed to find anything critical such as power couplings or hydraulics. The Dreadnought's claws sizzled and sparked with energy as they powered up, ready to rend flesh.

The avatar intercepted it.

Both were metal, but the living metal of the avatar's body moved with a smoothness and swiftness that the clumsy engineering of the orks could never hope to match. The edge of the Wailing Doom sheared off one of the Dreadnought's claws with a noise that sounded like souls bring ripped from their bodies, then the great daemon of the aeldari plunged its weapon to the hilt into its enemy's body.

The Dreadnought wobbled, but although the pilot was surely doomed, orks were nothing if not hardy. Even when outmatched, and with what remained of its living body now pierced by a blade longer than an aeldari was tall, the Dreadnought's operator still had the will to strike back one more time before death claimed it. Its weapons blazed in a point-blank barrage that thundered into the avatar, and triggered an explosion so bright that even Ilaethen had to turn his eyes away for a moment.

When he looked again, the Dreadnought was smoking wreckage on its back. The Avatar of Khaine was still standing, and the bright rents on its chest which revealed its internal fires were already healing over. It reached out with one hand and ripped the Wailing Doom from the Dreadnought's chassis, then raised it above its head with a bellowed challenge.

A volley of shells ripped out of the orks' ranks and smashed into the avatar. It had little appreciable effect other than enraging the daemon further, but Ilaethen could track the shots' origin, and his eyes narrowed behind his war helm as he made out what was approaching. It was another hulking metal shape, in dull black rather than brown, but although similar in size to the avatar's recently vanquished foe, this was not another war walker. This was perhaps the largest ork that Ilaethen had ever seen.

Its bulk was certainly greatly increased by the massive armour it was wearing, but there was no mistaking the fact that even beneath those thick metal plates, this was an ork of massive physique. One arm ended in the still-smoking barrels of the gun – more like a small cannon – which it had just fired, and the other in a gigantic three-pronged power claw. Two flame-tipped horns jutted forwards from beneath its jaw, and vomited fire ahead of it as it closed the distance. The avatar saw only another victim, and raised the Wailing Doom, ready to discharge a bolt of ravening energy from it at the onrushing ork.

Which might have been why it did not see the other ork until it was attacked from behind.

This was another huge ork, although neither as bulky nor as heavily armoured as the black-clad one. It wielded a massive axe with a powered head, and buried the blade deep into the avatar's side with a guttural bellow. Molten metal flew from the force of the blow, and the avatar staggered from this unexpected attack. It lashed out with the Wailing Doom, but the ork had already disengaged and ducked away, the avatar's white-hot blood spitting off the blade of its axe as it was purged by the power field. The avatar whirled, scattering burning droplets from the wound, and the other ork crashed into it.

It was a titanic clash, for this was not an ork commanding a war walker through a system of levers and crude bionic impulse links, but a massive, battle-hardened creature in full control of its own body. Its speed and economy of movement were almost frightening to witness, the very peak of the orkish culture of violence. Its first blow knocked the avatar down to one knee; its second was an almighty backhand which sent the daemon sprawling with its face caved in on one side.

Ilaethen tensed, and prepared to dive. He was unsure if the blade of his star glaive had either the length or the keenness needed to penetrate this ork's armour, but it was a foe that could not be allowed to live.

+Ilaethen. I have found the original beast – the one who brought these events to pass, and who must be stopped.+

Ilaethen blinked. +But the avatar–+

+Kaela Mensha Khaine can look after himself, Ilaethen.+

Ilaethen closed his eyes. He knew better than to doubt his farseer. He focused his thoughts once more.

+Guide me.+

Yria laid her casting over his eyes, and it picked out a single ork, lighting it up in his vision no matter where it moved. Ilaethen beat his wings once, and dived towards it.

Whether by chance, psychic awareness, or some form of bestial intuition, the ork detected him coming. Ilaethen felt its gaze lock with his for a moment, before green energy wrapped itself around the ork's head and blazed at him. He threw himself into a shallow roll and felt the blast scorch by him, leaving him untouched. The ork's eyes widened as it saw him evade its attack with the speed of thought, and raised the staff it carried as though to ward him off. Ilaethen saw something dangling from it that sparkled with a familiar light, and realised to his horror and anger that the creature was carrying a waystone as a trophy! He readied his star glaive to strike, to avenge the unfortunate spirit who had been denied the tranquillity of their craftworld's infinity circuit...

...and the ork disappeared.

One moment it was there, then there was a flash of green light, and it was gone. Ilaethen pulled up as his star glaive slashed through the space where the beast had been, but this was no illusion: it had used its power to transport itself away, somehow.

+Ilaethen! It is here! It–+

A brief, bloody vision seized Ilaethen. He was looking through lenses, not of his own helmet, but of a seer's ghosthelm. An unbearable pressure built within his head before he could react, a nuclear core of ferocious green energy which slammed outwards. He felt his head explode, cracking the ghosthelm with the sheer violence of it–

–and he was back in his own body as the psychic bleed from Yria Nightsong's communication died along with her spirit.

Ilaethen howled with grief and rage, his fury and sorrow further amplified by the presence of the avatar. One of Lugganath's greatest farseers had been slain by the trickery and foul sorceries of the orks, and he now wished only to slaughter them all. Thoughts of holding the gateway or defending the craftworld were washed away by bloodlust: he simply wanted to kill.

Had his perceptions not been so clouded by his emotions, he would have noticed the orks before they struck. They were a small group, arrayed as though ready to pounce upon the psyker who had just fled, but they were content enough to bury their long blades in an aeldari autarch instead. Ilaethen's star glaive killed one of them, but it was a death-blow reflex. The last thing he felt was the rough kiss of an ork's blade opening his throat from behind.

LOTZ

Armenius had sobbed. He would be the first to admit it.

He had been *free*. He had broken away from the orks and managed to liberate himself through nothing more than his own wits, cunning, and combat skills, which had remained undimmed despite his captivity. He had slain the filthy xenos in his way – only gretchin, admittedly, but he could hardly be blamed for that – and come up with a workable plan on a very limited timescale. He had navigated his way into Davidia's lowest reaches, successfully interpreted the frankly appallingly signed maze of tunnels until he found a local, and then impressed upon them the importance of his mission in order to secure their assistance.

He had been so close, *so* close to being able to transmit a message uphive and inform his superiors about the orkish threat from beneath (and once he had done that, he would also have found a way to let them know about the disgustingly heretical levels of xenos influence on the population down here). He had been within touching distance of acclaim, recognition, a promotion, and a return to as much safety as could be found on a planet overrun by an orkish Waaagh!, even one which currently lacked an overall leader. Had the orks united again and pushed upwards then Armenius Varrow would have been at the forefront of the defence, leading troops inspired to new levels of loyalty and ferocity by his heroism.

Instead, he had been betrayed. He *must* have been betrayed, even if he was currently unsure exactly who would or could have betrayed him, or why. Eza? The hunter had been eager to help once Armenius had coolly and calmly explained the situation in terms their somewhat primitive mind had been able to grasp. Had they been *too* eager? Were they simply a xenophile, eager to see humanity brought low by any alien race? Had they left a trail for the orks to follow, guiding them up into the hive? It spelled disaster for them and their community, of course, but such was the way with heretics of all stripes: they had no concept of the certain misery which awaited them should they turn their backs on the light of the Emperor. If they did, they would never do it.

And so, Armenius had wept. Not because of the horror of being imprisoned once again, of course – he would bear that with the same stolid resilience with which he had greeted all orkish blandishments so far – but because he had been unable to warn his comrades in the Golden Lions of the threat. What hope did the hive have without him?

Then the gate opened, as Armenius had feared it might from the moment he laid eyes on it, and horror surged forth.

Armenius read the *Regimental Standard* religiously, and he was well aware of the menace of the perfidious aeldari: or at least, as well aware as any reasonable officer of the Astra Militarum could be without delving into areas of knowledge best left to the Inquisition. He had recognised the heretical influences on the people of this hab-dome, and he knew what the true identity must have been of the 'warriors of the Emperor' who had come through that gate in ages past, or however the so-called seer had described them. All the same, seeing them in the flesh was another matter entirely. It shook him so badly that he actually attempted to communicate with the dull beast-machine to whose back his cage was strapped.

'Move!' he wailed, hammering desperately on the hull of the Killa Kan known as Sarge as the first aeldari warriors let loose a hail of shuriken from their weapons. 'Retreat! Run away! Get us *out* of here, you overgrown bloody grot!'

Sarge did no such thing. Instead, it opened fire with the hefty weapon serving as its right arm, which looked a bit like a heavy stubber if a heavy stubber had been designed by a member of the Mechanicus with an unshakeable conviction that bigger and louder was definitely better. Armenius covered his ears and howled as the racket thundered into his head, but Sarge was not yet done with his torment. The Killa Kan activated its speakers, bellowed '*WAAAGH!*' at the top of its tinny lungs, and lurched towards the enemy with quite un-grotlike enthusiasm. The massive saw blade on its left arm whined up to cutting speed, but Armenius had little faith in its chances of survival. He would not have liked to take on Sarge on his own, even if he had his power sword back, but this was the aeldari: their melee troops moved like quicksilver, most likely through a combination of disgusting xenos biology and foul alien sorcery, and their weapons made a mockery of armour plating. They were no match for the massed lasguns and overwhelming vehicular superiority of the Astra Militarum, of course – the *Regimental Standard* was very clear about that – but set against the crude, clanking hordes of the orks? It was scalpel against sledgehammer, and while Armenius' money might have been on the sledgehammer in the long haul, he had no wish to be strapped to the back of something making itself an obvious target for the scalpel's first incision.

They said that necessity was the mother of invention, in which case desperation was surely its father. Armenius gripped the bars of his cage and appealed to one of the beings in the galaxy he would have normally considered least likely to help him, without even going into how unlikely it would be for him to actually make such an appeal under virtually any other circumstance.

'Genrul! Genrul! *Help!*'

Sarge was Da Genrul's… pet? Bodyguard? Icon bearer? Armenius had no idea what the relationship between the two actually was, or even if he had a suitable lexicon for understanding it. The important thing was that the Killa Kan rarely left Uzbrag's side, and it was not unreasonable to assume that, given the wily Blood Axe kept Sarge around for some reason, he would not want it to run off and get itself destroyed.

Da Genrul was looking upwards as a grav-tank of a design the Imperium classed as a Wave Serpent thrummed overhead, and then began to disgorge melee troops that fell into the orks' ranks – insomuch as they had ranks, which they essentially did not – like particularly lethal, dark-green hail. At no point did he pay any attention to Armenius' increasingly panicked shouts, nor to the fact that Sarge was disappearing in the direction of the aeldari.

'Emperor preserve me,' Armenius whispered, as shuriken began *spanging* off Sarge's shoulders, razored shards of death pinwheeling away. The Killa Kan might have sufficient armour to stand up to the aeldari's basic weaponry – if monomolecular-edged killing discs could be said to be 'basic', which they were by the standards of these foul xenos – but Armenius certainly did not. If Sarge turned to flee now, or if the aeldari got behind it,

Armenius was a sitting waterfowl. He hardly thought that one species of xenos would recognise him as a captive rather than a willing collaborator with another species, let alone that they would care. The aeldari were heartless, aloof and arrogant, and known for the cruelty they inflicted on others, apparently for no reason other than the enjoyment it gave them. He could expect to be used for target practice if he was lucky, or as a living vivisection lesson if he was less so; nothing more.

…Better the daemon you knew?

He reared up as far as he could within the confines of his accursed cage, pressing the side of his face against the bars which formed the roof of it in order to get the best view he could of what Sarge was up against. It did not make for comforting viewing.

The aeldari did not hold to the human idea of ranks any more than the orks did, but there was at least a greater sense of organisation to them, fluid although it was. Armenius' experienced eyes picked out several distinct groups of warriors arrayed in front of the gateway, laying down fire from their shuriken catapults and the occasional support weapon, the latter mounted on their floating anti-grav platforms. Most wore the sort of orange-and-black combination he had seen on the inhabitants of Emperor's Gate, but these were the original, not human aping distorted by decades, centuries or even millennia of faulty memory. Every warrior's armour fit like a second skin, emphasising the slenderness of their build and belying the unnatural strength and resiliency Armenius knew them to possess. Every trained soldier of the Astra Militarum was aware that the aeldari were decadent, simpering aliens with no stomach for a fight, but also that you should never turn your back on one until you were certain it was dead, and preferably in several parts. It was well known that the treacherous xenos would wait until your back was turned to launch an underhanded attack with the last of their strength, instead of accepting their inferiority and dying with good grace.

Sarge was heading straight for the greatest concentration of them, with no coordinated support from the rest of the Waaagh!, and precisely zero tactical awareness. It was going to get them both killed, and so far as Armenius was concerned, the loss of a captain of the Aranuan 25th would be a greater blow to the Imperium than the death of one Killa Kan would be a gain.

'Left! Left, you brute!' he bawled, hammering on that side of its chassis as one of the support weapons began to swivel towards them. 'Big gun! Big gun *bad!*'

It was probably too much to hope for that the grot inside Sarge's shell was actually listening to him, or for that matter could understand his words. However, whether through luck, an unlikely communication between a man and a lower life-form, or even the divine intervention of the Emperor Himself, Sarge veered to the left just as the aeldari weapon fired.

Armenius had no idea what it was – some sort of unholy beam weapon which caused the very air to vibrate – but the important thing was that it missed. Sarge lumbered on unharmed, which meant in this instance that Armenius remained unharmed as well, and the large weapon on the Killa Kan's right arm tracked towards the weapon. Say what you wanted about grots, and Armenius certainly would given half a chance, but they tended to have a deal more accuracy to their shooting than their larger cousins. Large-calibre shells tore up the ground, ripped through a couple of Guardians who happened to be in the way, and then made a mess of both the support weapon's platform and its operator, who collapsed with at least three holes the size of Armenius' fist through their body.

'Hah haaaah!' Armenius cackled with relief, then ducked down hastily as another stray round whined and ricocheted past his head. At least, he hoped it was stray; if the aeldari cowards had got it into their heads to shoot at a helpless captive simply trying to stay alive, there was little hope for him. 'Saints' blood, what is wrong with you?' he yelled, just in case. 'I'm a prisoner!'

His protestations did nothing to help: the whine of shuriken catapults accelerating their ammunition met his ears a moment before another storm of blades clattered off Sarge. One deflected back off the bars of Armenius' cage, and sliced through the already-ragged left sleeve of his coat before tinkling away to Emperor knew where. He hissed in alarm, and examined his arm: a thin red wound and a trickle of blood met his wide eyes. Throne of Terra, he hadn't even felt it! Mercifully, this was little more than a scratch, but he immediately checked himself all over in case he had been dealt a more serious wound without realising. The stories of soldiers caught by an aeldari volley and falling apart into pieces without their nerves even registering that they had been hit suddenly seemed far more feasible.

He appeared to be otherwise unmarked, at least by the aeldari, although he had no guarantee for how long that state of affairs would continue. Sarge was nearly on the xenos now, and its saw blade was whining up to truly obscene speeds as the pilot sought to get to grips with its enemies and live out a gretchin's deep-seated desire to bloodily dismember other beings whilst being insulated from any reprisal. Armenius heard the whine of chainblades – a thin, eerie sound, very different to the guttural combustion-engine roar of orkish weapons of the same sort – and realised that the aeldari were going to be doing their utmost to make those reprisals stick, regardless of the Killa Kan's intentions.

He felt more than heard when combat was actually joined:

the rhythmic thunder of Sarge's steps hesitated for a moment longer than usual before the next impact, and its chassis tilted as its saw arm swung out. Armenius felt the juddering run through its body as the hideous weapon connected with a living body, and the spray of gore thrown out behind the Killa Kan into his field of view left him in no doubt as to the result. The aeldari were almost certainly fleeter of foot than the war machine to which Armenius was unwillingly strapped, but they were locked in place by their apparent determination to defend the gateway, and so they could not retreat before it, as they were known to often do when the noble armies of the Imperium tried to bring them to battle. Armenius could understand the xenos' rationale – they appeared to use this gateway, and others like it, to move around the galaxy somehow, and no one in their right mind would want their private highway infested by orks – but his superior tactical mind could see how it would be their weakness. The aeldari made war by striking hard, then fading away from counter-attacks. If their initial assault here did not debilitate the orks, they would be easy meat for the brute strength of their enemies.

Sarge's chassis rang with the sound of multiple impacts as aeldari close-combat Guardians struck back, seeking weak points with their blades. One flowed into view, its weapons drawn back in preparation to strike, and Armenius withdrew as far and as high as his cramped cage would allow.

'Don't hurt me!' he begged, waiting for the leaping lunge that would thrust the blade with its spinning, diamond-edged teeth in through the bars to spit him and rip out his innards, as the xenos recognised a hero of the Imperium.

The aeldari did not even look at him, so far as he could tell from its forbidding helm. It slashed at Sarge's body, throwing up sparks but causing no other damage that Armenius could discern, from his admittedly imperfect vantage point. Sarge was not satisfied with the blood it had shed so far, and its saw arm swung again. Armenius felt it connect once more, and then something landed wetly on top of the Killa Kan, just above his head. He looked up, and recoiled in horror as a pair of legs with no torso attached dropped past him.

The body followed a moment later, and clung to the bars of his cell.

It was a hideous, incongruous sight: the upper half of an aeldari Guardian, its battle helm unmarked and its body armour shining and splendid, until you got to the waist, at which point it became ragged fabric and even more ragged flesh, and a blood-soaked mass of gradually sagging viscera. Yet still, the foul xenos had found the strength and wherewithal to wrap one of its arms through the bars to arrest its fall, and was reaching in with the shuriken pistol in its other hand.

Armenius did not know for certain whether it was seeking to shoot Sarge in the back in a last gasp of desperate defiance at its killer, or attempting to execute him either as an orkish sympathiser, or simply as a human that it thought might, unlike the metal monstrosity carrying him, be within its capability to slay. Probably the latter. Well, he was going to prove the cowardly creature wrong.

He twisted as far away from the pistol's barrel as he could, seized the aeldari's wrist in both hands with a strength born of desperation, and began slamming its hand against the cage's solid floor. The aeldari hissed something at him, but Armenius let his rage take over and bellowed in anger as he continued his assault. After four, five, six such impacts, the pistol finally tumbled free of the aeldari's grasp. Armenius pivoted and lashed out with his foot, kicking it in what would have been its face had it not been wearing a helmet. The aeldari was knocked backwards and, stunned by his mighty strike, lost its grip on his cage. It dropped out of view without a further sound. Perhaps his blow had even killed it: broken its neck, perhaps?

More importantly, he now had a weapon.

He snatched the shuriken pistol up before Sarge's erratic movements could send it skittering over the floor and out through the bars, but even in his desperation he made sure to keep his fingers away from anything that might function as a trigger; the last thing he needed was to accidentally shoot himself with a xenos weapon designed for slicing through flesh and bone. He managed to get hold of it without incident, and arranged it into something approaching a ready position in his right hand, although it was poorly designed. The grip was too thin to feel properly secure, and what looked like the trigger-stud was a little too far forwards for his index finger to reach comfortably. Give him a regular-issue laspistol any day. However, needs must.

Sarge roared, its speakers emitting a static-edged screech of distortion and anger, or possibly pain, and the Killa Kan broke into a run. It lumbered off, away from the aeldari with which it had been locked in combat a moment ago. Armenius saw their receding figures, and hastily tried to hide the plundered pistol behind his body in case they got the wrong idea. What was going on? Had the gretchin pilot suddenly been overwhelmed by the fear common in its unarmoured kin and elected to flee? Had a chance blow caused some form of malfunction, sending it pelting away despite the wishes of the xenos nominally in control?

It didn't matter. What mattered was that another support weapon was swivelling towards Sarge as it ran, and this time the Killa Kan paid no attention to Armenius' frantic thumping and bellowed instructions.

The weapon fired.

Something below Armenius exploded, or possibly *im*ploded, and Sarge fell sideways.

The impact threw Armenius against the bars of his cage as they hit the ground, drove the breath from his lungs, and numbed the arm on which he landed. He kept hold of the pistol through a heroic effort of will, but his situation had drastically worsened. High up on Sarge's back, he had been lifted above the main level of fighting, and shielded from the worst impacts for as long as the Killa Kan had been facing its enemies. Now, the machine was immobilised, spluttering weakly, and missing at least one leg from what he could make out. Now, Armenius was an easy target for any pointy-eared aeldari wretch who wanted to get a metaphorical feather in its figurative cap by putting a murderous end to the career of perhaps the greatest captain of the Aranuan 25th.

Well, placing your faith in the Emperor of Mankind was a good and devout thing to do, but there came a time in every hero's life when he had to take a stand and strike out for himself. That time had come for Armenius.

He levelled the pistol at the crude lock on the door of his cage. High-velocity, razor-edged aeldari rounds against poorly forged ork steel. There could surely only be one winner in that contest, and it was the man inside the cage, who would be free again within moments.

On the other hand...

Armenius was as good as anyone at judging angles, but he was no artillery captain or Basilisk gunner. He *thought* he could point the pistol and fire it in a way which meant that any ricochets would spin harmlessly off – or harmlessly to him, anyway, which was all that mattered – but could he be sure? This was a xenos weapon, after all, and the aeldari were notorious for scoffing at concepts such as regular physics. And orkish metal: who could judge how that would react? It would be a poor service to the Imperium if Armenius were betrayed and slain by the same device he was attempting to use to gain his freedom, should a shuriken rebound in an unexpected manner and lodge itself in his heart, or neck, or bowel. He did not appear to be the centre of anyone's attention at the moment, so perhaps he should just–

An unearthly roar rang out, and a monstrous shape strode out of the still-shimmering aeldari gateway.

An avatar.

Armenius did not delve too deeply into xenos lore, of course he didn't, but there were some things you could not help but hear about once you had risen to a certain level within the Astra Militarum. There were whispers that ran around the officers' mess, whispers that you kept away from any member of the Commissariat as though your life depended upon it, because it probably did. Armenius had heard rumours of soulless metal men and how they could suck away the power of even the most potent psykers: which might not be such a bad thing, all things considered, had they not also been rumoured to blast Imperial citizens and troops into their component atoms. He had heard rumours of how some of the Traitor Space Marines which plagued the Imperium might not be the unnaturally preserved remainder of the great betrayal in ages past, but might actually be *new* traitors, turned from Chapters currently thought to be loyal.

And he had heard tales of the great metal daemons of the aeldari: gigantic molten figures of hatred and death, an alien war god incarnate.

That was what he was looking at now, and it drove all thoughts of caution from his mind. The thunder of its voice reached down into his soul and crushed it with white-hot fingers, and the momentary touch of its glowing eyes upon him as it scanned the battlefield withered his courage like a plant flash-burned by fire. Nothing mattered any more except *getting away from that Throne-damned thing*.

He pointed the shuriken pistol at the cage lock again and, his vision blurred by terrified tears, pressed the firing stud. The weapon thrummed slightly in his grasp, a faint but powerful vibration, and spat a stream of shining rounds. The lock was ruined within half a second; the bar to which it was attached was severed as well, before Armenius was able to coax his finger off the firing mechanism. He kicked out: the remains of the lock dropped away, and the door fell open with a clang.

He scrambled for it, this new promise of freedom, his insides so twisted by fear and hope that the combination reached up his throat and threatened to strangle him. He clawed his way out, still weeping, and ran. He ran away from the gunfire and bloodshed; he ran away from the alien gateway to a terrifying, unknown realm; and most importantly he ran away from the fiery metal daemon with its sword that sang a song of ruin as it swept through the air. He ran with a strength born of terror, ducking and cowering as ork shootas stitched glowing lines towards the gateway and the aeldari sent streams of whisper-thin shuriken back. He rolled desperately to one side as ork vehicles roared past, their drivers and gunners paying no attention to him in favour of targeting the gateway's defenders. He ran on, between the buildings of Emperor's Gate, keeping away from the shadows which he knew all too well might hide Da Genrul's kommandos from his view.

He ran towards the side of the dome opposite the one by which he had entered, praying as he ran that he might find an escape there. Orks were still streaming in from either side, but one lone, running human was of no interest to them compared to the battle. All the same, he did not slow once he had left the fighting behind him. He would not stop until he had escaped the dome completely.

Or, as it turned out, until he came upon a dark tunnel leading through the dome wall which was not disgorging orks, and ran into a thicket of lasgun barrels.

'Don't shoot!' he shouted, raising his hands and blinking into the light of photo-lumens, and making sure to avoid triggering the shuriken pistol. 'Don't shoot!'

'Who goes–' a voice began, and then stopped in shock. 'Captain Varrow?!'

'Who's that?' Armenius said. It was a human voice, and it knew his name, but his insides were wound far too tight by now to give in to anything approaching relief. This could be a mind-reading witch with their armed escort of underhive scummers, or, or…

'Captain Varrow,' a new voice said, and Armenius' throat tightened as the speaker stepped out in front of the lasguns and into the dim light of the dome, sufficient for him to see the peaked cap, the black greatcoat, and the iron-grey hair. Commissar Elushka Bone.

Throne, he would almost prefer the mind-reading witch to Old Bones.

'Commissar,' he said, his feet coming to attention without receiving a conscious instruction from his brain, although his hands remained raised in dim acknowledgement of the gun barrels still trained on him.

'You are recorded as lost in action, captain,' Bone said, her voice as sharp as a flensing knife. 'What are you doing here? And by the God-Emperor, what is happening in there?'

'The orks took me prisoner, commissar,' Armenius said. 'The suffering I've endured, I…' He swallowed back the emotion that threatened to choke his words. Just living through it had been bad enough – now he actually had to verbalise it to another human, it all came crashing back in even more intensely than before. 'They managed to gain entry to the hive, and I escaped.' He declined to mention how he had already escaped once, but then been captured again: even in his ragged-nerved state, that did not seem a sensible thing to admit. 'Commissar, there is… *something* down there. I believe it's a heretical aeldari construct, one of their infernal devices which allow them to move around the galaxy. The orks are trying to enter it, I think, and the aeldari have, er, emerged. To fight them.'

Bone looked at him, then past him. The expression on her face quite plainly said that she would have no intention of believing him were she not able to see the flashes of explosions and hear the rumble of gunfire, and was still having doubts about it despite those details.

The avatar roared again, and Armenius flinched despite the fact that it was far more distant now than the first time. You simply did not hear the voice of an alien god and remain the same man afterwards.

'We were aware of the orkish incursion,' Bone said, almost absently. Armenius could see explosions reflected in her dark eyes. 'Colonel Sudliff ordered a team of volunteers to gather intelligence on what is occurring.'

'Very sensible,' Armenius said, nodding like a fool.

'I have executed the colonel for cowardice,' Bone said, her eyes boring into him. 'We are not here to gather intelligence. We are here in full force, under the command of myself and Brevet Colonel Bruja, to destroy the enemy.'

'Ah,' Armenius stammered. 'E-even more sensible?'

'You say you were captured by the orks, and that is why you are still alive?'

Armenius breathed out. At last, he would get to deliver his hard-won information! 'Yes, commissar! Their warboss was killed, and I have discovered that the three largest remaining orks are in a struggle for dominance. They are an Evil Sun named Zagnob Thundaskuzz, a Goff called Mag Dedfist, and a Blood Axe known as Genrul Uzbrag, or simply Da Genrul. Our tactics should be varied depending on which of them gains supremacy, but we could capitalise on their current disarray by–'

'We need explosives,' Bone interrupted, turning to look at the soldiers in the tunnel. 'Send three teams to drill them into the ceiling from the dome above. All other units will advance on the xenos. Should we fall, the explosives are to be detonated. We'll drop a few thousand tonnes of rockcrete on these bastards and see how much they like that.'

'Commissar,' Armenius said, feeling his tentative footing begin to slip away. 'Should we not–'

'Armenius Varrow, you were captured by the enemy and have undoubtedly aided them,' Bone said, cutting him off again. She still was not looking at him. 'You are, even now, holding a prohibited xenos weapon. You should have taken your own life rather than let yourself be corrupted in this manner.'

Armenius swallowed. 'But commissar, I can–'

'I will now correct your error.'

Armenius just had time to register that Elushka Bone had drawn her bolt pistol from its holster and levelled it against his forehead, before he was incapable of registering anything, ever again.

LOTZ

Mag Dedfist was pissed off.

He'd done everything he was supposed to. He'd obeyed both the vision, and Old Morgrub's explanation of it. He'd smashed straight through the walls of the humie city with the sort of speed and violence that would be expected of the very best of the Goffs, and slaughtered everything in his way. That should have been an end to it.

It was those zoggin' grots, that was the problem. He hadn't trusted it when he'd seen them racing off as though they had a mind of their own, rather than doing whatever it was a runtherd told them to do. It turned out that he'd been right to be suspicious: the little gits had scampered off ahead of him, almost as if they were trying to find Morgrub's gate in their own right. If he hadn't bothered with following them, and had forged his own path instead, he was certain he would have got to the gate quicker. Instead, Da Genrul was already there, looking as smug as a squig in a feed trough.

All that effort, and for what? Back to where he'd started, facing down Uzbrag and Thundaskuzz, with Old Morgrub giggling in the background. That was the last time he paid attention to anything a weirdboy said, even if he *was* a warphead.

Mag's mood hadn't even improved much once the gateway had opened and the skrawniez had come pouring out. They were thin gits that broke easily. It was like punching a tent: no real resistance, and a similar lack of satisfaction from the inevitable collapse which followed. Still, Mag rampaged around for a bit, blowing them apart with his kustom shoota and clobbering them with his power klaw, trying to get at least some enjoyment from the whole situation.

Then he heard the hot-git yelling, and his day got a lot better.

Mag *knew* about hot-gits. If you got the skrawniez really riled, sometimes they showed up with one: a big metal skrawnie, only it wasn't really that scrawny any more, which blazed with heat and carried a massive choppa or spear. He'd seen one once, back when he was nothing more than a boy with a shoota. It had torn through a battlewagon like it was made of sticks, and he'd actually admired how killy it was, although he never got close enough to have a go at it himself.

That was going to change today.

The hot-git wasn't hard to make out: it was about three times the height of a regular skrawnie, and when it moved, the dark, dull red of what passed for its skin cracked open to reveal the white-hot fire within. They were made of metal, Mag had heard, although he wasn't sure how that worked. Typical skrawnie nonsense, he reckoned.

Still, it seemed that this hot-git was just as good at scrapping as the one he saw all those years ago. It cut down half a dozen boyz with one sweep of its massive blade, and when a trio of squighog boyz pelted towards it, all whooping and hollering, it fired a blast of *something* from its choppa that atomised the middle rider in the time it took for Mag to blink. That was enough to send all three squigs squealing away in terror, with the two remaining beast snaggas on their backs yelling and cursing futilely. Mag laughed at them as they careered past him, then swatted aside a skrawnie that had got too close, and set off towards this most worthy of foes.

A Deff Dread got there first: a rare Snakebite Deff Dread, cobbled together by one of the few mekboyz the clan produced. Skrawnie cutty-discs rattled off its armour with no effect, and its power klaws were just charging up for some proper scragging when the hot-git jumped in to ruin its fun. That huge choppa took off one of the Dread's klaws, as clean as you like, then the hot-git rammed it straight through the main chassis.

The pilot was no cowardly squig, and fired off all his weapons at point-blank range. The explosions – or possibly the hot-git's flaming blood – must have cooked off the rest of the machine's ammo stores, because there was a massive bang. However, in the aftermath of it, the Deff Dread was in a smoking heap on its back, and the hot-git was still standing. Not only was it still standing, but it was *healing*: the damage was already scabbing over, as dull metal skin replaced the blazing innards which had been exposed. It ripped its huge choppa out, held it above its head, and roared what could only be a challenge.

Mag grinned. An enemy that healed that quickly would be *very* fun to fight. It would last for ages!

He took general aim with his kustom shoota, and let rip. The hot-git was so large that he couldn't really miss, and his shells slammed into it. They did little except anger it, and Mag practically felt its eyes land on him, so powerful was its gaze. The very air around it was shimmering from the heat it was giving off. This was going to be a fight to remember.

He lumbered forwards into a run. Mega armour didn't make

an ork any faster, but it certainly added momentum – enough momentum to give even this massive thing some problems. The hot-git levelled its choppa at him and furious energy began to build around the blade. Mag gritted his teeth: he had no idea if he could stand up to the sort of blast that had destroyed the squighog nob, but he wasn't going to give this bloody skrawnie monster the satisfaction of seeing him flinch or dodge. Goffs met the enemy head-on, no matter what was thrown at them...

And then Genrul zoggin' Uzbrag appeared from *behind* the hot-git, and laid into it with his power choppa.

The energised blade bit into the hot-git's side, and molten metal spilled out. The hot-git roared in pain and anger, and spun around to take a swing at Da Genrul, but Uzbrag was a typical sneaky Blood Axe, and was already running like he was some sort of grot.

Mag was furious. He'd waited *years* to have a crack at one of these, and now Da Genrul wanted to steal his thunder? It was outrageous is what it was. He wound up all that rage into his klaw arm, and expressed it with a cataclysmic punch that connected with the hot-git's chest.

This was satisfying. *This* had substance. The aftershock shuddered back up Mag's arm as he made contact. The blow sounded like an explosion in a furnace, and the hot-git was driven down to one knee by the force of it, bringing its monstrous head more or less level with his own. The hot-git began to bring its choppa around, but Mag was too quick: he dealt it a thunderous backhand across the face, sending it sprawling with its head caved in on one side.

The hot-git roared through its broken mouth, but Mag could sense that there was pain there as well as rage. He took one more step to stand over it, raised his klaw, and drove the talons of it down into the hot-git's chest. The monster roared again, even louder, and Mag bellowed in triumphant answer as he sank his weapon deeper and deeper, searching for its heart.

However, the zoggin' thing apparently didn't have one.

Both of its hands came up to clamp around Mag's power klaw. He just had time to notice that one of those hands seemed to be dripping with blood before he felt the tremendous heat seeping through the thick metal around his arm, and the damned stuff began to *soften*.

It was shock more than pain that caused Mag to jerk his arm backwards, but the power klaw didn't come with him: the metal attaching it to his armour melted away, and his weapon remained in the hot-git's grasp, and still partially embedded in its chest. He swore violently as molten bits of metal dropped onto his arm, and swore some more as the hot-git plucked his power klaw out and tossed it aside, then flowed back up to its feet and took up its massive choppa once more.

Mag Dedfist began to wonder whether having an enemy who healed so quickly was such a good thing after all.

Still, he'd hurt it, and hurt it good. He raised his kustom shoota again, ready to give the hot-git another salvo, at least make it walk through pain to get to him. Gork and Mork couldn't fault him if he died fighting this monster; it would be a death to be proud of.

The hot-git took a step forwards, and then a harpoon smashed through its neck and came out the other side in a spray of molten metal.

'Gotcha!' Zagnob Thundaskuzz bawled, as his snagga klaw took the hot-git in what probably counted as its throat. 'Hot-git' was certainly the right name for it – he could feel the heat coming off its body from here, although to be fair, the torn-up side of his face could feel a lot of things at the moment, down to and including minuscule air currents. He expertly clamped the harpoon chain to his wartrike's chassis, because while Zagnob might not pay much attention to a lot of extraneous detail in life, he understood weight and balance and momentum. Trying to bring this thing down himself would simply see him falling off his own vehicle for the second time in one day.

'Come around!' he yelled at Duffrak, and pulled out one of his twin boomstikks. It coughed twice, sending bolts as thick as a humie's fist into the hot-git's chest and spattering more of the molten metal which seemed to serve the thing as blood. Duffrak obeyed his order, expertly skidding into a turn, then hammering the engines up again and taking off in a new direction. The hot-git, which had just taken one lumbering step after them, was taken off guard and off balance: the harpoon chain jerked tight and the wartrike shuddered to a halt, but the skrawnie beast was tugged off its feet.

'YES!' Zagnob cheered. 'Drag it! Drag it!' This would be his greatest success yet as speedboss, if he could ride through the battle dragging *that* behind him.

'Tryin', boss!' Duffrak assured him, but the hot-git's weight was simply too great: the tyres were spinning and sending up smoke, but not getting enough purchase.

Time for special measures.

'Skitta!' Zagnob ordered imperiously, pointing. The grot screamed, and hammered the red button once more. The engines howled even louder, and there was the slightest of lurches. They were doing it!

Then Zagnob saw Mag Dedfist coming up behind the hot-git, raising his kustom shoota to take aim at the back of its head.

'Oh no ya don't,' Zagnob muttered. He grabbed his other boomstikk and opened fire. The first shot missed; the second hit Mag in the shoulder, staggering the Goff backwards. Zagnob broke his weapon open to reload, but the hot-git reached up with one hand that was glowing with heat, and took hold of the chain...

The chain softened and snapped. The wartrike, no longer tethered to its metal anchor, lurched forwards so violently that Zagnob had to hang on desperately to avoid tumbling off. There was a wet splattering noise as they went into, through, and over a brawling ruck of boyz and skrawniez at full speed, but while this would normally have brought a smile to Zagnob's face, now he could only think about the prey that had got away.

'Back dat way!' he yelled at Duffrak, who hauled the steering bars around obediently. 'I want anuvver crack at dat fing!' They swerved around, dodged a plummeting skrawnie sky-bike that crashed and exploded close enough to spray them with shrapnel, and accelerated towards the hot-git again. It was now back on its feet, and it drew its arm back, then threw its massive choppa overhanded.

The weapon whirled through the air faster than Zagnob would have believed possible, and slammed straight through his wartrike, point first, pinning it to the ground. Duffrak was impaled; the vehicle itself came to a dead stop.

Zagnob himself did not. He was catapulted directly forwards, flying through the air towards the creature that had just wrecked his ride.

Perhaps the hot-git was not expecting Zagnob to have the presence of mind to turn his unexpected flying lesson into an attack, but no one and nothing had faster reflexes than an Evil Sunz speedboss. Zagnob lashed out with his snagga klaw, and hammered the warboss of all punches straight into the hot-git's face.

And it went *down*.

Molten blood spattered up Zagnob's arm, but the pain was

as nothing compared to the triumph that rushed through him. He'd done it! He'd taken out the biggest, baddest skrawnie in the place!

The ground came up to meet him, but not with any intent to congratulate. He landed hard, and skidded through dust and rubble to come to an undignified halt at the base of a half-ruined wall.

'Waaagh!' he bellowed, fighting his way back up. 'Dat's wot I'm talkin' about! 'Ave it, ya great big–'

The hot-git was getting up again.

'Oh, zoggin' 'eck,' Zagnob said with feeling. What did it take to put this thing down properly? He broke into a run, hoping against hope that he could land another punch before it rose to its full height and he was reduced to taking gut shots.

Mag Dedfist had recovered himself and was lining up a shot again, but the hot-git seemed to have its own ideas. It reached out behind it, still on one knee, and opened its hand. The choppa with which it had killed Duffrak – and more importantly, Zagnob's wartrike – shuddered, then freed itself with a screech of metal-on-metal, and flew through the air towards it.

Mag saw the huge weapon coming, and managed to get his mega-armoured bulk out of the way. The choppa settled into the hot-git's hand with a *thunk*, it extended it towards Zagnob, and the air above it began to shimmer with heat...

...and Da Genrul buried his power choppa into its shoulder, knocking its arm and sending a bolt of ravening energy scoring across the ground instead of straight into Zagnob.

Da Genrul ducked under the hot-git's blade as it swung around for him once more, but he felt the heat of it as it passed rather closer to his head than he would have liked. He retreated again, wary of his injured leg, and looking for an opening: there was no point rushing in against this enemy, one who could end you with one shot–

Zagnob Thundaskuzz pelted up behind it and clobbered it with his snagga klaw, drawing another howl of ire, which just showed how much sense Evil Sunz had.

'Wot da zog do ya fink ya doin'?' Mag Dedfist roared at Da Genrul, as the hot-git rounded on Zagnob. The Goff was punching his kustom shoota, which had apparently jammed.

'Tryin' to kill dat fing!' Uzbrag told him angrily. 'What do *yoo* fink I'm doin'?'

'Dat's mine!' Mag bellowed.

'Yoo had yer shot, an' ya missed!' Uzbrag retorted. 'Tell ya wot, let's *all* scrag da zogger, an' sort everyfing else out afterwards!'

Mag opened his massive mouth to argue, then looked over at where Zagnob was desperately scrambling away from the massive choppa as it swung down and buried itself into the ground, and shrugged. 'Wotever. First decent plan yoo've ever had.'

Da Genrul spun his power choppa. 'Alright den. Let's do dis.'

Mag wrenched his malfunctioning kustom shoota off through sheer brute force, then picked up what turned out to be the severed arm of a Deff Dread, which he wielded like a club. Uzbrag nodded at him, and they charged.

'Waaagh!'

Zagnob had just landed another blow, tearing through the hot-git's right knee. It staggered, but managed to grab Thundaskuzz with the hand that wasn't holding its choppa. The Evil Sun howled in pain as the hot metal closed on his shoulder and began to burn him, but only until Mag Dedfist clobbered the hot-git on the back of its head with his makeshift bludgeon.

The skrawnie beast toppled forwards, releasing Zagnob and throwing out its hands to break its fall. Da Genrul swung his power choppa again, and felt the shudder as the blade bit into the hot-git's side. Consistent damage, that was the key: they had to keep hitting it, faster and harder than it could heal.

'Keep at it!' he yelled. 'If we work togevva, we can–'

Zagnob raised his snagga klaw to take a shot at the hot-git's neck, but Mag shoved him aside. The Goff grinned so widely it could be seen even above the massive metal underjaw of his armour, and lined up his own blow with his salvaged weapon.

The hot-git's choppa speared right through his mega armour, transfixing him.

Mag howled in pain and staggered back, the Deff Dread's arm falling from his grip and landing on his own head. The hot-git was exposed, and Zagnob had the perfect opportunity to take its head off with his snagga klaw before it could protect itself, but he swung at Mag instead, punching through the Goff's armour and burying the twin prongs of his weapon in Dedfist's chest. Mag went down, and Zagnob whooped in joy and revenge.

The hot-git staggered up, reached out, and clamped one hand around Zagnob's head while he was still cheering over the fallen Mag. Zagnob's howls of pain were muffled by the massive metal fingers as they began to cook his brain inside his own skull. Uzbrag brought his own power choppa back for another blow, but the hot-git's choppa leaped out of Mag's corpse at its gesture and landed in its hand again, and its backswing took Da Genrul in the chest.

It was, by some freak of chance, only the flat of the blade, but that didn't prevent him from being knocked a couple of trukk-lengths away by the blow, and he felt something inside him break from the force of it. He struggled up again, leaning on the haft of his power choppa, just in time to see the hot-git run Zagnob Thundaskuzz through as well.

'Zoggin' idiots,' Uzbrag muttered. 'We could've taken it!' Well, there was only one thing for it. It was still a bit busted up, so if he got really lucky…

Uzbrag's ears twitched, and he became aware of a new noise, audible even over the thunder of battle going on around him. All orks knew the sound of boots on the ground, but these weren't orkish boots.

It sounded like the humies had decided to join the party properly at last.

They poured into view from between the buildings beyond the hot-git, yelling and whooping like they were orks themselves, although Uzbrag reckoned they had a better chance of scaring themselves than anyone else. A whole mob of them opened up with their zappy light-guns, firing indiscriminately into the battling orks and skrawniez. Notably, a lot of the shots hit the hot-git.

'Whoops,' Uzbrag said. 'Yoo didn't want to do dat, humies.'

The hot-git never seemed to be anything less than furious, but this new attack appeared to stoke its rage to new heights. It flung Zagnob's body off its choppa with a scream, and stormed away from Uzbrag and towards these new irritants, stomping Mag Dedfist underfoot as it went. If there had been any life left in the big Goff's body, it undoubtedly fled when half his chest was flattened.

It probably would have been bad enough for the humies if it had only been the hot-git heading for them, given how terrified they sounded as it approached with their shots bouncing harmlessly off it. However, a few of the boyz nearby decided to pile in as well, and more surprisingly, a large chunk of the skrawniez seemed to get caught up in the hot-git's anger. They moved with deadly swiftness, following in its wake almost like boyz tailing a Deff Dread into the heart of a fight.

'Oi!' Da Genrul shouted. 'I haven't finished wiv yoo yet!' But the hot-git took no notice, and began slaughtering humies by the handful, while they desperately brought up bigger and bigger guns to shoot it with.

'Well, I ain't chasin' ya,' Uzbrag muttered, poking at his ribs and wincing. 'When yoo're zoggin' ready, eh? Coward.'

He turned around, and realised that they'd won.

LOTZ

If there was one good thing about being a grot, Snaggi thought, it was that enemies would usually pass up the chance to shoot at you if they could shoot at an ork instead.

The orks sometimes didn't give them a choice, of course. Many a mob of grots had been prodded into place on a battlefield by an enterprising runtherd with a good knowledge of when to duck, precisely so that the enemy would literally have to go through Snaggi's kin in order to get to the orks behind. This was just another example of how unfair the galaxy was, given that most of those grots didn't want to be there in the first place, and the orks universally *did*.

However, in this case, when Snaggi threw himself onto the floor and covered his head with his hands, the skrawniez didn't waste their time and ammunition on him and his ladz. Snaggi heard the first volley whisper by overhead and bite into the orks behind him, which under the circumstances was about as good an outcome as he could have expected, given that Da Genrul had been about to shoot him. Of course, that didn't mean he could be complacent.

'Run for it!' he yelled, and the grots with him scattered. Since they had been surrounding the gateway, that basically meant each one of them ran directly away from it, and the terrifying warriors it had just disgorged. Granted, that meant they were running towards the orks they had just been defying, but the orks quite literally had bigger things to think about. Kicking a cheeky grot was something they could – and indeed, did – do any day, whereas mixing it up with a bunch of skrawniez was a far rarer opportunity. Snippa One-Ear abruptly became Snippa No-Face when he ran headlong into the blade of Da Genrul's power choppa, which the Blood Axe was spinning to warm himself up for the fight to come, but if Snippa couldn't look where he was going then the git only had himself to blame.

'Wot's da plan now?' Skrawk asked, as a small group of them dived for cover in a humie hut. The former occupants had clearly already decided that staying put around this many orks was a bad plan and had legged it, so there was no one to pop up with a gun and an inconvenient attitude to property ownership.

'Da plan is not to die,' Snaggi said firmly. 'Dat's da first an' most important part of it, an' look! Dere's already gits out dere who ain't even managin' dat.'

Two orks collapsed a short distance away from where the grots had taken cover, their heads sliced clean in half by the skrawniez' cutty-discs. Snaggi shook his head, and tutted.

'See? Dat's wot ya get when dere ain't proppa leadership. Da big gits can't even follow a simple plan.'

'An' supposin' we manage to not die, is dere any more to da plan?' another grot asked. He was one of Snippa's old lot: Snaggi thought his name was Lunk, and already had him pegged as a potential troublemaker.

'Only fools rush in,' he said loftily.

'Waaagh!'

'Well, an' Goffs,' he amended, as the black-clad part of the orkish forces charged into the teeth of the skrawniez' guns with typical enthusiasm, if such a word could be said to apply to orks who were never happy with the quality of the fight once they found it. 'But anyway, my point is... Look, dere's loads more skrawniez comin' outta dat gate, so da sensible fing is to wait an' see wot happens, right?'

'Not sure dat "wait an' see" is a great battle cry for da Grot-Waaagh!, dat's all I'm sayin',' Lunk muttered. Snaggi scowled at him, because he was fairly sure that that was not, in fact, all that Lunk was saying.

'I'm gettin' da feelin' dat yer castin' aspershuns over me leadership qualities,' he said menacingly, standing up to his full height and glowering at the other grot. 'Wotcha got to say to dat, eh?'

'Wot've I got to say?' Lunk repeated. He rose up to his feet as well, out of the instinctive crouch he had been in, and folded his arms. 'I reckon... I reckon dat ya ain't no ork, Snaggi Little toof, an' ya haven't got da faintest idea wot da best fing to do is, dat's wot I got to say.'

Snaggi laughed loudly and falsely, and pointed at Lunk. 'See? Dis is da sort of finking we've got to deal wiv, ladz! No, I ain't an ork,' he continued, staring fiercely at Lunk, 'an' I'm proud of it! Wot good am I gonna do, goin' around pretendin' to be an ork? Ya gotta get dis idea dat orks are better dan us just cos dey're bigger outta ya head! Dey ain't *kunnin'*! Both da gods have got space for kunnin', but da orks mainly focus on the "brutal" part, cos dat's wot dey're best at! But just fink about it for a second! Wot if ya could get proper orky brutal, but wiv grot kunnin? Dat's wot da GrotWaaagh! is gonna be about, ladz! *We* give da orders, *dey* do da fightin', everyone wins, an' everyone's happy! Well, except whoever it is we're fightin',' he admitted, 'but who gives a zog about dose gits?'

'Da orks ain't gonna follow a grot wot don't wanna rush in,' Lunk said stubbornly. 'I ain't seen no sign dat da gods talk to ya, Snaggi, no matter wot ya say.'

'Yeah?' Snaggi wanted to give Lunk a taste of his boomstikk, but that seemed like a very orky thing to do. 'Is dat so? Well alright den. Da gods are still tellin' me dat we should get to dat gate an' get froo it, but dey're also tellin' me dat if we was to make a run for it now, it'd be a very bad fing for us, an' we should wait.'

Guffink poked his head around the door frame. 'I mean, dere's a lotta fightin' goin' on out dere right now, so I ain't sure dat's much of a prediction, Snaggi.'

'No, just wait,' Snaggi said. 'Just wait.' He fixed Lunk with a stern look, and dared the universe to prove him wrong. Damn it all, *he* knew that the gods were speaking to him! And yes, okay, most of the time they definitely wanted him to go and get stuck in, but it wasn't his fault if the gods had a slightly inflated idea of what he could manage. Gork and Mork were used to dealing with orks, after all, it only made sense that they might get a bit mixed up now they had shifted their favour to a grot–

A blood-curdling roar split the air. Snaggi, despite knowing that something awful was coming, jumped so much he nearly dropped the grabba stikk.

'Yeah,' Guffink managed weakly, as a gigantic daemon of molten metal holding an enormous choppa emerged from the gateway. 'I fink dat counts as a bad fing.'

'I really don't wanna be stuck in here wiv dat!' Skrawk wailed. 'Snaggi! Can we get outta here?'

Snaggi swallowed, and tried to maintain his composure. The big glowing fing wasn't coming towards them, at least – it seemed to be heading in the general direction of Mag Dedfist's lot, which really drove home Snaggi's point about not rushing in – but Skrawk had the right idea: this really was no place to be hanging about. The traditional grot thing to do in such circumstances was to do a runner back the way you'd come and try to avoid any runtherds you might meet along the way, but Snaggi was not going to run from his destiny. He'd led them here, by Gork and Mork, and he was not going to turn around now. He was going through that gateway, and Old Morgrub *was* going to acknowledge Snaggi Littletoof as Da Grotboss!

He caught a glimpse of Da Genrul running off towards the skrawniez' monster, and snorted in grim amusement. Well, that should take care of one of his rivals, at least. Mag Dedfist was certain to get stuck in as well, if he was anywhere nearby. With any luck, the three of them would scrag each other. However, there was still one other pretender who needed taking care of.

'Anyone see Thundaskuzz?' Snaggi asked, trying his best to see through the scrapping going on directly in front of them.

'Da speed freeks have split up,' Guffink said, pointing to a trio of warbikers hurtling towards a group of orange skrawniez and unloading their dakkaguns into them, and then at what looked like the boomdakka snazzwagon of Skrappit the mek, exchanging fire with a floaty-tank. 'He could be anywhere.'

'But he ain't gone froo da gate?' Snaggi said.

'Nuffink's gone froo da gate from dis side, uvver dan some dakka,' Guffink replied, shaking his head. 'Da skrawniez have got it closed up tighter'n a painboy's stitch job.'

'Dat's not usually very tight,' Skrawk pointed out. 'Dere's often quite big gaps.'

'Yeah, dat's why I said dey've done it "tight*er*", not "tight *as*". Obvious, innit?'

So, there was still a chance to be first, Snaggi thought, ignoring the bickering of his underlings. That was the goal. He'd got *to* the gate first, but none of the orks had cared about that: not even Old Morgrub, who had clearly gone deaf to the will of the gods. However, surely no one could argue with Snaggi's claim to the title of warboss if he actually went where no grot had gone before, and made it *through* the gate first.

He was going to need more than just his own legs to do that, though, because while Snaggi was quite fond of his own legs – certainly enough that he wouldn't want anyone to take them off him – he was not overly confident in their ability to get him through the gate before any of the skrawniez could shoot him. Luckily, the sort of ingenuity which had made him an obvious choice for grotboss had not deserted him.

He looked at the grots with him. Five in total: Skrawk, Guffink, Lunk, and two more by the names of Pukk and Wizza.

'Follow me, ladz,' he said boldly, and scampered back out into the fight.

He didn't wait to see if they were following him. Rather, he led the way and made it obvious by so doing that he expected them to follow him, and hoped that reality would just sort itself out accordingly. Somewhat shockingly, reality obliged: at least, if the squeals of alarm from behind him when explosions went off nearby were anything to go by. Snaggi experienced another surge of pride. What other grot could boast such loyalty from his fellows? Even a runtherd couldn't manage this sort of thing without some well-placed threats.

Of course, even the most loyal of followers needed to see some sort of results if they were to continue placing themselves at risk at their leader's behest, which was why Snaggi was grateful that it was not far to what he had identified as their objective.

The wartrakk was still upright, but that was more than could be said for its crew. The driver was slumped over the controls, missing most of his head thanks to some typically cowardly long-ranged skrawnie pot-shotting. The gunner was nowhere

to be seen, but a spray of dark blood over the weapon platform suggested that he had not just nipped off to get a nice
juicy squig for a snack.

'Right, we're gonna take dis, an' we're gonna drive it straight
at dat gate,' Snaggi said, patting the trakk on its flank as though
it were a smasha squig that needed soothing. 'Blast right froo
dem skrawniez, an' make history! Dat'll really show da orks wot
grots can do. *An'* it means we get out of here,' he added, looking meaningfully at Skrawk.

'Well, yeah,' Skrawk managed, 'but only by drivin' straight at
da gits wiv da big guns!'

'Ah, but we've got a big gun now, too!' Snaggi said, pointing
at the double big shoota on its mount. 'If Lunk stands at da
bottom an' yoo sit on his shoulders, yoo can dakka 'em before
dey get us, can't ya! An' if Pukk pushes da pedals an' Guffink
steers, we can drive it no trouble!'

'Wot about yoo an' Wizza, den?' Lunk demanded, seeming
less than happy about being Skrawk's seat.

'Wizza's gonna be da spare, ready to fill in if one of ya...' *dies*,
Snaggi's brain supplied, but he shunted it away. 'Needs a rest,'
he finished, daring any of them to disagree with him. 'I'm Da
Grotboss, so I'm gonna be directin' ya all, right? Now get to it!'

The driver was pushed unceremoniously off his seat, and
they arranged themselves as Snaggi had instructed. Lunk was
still grumbling, but Snaggi pointed out that at least Skrawk
was the smallest of them, so he swallowed his complaints
and let the other grot climb up on him. Then Guffink pressed
the starter button, the engine roared into life, and they were
ready to go.

Grots, driving a trakk! And Snaggi Littletoof, standing proud
right behind the driver's seat, with a boomstikk in one hand
and the symbol of his kind's oppression in the other! It was

like a moment out of legend. It was a moment that deserved to *become* a legend. Snaggi Littletoof deserved to become a legend.

Well, he was on his way.

'Forwards!' he yelled, and Pukk stamped on the go pedal.

The trakk's engine roared, and it lurched away in a shower of gravel and surprised cursing from its crew. Snaggi swayed, but managed to remain on his feet: it would not do for Da Grotboss to be sent tumbling at the moment of his greatest triumph (to date). Lunk nearly didn't manage it, but was held up by Skrawk's death grip on the big shoota. However, said death grip involved clamping his fingers on the triggers, and the twin weapon sent a ragged burst of fire ripping upwards into the air.

It was an appropriate enough way to mark the start of their progress towards glory, but it was going to attract attention. A few ork heads turned towards them as the guns went off, since orks were always attracted to the noise of dakka, and Snaggi felt the slight bite of anxiety in his throat. He knew in his heart that there was absolutely no reason why grots *shouldn't* be driving a trakk, especially since the previous owners had come to a sticky end through no doing of his or his ladz, but he was not quite sure whether the orks would feel the same way about it.

Well, he was committed. He might as well make sure that the orks saw the grot who would soon be giving them their orders.

'To da gateway!' he yelled at the top of his lungs, striking a pose and gesturing with the grabba stikk as they raced across the ground.

'We're already goin' to da gateway!' Guffink protested, not looking around from where he was wrestling with the handlebars.

'Yeah, I know,' Snaggi said, out of the corner of his mouth. 'I'm tryin' to be inspirashunal.'

'Uh, boss?' Wizza said tentatively.

'Wot?'

'Shouldn't we be goin' a bit faster? Only dese fings normally get ahead of da boyz, but some of 'em are catchin' us up...'

Snaggi looked over his shoulder, sudden uncertainty seizing him. Sure enough, there was indeed a mob of orks charging after them, and they were getting closer. That didn't seem right.

He looked over the side of the trakk. It *felt* like they were going fast, but then Snaggi had never ridden on a trakk before, so maybe he had been deceived. Other evidence, such as the gradually closing bellows of 'bloody cheeky grots!' and the like, certainly seemed to suggest that it was his perception which was in error, rather than the world.

'Pukk!' he barked. 'Wot's da problem? Why ain't we goin' faster?'

'Da pedals are well stiff, boss!' Pukk panted, from somewhere just past Guffink's crotch. 'I fink ya need ork legs to press 'em down proper!'

Snaggi cursed everything. Why did ork meks make vehicles that only orks could drive? That was just inconsiderate. Luckily, he had a plan for just such an eventuality. 'Wizza! Get up dere an' help wiv da pedals!'

'Yes, boss!' Wizza replied, scuttling forwards. If that was partly just to get that bit further away from the orks catching them up, well, at least Snaggi knew how to motivate those under his command.

It took Wizza a couple of moments to negotiate his way past Guffink, but when he managed to do so the effect was immediate: the trakk lurched and accelerated, and the outraged shouts of the boyz behind them got angrier, but began to fade as the trakk pulled away.

'Hah!' Snaggi gloated, abandoning any ideas of being an inspirational figure, in favour of outright mockery. 'Yeah, zog da lot of ya!'

A roar of engines grabbed his attention, and he looked away from the receding footsloggers to see other red-painted vehicles pulling alongside them. And then pulling past them, because two grots together might manage to make a wartrakk go faster than a bunch of orks on foot, but they still couldn't match up to an actual ork in control of a vehicle. Snaggi caught a brief glimpse of a confused expression on what was left of the face of Zagnob Thundaskuzz as his Deffkilla wartrike overtook them, and then the speedboss was gone.

Heading for the gate, with a bunch of others behind him.

'No!' Snaggi yelled desperately. 'Dis was my idea, ya zoggin' great gits! *My* idea!' Why did he have to be cursed with *grots* taking his orders? All he'd needed was one decent ork driver and he'd have been away! He fumbled with his boomstikk as the gate drew closer – but not quickly enough, not for him – and wrestled with the idea of shooting Zagnob Thundaskuzz in the back. On the one hand, it was undoubtedly a very bad idea, but what did he have to lose at this point?

Well, head, legs, arms, potentially fingers one by one...

He was still caught in the web of indecision when light erupted near the gate: not the strange, cold, shimmering light of the gate itself, but good, strong, green light. It faded away almost immediately to reveal the shape of Old Morgrub, right in amongst some of the fanciest-looking skrawniez. One of the skrawniez drew a blade which flickered with darkness, and Snaggi thought for a moment that the warphead had had it, but Morgrub had already raised his staff and was bellowing something, and then heads exploded all around him.

It hadn't been planned – it couldn't have been planned, not least because that would have involved Zagnob Thundaskuzz having a concept of something more to do a few moments into the future other than 'continue to go fast' – but the speed freeks chose that moment to open up with their weapons. The remaining skrawniez around the gate, the ones who hadn't followed their big glowing metal friend, did not do well in the next few seconds. The Kult of Speed were no more accurate than most orks, but by Gork and Mork, they made up for quality with quantity. The skrawniez had no defence against the hail of fire that swept across them, and nowhere to hide from it. Only one of their big floaty guns got a shot away before its crew was gunned down, but to give the skrawniez due credit, it ripped a hole in the world for a moment and pulled two warbikes through into whatever lay beyond, turning them into a crumpled mess as it did so.

'Zoggin' 'eck!' Guffink exclaimed, twitching the handlebars and jerking them slightly further away from the rapidly diminishing rip in reality. 'Dat fing's dangerous!'

It certainly was, but it hadn't hit Zagnob Thundaskuzz, and the speedboss was nearly at the gateway now. Old Morgrub had somehow survived the barrage which had killed the skrawniez around him, and Snaggi waited for the warphead's eyes to light up with that green fire again, and for him to call down the Foot of Gork, or explode some more heads, or do *something* to prevent Thundaskuzz from getting through.

No such thing happened, but the Evil Sunz speedboss did not roar through the skrawnie gate as Snaggi had feared. Instead he veered off to one side, heading for the massive scrap that seemed to be shaping up around Mag Dedfist, Da Genrul, and the hot-git.

Snaggi punched the air in delight with the hand that held the grabba stikk. He should have known that the gods would intervene on his behalf! Thundaskuzz was too interested in a fight to claim the destiny which was Snaggi's by rights, showing the typical lack of forward thinking with which orks were cursed. This was why it should be grots in charge!

'Alright, ladz,' he gloated. 'Straight on! We've got dis in da bag!'

A moment later, he frowned. If he went through the gateway like this, on the trakk, then technically he wasn't going to be the first. That honour would go to Pukk and Wizza, working the pedals, since they were at the front. Should he order them to stop?

As it turned out, the gods had taken care of this as well. Unfortunately for Snaggi, this took the shape of one skrawnie who wasn't properly dead yet managing to claw his way back up behind the disappear-kannon, and activating it.

Snaggi threw himself clear of the trakk, but the rest of his crew lacked his superb reflexes, given as how they were stupidly holding onto things, or had another grot sitting on their shoulders, or what have you. The disappear-kannon ripped open the world again, and a swirl of unnatural colours that made Snaggi's head hurt to look at engulfed the trakk. Snaggi felt it pulling at him, and he scrabbled desperately in the dirt and dust as he landed, trying to get a grip on it. He felt himself starting to slide backwards...

...and the awful tugging sensation ceased. He looked around. Half a front wheel, crumpled; a few trakk links, buckled; someone's leg, without even a decent boot on the foot for him to take. That was all the kannon had left of his ride, and his ladz.

Thin, vicious, green rage surged through Snaggi's body. He scrambled back up to his feet, and levelled his grabba stikk at the skrawnie who had so insulted him.

'You!'

The skrawnie's helmet was emotionless, of course, but Snaggi could practically feel the fear his shout had engendered in the wearer. Some might have thought that the shakiness as it started to line the kannon up on him was due to the hideous injuries it had sustained, but Snaggi knew better: it was terrified of him! And with good reason, for he was vengeance incarnate. He charged towards it, determined to punish this pointy-eared git who had dared to destroy Da Grotboss' wartrakk... and also his ladz, but Snaggi could find new ladz anywhere, whereas trakks tended to have ork owners who were not inclined to part with them.

He had a moment's warning as the business end of the disappear-kannon glowed, and threw himself to one side. The weird krumpy-light missed: something behind him got chewed up and vanished, but the gods were still smiling on Snaggi Littletoof! Everyone knew that the skrawniez were good at shooting, didn't they? It must have been the favour of the gods which saved his life.

The skrawnie didn't get another chance to defy the gods. Snaggi fired the boomstikk into its face, splintering its helmet's faceplate – *he* didn't miss, because he was better than any skrawnie – and then latched onto its skinny neck with the grabba stikk. The skrawnie spasmed as he zapped it with the grabba stikk's full force, then fell bonelessly to the ground when he opened the jaws again. Snaggi whooped in triumph, then stopped as he noticed the skrawnie's chest was still moving up and down. How much did it take to kill one of these gits? He racked another shell into his boomstikk, and took aim.

A big green hand came down on his gun.

'Leave it,' Old Morgrub said. The warphead reached down and plucked the injured skrawnie off the ground, holding it by the neck with one hand. 'We're gonna need one of 'em alive.'

'Wot for?' Snaggi asked.

'Weirdboy stuff,' Morgrub said, with a wink. 'Look at da gate.' Snaggi did so, and his jaw dropped open in despair. 'Wot? *No!*' It was closed.

Well, it wasn't *closed*, you couldn't really close something that was just an arch. However, the weird light which had filled it had disappeared, and it was once more just a curve of stone-like stuff with nothing but clear air in the middle.

'I can open it again wiv dis git, don't worry about dat,' Morgrub said. 'An' yoo'll go froo first,' he added. 'I'll make sure of dat. Yoo've proved yerself to da gods.'

Snaggi gaped at him. 'Really?!'

'Oh yeah,' Morgrub grinned. 'Now we just gotta wait for somefing.'

Snaggi squinted. On the other side of the gate, he could just make out what looked like the hot-git piling into a bunch of humies in the distance, with the small shapes of other skrawniez around it.

He looked around. 'Where are all da uvver skrawniez?'

'Dead,' Morgrub said happily. 'Or on da way to it.'

Sure enough, the rest of what had once been Waaagh! Goresnappa were mopping up the few remaining skrawniez, and looking around for what to do next. Snaggi's chest swelled with pride. They would look towards the gate, they would see him standing next to Old Morgrub, and they would–

'Attennnnnnnnnnnn-SHUN!'

And they would see, Snaggi realised with a sinking feeling, the limping but unquestionably still alive figure of Da Genrul.

LOTZ

Da Genrul's leg was giving him grief, and his ribs were none too happy either, but he was still armed and upright, and quite definitely the largest ork in the vicinity since Mag Dedfist got stomped. All around him, orks were polishing off the skrawniez that had not followed the hot-git off on its rampage. They'd given the Waaagh! a good scrap, Uzbrag would admit that, but when it came down to it, nothing could beat orks in a straight-up fight.

He was ignoring the fact that there was still dakka going off behind him. So far as he was concerned, the Waaagh! had won *this* fight, given that the skrawniez appeared to have given up on it and run off to start scragging humies. If they came back again, they could call it a new fight, and start over.

His eyes lit on Old Morgrub, standing near the gate, next to that ridiculous grot who'd given Uzbrag some lip earlier. The gate itself, he noticed with displeasure, now lacked the shimmering light through which the skrawniez had come. Uzbrag was no expert in artefacts created by the pointy-earz, but he had an inkling that you couldn't just step through it at any point and have it work. Had that zoggin' warphead dragged them all under this giant humie camp just for his promised gateway to the stars to stop working?

Kaptin Skulsnik and the Guttas materialised at Uzbrag's left elbow.

'Want us to do 'im over, boss?' Skulsnik muttered. 'We were gonna stick 'im earlier, but da git went all green an' disappeared on us. We scragged a fancy flyin' skrawnie instead, tho.'

'Leave 'im for da moment,' Uzbrag replied in a low voice. 'If he can get da gate open again, he's still got a use.'

'Gotcha, boss.'

Da Genrul inhaled. Time to take control.

'Attennnnnnnnnnn-SHUN!'

Only the Blood Axes really knew what he was yelling, of course, but the eyes of the rest of the Waaagh! gravitated to him nonetheless. Uzbrag felt their gazes land on him, and could tell that the various nobs and kaptins were weighing him up, deciding whether now was the time they wanted to make a bid for leadership themselves. He glowered around at them, meeting each pair of eyes that dared to hold his gaze, and watched them drop, one after another.

Apparently not, then.

'Mag Dedfist is dead!' Da Genrul bellowed. 'Zagnob Thunda-skuzz is dead! I'm warboss now, an' yoo're all a part of Waaagh! Uzbrag! You got it?'

A cheer went up. Orks didn't like uncertainty, and fun though the race to get here had been, everyone felt better now they only had one warboss to worry about displeasing. Uzbrag stomped towards Old Morgrub, secure in the knowledge that the Waaagh!

was behind him. Let the warphead try something funny now he didn't have two other big bosses to play him off against!

'Wot's dat for?' he demanded, pointing at the half-dead skrawnie that was limp in Morgrub's grasp.

'For da gate,' Morgrub replied. He gave Uzbrag a sly grin. 'Assumin' ya still wanna go froo it?'

Uzbrag drummed his fingers on the haft of his power choppa, and gave the matter some thought. He looked over at where the fight was still going on, skrawniez against humies, accompanied by screams, flashes of light and explosions: all the good stuff. A lot of the ladz were starting to shuffle in that direction as well, drawn by the incessant lure of a fight they weren't part of. Most of them were looking at him, waiting for the new warboss to give the order for them to pile in.

It was the order Gazrot Goresnappa would have given. It was the order Mag Dedfist would have given. As for Zagnob Thunda-skuzz, he wouldn't have given an order so much as set off for the fight at top speed and expected everyone to follow him. It was the expected order.

So maybe, Da Genrul thought, it was an order he shouldn't give.

'Ya see dat over dere?' he yelled, pointing at the fight. 'Ya see dat? Dat's skrawniez an' humies kickin' da snot out of each uvver! An' ya see dat big fing with da massive choppa? Dat's a hot-git! It's dead fighty! It killed Mag Dedfist and Zagnob Thundaskuzz! Didn't get me, cos I'm *smart!* An' I bet ya all want to go an' get stuck in, am I right?'

Another cheer greeted these words, as was to be expected. It was easy to get orks to cheer, if it sounded like you were promising them a fight.

'Well,' Uzbrag said. 'I've got a better idea.'

That statement was met with confused blinks. Better than

a fight? This was a concept the Waaagh! had not encountered before. Da Genrul had to get them back onside quickly, but he reckoned he knew how to do that.

'See, we've been fightin' humies ever since we landed on dis planet!' he shouted. 'An' it's been fun an' all, but it gets a bit samey after a while, dunnit? Maybe we should go an' find somefing else to clobber? An' yeah, dat hot-git's well fighty, but da fing about dat is, it came out of *here*.'

He pointed at the gateway.

'So I reckon dere's more of 'em on da uvver side! Maybe a lot more! We could have da best scrap of our lives if we go froo dis gate! We could find all sorts of interestin' fings to give some dakka to! So whaddya say, ladz? Dere ain't many humies an' skrawniez left. It's almost a shame to ruin da fun for 'em, an' it wouldn't be a challenge for us to finish 'em off. Let's leave 'em to it, an' go an kick da rest of the galaxy's faces in instead!'

It turned out that orks could grasp the concept of something better than a fight, so long as it was a *bigger* fight. Another cheer went up, and the Waaagh! began to pile forwards eagerly.

'Over to yoo,' Uzbrag said smugly, turning to Morgrub. 'Can ya ackcherly get it–'

He stopped. Morgrub had one hand around the skrawnie's head, and the gate was filled with shimmering light again.

'Oh. Alright.' Da Genrul shrugged. If the warphead hadn't been able to do what he'd promised, way back before they'd even got inside the walls, Uzbrag could have blamed the failure on him and had the full support of the Waaagh! in taking Morgrub out of the reckoning for good. As it was, it looked like they were good to go.

Or were they?

Uzbrag eyed the curtain of cold light and took another look at Old Morgrub. The warphead hardly looked trustworthy at the best of times, so it was difficult to work out what he might be thinking. All the same, Uzbrag had seen various force fields and the like at work, and he was aware of the notion that sometimes you could get through something in one direction, but definitely not the other. Might this be a trick to get Uzbrag out of the way, so Morgrub could turn this into a WeirdWaaagh! under his command?

That grot with the grabba stikk was looking expectantly at Old Morgrub. Da Genrul came to a decision.

'Oi, you!'

The grot turned towards him, its mouth opening almost as though it was going to answer him back, but it never got the chance: Uzbrag's boot connected solidly with its midsection, and sent it sailing through the air. It wailed, still somehow holding onto the grabba stikk, hit one side of the arch, and ricocheted off it through the lights and out of sight. Old Morgrub practically bent double laughing, which at least showed the old weirdboy still had something approaching a normal sense of humour somewhere.

'Huh,' Da Genrul grunted. 'Reckon it works.'

'How d'ya know, boss?' Skulsnik asked.

'Well, da grot didn't bounce off and catch fire, or just disintegrate into little bits of wotnot,' Uzbrag said confidently. 'It went froo, so it's all good.'

'Yeah, but goin' froo might've killed it,' Skulsnik pointed out. 'Da skrawniez are well strange.'

'Eh, it's a grot,' Uzbrag said dismissively. 'Goin' froo *might've* killed it, but lotsa fings'll kill a grot wot won't kill an ork. I'm warboss now – can't let a little fing like gettin' killed stop me.' He raised his power choppa. 'Come on, ladz! It's time to take da Waaagh! *to da stars!*'

He charged. And Waaagh! Uzbrag charged with him.

DA BIT WOT
COMES AFTER DA FING

The ork frowned.

'Ya didn't shorten dat at all. And ya ain't explained how ya ended up *here*.'

Snaggi grinned hopefully. He had been hoping to impress his captor with his obvious ingenuity and leadership potential. 'But I told ya wot ya wanted to know, boss!'

'No, ya didn't,' the ork rumbled, picking up a large and extremely dangerous-looking hammer with an axe head on the back of it. 'Guess we'll ask da next one.'

'No! No, wait!' Snaggi yelped. 'I fort it was obvious! I mean, dat is,' he added hastily, aware that he had just implied the ork wasn't intelligent enough to understand what he'd been saying, 'it's da skrawniez! Ya gotta have a skrawnie to get froo da gate!'

The ork paused, the hammer halfway raised. 'A skrawnie?'

'Yeah!' Snaggi confirmed, nodding furiously. 'Da tunnels are wot dey use to get around! Dey're da ones who can turn da gates on an' off! So if ya wanna get in, yoo're gonna need one!' he added, helpfully.

The ork studied him carefully for a few seconds. Snaggi did his best not to squirm, but it was difficult. Not only was this ork massive, he also gave off the impression of being quite smart, for an ork. That was not a combination with which Snaggi felt particularly comfortable.

'We did see wot looked like a skrawnie hangin' around just before we nabbed dis git, boss,' the other grot said. Snaggi glared at him. So this was the traitor who'd captured him! He'd make sure to get his revenge, assuming the ork didn't hammer him flat.

The ork nodded. 'Right, skrawniez it is.' He leaned down, until his face was a few inches away from Snaggi's. Given the ork's head was roughly the same size as all of Snaggi, this did not do much for Snaggi's general state of mind.

'Yoo're my grot, now,' the ork rumbled. 'Ya do wot I say, when I say it, or I feed ya to me squig. Ya got dat?'

Snaggi hated himself, but there was nothing he could do. He nodded his head. 'Yes, boss. An', uh, who're yoo? Just so I can say, if someone asks who me boss is.'

The ork's face split into an entirely unpleasant grin. 'I'm Ufthak Blackhawk, an' I'm da big boss around 'ere.' He straightened up again. 'Nizkwik, show dis one wot to do. I'm gonna talk to Da Meklord.'

Snaggi watched the massive ork thud away, each step like a Deff Dread's, then turned his attention to the other grot.

'So, yoo're Nizkwik, den?'

'Dat's right.' Nizkwik untied Snaggi's hands and smirked at him. 'I'm da grot da boss kicks least! An' he's never fed me to his squig!' He squared up to Snaggi, trying to make himself look taller, even though they were the same height. 'So I'm not gonna have any trouble outta ya, am I, Snaggi Littletoof?'

'No,' Snaggi said, shaking his head. He waited until Nizkwik had turned his back before sticking out his tongue.

Yet.

Orks, grots, squigs, skrawniez: it made no difference. Gork and Mork had spoken to Snaggi Littletoof, and if he knew one thing for sure, it was that his destiny would *not* be denied...

ABOUT THE AUTHOR

Mike Brooks is a science fiction and fantasy author who lives in Nottingham, UK. His work for Black Library includes the Horus Heresy Primarchs novel *Alpharius: Head of the Hydra*, the Warhammer 40,000 novels *Rites of Passage*, *Warboss* and *Brutal Kunnin*, the Necromunda novel *Road to Redemption* and the novellas *Wanted: Dead* and *Da Gobbo's Revenge.* When not writing, he plays guitar and sings in a punk band, and DJs wherever anyone will tolerate him.